TERRA TEMPO

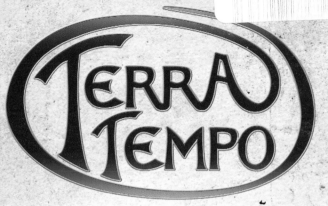

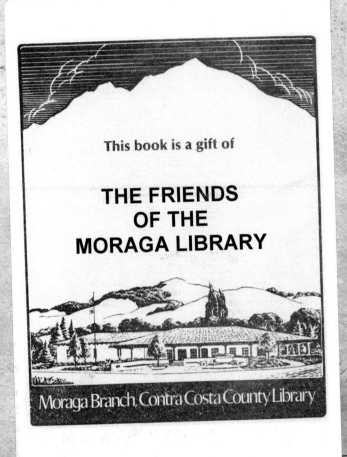

TERRA TEMPO

The Academy of Planetary Evolution

Academy of Planetary Evolution

1898

Written by **David R. Shapiro**
Illustrated by **Christopher Herndon**

CRAIGMORE
CREATIONS

Portland, Oregon

Production: Brian David Smith
Cover Design and Art: Christopher Herndon
Color and Lettering: Erica Melville and Christopher Herndon

Library of Congress Cataloging-in-Publication Data

Shapiro, David, 1977-
The Academy of Planetary Evolution / written by David R. Shapiro ; illustrated
by Christopher Herndon ; color and lettering by Erica Melville. -- First edition.
pages cm. -- (Terra tempo ; 3)
Summary: The kids of the Academy of Planetary Evolution race from the
Cenozoic era to the modern age, making their way through the evolution of
mammals, but when the Bone Wars of the late 1800s threaten to break over to
the modern age, Jenna, Caleb, and Ari find themselves in a fight alongside some
of history's most notable figures as they race to ensure the safety of the world's
history, and its future.
ISBN 978-1-940052-09-0 (paperback)
1. Graphic novels. [1. Graphic novels. 2. Natural history--Fiction.
3. Evolution--Fiction. 4. Time travel--Fiction. 5. Earth (Planet)--History--
Fiction.] I. Herndon, Christopher, illustrator. II. Title.

PZ7.7.S4535Ac 2014
741.5'973--dc23

2014021305

Printed in the United States of America

ISBN: 978-1-940052-09-0

CRAIGMORE
CREATIONS

Portland, OR
www.craigmorecreations.com

To Acacia and Miles.
—DS

To Joshua, Jen, Megan, and the rest
of the folks at John Day Fossil Beds.
—CH

INTRODUCTION

Previously in Terra Tempo: While working with his parents on a dig in Arizona's Painted Desert, Ari discovered another time travel map—this time of the Colorado Plateau. Uncle Al and Aunt Maddie rented an RV to take Jenna, Caleb, and Ari on a tour of Southwestern national and tribal parks. After picking Ari up at the Petrified Forest National Park, the trio was reunited for an adventure that touched on the Grand Canyon and the Four Corners through 550 million years of Earth history.

Ari excitedly shared his new find with his friends, but they hid the time map from the grown-ups. The adventure started out innocently enough, but lack of oxygen in the Cambrian Period forced the kids to jump ahead 100 million years to the Devonian Period, the time of ancient fish. Dangers lurked in the waters leaving nowhere in the past safe enough to stay for long. Returning to the present, the kids armed themselves with weapons purchased from the Navajo reservation, but Jenna, Caleb, and Ari quickly realized that they would need more than a bow, arrows, and a hatchet to protect themselves from the animals and the ongoing war over the time travel maps.

The fight between the Geosophists, who sought to study the Earth for the understanding of all, and the Treasure Hunters, who desired to own Earth's resources for the benefit of the few, had been going on for many years even before Ari found his map—a map which had been hidden by a Geosophist in hopes of keeping it from the Treasure Hunters. Seth, leader of the Treasure Hunters, had been searching for the map when he found the kids in the deep swamps of the Carboniferous Period. Discovering they held the map he'd been searching for, Seth and his goon chased the kids through the swamp until Jenna safely opened a portal to the Permian Period, escaping but not quickly enough before Seth and his goon had followed. The thunderbird Yakama returned and flew the kids to Levi Wilson, the leader of the Geosophists and Seth's twin brother. Levi introduced himself to the kids and told the story of Teddy Roosevelt's army of Rough Riders, their quarantine camp after the end of the Spanish American War in 1898, and the creation of the time travel maps. Hunted down by his twin, Levi escaped the Permian in a blaze of glory, distracting Seth from his hunt for the kids.

Not deterred, Seth and his goon picked up the trail after the kids missed their mark, winding up in Navajo land in 1986, and meeting Robbie, a Navajo guide to Monument Valley Tribal Park. With Robbie's help, they gave Seth and his goon the slip, but the chase continued through millions of years until the Triassic where they met Peregrina Sandoval, a time traveler and explorer, deepening their knowledge of the time map mythos. Through Peregrina the kids learn they are involved in something much bigger than they had previously conceived. Leaving behind the Triassic for the Jurassic Period, Jenna, Caleb, and Ari meet the wandering poet and artist Everett Ruess where he was pursuing a dinosaur that was named after him. He encouraged the kids to finish their journey through the map's time periods.

In the most dangerous of times, the Cretaceous—filled with giant relatives of the T. rex and other huge dinosaurs, the kids had their final showdown with Seth and his goon. Yakama was no match and went down against the giant Quetzalcoatlus, leaving Jenna, Ari, and Caleb on their own against Seth, his goon, and a hungry Bisti Beast. The kids were saved only by the grace of a tail swinging Ankylosaurus, trapping Seth and his goon under the fallen body of Bistahieversor, a late Cretaceous Tyrannosaurid. With the help of Yakama, still flying after the battle with Quetzalcoatlus, the kids made it back to the present where they received an invitation delivered by Peregrina to attend the Academy of Planetary Evolution.

With their invitations to the prestigious academy in hand, and the practical experience of time travel under their belts, the time has come for Jenna, Caleb, and Ari to gain more knowledge of the Earth's deep past and go on an educational adventure through the hidden halls of America's finest natural history museums.

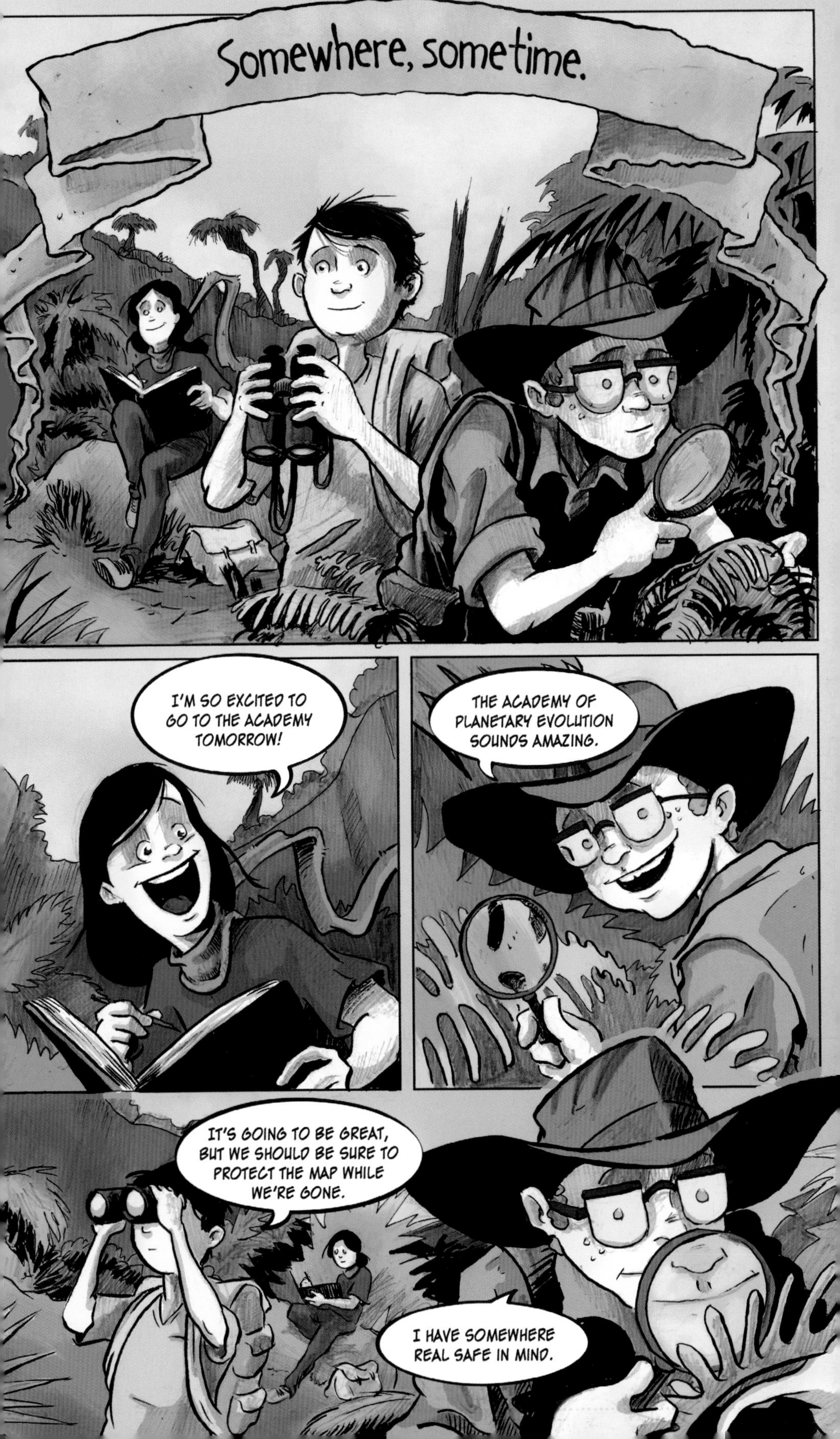
Somewhere, sometime.
I'M SO EXCITED TO GO TO THE ACADEMY TOMORROW!
THE ACADEMY OF PLANETARY EVOLUTION SOUNDS AMAZING.
IT'S GOING TO BE GREAT, BUT WE SHOULD BE SURE TO PROTECT THE MAP WHILE WE'RE GONE.
I HAVE SOMEWHERE REAL SAFE IN MIND.

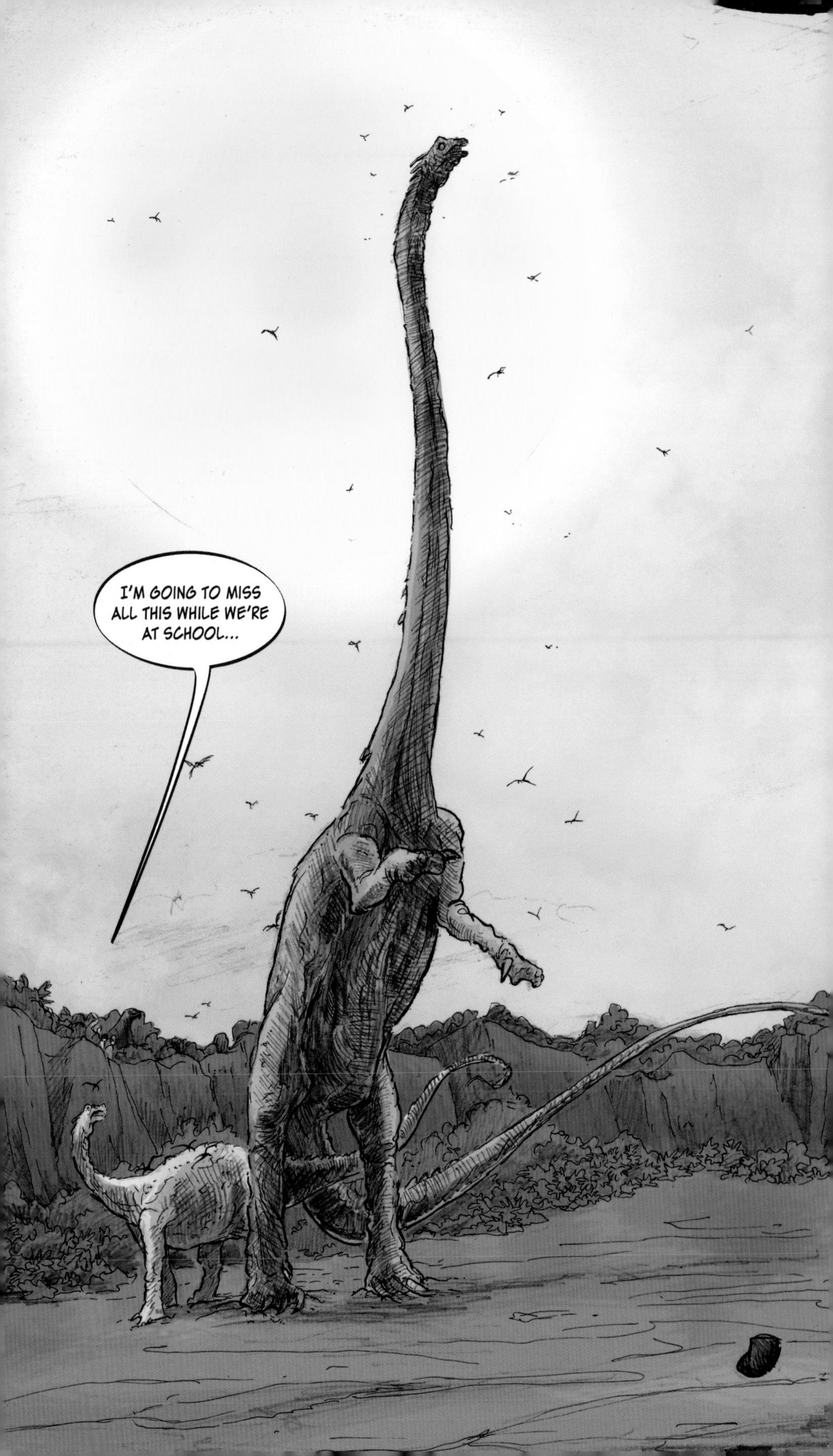
I'M GOING TO MISS ALL THIS WHILE WE'RE AT SCHOOL...

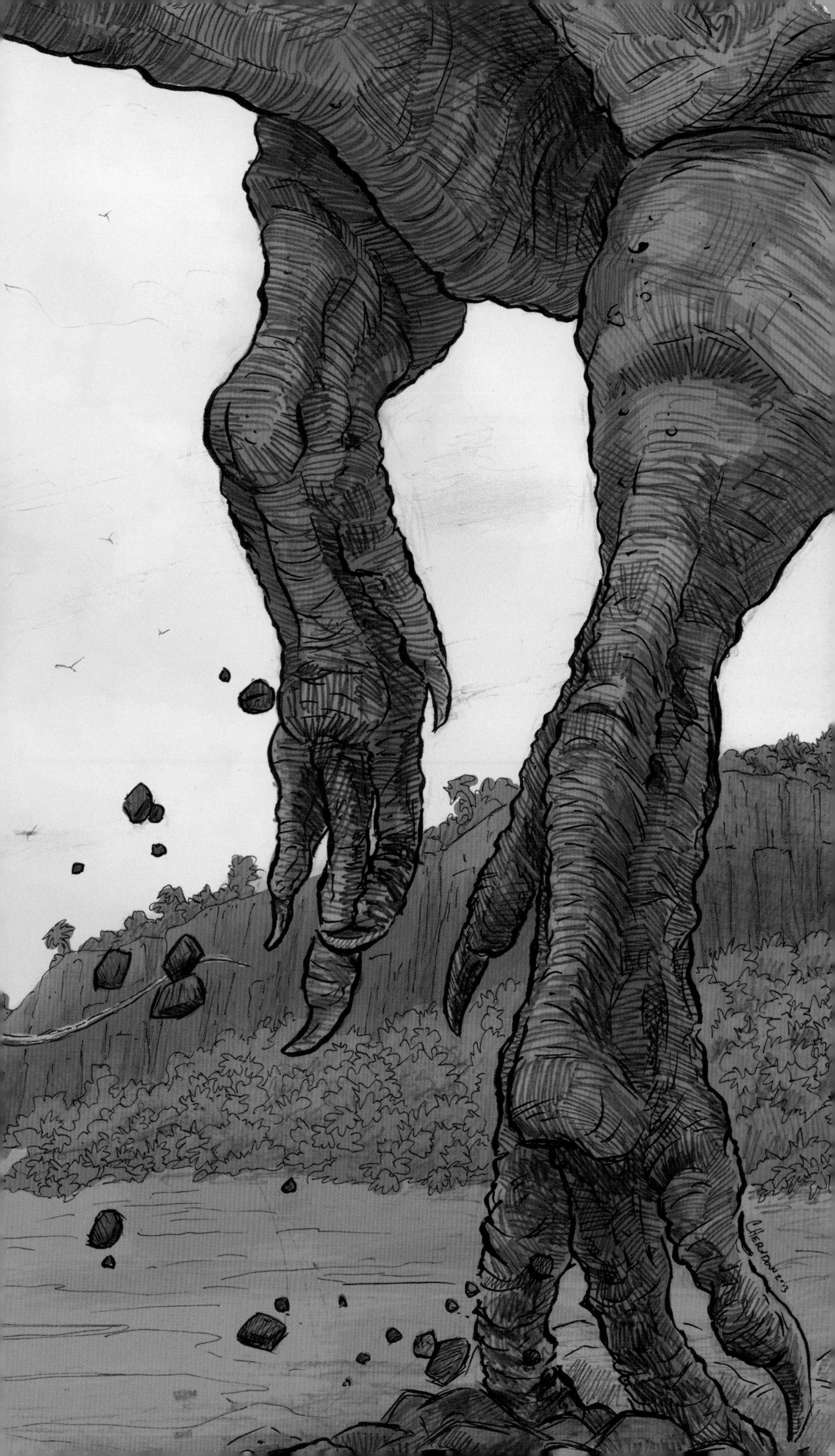

STUDENT HANDBOOK

Academy of
Planetary
Evolution

1

"Back to School"

MONTAUK INDUSTRIES

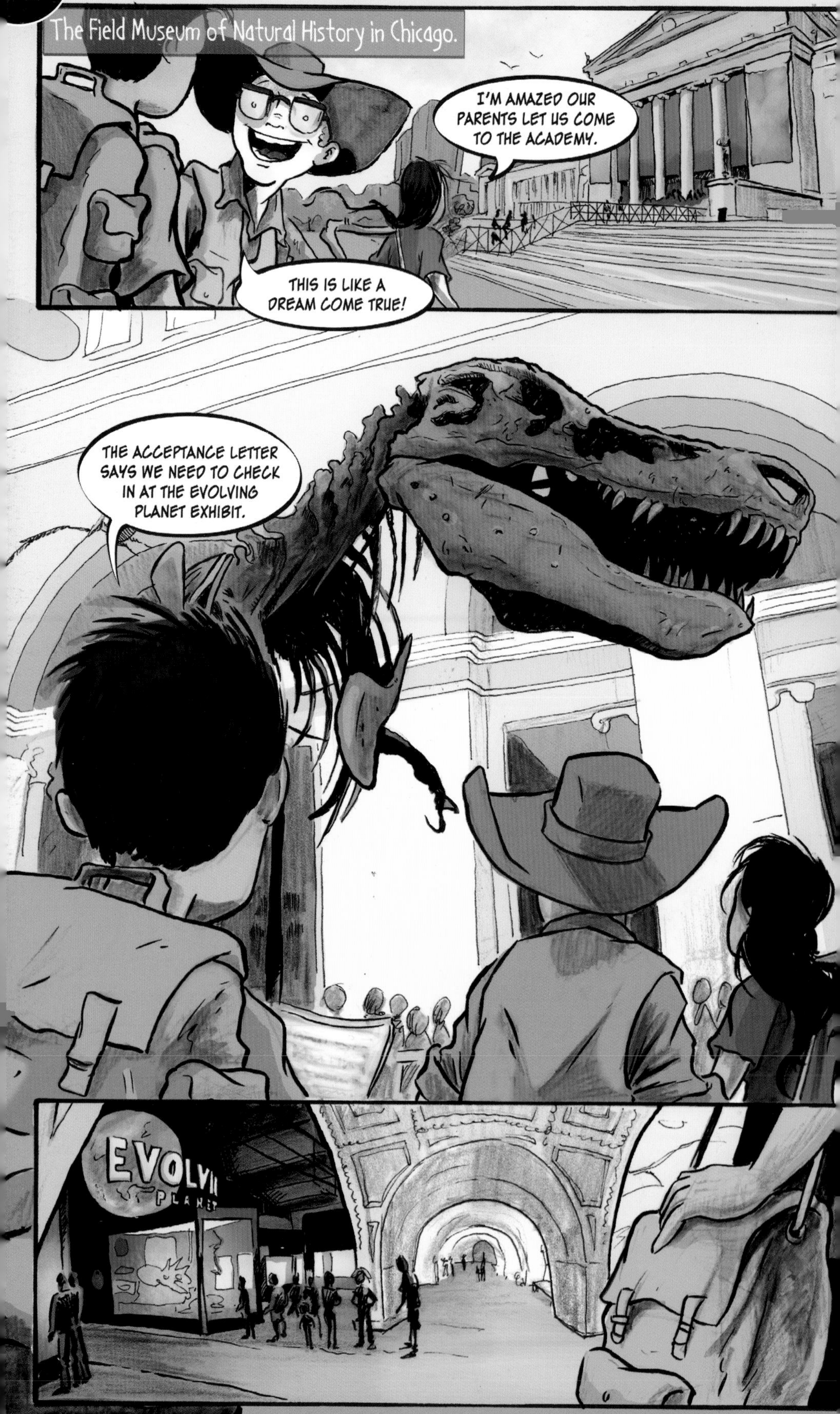
The Field Museum of Natural History in Chicago.
I'M AMAZED OUR PARENTS LET US COME TO THE ACADEMY.
THIS IS LIKE A DREAM COME TRUE!
THE ACCEPTANCE LETTER SAYS WE NEED TO CHECK IN AT THE EVOLVING PLANET EXHIBIT.
EVOLVI
PLANET

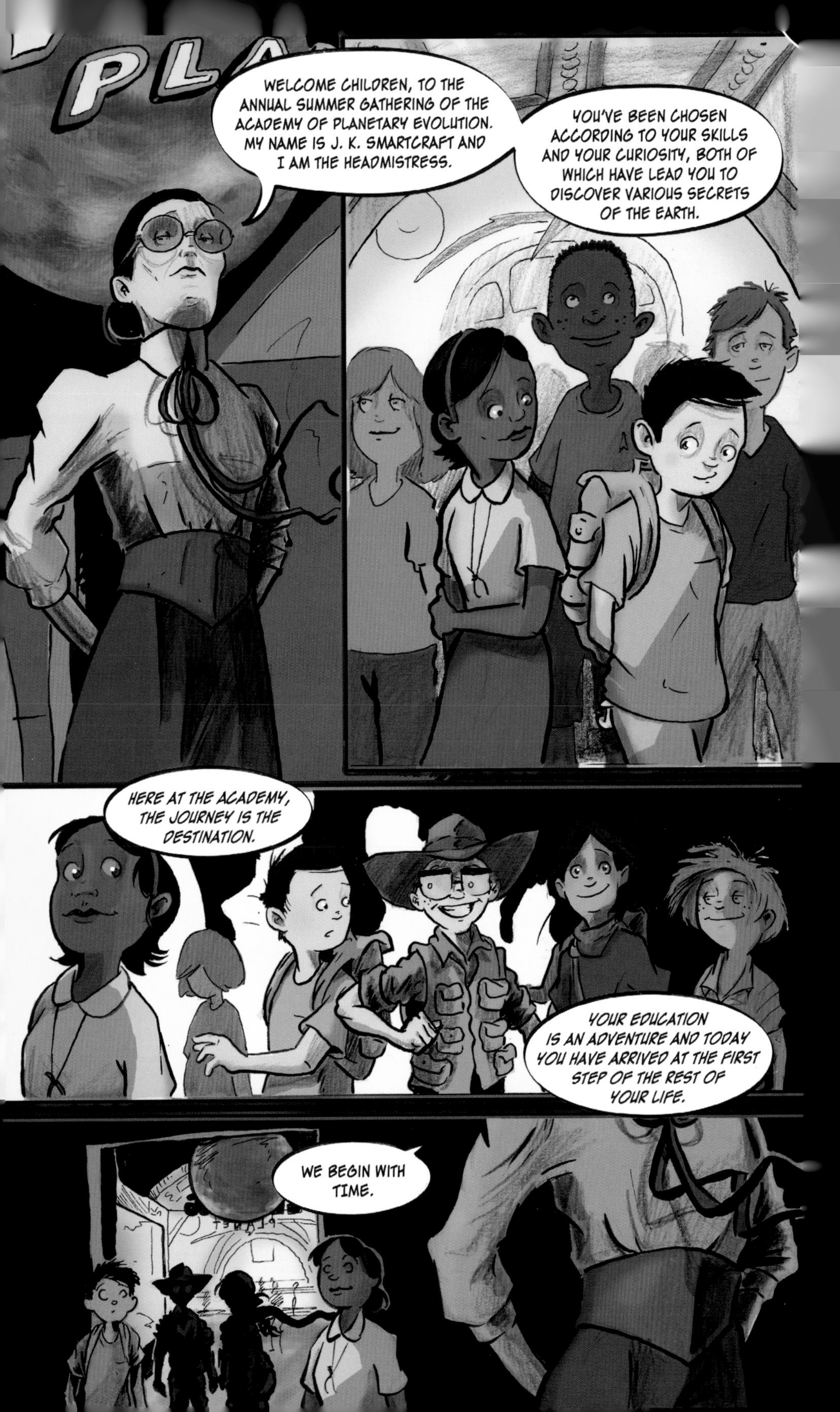
PLA
WELCOME CHILDREN, TO THE ANNUAL SUMMER GATHERING OF THE ACADEMY OF PLANETARY EVOLUTION. MY NAME IS J. K. SMARTCRAFT AND I AM THE HEADMISTRESS.
YOU'VE BEEN CHOSEN ACCORDING TO YOUR SKILLS AND YOUR CURIOSITY, BOTH OF WHICH HAVE LEAD YOU TO DISCOVER VARIOUS SECRETS OF THE EARTH.
HERE AT THE ACADEMY, THE JOURNEY IS THE DESTINATION.
YOUR EDUCATION IS AN ADVENTURE AND TODAY YOU HAVE ARRIVED AT THE FIRST STEP OF THE REST OF YOUR LIFE.
WE BEGIN WITH TIME.

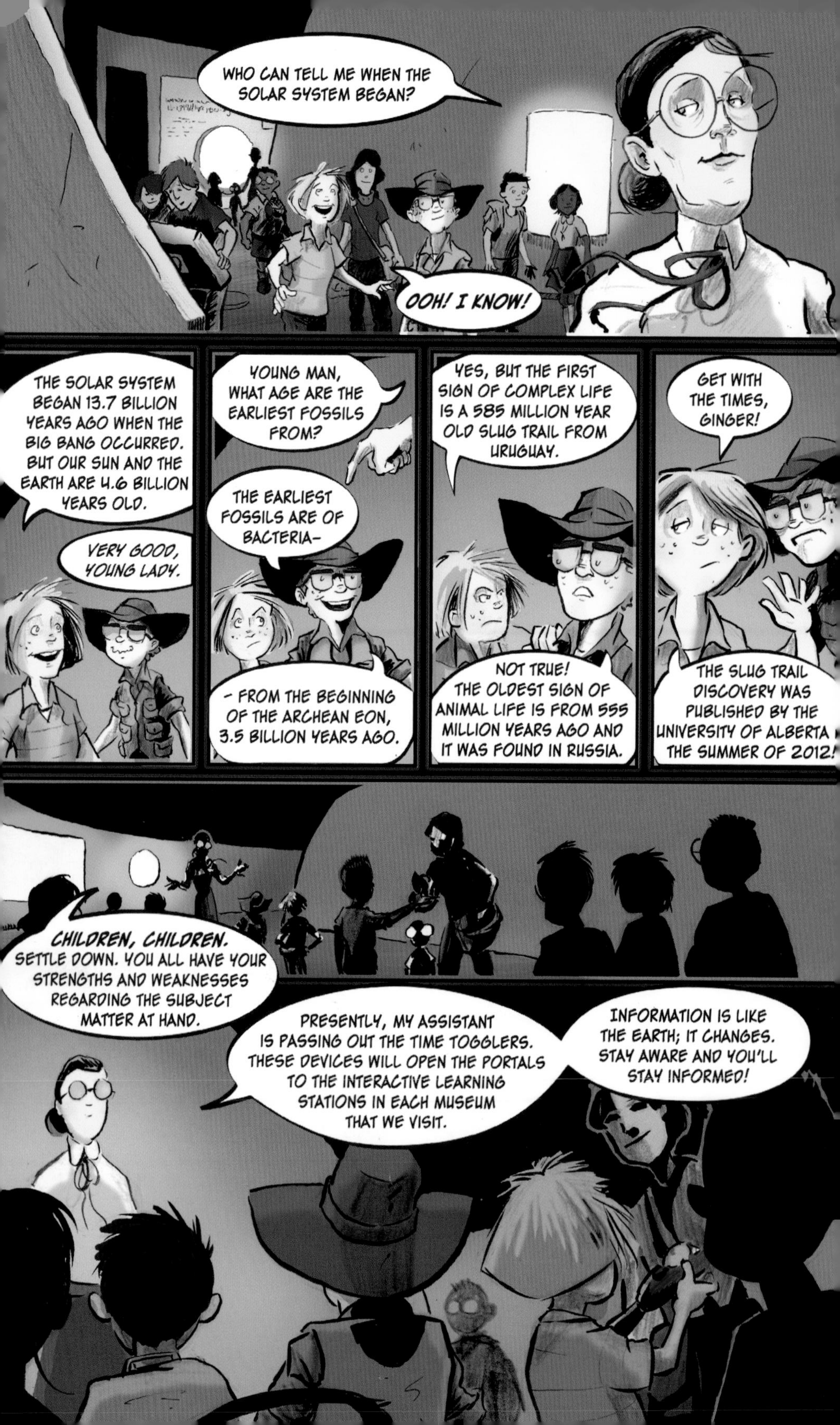
WHO CAN TELL ME WHEN THE SOLAR SYSTEM BEGAN?
OOH! I KNOW!
THE SOLAR SYSTEM BEGAN 13.7 BILLION YEARS AGO WHEN THE BIG BANG OCCURRED. BUT OUR SUN AND THE EARTH ARE 4.6 BILLION YEARS OLD.
VERY GOOD, YOUNG LADY.
YOUNG MAN, WHAT AGE ARE THE EARLIEST FOSSILS FROM?
THE EARLIEST FOSSILS ARE OF BACTERIA-
- FROM THE BEGINNING OF THE ARCHEAN EON, 3.5 BILLION YEARS AGO.
YES, BUT THE FIRST SIGN OF COMPLEX LIFE IS A 585 MILLION YEAR OLD SLUG TRAIL FROM URUGUAY.
NOT TRUE! THE OLDEST SIGN OF ANIMAL LIFE IS FROM 555 MILLION YEARS AGO AND IT WAS FOUND IN RUSSIA.
GET WITH THE TIMES, GINGER!
THE SLUG TRAIL DISCOVERY WAS PUBLISHED BY THE UNIVERSITY OF ALBERTA THE SUMMER OF 2012!
CHILDREN, CHILDREN. SETTLE DOWN. YOU ALL HAVE YOUR STRENGTHS AND WEAKNESSES REGARDING THE SUBJECT MATTER AT HAND.
PRESENTLY, MY ASSISTANT IS PASSING OUT THE TIME TOGGLERS. THESE DEVICES WILL OPEN THE PORTALS TO THE INTERACTIVE LEARNING STATIONS IN EACH MUSEUM THAT WE VISIT.
INFORMATION IS LIKE THE EARTH; IT CHANGES. STAY AWARE AND YOU'LL STAY INFORMED!

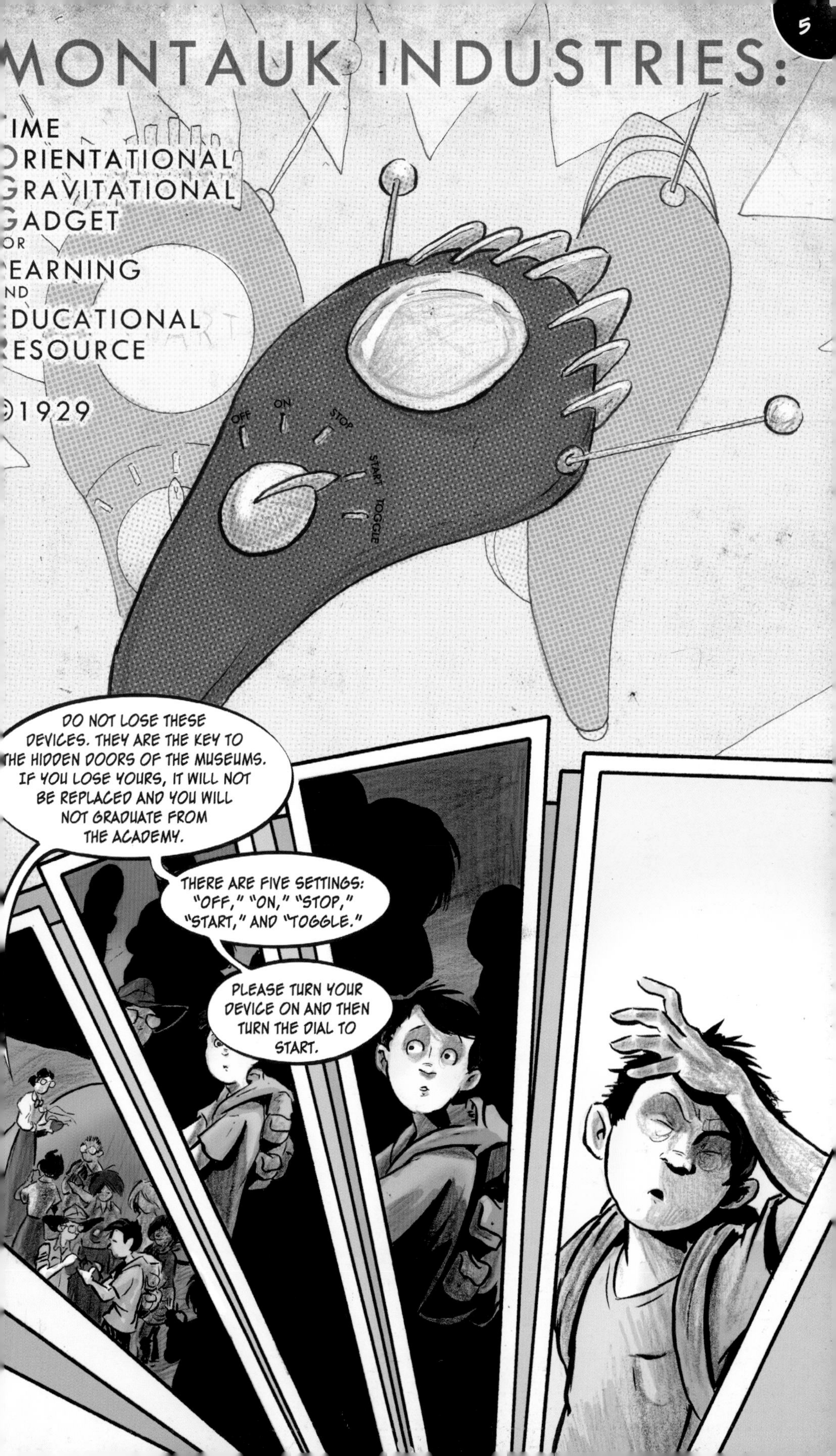
MONTAUK INDUSTRIES:
IME
RIENTATIONAL
RAVITATIONAL
ADGET
OR
EARNING
ND
DUCATIONAL
ESOURCE
1929
OFF
ON
STOP
START
TOGGLE
DO NOT LOSE THESE DEVICES. THEY ARE THE KEY TO THE HIDDEN DOORS OF THE MUSEUMS. IF YOU LOSE YOURS, IT WILL NOT BE REPLACED AND YOU WILL NOT GRADUATE FROM THE ACADEMY.
THERE ARE FIVE SETTINGS: "OFF," "ON," "STOP," "START," AND "TOGGLE."
PLEASE TURN YOUR DEVICE ON AND THEN TURN THE DIAL TO START.

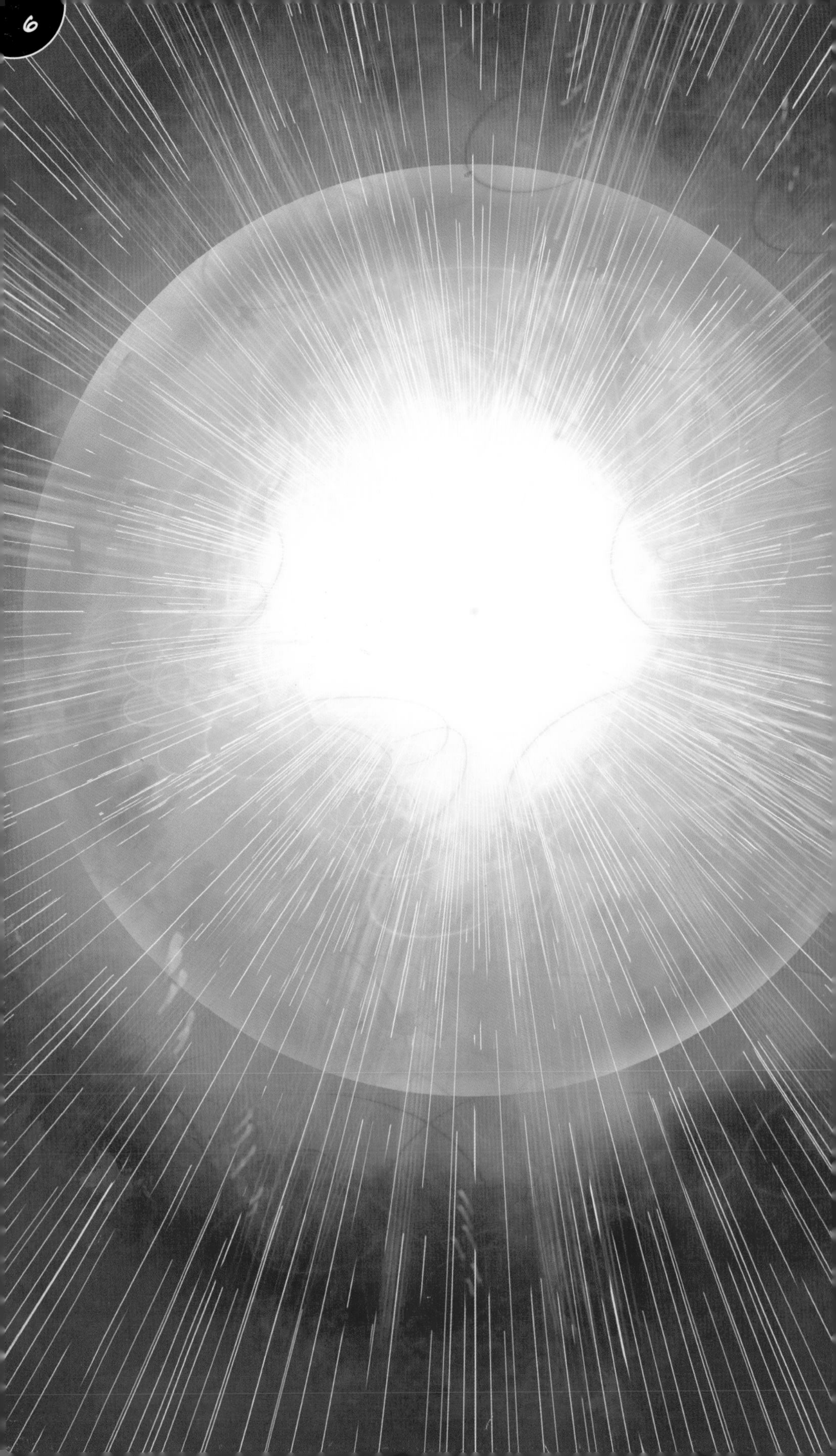

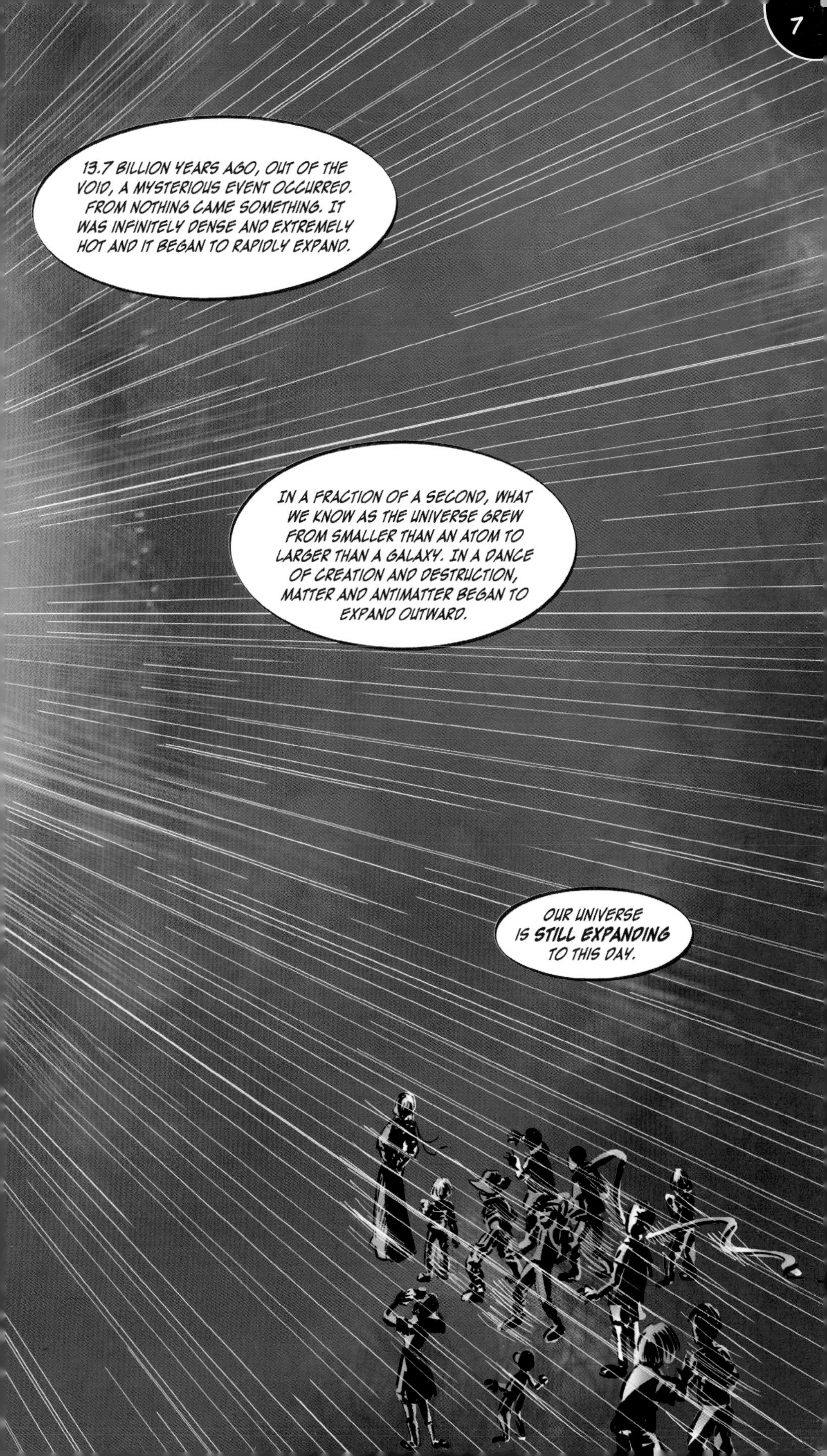
13.7 BILLION YEARS AGO, OUT OF THE VOID, A MYSTERIOUS EVENT OCCURRED. FROM NOTHING CAME SOMETHING. IT WAS INFINITELY DENSE AND EXTREMELY HOT AND IT BEGAN TO RAPIDLY EXPAND.
IN A FRACTION OF A SECOND, WHAT WE KNOW AS THE UNIVERSE GREW FROM SMALLER THAN AN ATOM TO LARGER THAN A GALAXY. IN A DANCE OF CREATION AND DESTRUCTION, MATTER AND ANTIMATTER BEGAN TO EXPAND OUTWARD.
OUR UNIVERSE IS **STILL EXPANDING** TO THIS DAY.

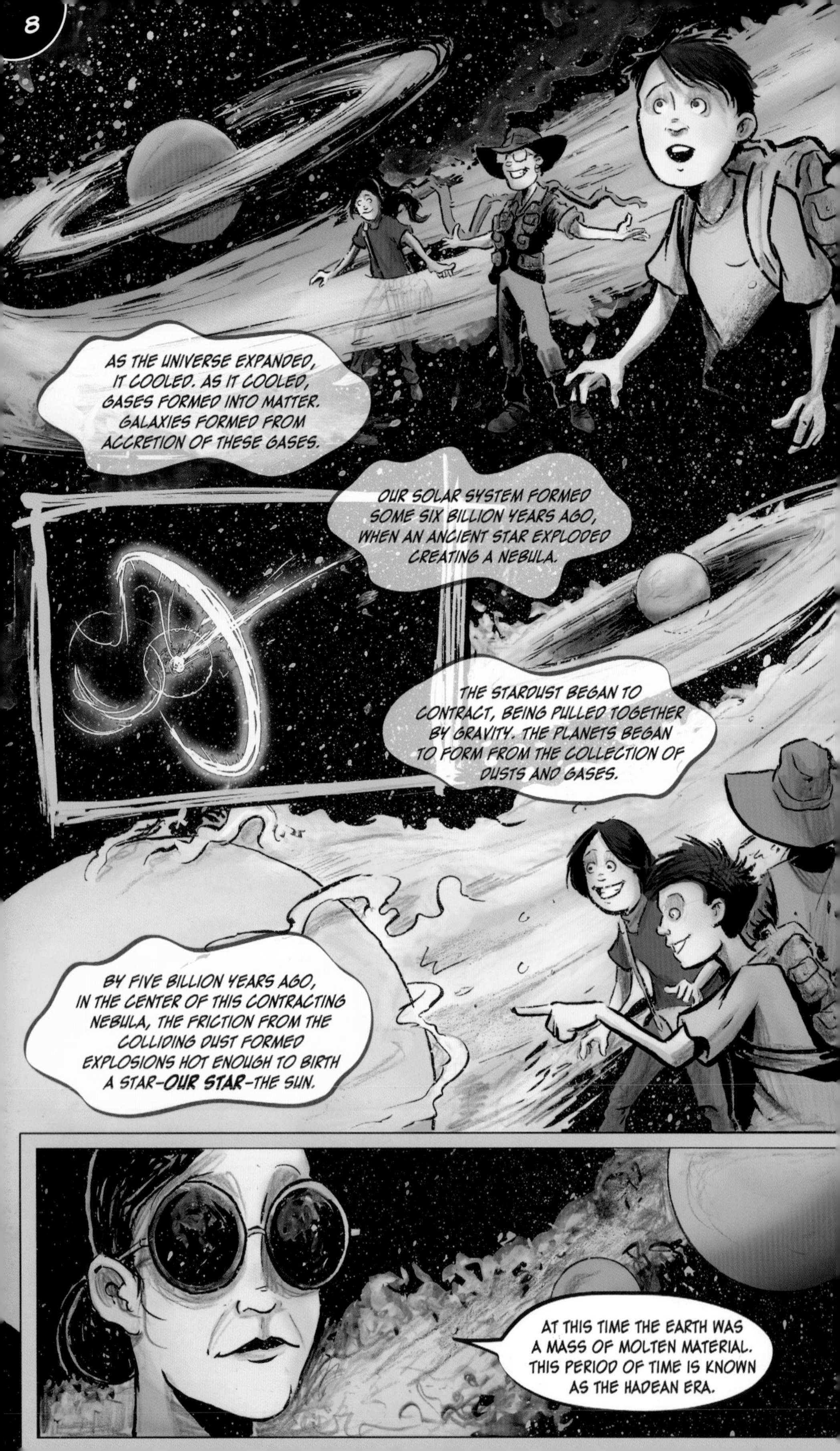
AS THE UNIVERSE EXPANDED, IT COOLED. AS IT COOLED, GASES FORMED INTO MATTER. GALAXIES FORMED FROM ACCRETION OF THESE GASES.
OUR SOLAR SYSTEM FORMED SOME SIX BILLION YEARS AGO, WHEN AN ANCIENT STAR EXPLODED CREATING A NEBULA.
THE STARDUST BEGAN TO CONTRACT, BEING PULLED TOGETHER BY GRAVITY. THE PLANETS BEGAN TO FORM FROM THE COLLECTION OF DUSTS AND GASES.
BY FIVE BILLION YEARS AGO, IN THE CENTER OF THIS CONTRACTING NEBULA, THE FRICTION FROM THE COLLIDING DUST FORMED EXPLOSIONS HOT ENOUGH TO BIRTH A STAR–**OUR STAR**–THE SUN.
AT THIS TIME THE EARTH WAS A MASS OF MOLTEN MATERIAL. THIS PERIOD OF TIME IS KNOWN AS THE HADEAN ERA.

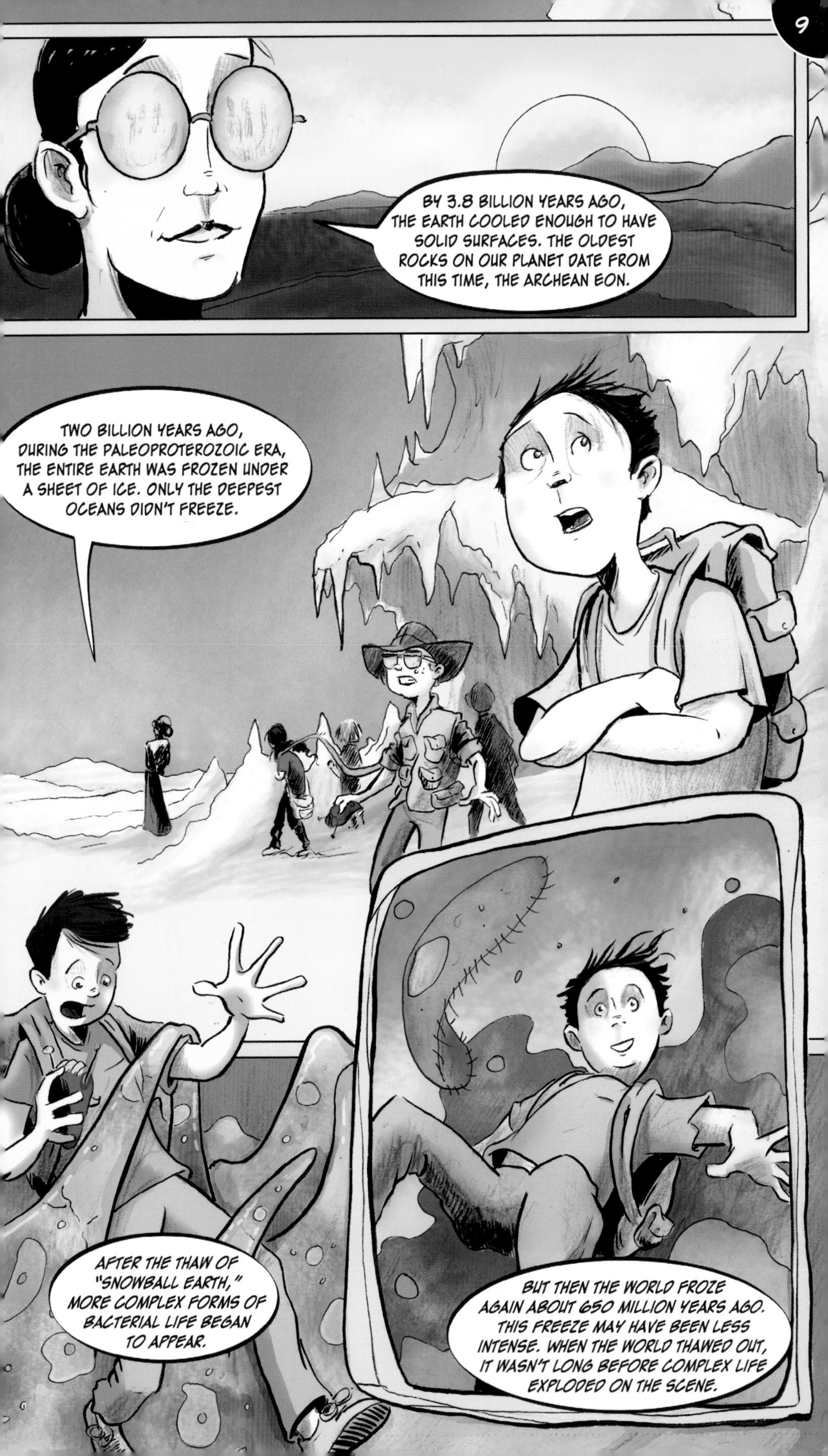
BY 3.8 BILLION YEARS AGO, THE EARTH COOLED ENOUGH TO HAVE SOLID SURFACES. THE OLDEST ROCKS ON OUR PLANET DATE FROM THIS TIME, THE ARCHEAN EON.
TWO BILLION YEARS AGO, DURING THE PALEOPROTEROZOIC ERA, THE ENTIRE EARTH WAS FROZEN UNDER A SHEET OF ICE. ONLY THE DEEPEST OCEANS DIDN'T FREEZE.
AFTER THE THAW OF "SNOWBALL EARTH," MORE COMPLEX FORMS OF BACTERIAL LIFE BEGAN TO APPEAR.
BUT THEN THE WORLD FROZE AGAIN ABOUT 650 MILLION YEARS AGO. THIS FREEZE MAY HAVE BEEN LESS INTENSE. WHEN THE WORLD THAWED OUT, IT WASN'T LONG BEFORE COMPLEX LIFE EXPLODED ON THE SCENE.

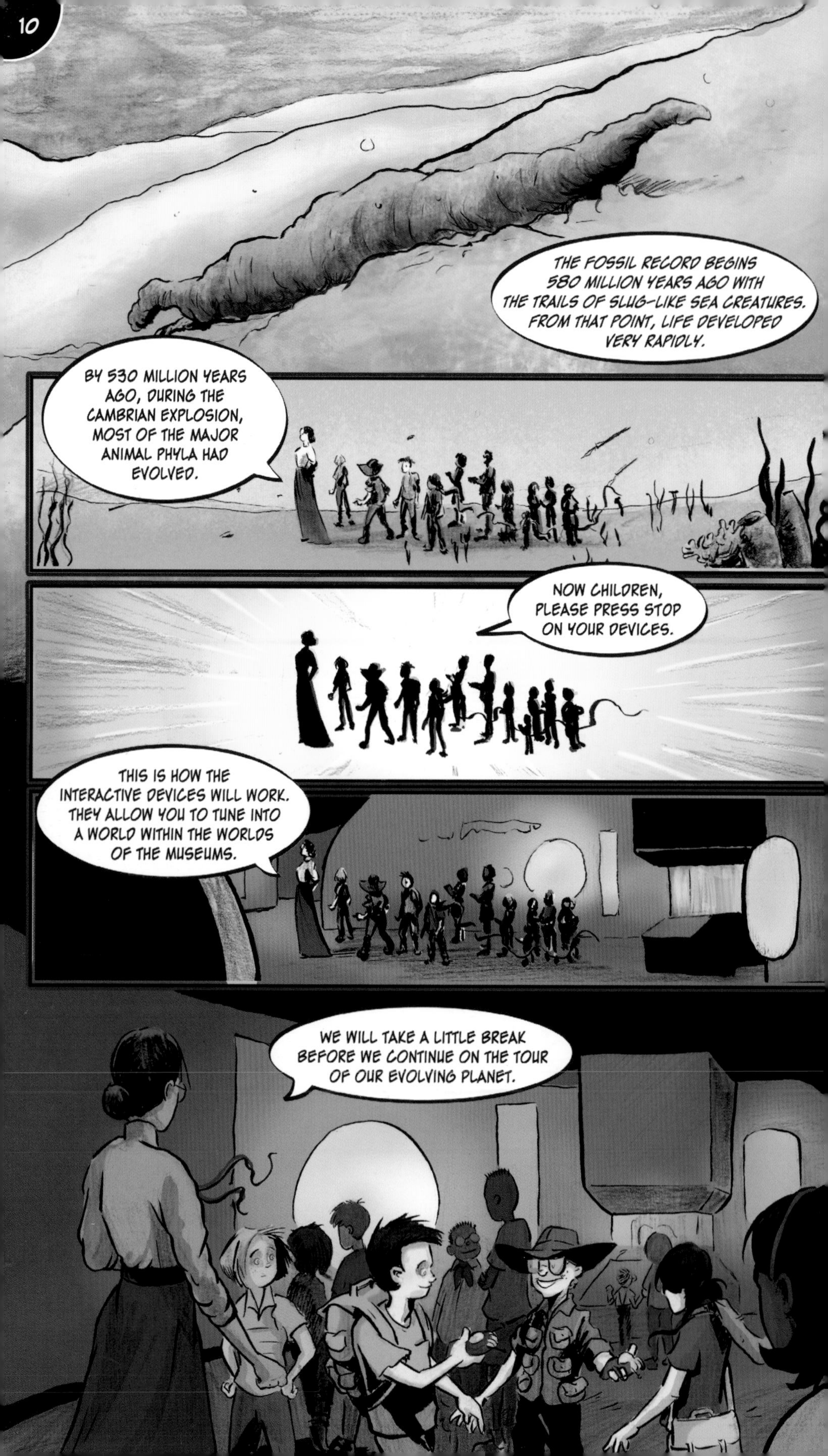
THE FOSSIL RECORD BEGINS 580 MILLION YEARS AGO WITH THE TRAILS OF SLUG-LIKE SEA CREATURES. FROM THAT POINT, LIFE DEVELOPED VERY RAPIDLY.
BY 530 MILLION YEARS AGO, DURING THE CAMBRIAN EXPLOSION, MOST OF THE MAJOR ANIMAL PHYLA HAD EVOLVED.
NOW CHILDREN, PLEASE PRESS STOP ON YOUR DEVICES.
THIS IS HOW THE INTERACTIVE DEVICES WILL WORK. THEY ALLOW YOU TO TUNE INTO A WORLD WITHIN THE WORLDS OF THE MUSEUMS.
WE WILL TAKE A LITTLE BREAK BEFORE WE CONTINUE ON THE TOUR OF OUR EVOLVING PLANET.

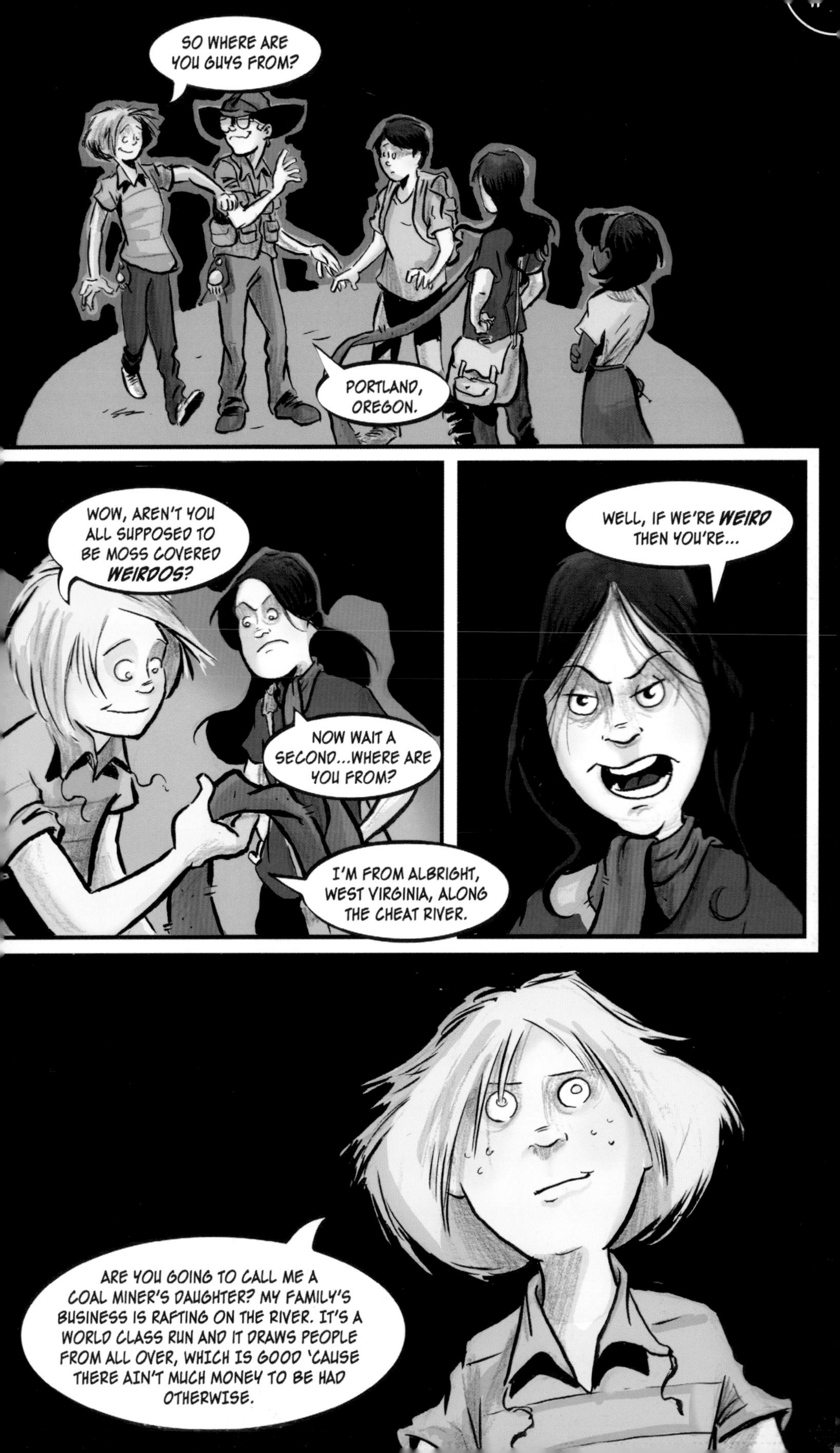
SO WHERE ARE YOU GUYS FROM?
PORTLAND, OREGON.
WOW, AREN'T YOU ALL SUPPOSED TO BE MOSS COVERED WEIRDOS?
NOW WAIT A SECOND...WHERE ARE YOU FROM?
I'M FROM ALBRIGHT, WEST VIRGINIA, ALONG THE CHEAT RIVER.
WELL, IF WE'RE WEIRD THEN YOU'RE...
ARE YOU GOING TO CALL ME A COAL MINER'S DAUGHTER? MY FAMILY'S BUSINESS IS RAFTING ON THE RIVER. IT'S A WORLD CLASS RUN AND IT DRAWS PEOPLE FROM ALL OVER, WHICH IS GOOD 'CAUSE THERE AIN'T MUCH MONEY TO BE HAD OTHERWISE.

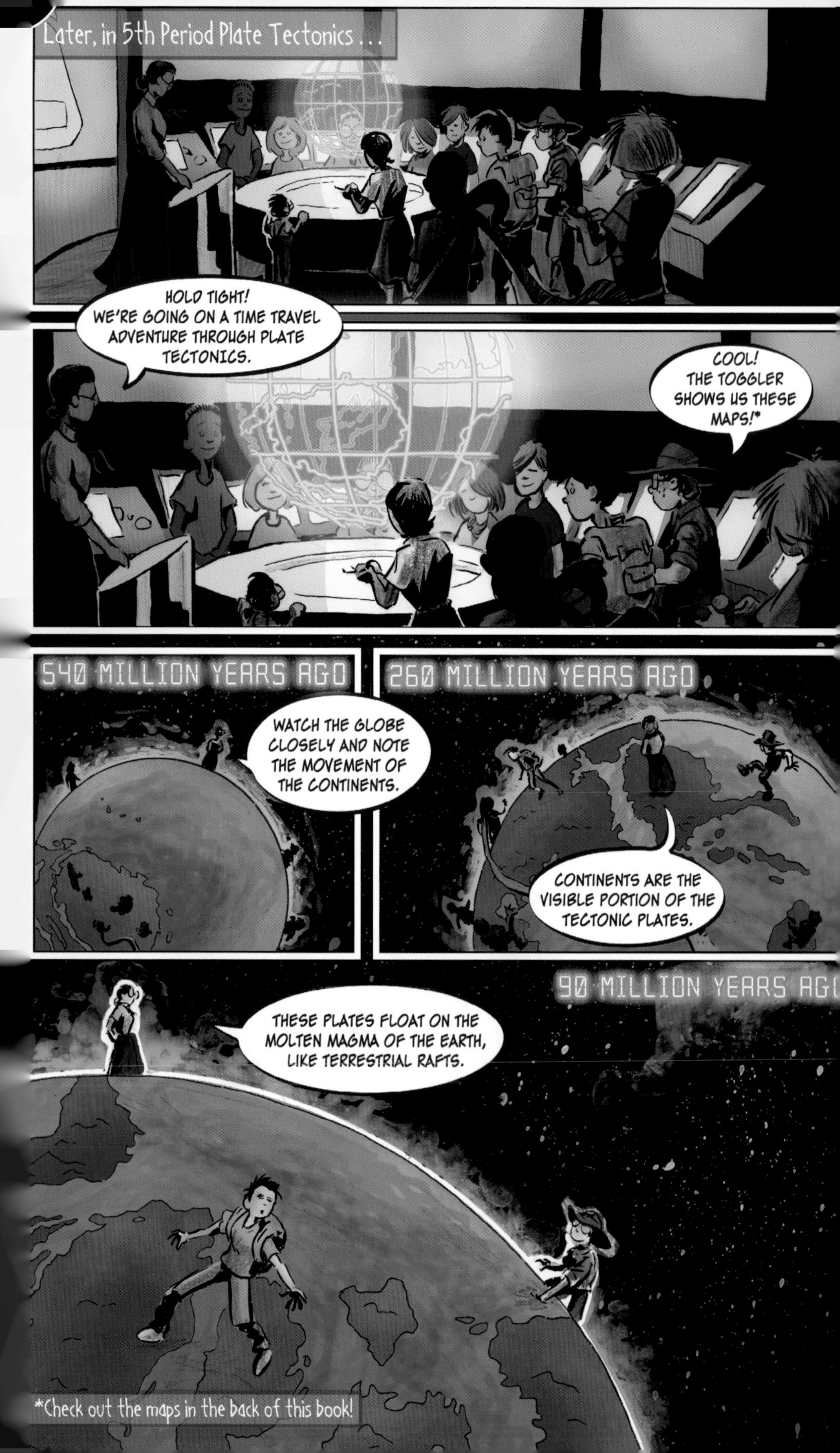
Later, in 5th Period Plate Tectonics . . .
HOLD TIGHT! WE'RE GOING ON A TIME TRAVEL ADVENTURE THROUGH PLATE TECTONICS.
COOL! THE TOGGLER SHOWS US THESE MAPS!*
540 MILLION YEARS AGO
WATCH THE GLOBE CLOSELY AND NOTE THE MOVEMENT OF THE CONTINENTS.
260 MILLION YEARS AGO
CONTINENTS ARE THE VISIBLE PORTION OF THE TECTONIC PLATES.
90 MILLION YEARS AGO
THESE PLATES FLOAT ON THE MOLTEN MAGMA OF THE EARTH, LIKE TERRESTRIAL RAFTS.
*Check out the maps in the back of this book!

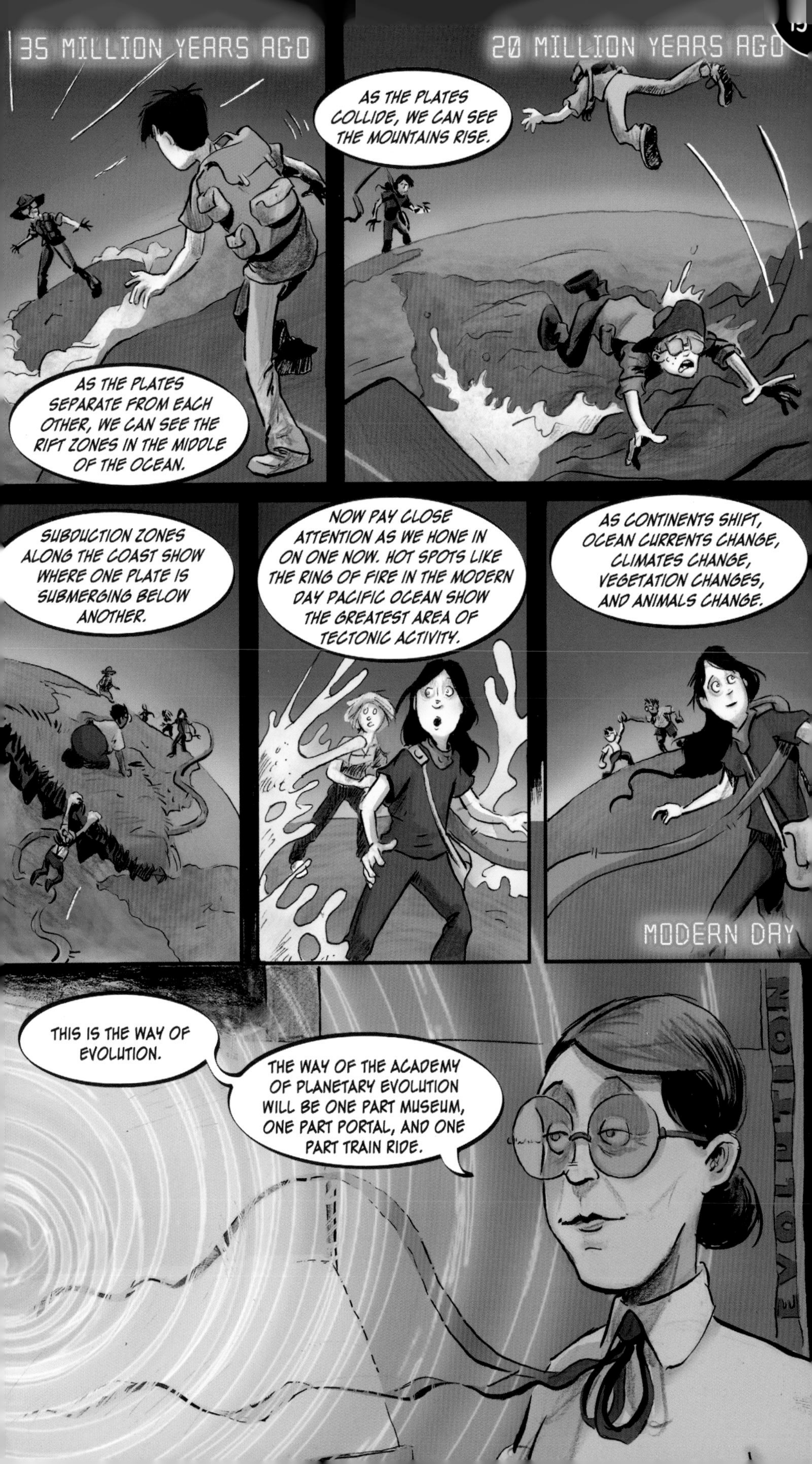
35 MILLION YEARS AGO
AS THE PLATES SEPARATE FROM EACH OTHER, WE CAN SEE THE RIFT ZONES IN THE MIDDLE OF THE OCEAN.
20 MILLION YEARS AGO
AS THE PLATES COLLIDE, WE CAN SEE THE MOUNTAINS RISE.
SUBDUCTION ZONES ALONG THE COAST SHOW WHERE ONE PLATE IS SUBMERGING BELOW ANOTHER.
NOW PAY CLOSE ATTENTION AS WE HONE IN ON ONE NOW. HOT SPOTS LIKE THE RING OF FIRE IN THE MODERN DAY PACIFIC OCEAN SHOW THE GREATEST AREA OF TECTONIC ACTIVITY.
AS CONTINENTS SHIFT, OCEAN CURRENTS CHANGE, CLIMATES CHANGE, VEGETATION CHANGES, AND ANIMALS CHANGE.
MODERN DAY
THIS IS THE WAY OF EVOLUTION.
THE WAY OF THE ACADEMY OF PLANETARY EVOLUTION WILL BE ONE PART MUSEUM, ONE PART PORTAL, AND ONE PART TRAIN RIDE.

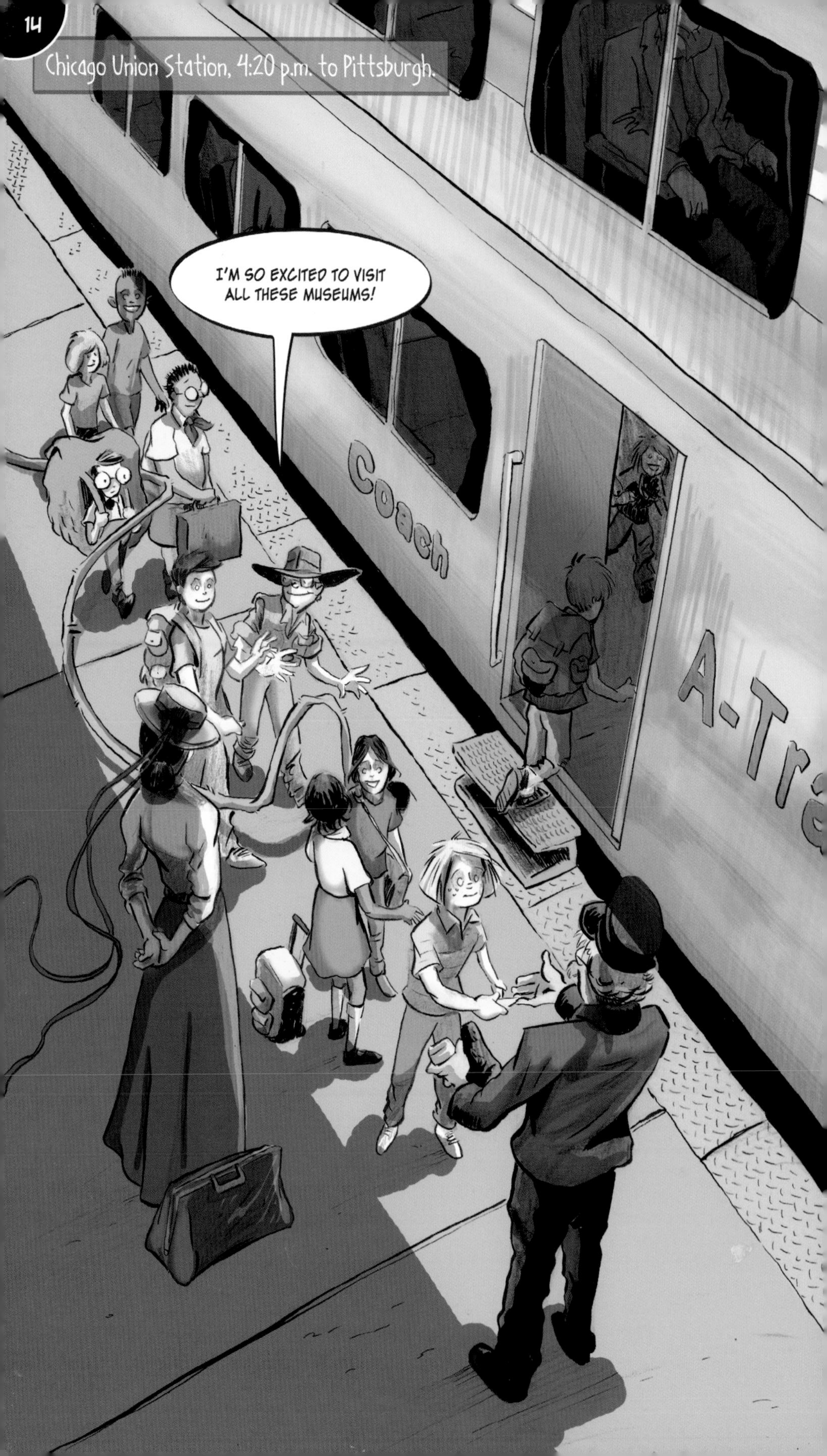
Chicago Union Station, 4:20 p.m. to Pittsburgh.
I'M SO EXCITED TO VISIT ALL THESE MUSEUMS!
Coach
A-Tra

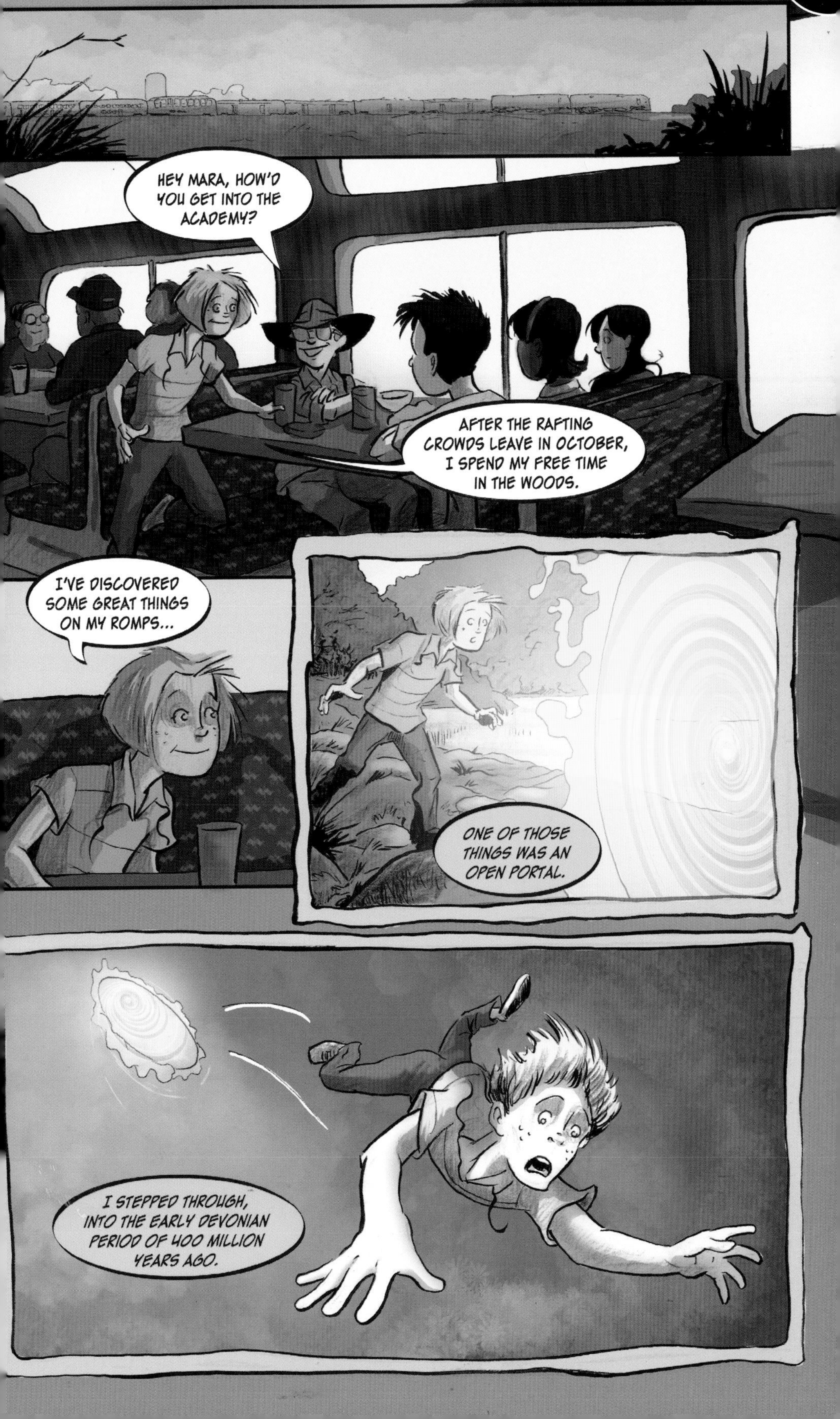
HEY MARA, HOW'D YOU GET INTO THE ACADEMY?
AFTER THE RAFTING CROWDS LEAVE IN OCTOBER, I SPEND MY FREE TIME IN THE WOODS.
I'VE DISCOVERED SOME GREAT THINGS ON MY ROMPS...
ONE OF THOSE THINGS WAS AN OPEN PORTAL.
I STEPPED THROUGH, INTO THE EARLY DEVONIAN PERIOD OF 400 MILLION YEARS AGO.

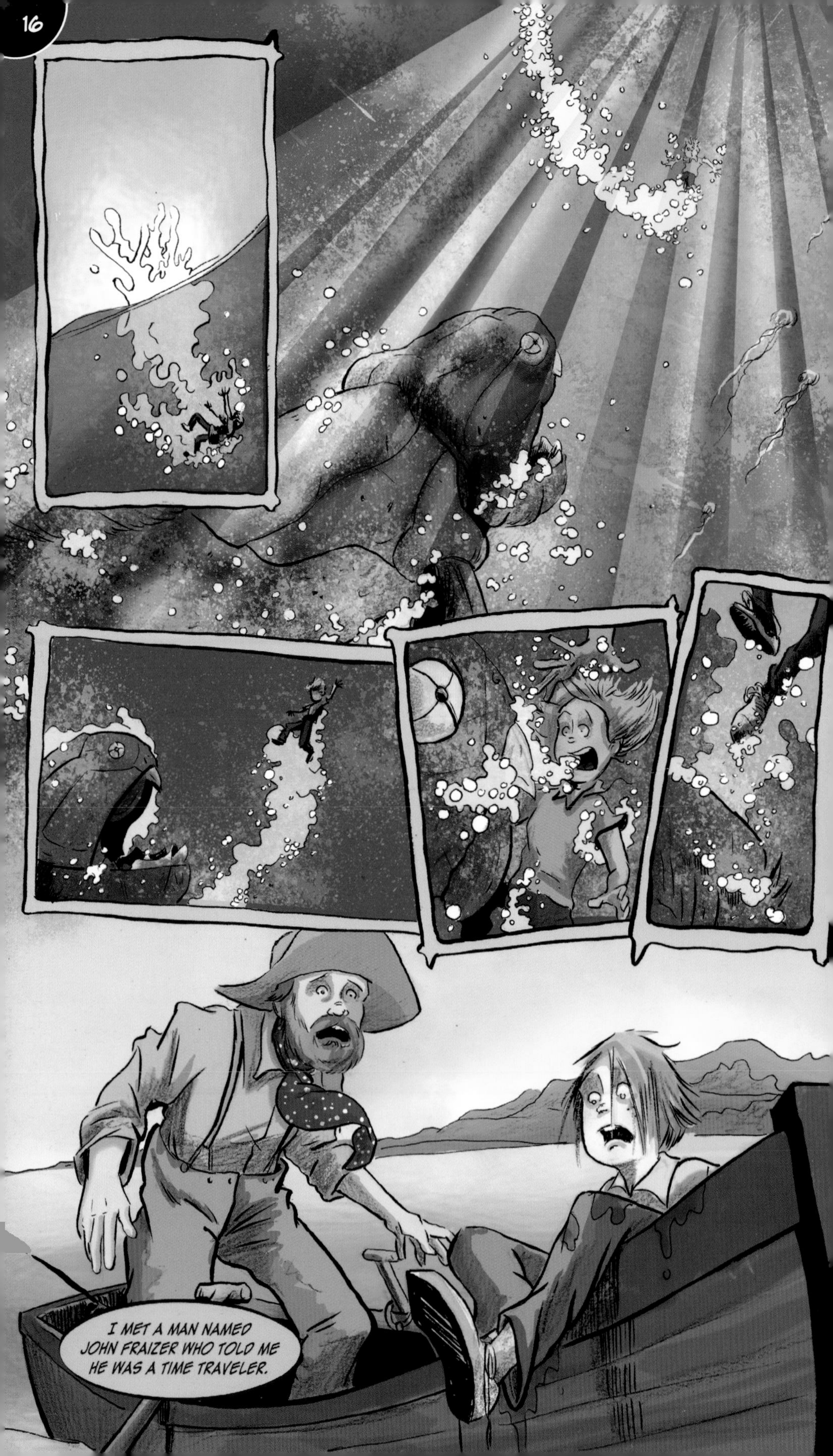
I MET A MAN NAMED
JOHN FRAIZER WHO TOLD ME
HE WAS A TIME TRAVELER.

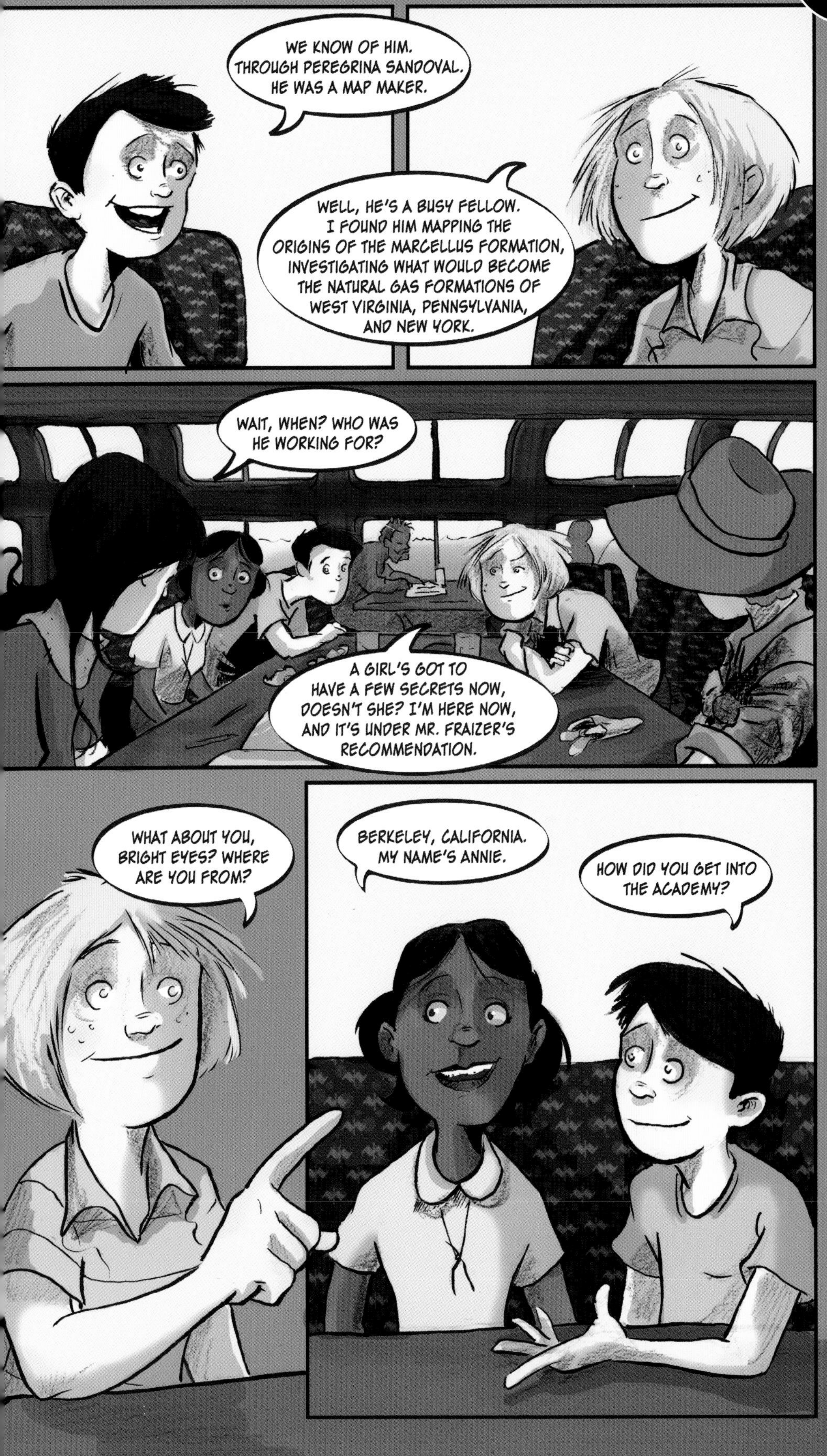
WE KNOW OF HIM. THROUGH PEREGRINA SANDOVAL. HE WAS A MAP MAKER.
WELL, HE'S A BUSY FELLOW. I FOUND HIM MAPPING THE ORIGINS OF THE MARCELLUS FORMATION, INVESTIGATING WHAT WOULD BECOME THE NATURAL GAS FORMATIONS OF WEST VIRGINIA, PENNSYLVANIA, AND NEW YORK.
WAIT, WHEN? WHO WAS HE WORKING FOR?
A GIRL'S GOT TO HAVE A FEW SECRETS NOW, DOESN'T SHE? I'M HERE NOW, AND IT'S UNDER MR. FRAIZER'S RECOMMENDATION.
WHAT ABOUT YOU, BRIGHT EYES? WHERE ARE YOU FROM?
BERKELEY, CALIFORNIA. MY NAME'S ANNIE.
HOW DID YOU GET INTO THE ACADEMY?

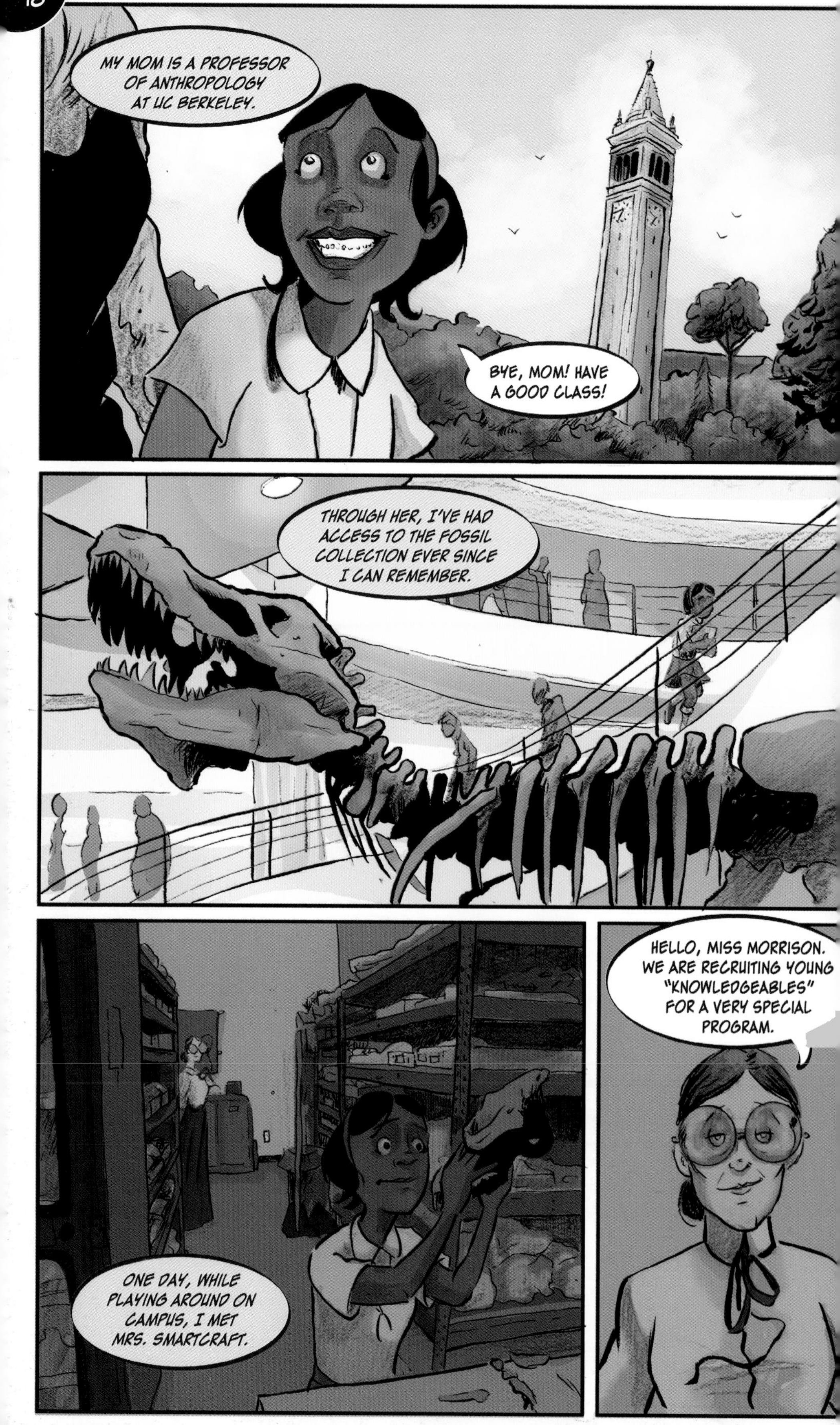
MY MOM IS A PROFESSOR OF ANTHROPOLOGY AT UC BERKELEY.
BYE, MOM! HAVE A GOOD CLASS!
THROUGH HER, I'VE HAD ACCESS TO THE FOSSIL COLLECTION EVER SINCE I CAN REMEMBER.
ONE DAY, WHILE PLAYING AROUND ON CAMPUS, I MET MRS. SMARTCRAFT.
HELLO, MISS MORRISON. WE ARE RECRUITING YOUNG "KNOWLEDGEABLES" FOR A VERY SPECIAL PROGRAM.

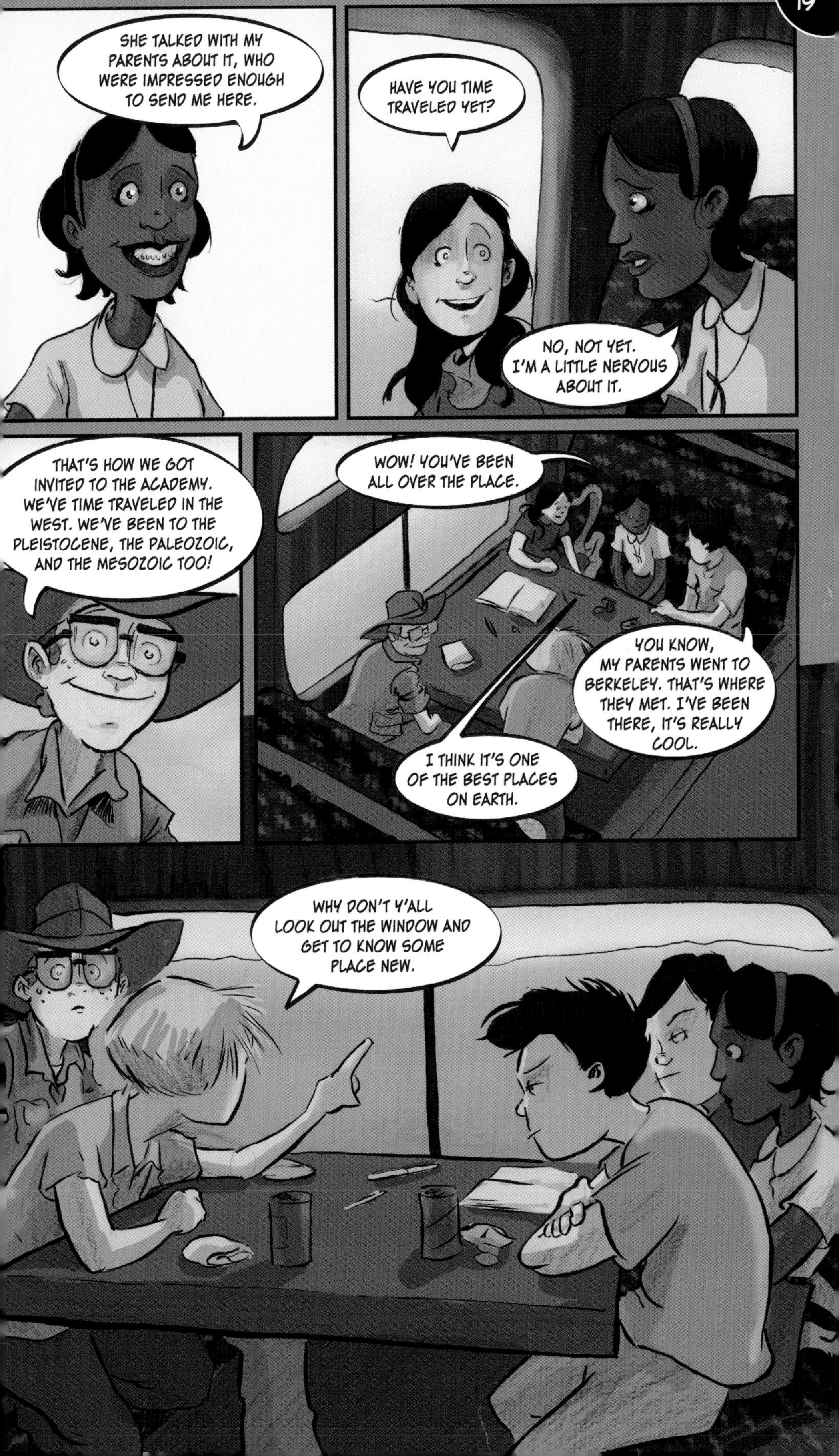
SHE TALKED WITH MY PARENTS ABOUT IT, WHO WERE IMPRESSED ENOUGH TO SEND ME HERE.
HAVE YOU TIME TRAVELED YET?
NO, NOT YET. I'M A LITTLE NERVOUS ABOUT IT.
THAT'S HOW WE GOT INVITED TO THE ACADEMY. WE'VE TIME TRAVELED IN THE WEST. WE'VE BEEN TO THE PLEISTOCENE, THE PALEOZOIC, AND THE MESOZOIC TOO!
WOW! YOU'VE BEEN ALL OVER THE PLACE.
YOU KNOW, MY PARENTS WENT TO BERKELEY. THAT'S WHERE THEY MET. I'VE BEEN THERE, IT'S REALLY COOL.
I THINK IT'S ONE OF THE BEST PLACES ON EARTH.
WHY DON'T Y'ALL LOOK OUT THE WINDOW AND GET TO KNOW SOME PLACE NEW.

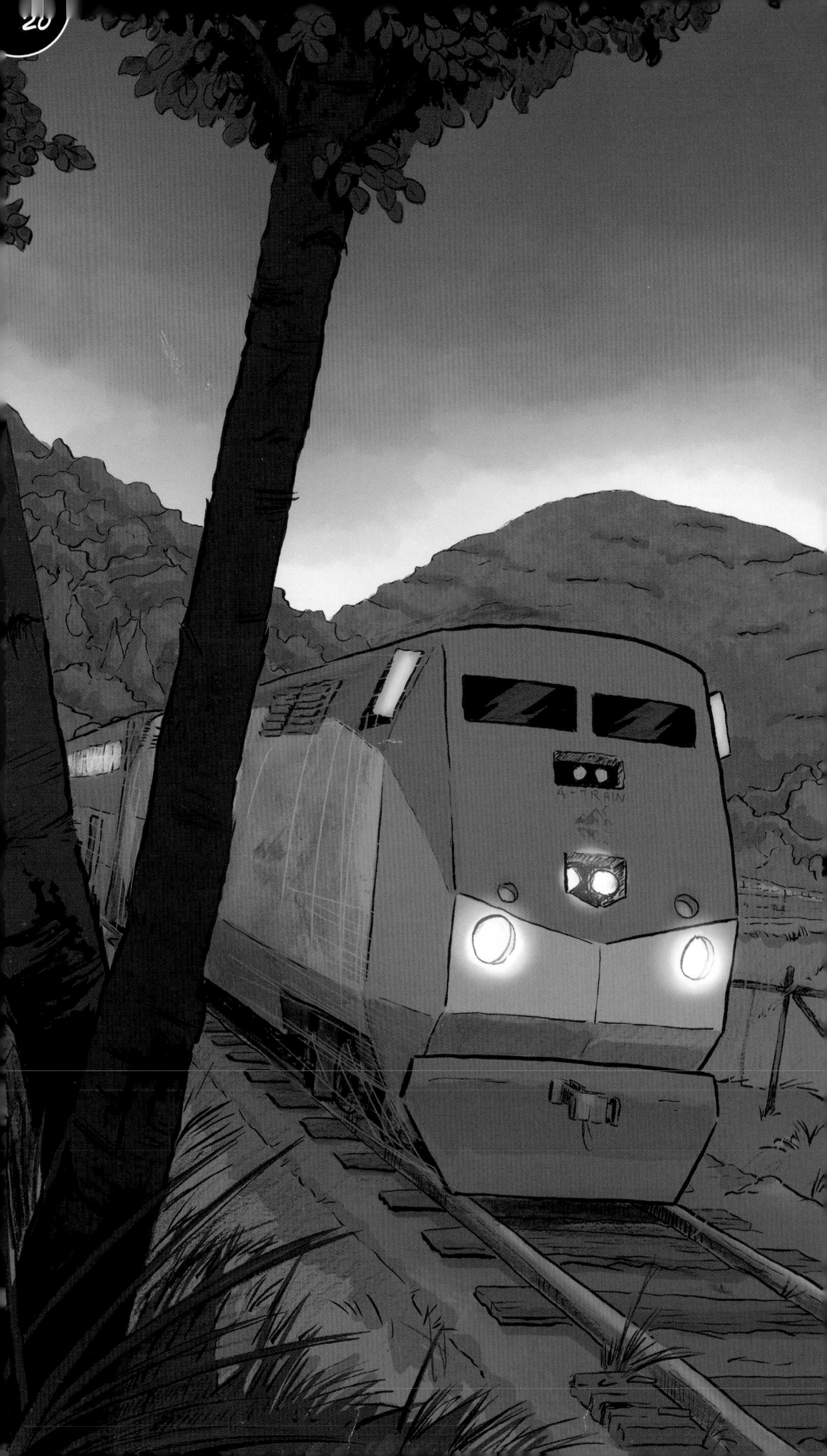
A-TRAIN

STUDENT HANDBOOK

Academy of
Planetary
Evolution

2

"Carnegie Hall"

2

MONTAUK INDUSTRIES

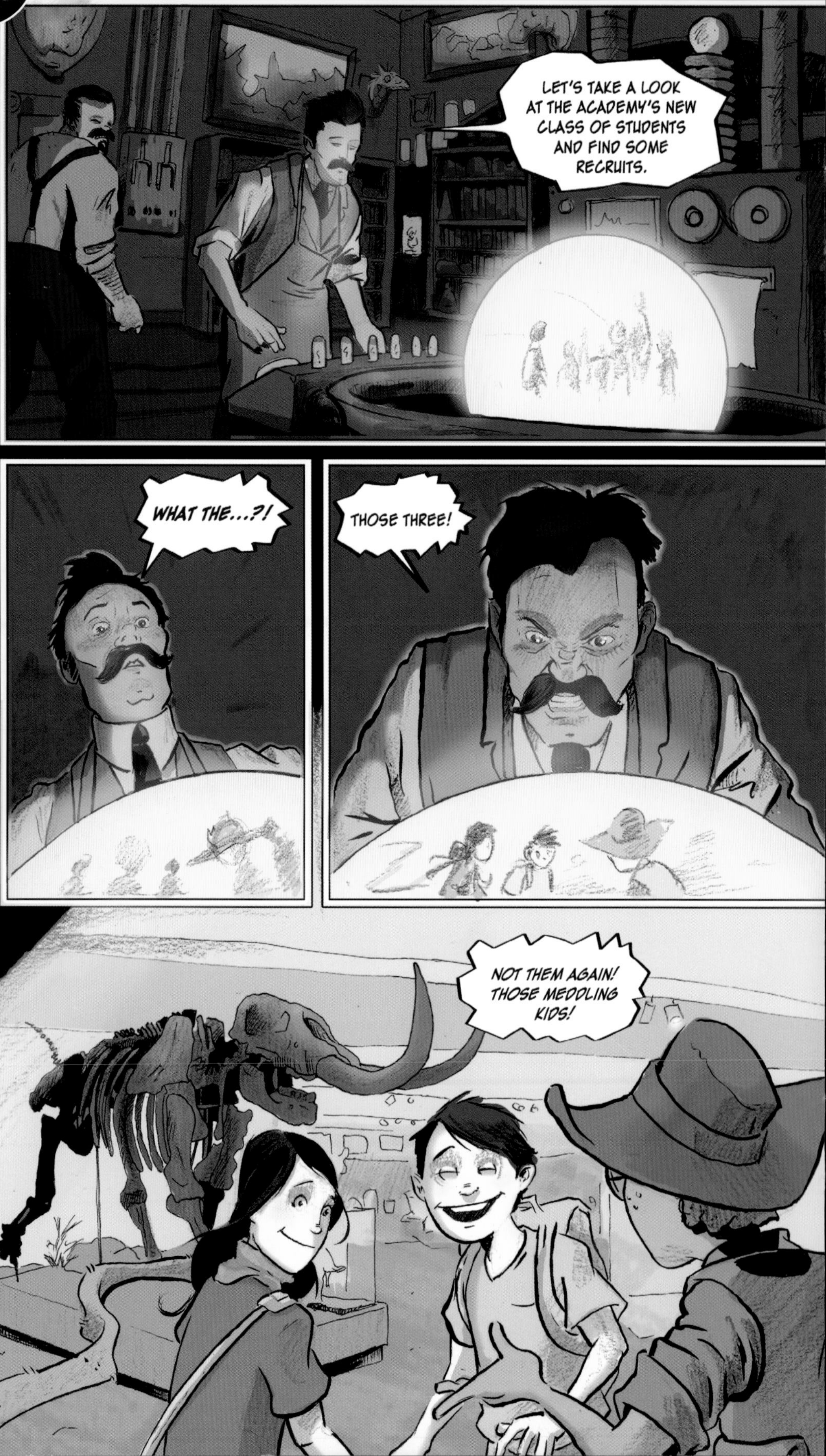
LET'S TAKE A LOOK AT THE ACADEMY'S NEW CLASS OF STUDENTS AND FIND SOME RECRUITS.
WHAT THE...?!
THOSE THREE!
NOT THEM AGAIN! THOSE MEDDLING KIDS!

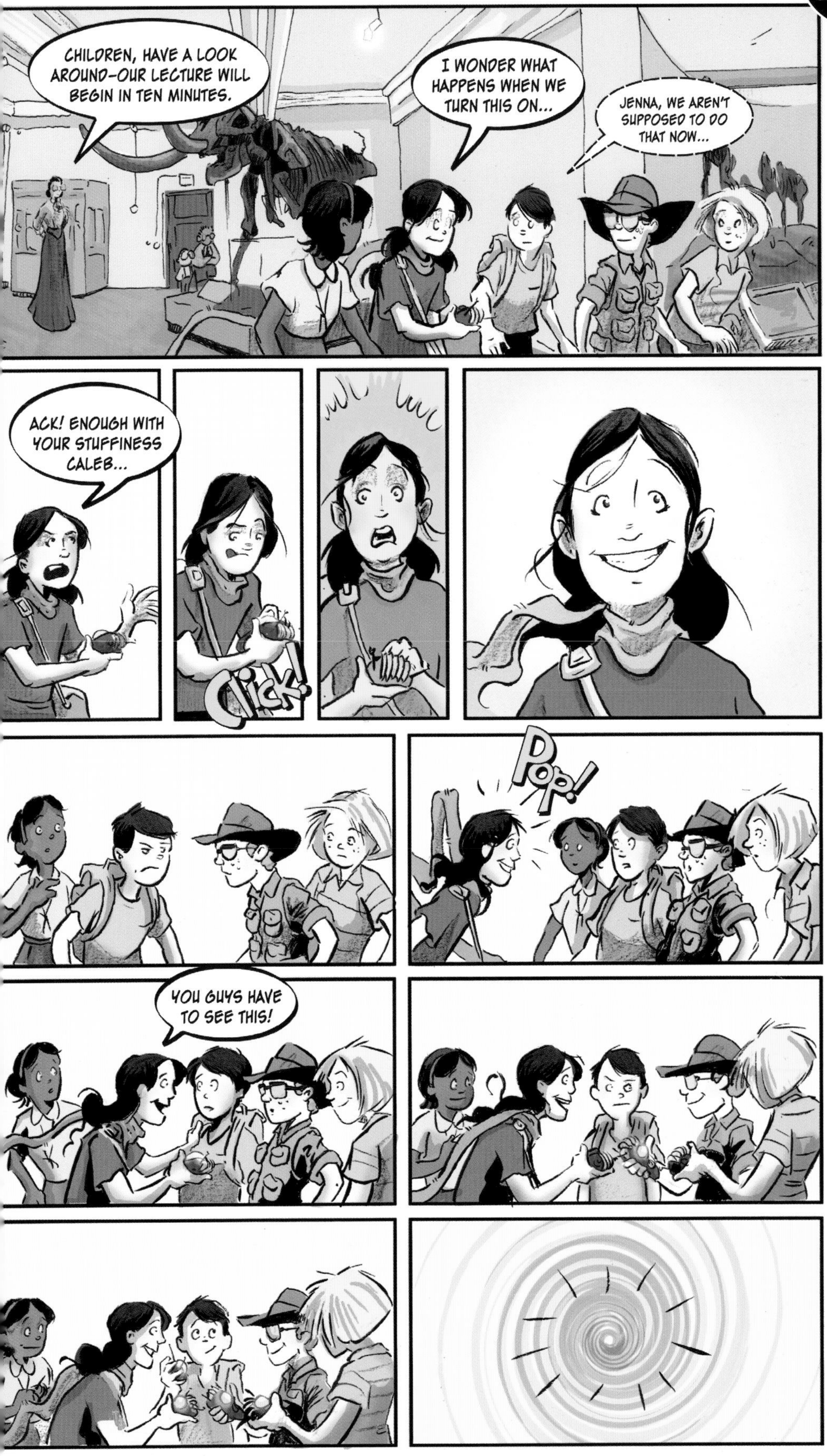
CHILDREN, HAVE A LOOK AROUND–OUR LECTURE WILL BEGIN IN TEN MINUTES.
I WONDER WHAT HAPPENS WHEN WE TURN THIS ON...
JENNA, WE AREN'T SUPPOSED TO DO THAT NOW...
ACK! ENOUGH WITH YOUR STUFFINESS CALEB...
CLICK!
POP!
YOU GUYS HAVE TO SEE THIS!

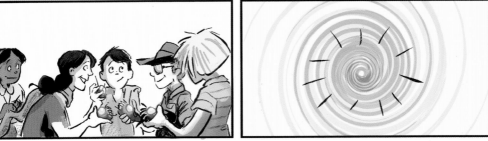

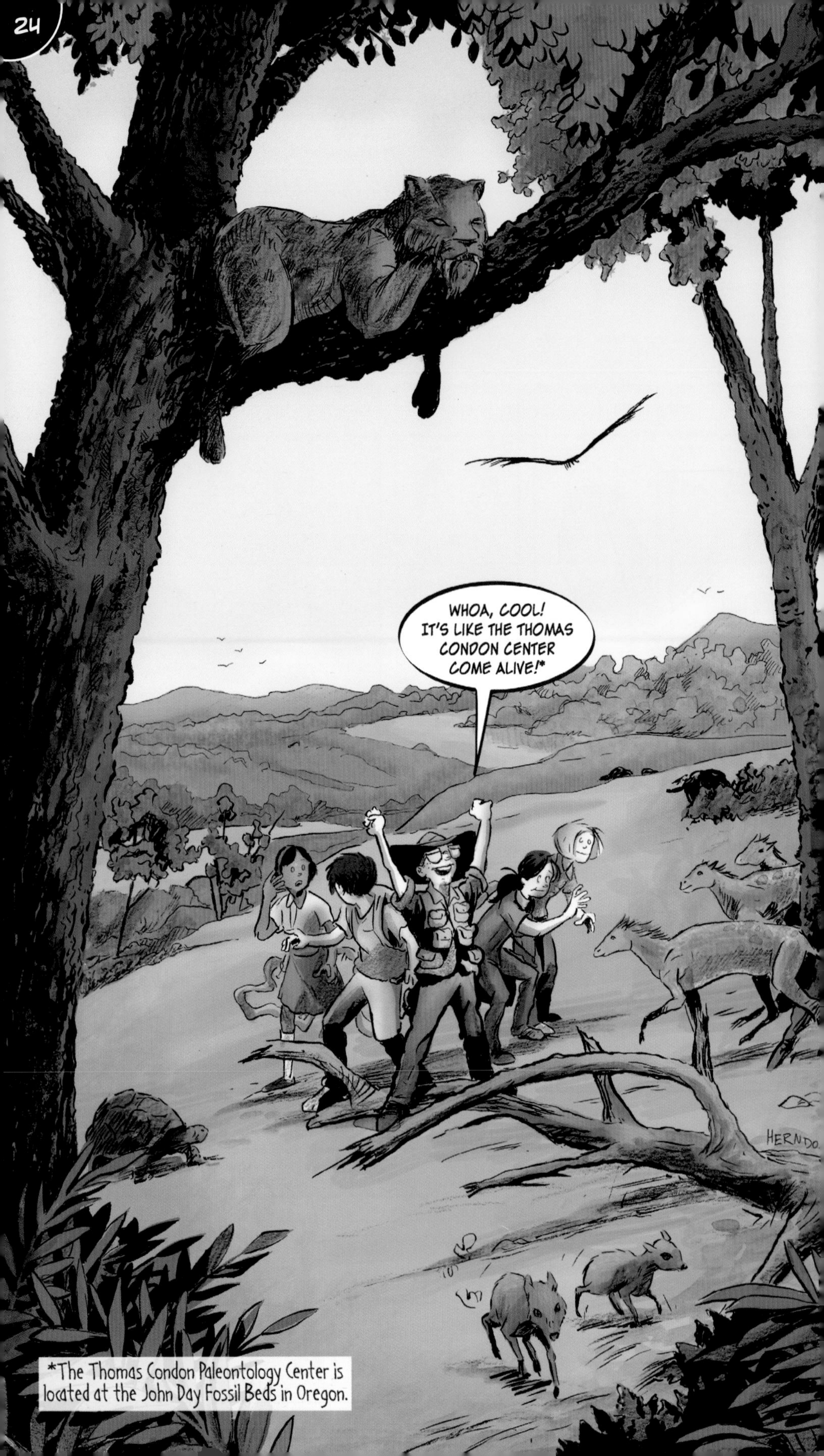
WHOA, COOL! IT'S LIKE THE THOMAS CONDON CENTER COME ALIVE!*
HERNDO.

*The Thomas Condon Paleontology Center is located at the John Day Fossil Beds in Oregon.

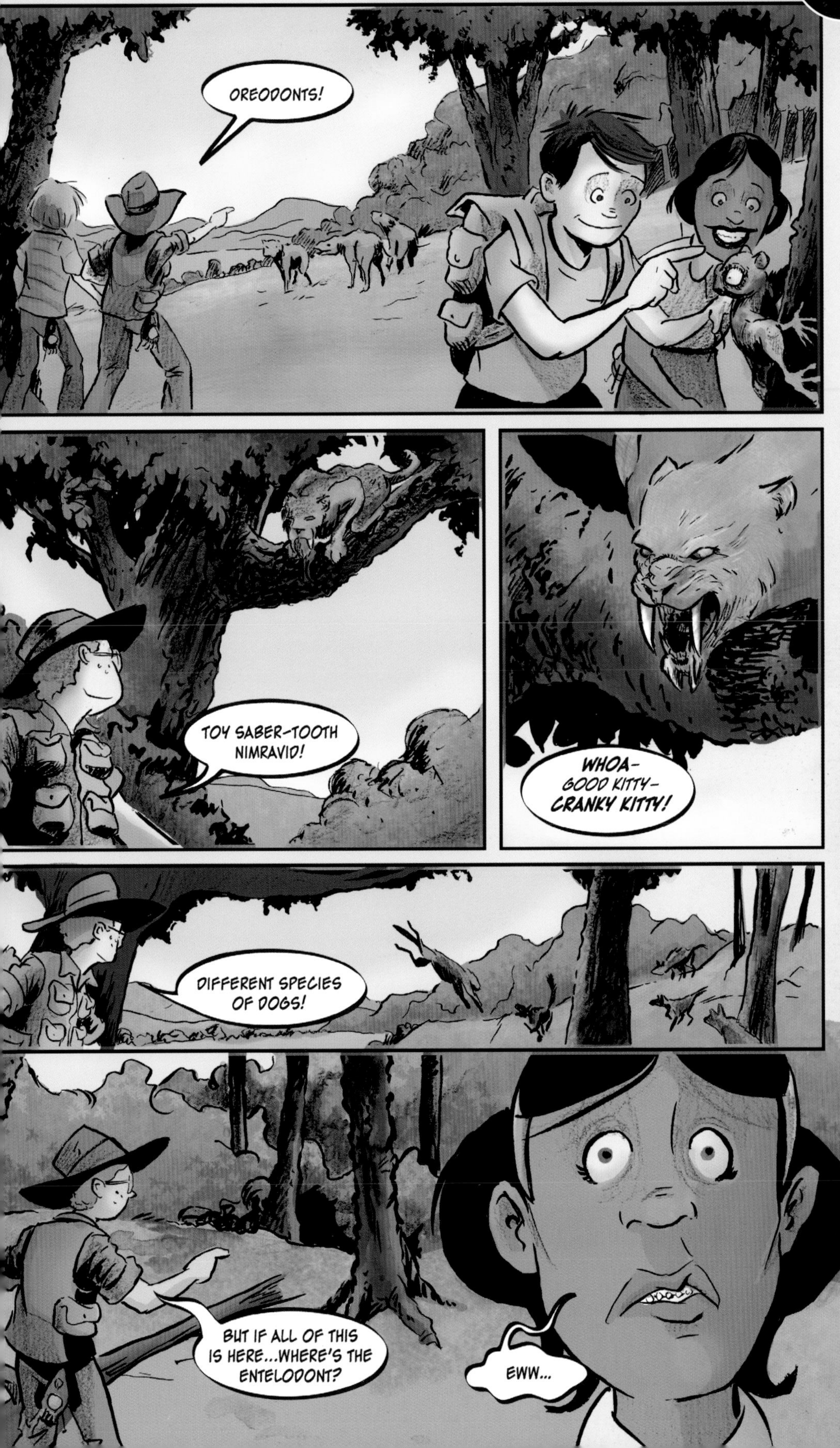
OREODONTS!
TOY SABER-TOOTH NIMRAVID!
WHOA-
GOOD KITTY-
CRANKY KITTY!
DIFFERENT SPECIES OF DOGS!
BUT IF ALL OF THIS IS HERE...WHERE'S THE ENTELODONT?
EWW...

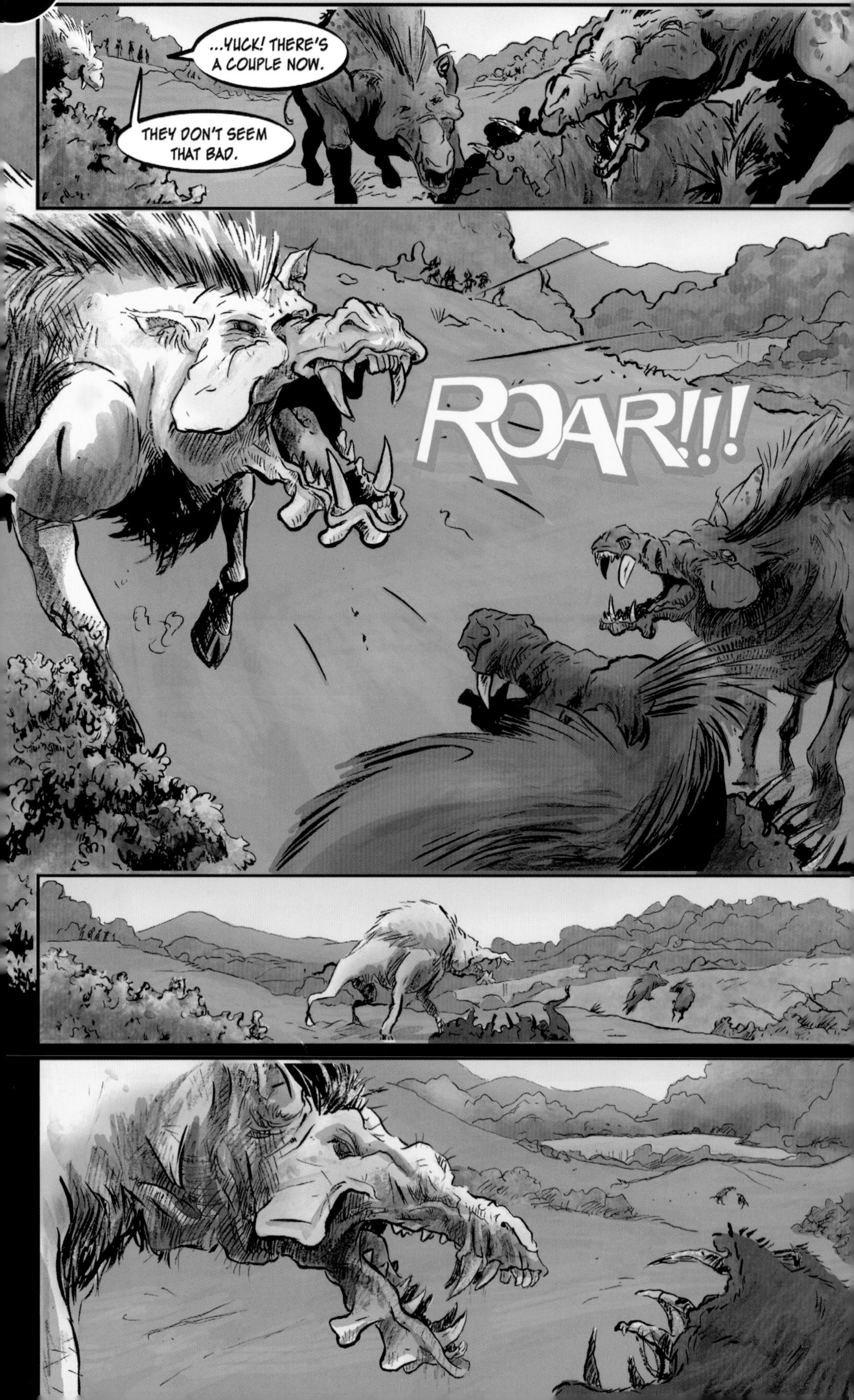
...YUCK! THERE'S A COUPLE NOW.
THEY DON'T SEEM THAT BAD.
ROAR!!!

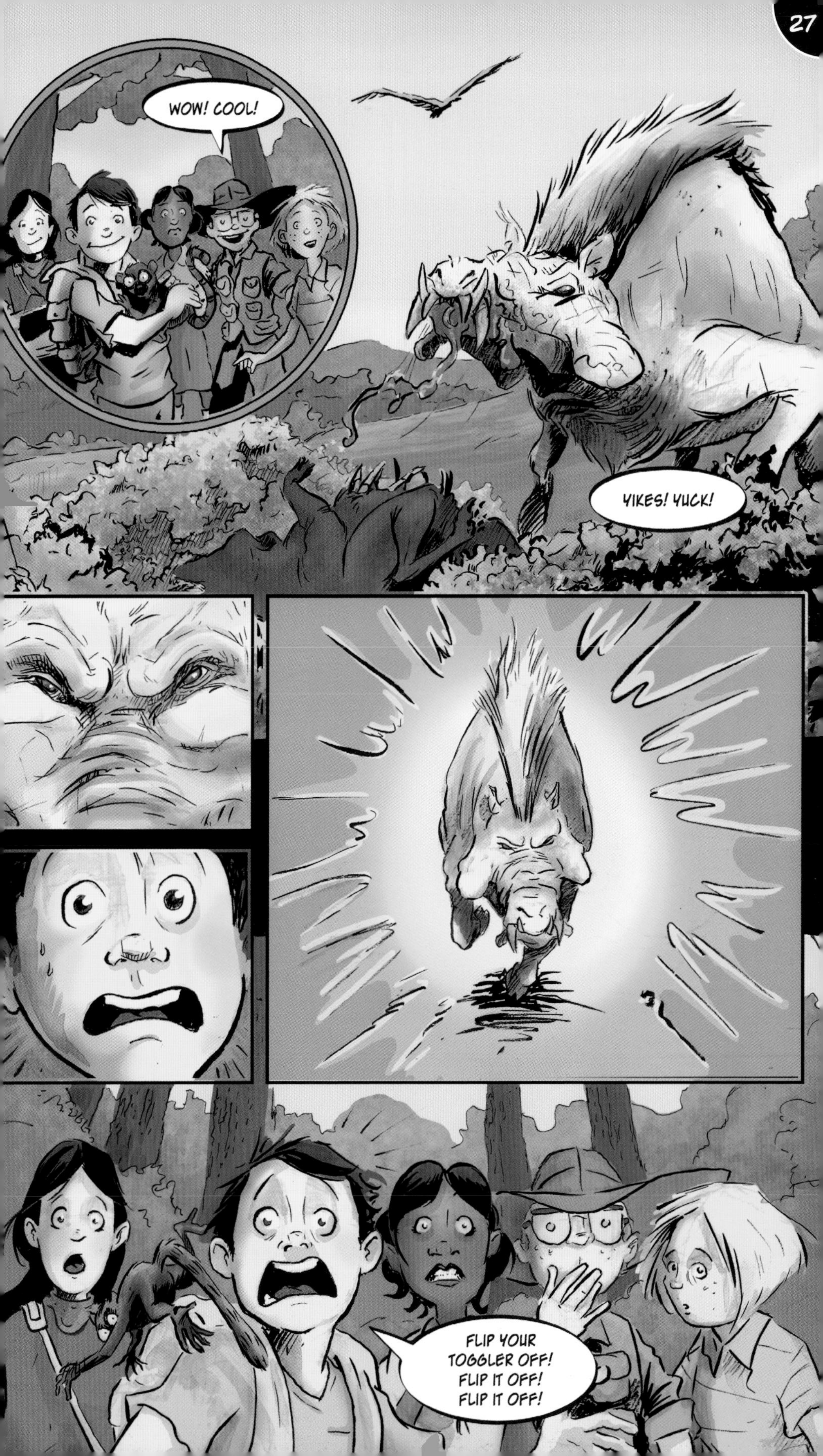
WOW! COOL!
YIKES! YUCK!
FLIP YOUR TOGGLER OFF! FLIP IT OFF! FLIP IT OFF!

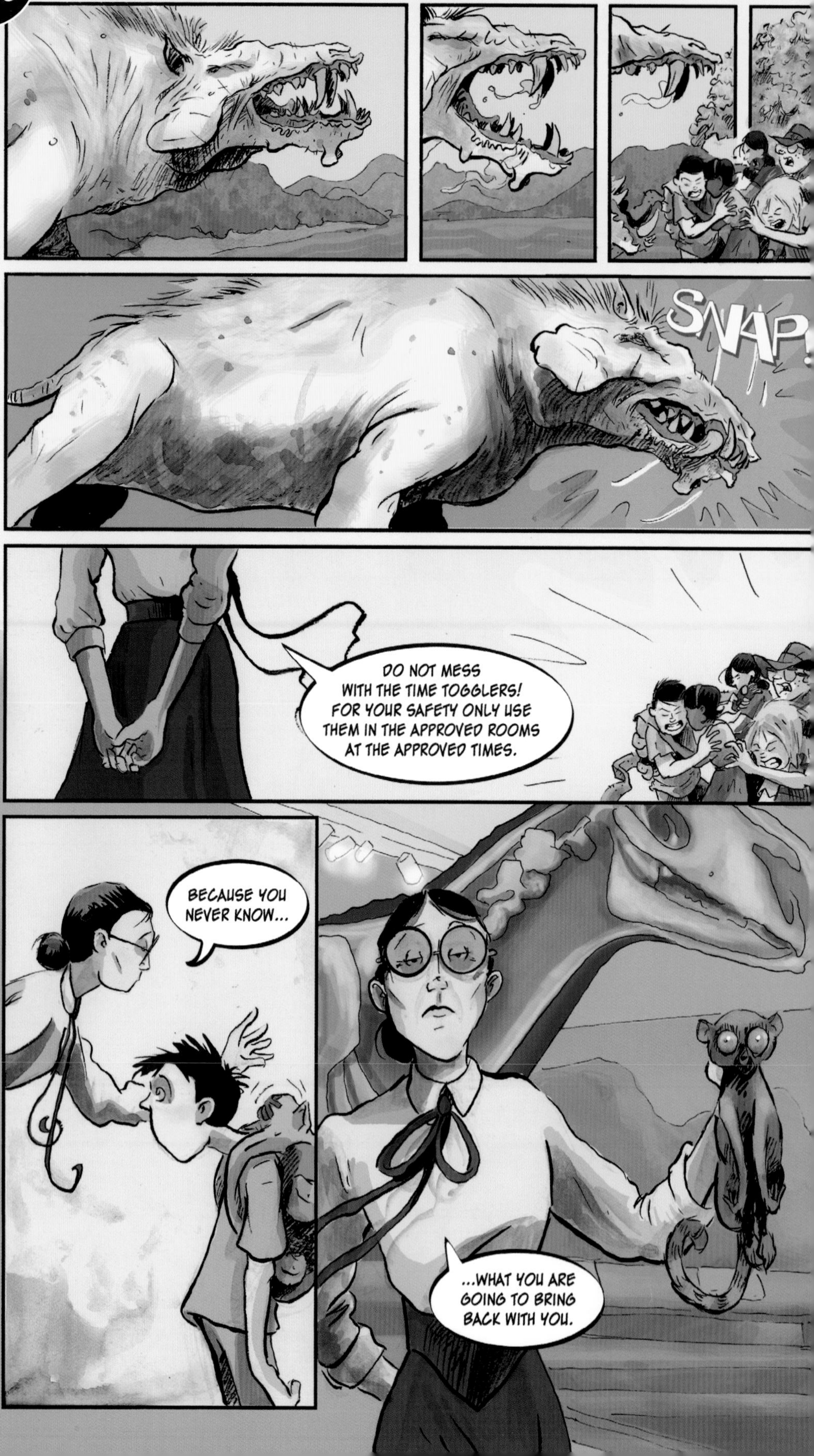
SNAP!
DO NOT MESS WITH THE TIME TOGGLERS! FOR YOUR SAFETY ONLY USE THEM IN THE APPROVED ROOMS AT THE APPROVED TIMES.
BECAUSE YOU NEVER KNOW...
...WHAT YOU ARE GOING TO BRING BACK WITH YOU.

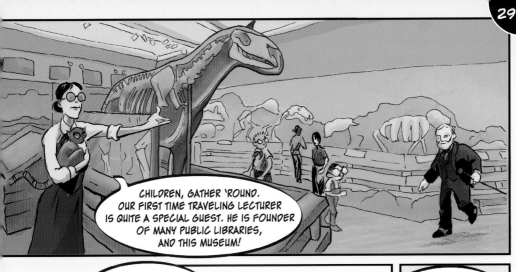

CHILDREN, GATHER 'ROUND. OUR FIRST TIME TRAVELING LECTURER IS QUITE A SPECIAL GUEST. HE IS FOUNDER OF MANY PUBLIC LIBRARIES, AND THIS MUSEUM!

WELCOME TO MY MUSEUM! I AM ANDREW CARNEGIE, A DENIZEN OF THE TURN OF THE CENTURY. THE PAST CENTURY, THAT IS!

MRS. SMARTCRAFT HAS ASKED ME TO INTRODUCE ONE OF THE GREATEST STORIES OF THE PAST 65 MILLION YEARS— HORSE EVOLUTION THROUGHOUT THE CENOZOIC ERA!

I JUMP AT THE CHANCE TO PUT ONE OF THESE ON MY HEAD.

PLEASE TURN YOUR DEVICES TO "START."

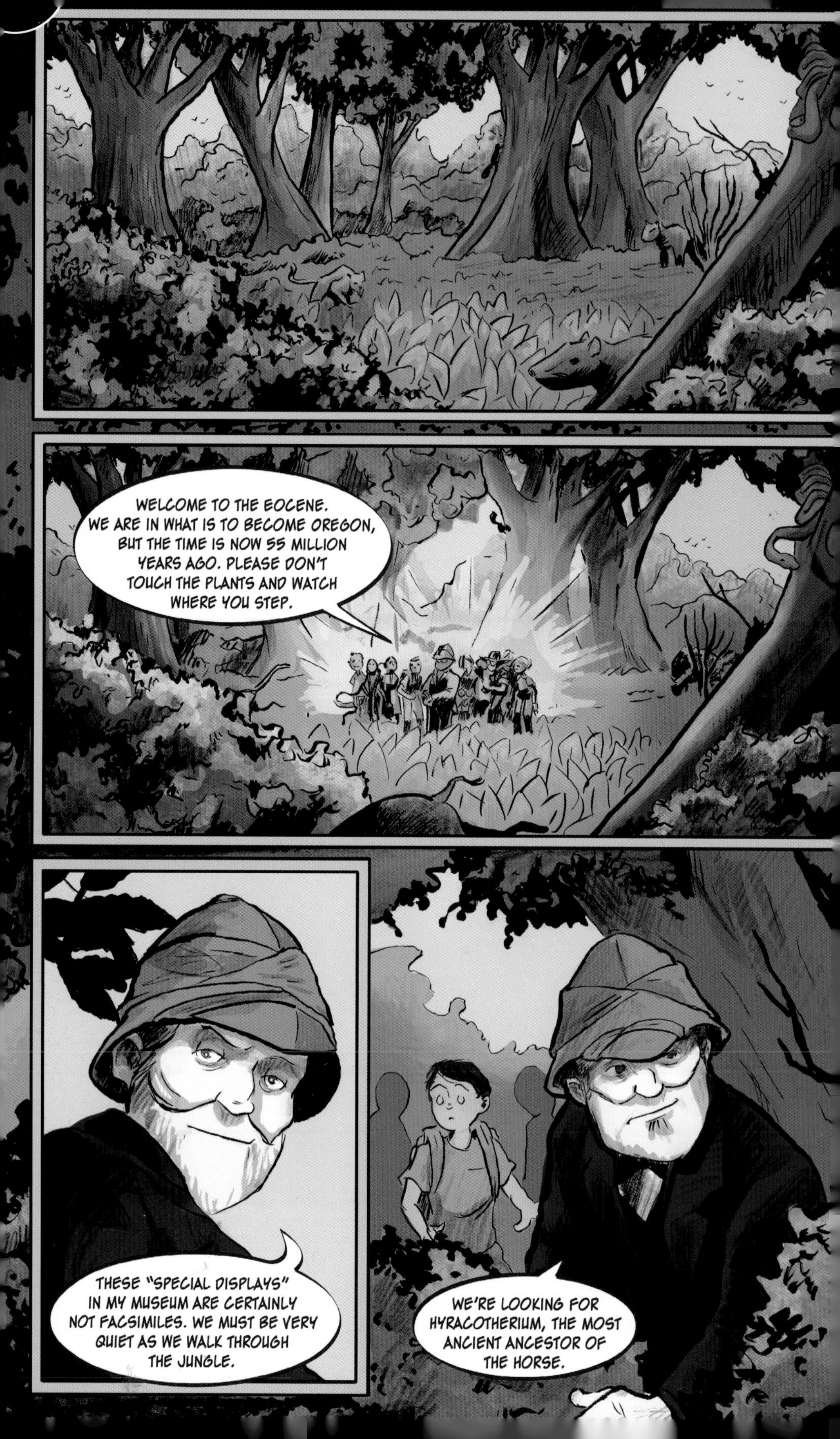
WELCOME TO THE EOCENE. WE ARE IN WHAT IS TO BECOME OREGON, BUT THE TIME IS NOW 55 MILLION YEARS AGO. PLEASE DON'T TOUCH THE PLANTS AND WATCH WHERE YOU STEP.
THESE "SPECIAL DISPLAYS" IN MY MUSEUM ARE CERTAINLY NOT FACSIMILES. WE MUST BE VERY QUIET AS WE WALK THROUGH THE JUNGLE.
WE'RE LOOKING FOR HYRACOTHERIUM, THE MOST ANCIENT ANCESTOR OF THE HORSE.

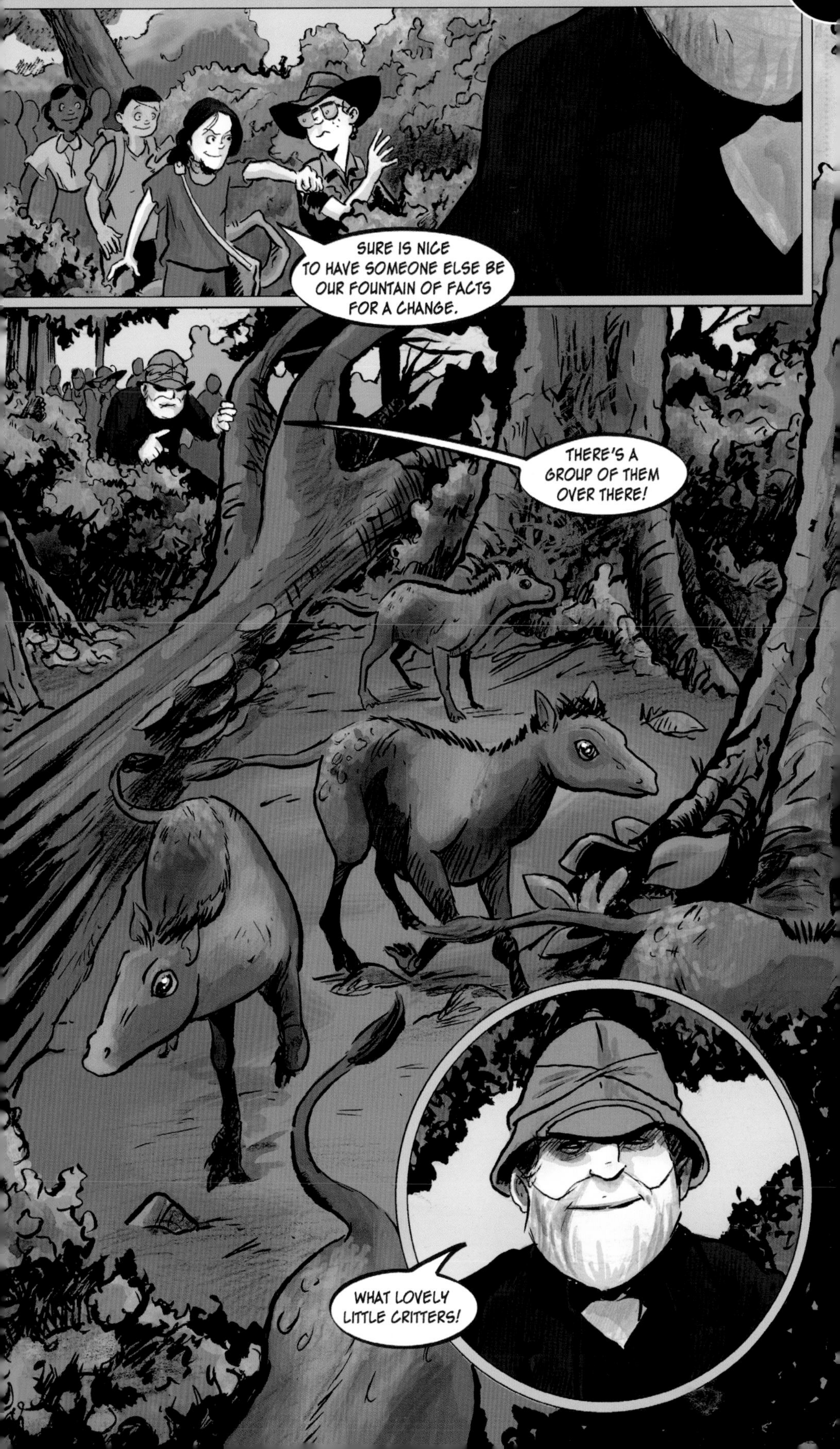
SURE IS NICE TO HAVE SOMEONE ELSE BE OUR FOUNTAIN OF FACTS FOR A CHANGE.
THERE'S A GROUP OF THEM OVER THERE!
WHAT LOVELY LITTLE CRITTERS!

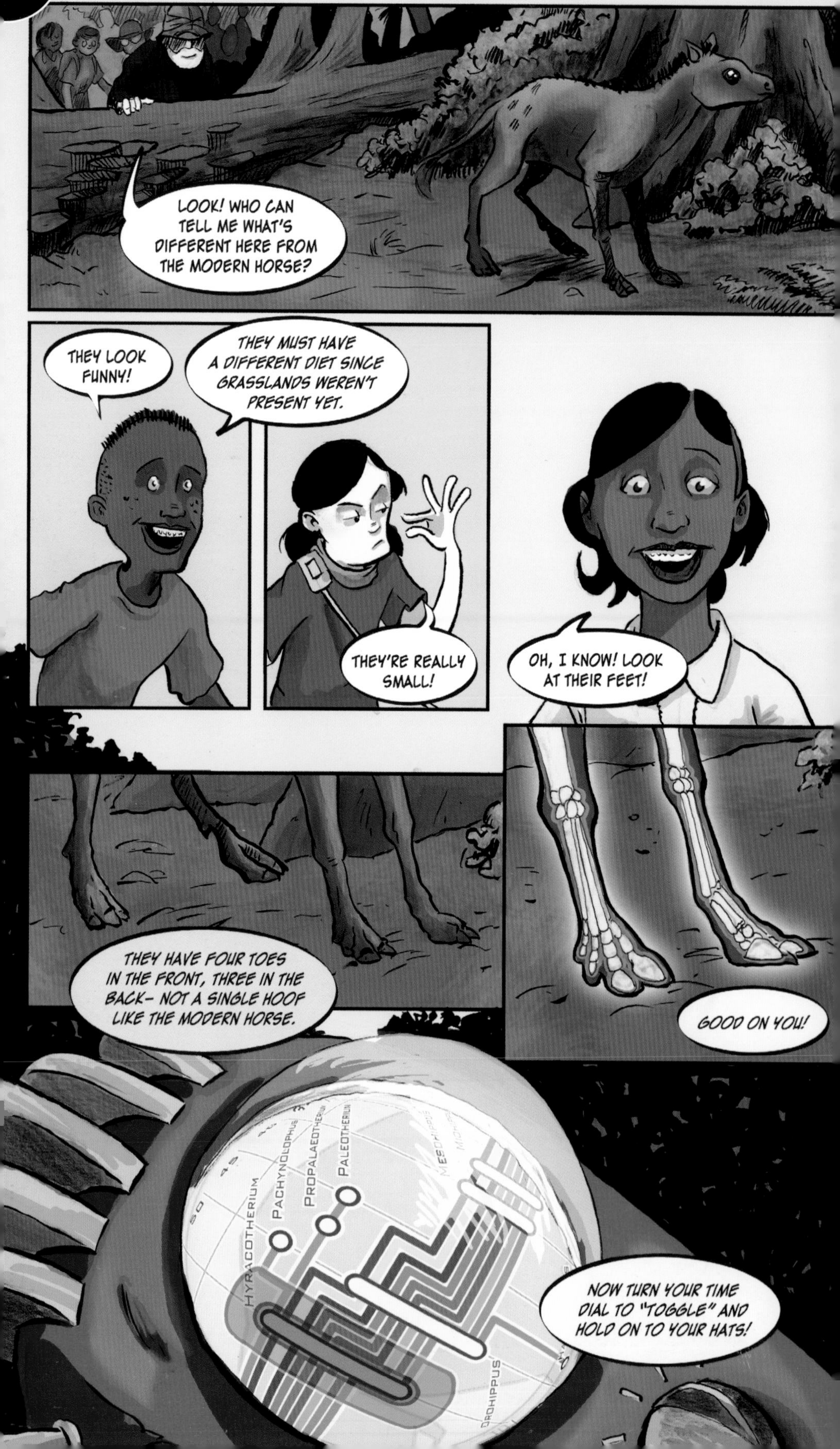
LOOK! WHO CAN TELL ME WHAT'S DIFFERENT HERE FROM THE MODERN HORSE?
THEY LOOK FUNNY!
THEY MUST HAVE A DIFFERENT DIET SINCE GRASSLANDS WEREN'T PRESENT YET.
THEY'RE REALLY SMALL!
OH, I KNOW! LOOK AT THEIR FEET!
THEY HAVE FOUR TOES IN THE FRONT, THREE IN THE BACK– NOT A SINGLE HOOF LIKE THE MODERN HORSE.
GOOD ON YOU!
HYRACOTHERIUM
PACHYNOLOPHUS
PROPALAEOTHERIUM
PALEOTHERIUM
MESOHIPPUS
MIOHIPPUS
OROHIPPUS
NOW TURN YOUR TIME DIAL TO "TOGGLE" AND HOLD ON TO YOUR HATS!

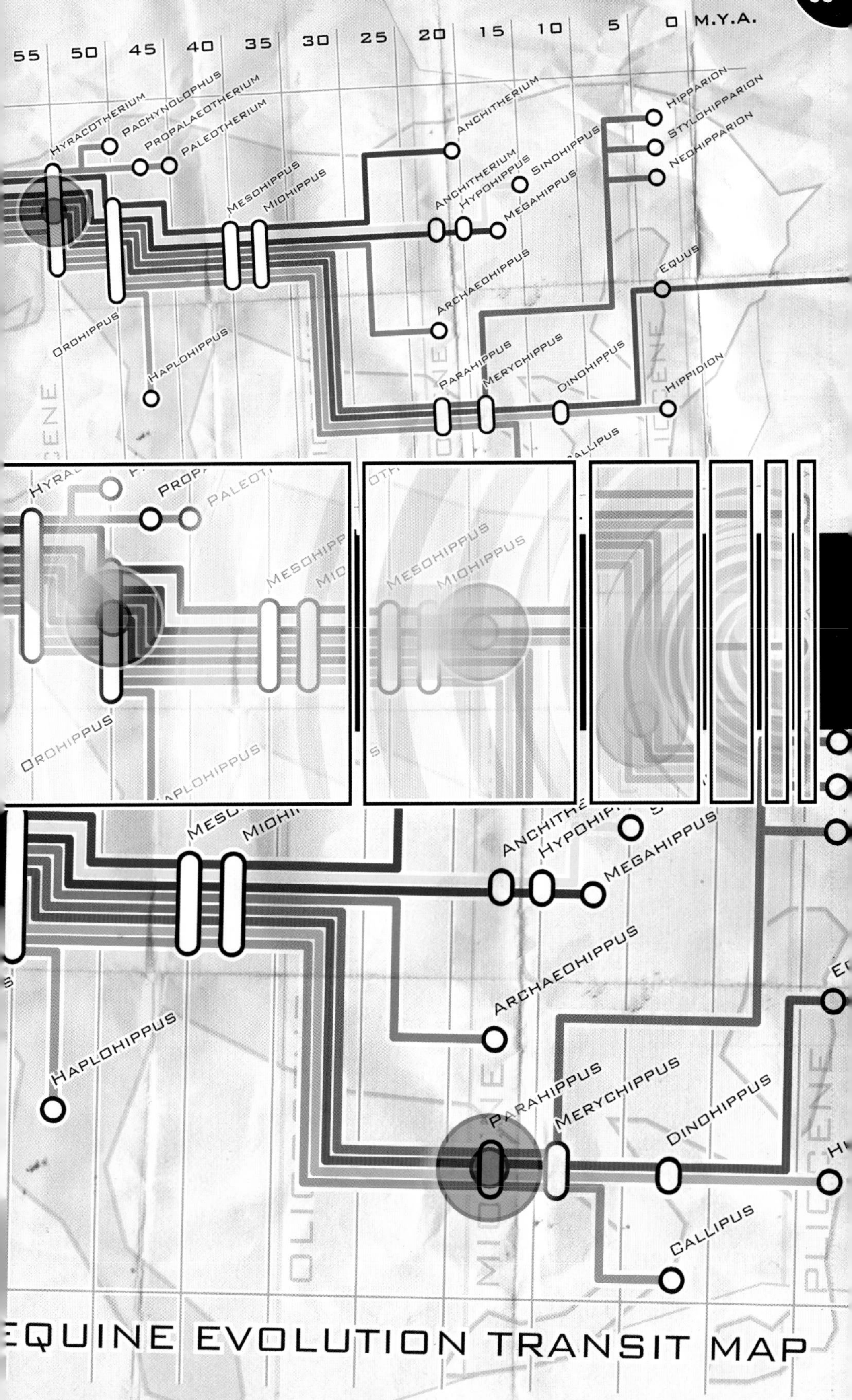
55
50
45
40
35
30
25
20
15
10
5
0 M.Y.A.
Hyracotherium
Pachynolophus
Propalaeotherium
Paleotherium
Orohippus
Haplohippus
Mesohippus
Miohippus
Anchitherium
Archaeohippus
Anchitherium
Hypohippus
Sinohippus
Megahippus
Parahippus
Merychippus
Dinohippus
Callipus
Hipparion
Stylohipparion
Neohipparion
Equus
Hippidion
Eocene
Oligocene
Miocene
Pliocene

EQUINE EVOLUTION TRANSIT MAP

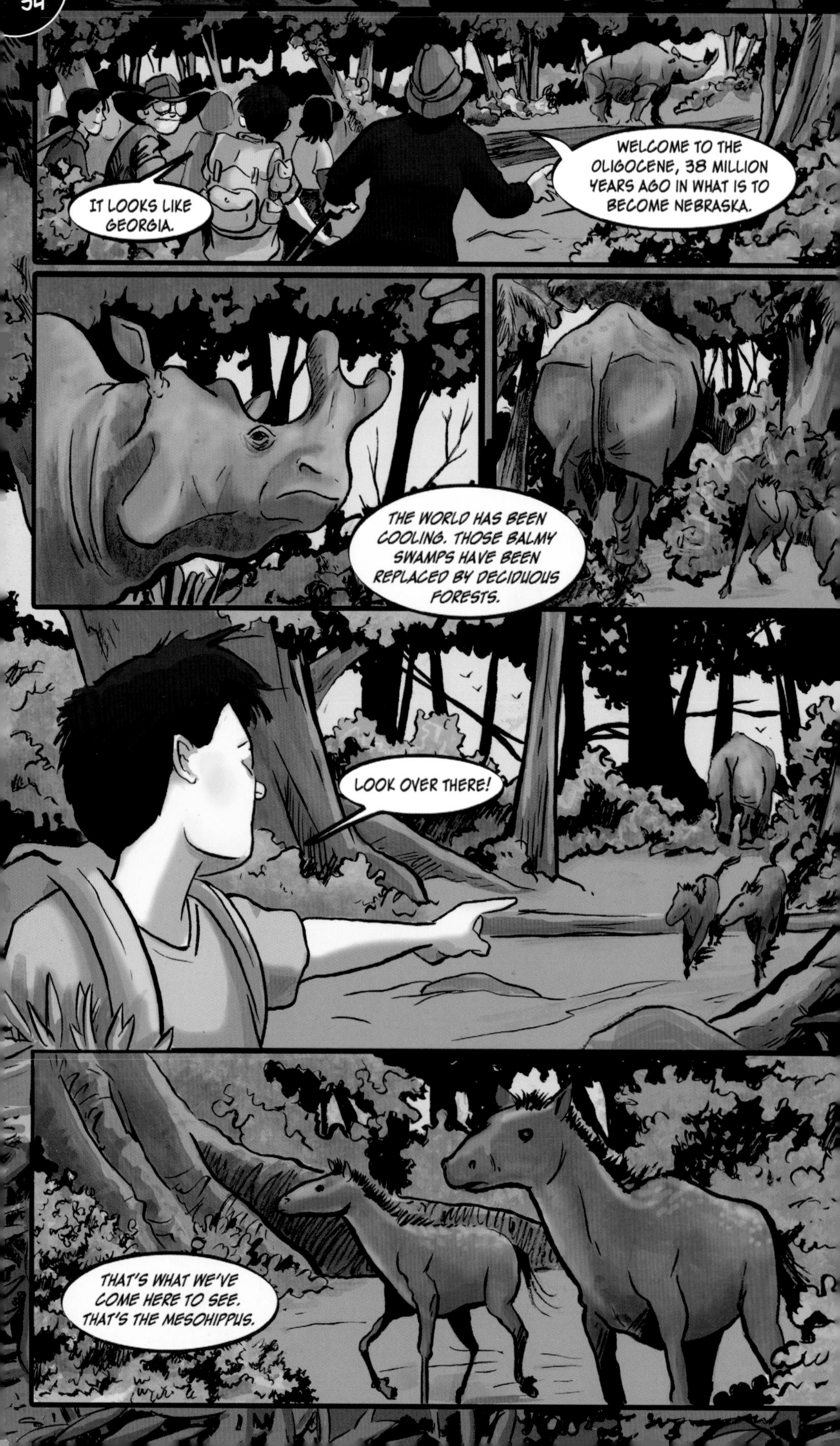
IT LOOKS LIKE GEORGIA.
WELCOME TO THE OLIGOCENE, 38 MILLION YEARS AGO IN WHAT IS TO BECOME NEBRASKA.
THE WORLD HAS BEEN COOLING. THOSE BALMY SWAMPS HAVE BEEN REPLACED BY DECIDUOUS FORESTS.
LOOK OVER THERE!
THAT'S WHAT WE'VE COME HERE TO SEE. THAT'S THE MESOHIPPUS.

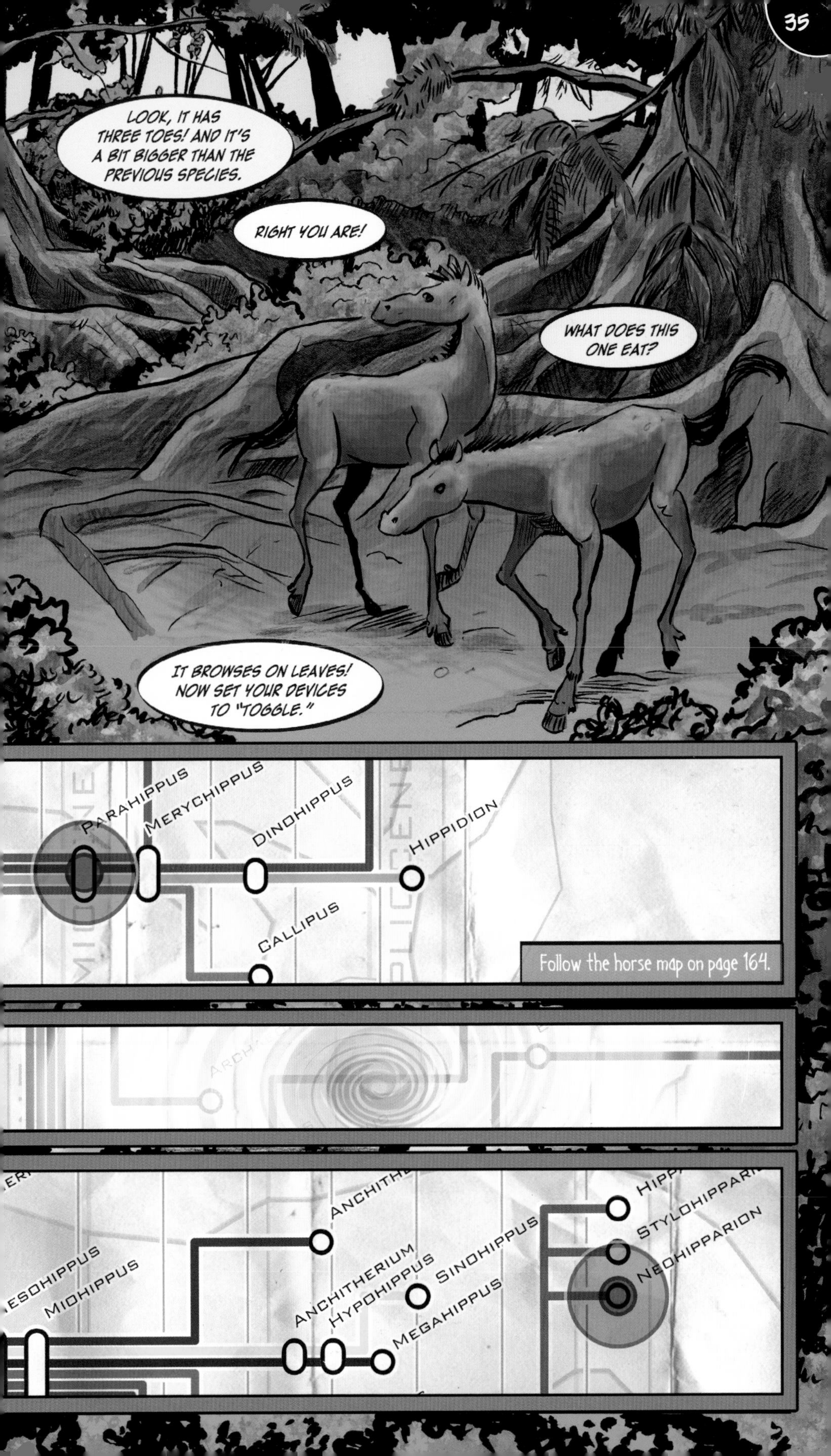
LOOK, IT HAS THREE TOES! AND IT'S A BIT BIGGER THAN THE PREVIOUS SPECIES.
RIGHT YOU ARE!
WHAT DOES THIS ONE EAT?
IT BROWSES ON LEAVES! NOW SET YOUR DEVICES TO "TOGGLE."
PARAHIPPUS
MERYCHIPPUS
DINOHIPPUS
HIPPIDION
CALLIPUS
Follow the horse map on page 164.
MIOHIPPUS
ANCHITHERIUM
HYPOHIPPUS
SINOHIPPUS
MEGAHIPPUS
STYLOHIPPARION
NEOHIPPARION

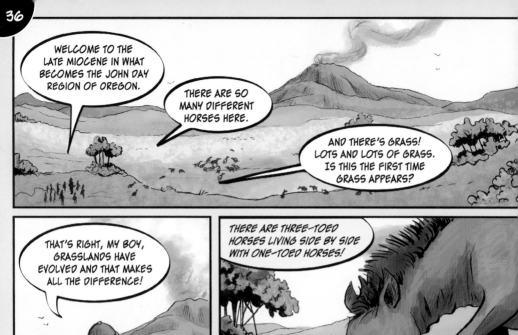

WELCOME TO THE LATE MIOCENE IN WHAT BECOMES THE JOHN DAY REGION OF OREGON.

THERE ARE SO MANY DIFFERENT HORSES HERE.

AND THERE'S GRASS! LOTS AND LOTS OF GRASS. IS THIS THE FIRST TIME GRASS APPEARS?

THAT'S RIGHT, MY BOY, GRASSLANDS HAVE EVOLVED AND THAT MAKES ALL THE DIFFERENCE!

THERE ARE THREE-TOED HORSES LIVING SIDE BY SIDE WITH ONE-TOED HORSES!

YES! AND THAT'S IMPORTANT TO REALIZE! EVOLUTION ISN'T ALWAYS ABOUT ONE SPECIES REPLACING ANOTHER.

IT'S LIKE WHEN THERE ARE MULTIPLE TYPES OF SPECIES WITHIN A GIVEN GENERA, LIKE MODERN FELINE SPECIES DIVERSITY AS OPPOSED TO THE GREATER DIFFERENCES BETWEEN MODERN FELINES AND HYENAS—TWO DIFFERENT GENERA, WITH A COMMON ANCESTRY.

THAT'S RIGHT, MY BOY, ANAGENESIS VERSUS CLADOGENESIS!

ANAGENESIS IS EVOLUTION WITHIN A LINEAGE...LIKE THE CHANGES THAT THE MODERN HORSE EQUUS HAS GONE THROUGH SINCE THE PLIOCENE.

CLADOGENESIS IS THE SPLITTING OF A LINE, AS IN THE BRANCHING OF THE HORSE EVOLUTIONARY TREE SINCE MERYCHIPPUS.

TELLING BY THE SMOKE ON THE HORIZON, I'D SAY IT'S TIME TO MOVE ON. SET YOUR DEVICES TO "TOGGLE."

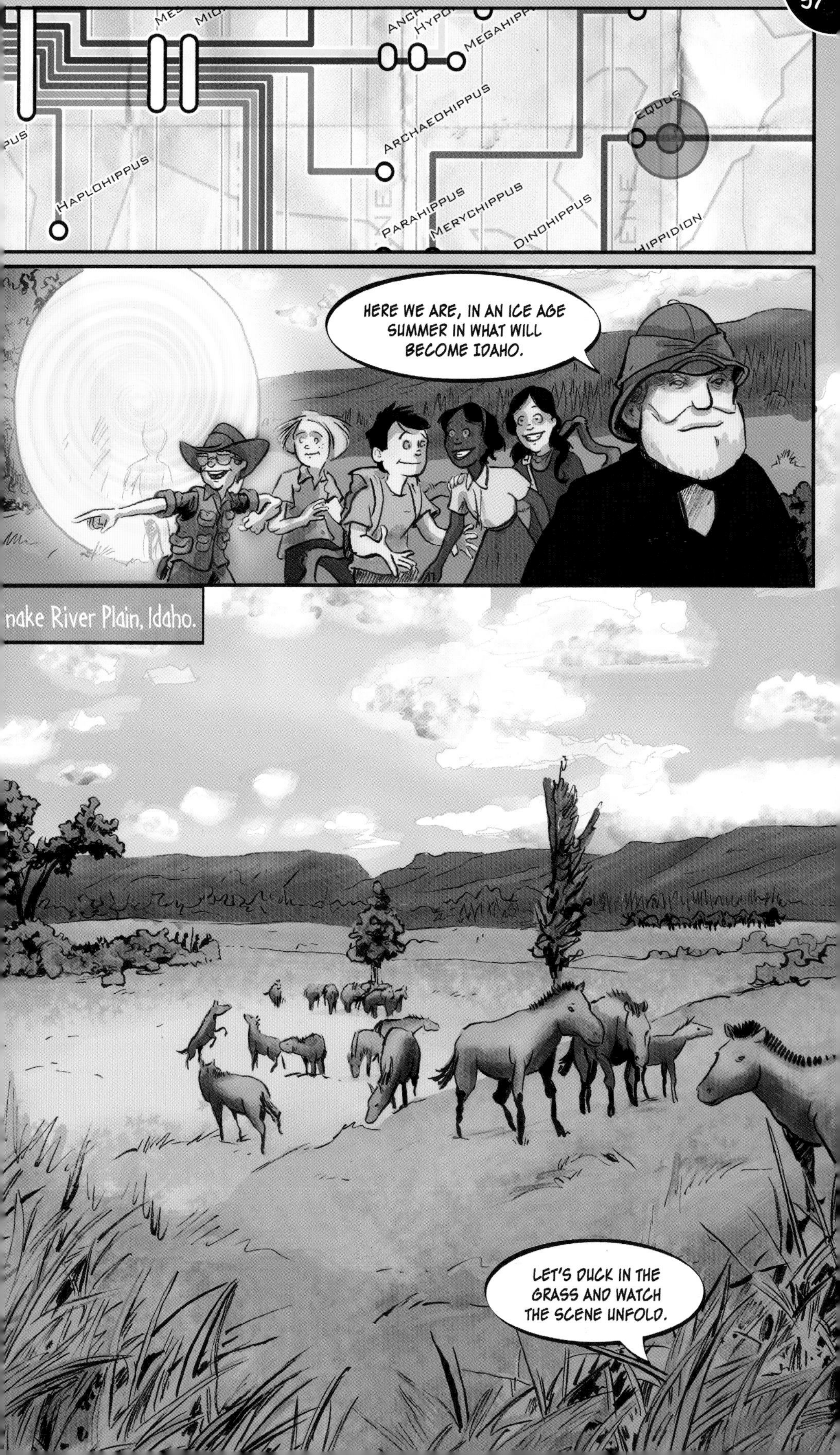
MEGAHIPPUS
ARCHAEOHIPPUS
EQUUS
HAPLOHIPPUS
PARAHIPPUS
MERYCHIPPUS
DINOHIPPUS
HERE WE ARE, IN AN ICE AGE SUMMER IN WHAT WILL BECOME IDAHO.
nake River Plain, Idaho.
LET'S DUCK IN THE GRASS AND WATCH THE SCENE UNFOLD.

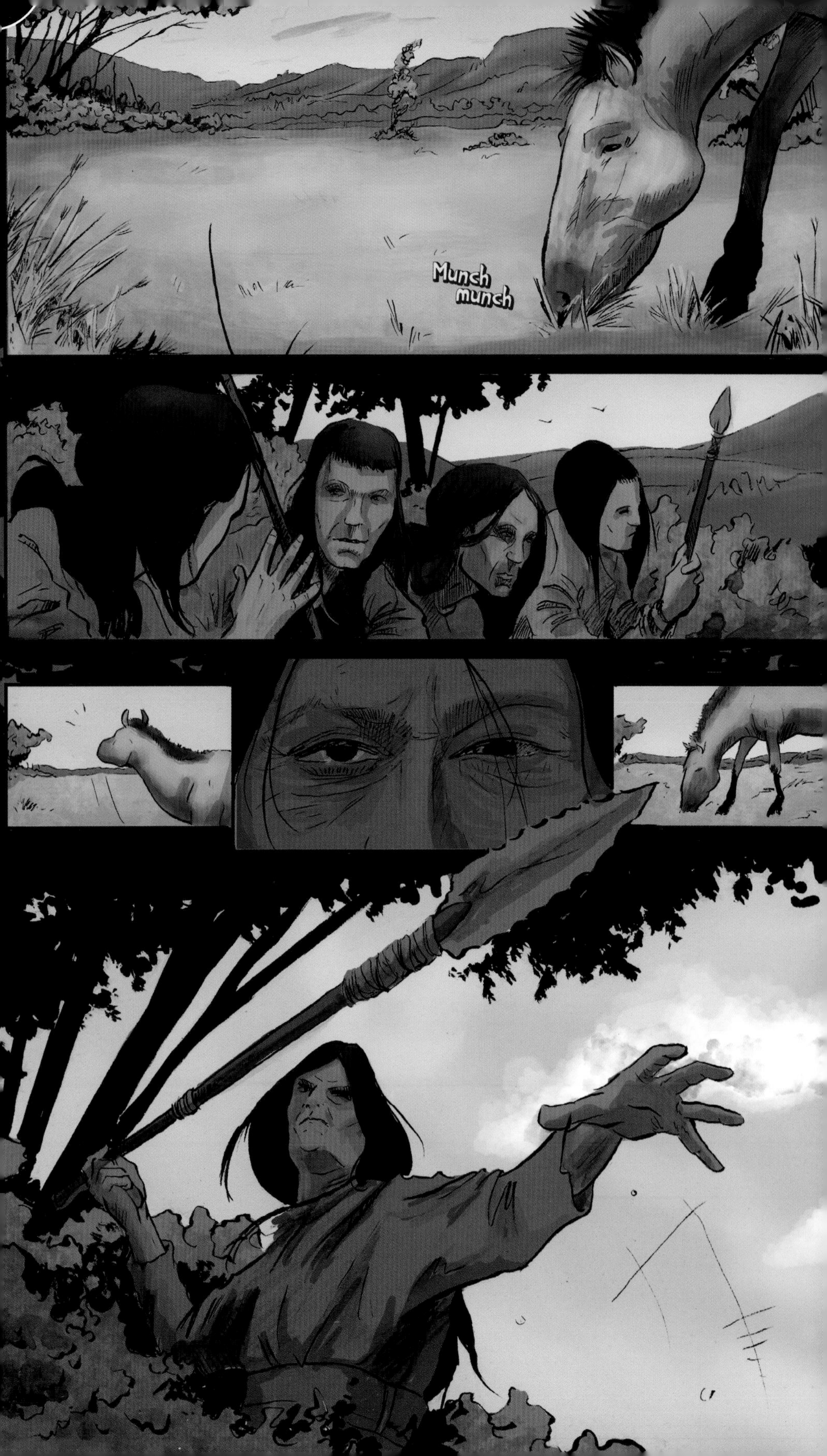
Munch
munch

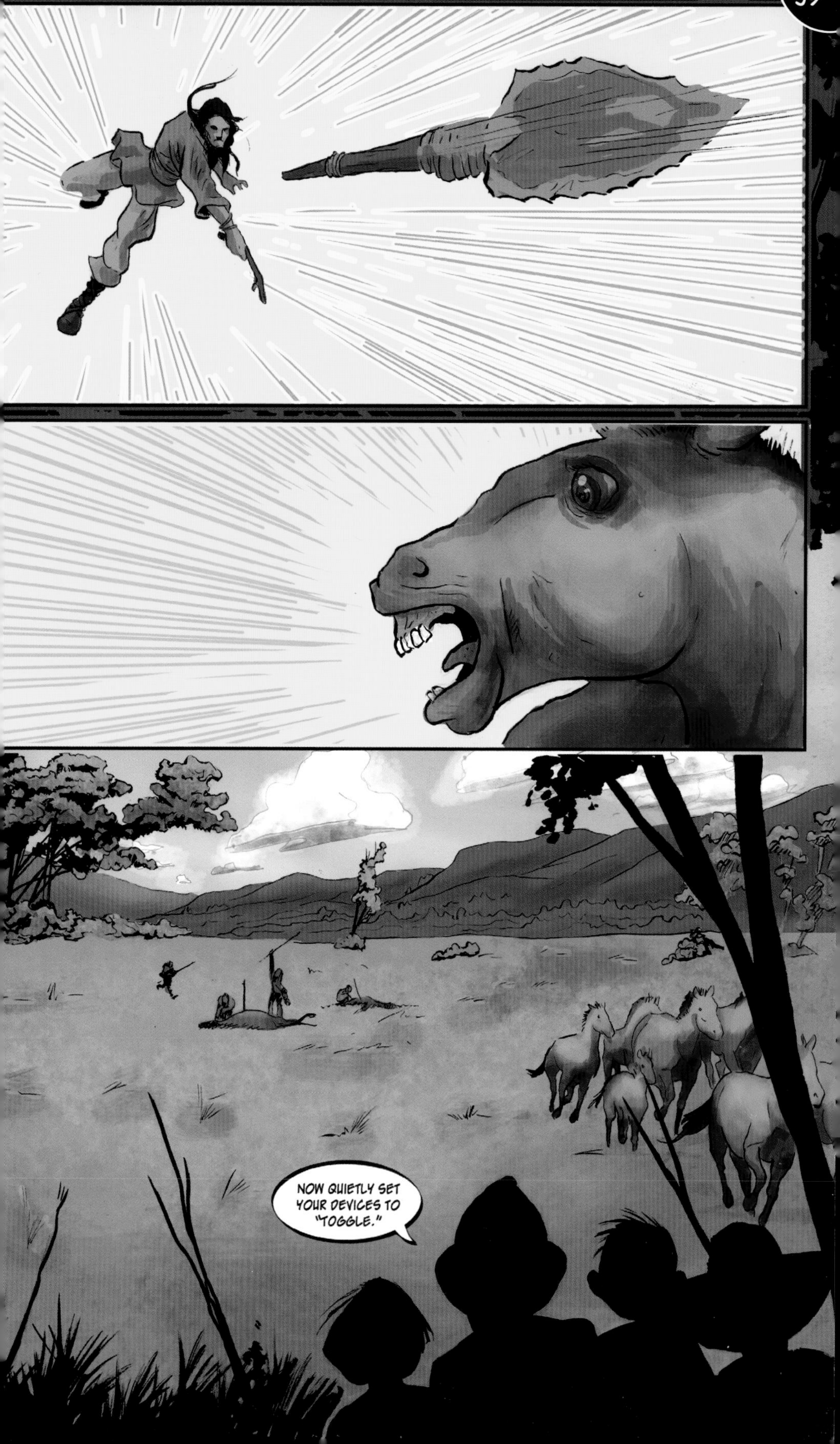
NOW QUIETLY SET YOUR DEVICES TO "TOGGLE."

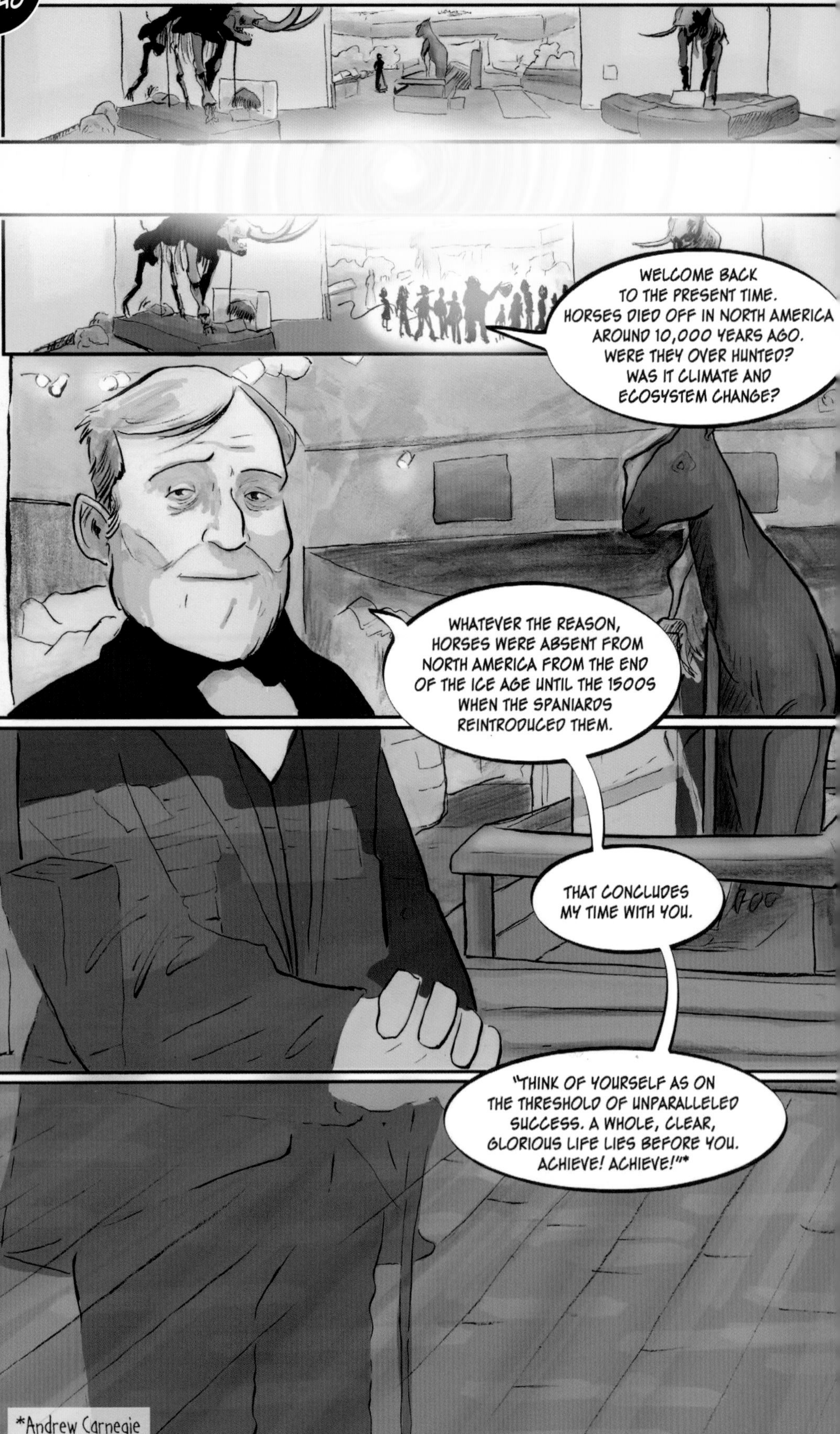
WELCOME BACK TO THE PRESENT TIME. HORSES DIED OFF IN NORTH AMERICA AROUND 10,000 YEARS AGO. WERE THEY OVER HUNTED? WAS IT CLIMATE AND ECOSYSTEM CHANGE?
WHATEVER THE REASON, HORSES WERE ABSENT FROM NORTH AMERICA FROM THE END OF THE ICE AGE UNTIL THE 1500S WHEN THE SPANIARDS REINTRODUCED THEM.
THAT CONCLUDES MY TIME WITH YOU.
"THINK OF YOURSELF AS ON THE THRESHOLD OF UNPARALLELED SUCCESS. A WHOLE, CLEAR, GLORIOUS LIFE LIES BEFORE YOU. ACHIEVE! ACHIEVE!"*
*Andrew Carnegie

STUDENT HANDBOOK

A cademy of
P lanetary
E volution

3

"Bone Wars"

MONTAUK INDUSTRIES

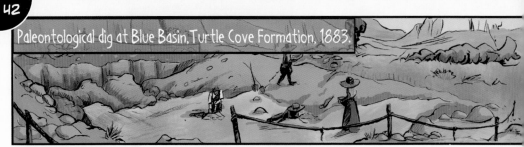

Paleontological dig at Blue Basin, Turtle Cove Formation, 1883.

NOT YOU! WHAT DO YOU WANT?

BY ORDER OF THE FEDERAL GOVERNMENT, YOU ARE TO LEAVE THIS DIG SITE AT ONCE. ME AND MY TEAM ARE TAKING OVER.

YOU SCOUNDREL! YOU'RE NOT GOING TO GET AWAY WITH THIS— BELIEVE ME, THE RIGHT PEOPLE WILL FIND OUT!

WHAT ARE YOU GOING TO DO? TELL THE PAPERS? HA!

YOU DON'T HAVE A LEG TO STAND ON. PACK IT UP.

YOU SIR, ARE NOT A GENTLEMAN OF SCIENCE. YOU'RE A BULLY AND A BRUTE!

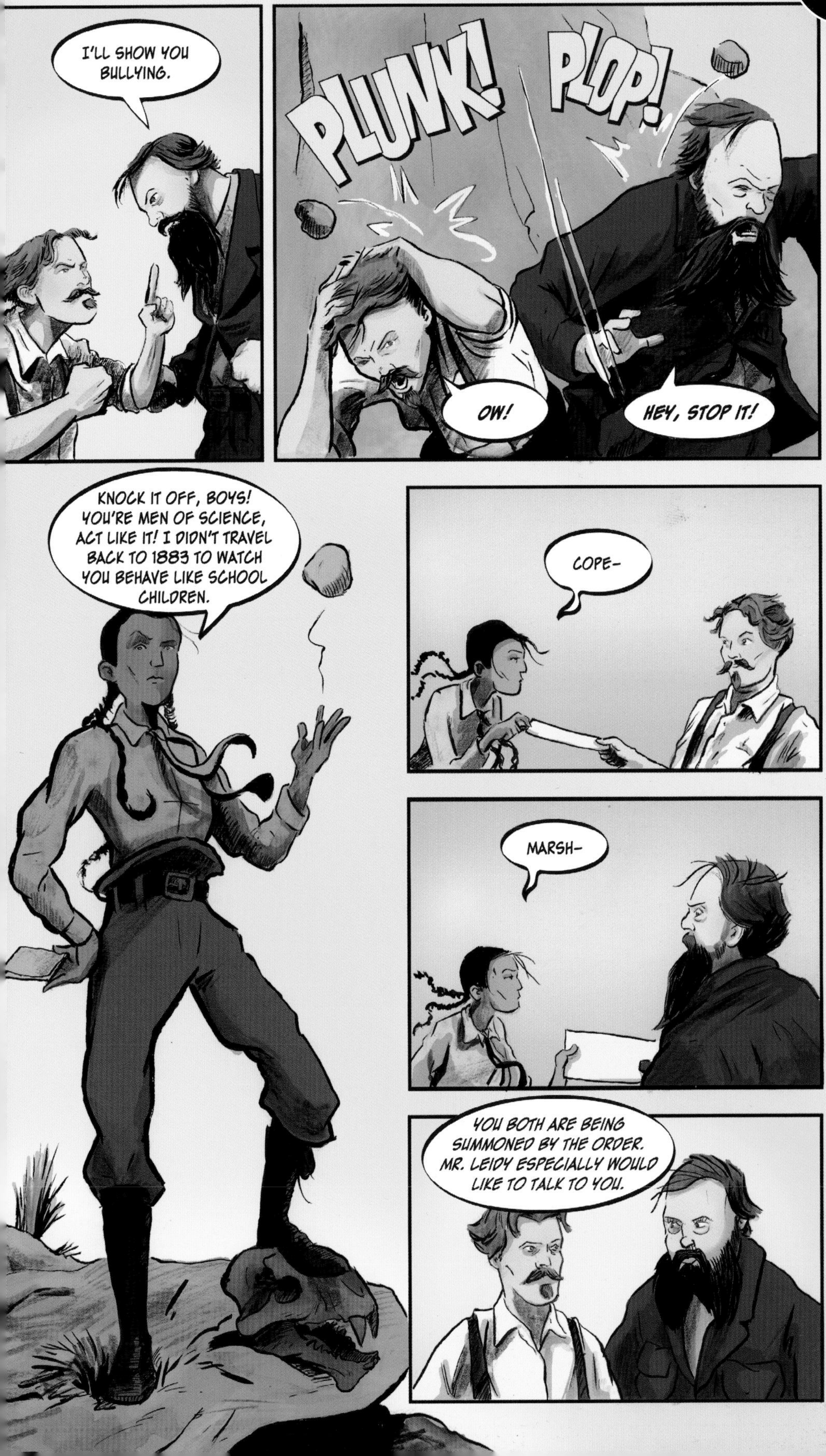
I'LL SHOW YOU BULLYING.
PLUNK!
PLOP!
OW!
HEY, STOP IT!
KNOCK IT OFF, BOYS! YOU'RE MEN OF SCIENCE, ACT LIKE IT! I DIDN'T TRAVEL BACK TO 1883 TO WATCH YOU BEHAVE LIKE SCHOOL CHILDREN.
COPE-
MARSH-
YOU BOTH ARE BEING SUMMONED BY THE ORDER. MR. LEIDY ESPECIALLY WOULD LIKE TO TALK TO YOU.

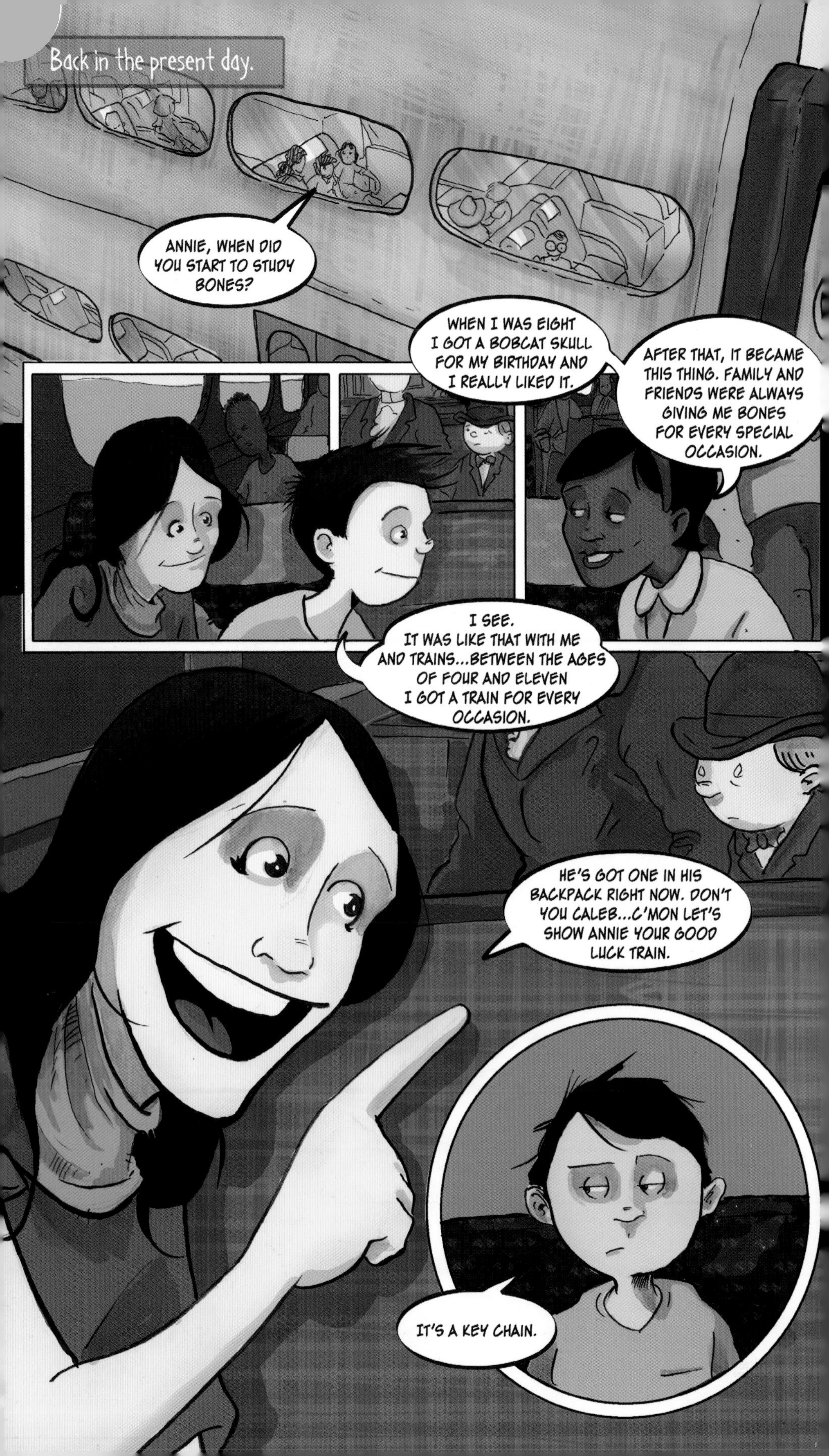
Back in the present day.
ANNIE, WHEN DID YOU START TO STUDY BONES?
WHEN I WAS EIGHT I GOT A BOBCAT SKULL FOR MY BIRTHDAY AND I REALLY LIKED IT.
AFTER THAT, IT BECAME THIS THING. FAMILY AND FRIENDS WERE ALWAYS GIVING ME BONES FOR EVERY SPECIAL OCCASION.
I SEE. IT WAS LIKE THAT WITH ME AND TRAINS...BETWEEN THE AGES OF FOUR AND ELEVEN I GOT A TRAIN FOR EVERY OCCASION.
HE'S GOT ONE IN HIS BACKPACK RIGHT NOW. DON'T YOU CALEB...C'MON LET'S SHOW ANNIE YOUR GOOD LUCK TRAIN.
IT'S A KEY CHAIN.

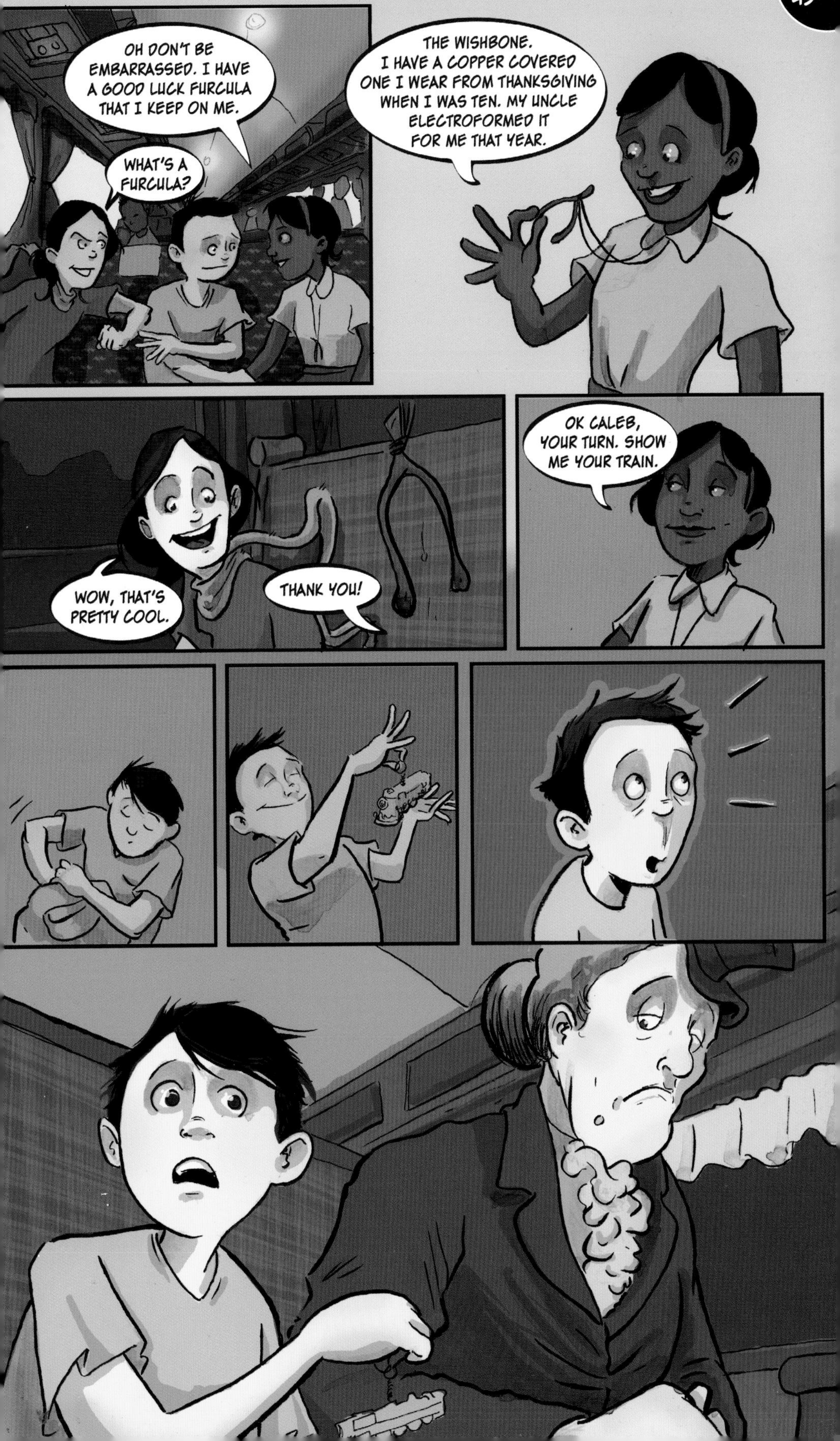
OH DON'T BE EMBARRASSED. I HAVE A GOOD LUCK FURCULA THAT I KEEP ON ME.
WHAT'S A FURCULA?
THE WISHBONE. I HAVE A COPPER COVERED ONE I WEAR FROM THANKSGIVING WHEN I WAS TEN. MY UNCLE ELECTROFORMED IT FOR ME THAT YEAR.
WOW, THAT'S PRETTY COOL.
THANK YOU!
OK CALEB, YOUR TURN. SHOW ME YOUR TRAIN.

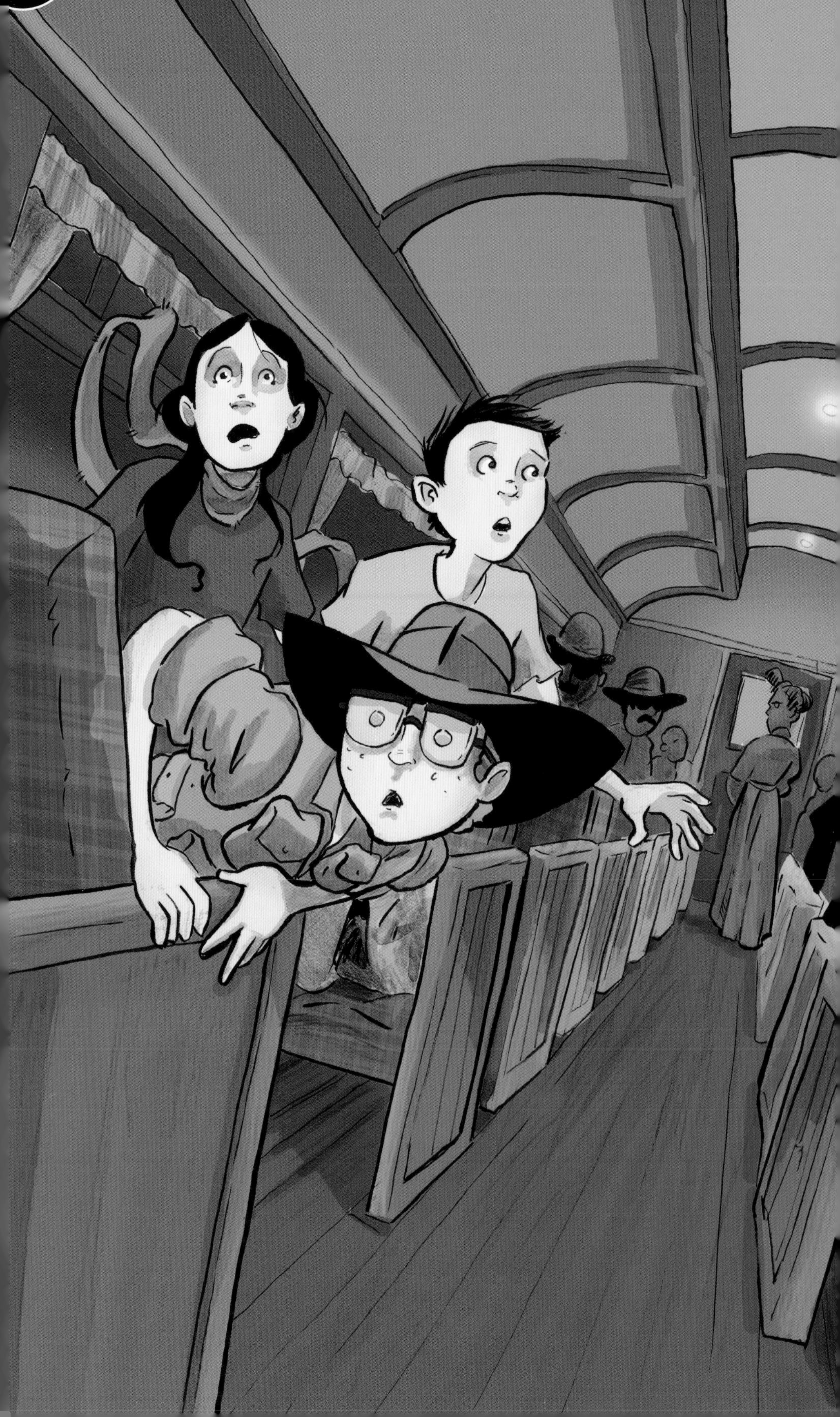

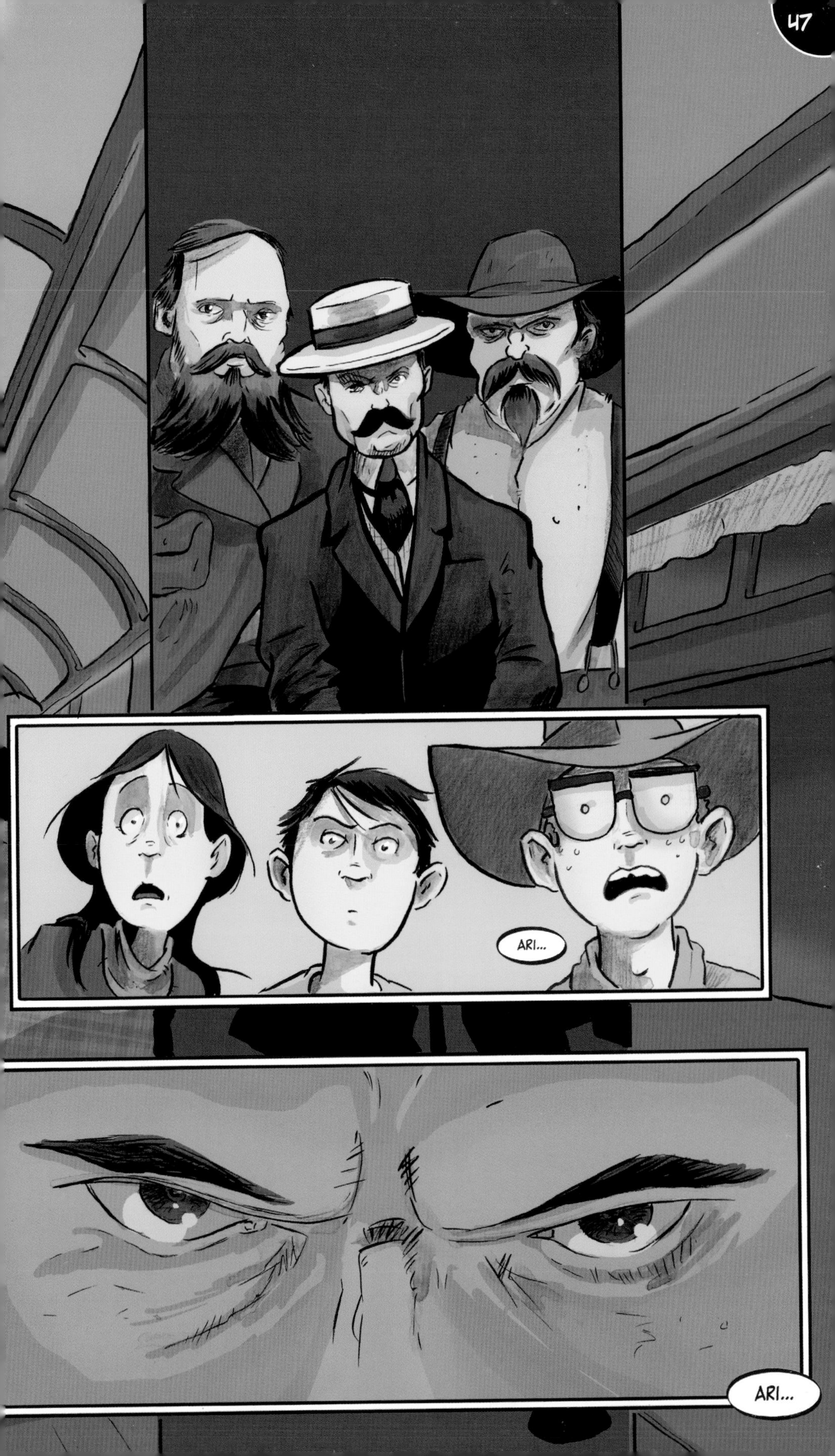
ARI...
ARI...

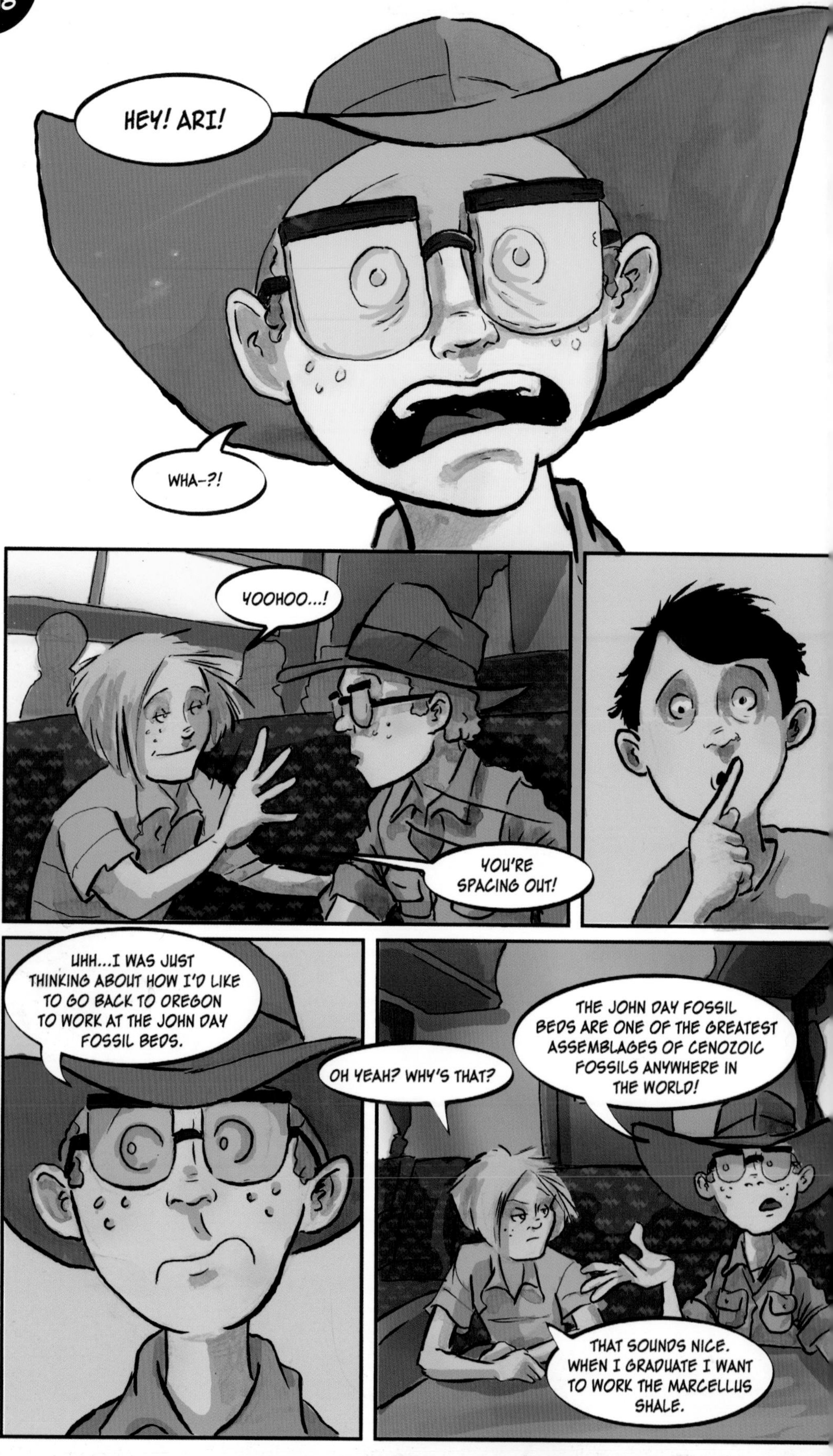
HEY! ARI!
WHA-?!
YOOHOO...!
YOU'RE SPACING OUT!
UHH...I WAS JUST THINKING ABOUT HOW I'D LIKE TO GO BACK TO OREGON TO WORK AT THE JOHN DAY FOSSIL BEDS.
OH YEAH? WHY'S THAT?
THE JOHN DAY FOSSIL BEDS ARE ONE OF THE GREATEST ASSEMBLAGES OF CENOZOIC FOSSILS ANYWHERE IN THE WORLD!
THAT SOUNDS NICE. WHEN I GRADUATE I WANT TO WORK THE MARCELLUS SHALE.

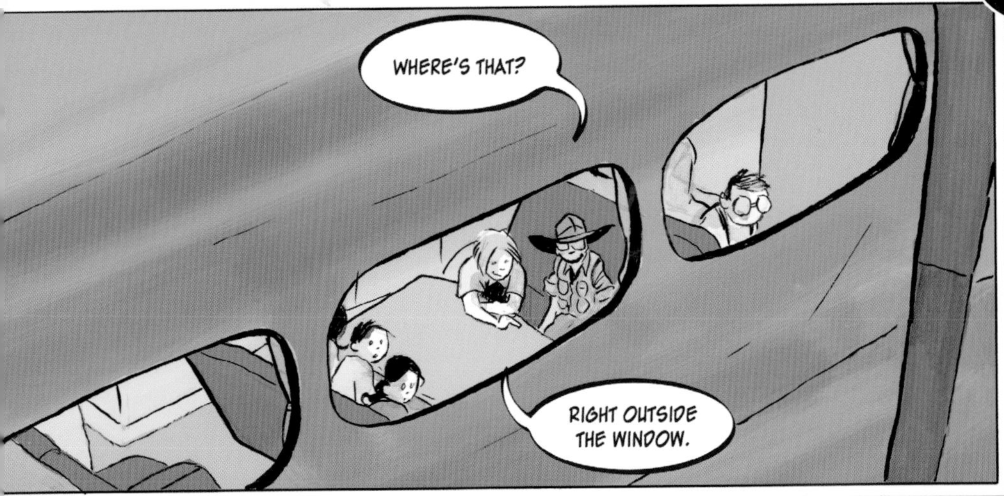
WHERE'S THAT?
RIGHT OUTSIDE THE WINDOW.

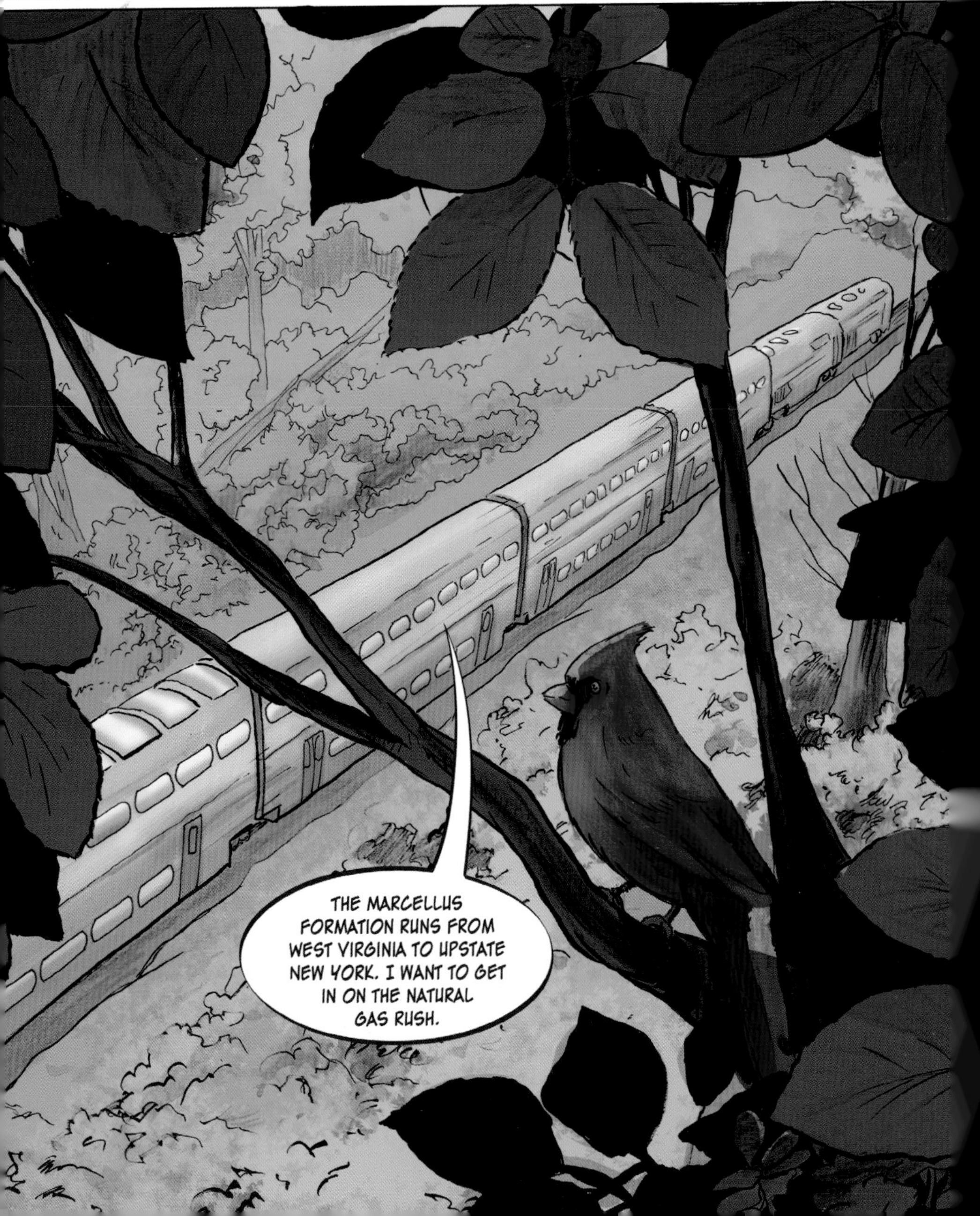
THE MARCELLUS FORMATION RUNS FROM WEST VIRGINIA TO UPSTATE NEW YORK. I WANT TO GET IN ON THE NATURAL GAS RUSH.

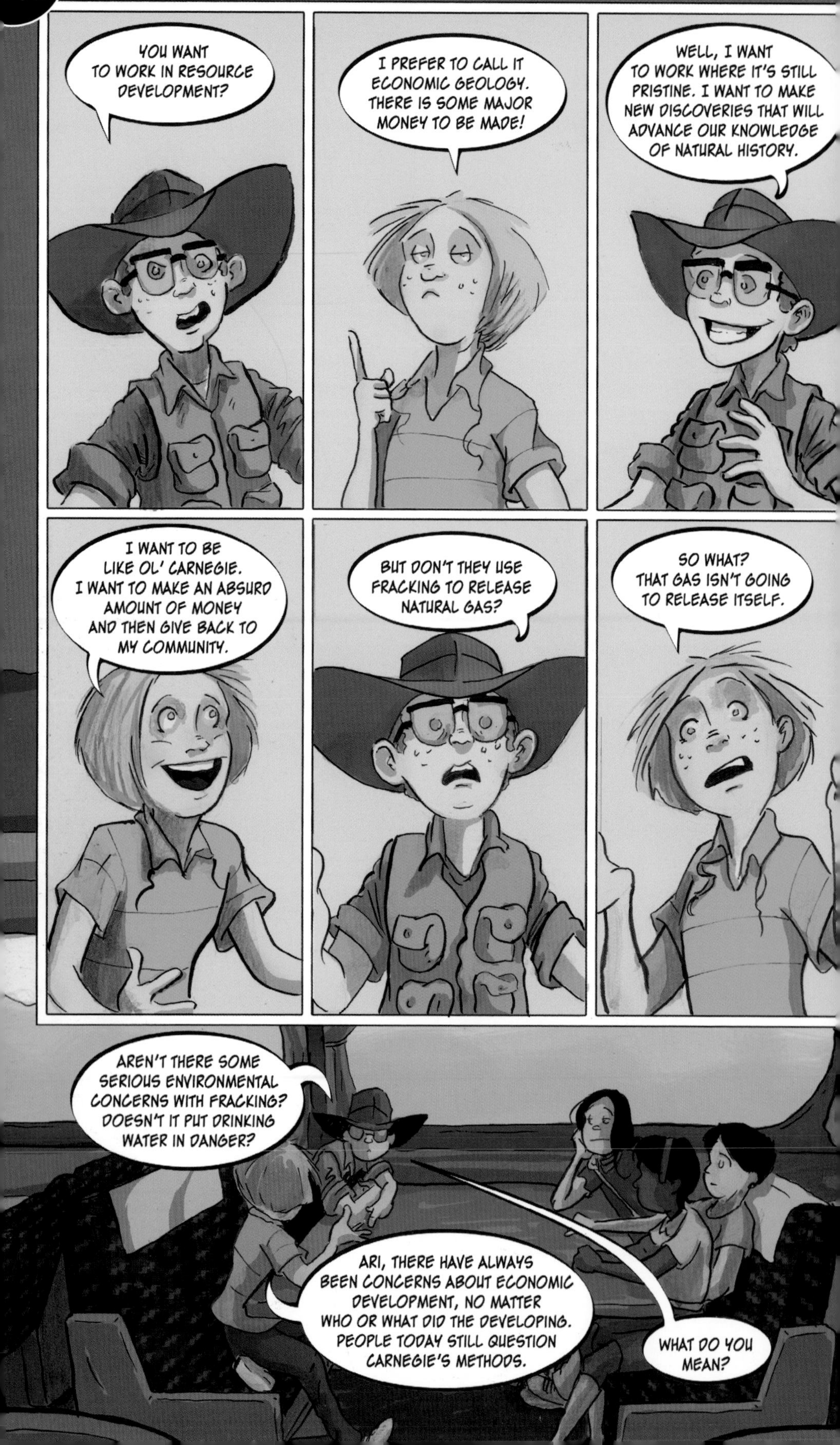
YOU WANT TO WORK IN RESOURCE DEVELOPMENT?
I PREFER TO CALL IT ECONOMIC GEOLOGY. THERE IS SOME MAJOR MONEY TO BE MADE!
WELL, I WANT TO WORK WHERE IT'S STILL PRISTINE. I WANT TO MAKE NEW DISCOVERIES THAT WILL ADVANCE OUR KNOWLEDGE OF NATURAL HISTORY.
I WANT TO BE LIKE OL' CARNEGIE. I WANT TO MAKE AN ABSURD AMOUNT OF MONEY AND THEN GIVE BACK TO MY COMMUNITY.
BUT DON'T THEY USE FRACKING TO RELEASE NATURAL GAS?
SO WHAT? THAT GAS ISN'T GOING TO RELEASE ITSELF.
AREN'T THERE SOME SERIOUS ENVIRONMENTAL CONCERNS WITH FRACKING? DOESN'T IT PUT DRINKING WATER IN DANGER?
ARI, THERE HAVE ALWAYS BEEN CONCERNS ABOUT ECONOMIC DEVELOPMENT, NO MATTER WHO OR WHAT DID THE DEVELOPING. PEOPLE TODAY STILL QUESTION CARNEGIE'S METHODS.
WHAT DO YOU MEAN?

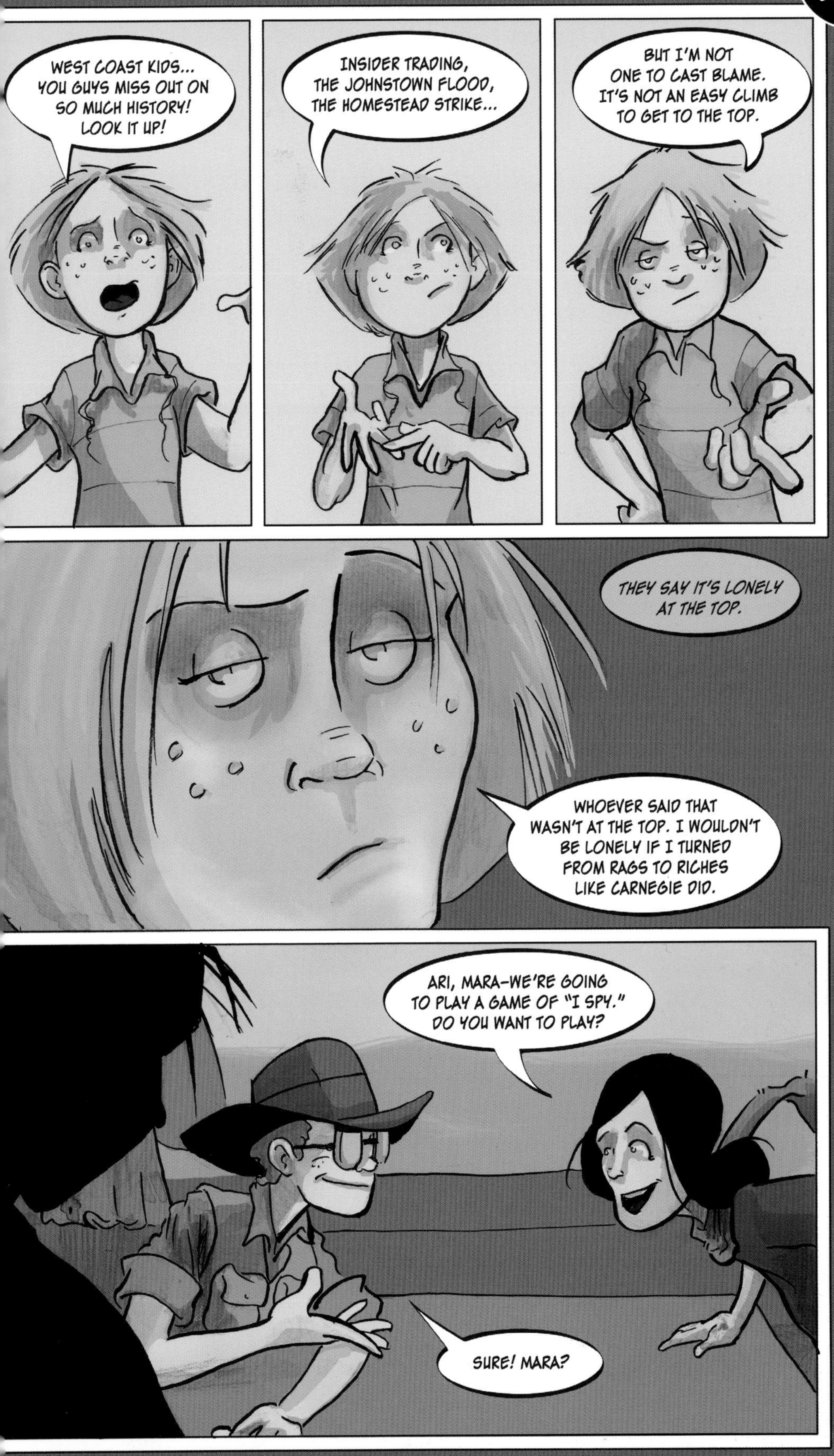
WEST COAST KIDS... YOU GUYS MISS OUT ON SO MUCH HISTORY! LOOK IT UP!
INSIDER TRADING, THE JOHNSTOWN FLOOD, THE HOMESTEAD STRIKE...
BUT I'M NOT ONE TO CAST BLAME. IT'S NOT AN EASY CLIMB TO GET TO THE TOP.
THEY SAY IT'S LONELY AT THE TOP.
WHOEVER SAID THAT WASN'T AT THE TOP. I WOULDN'T BE LONELY IF I TURNED FROM RAGS TO RICHES LIKE CARNEGIE DID.
ARI, MARA—WE'RE GOING TO PLAY A GAME OF "I SPY." DO YOU WANT TO PLAY?
SURE! MARA?

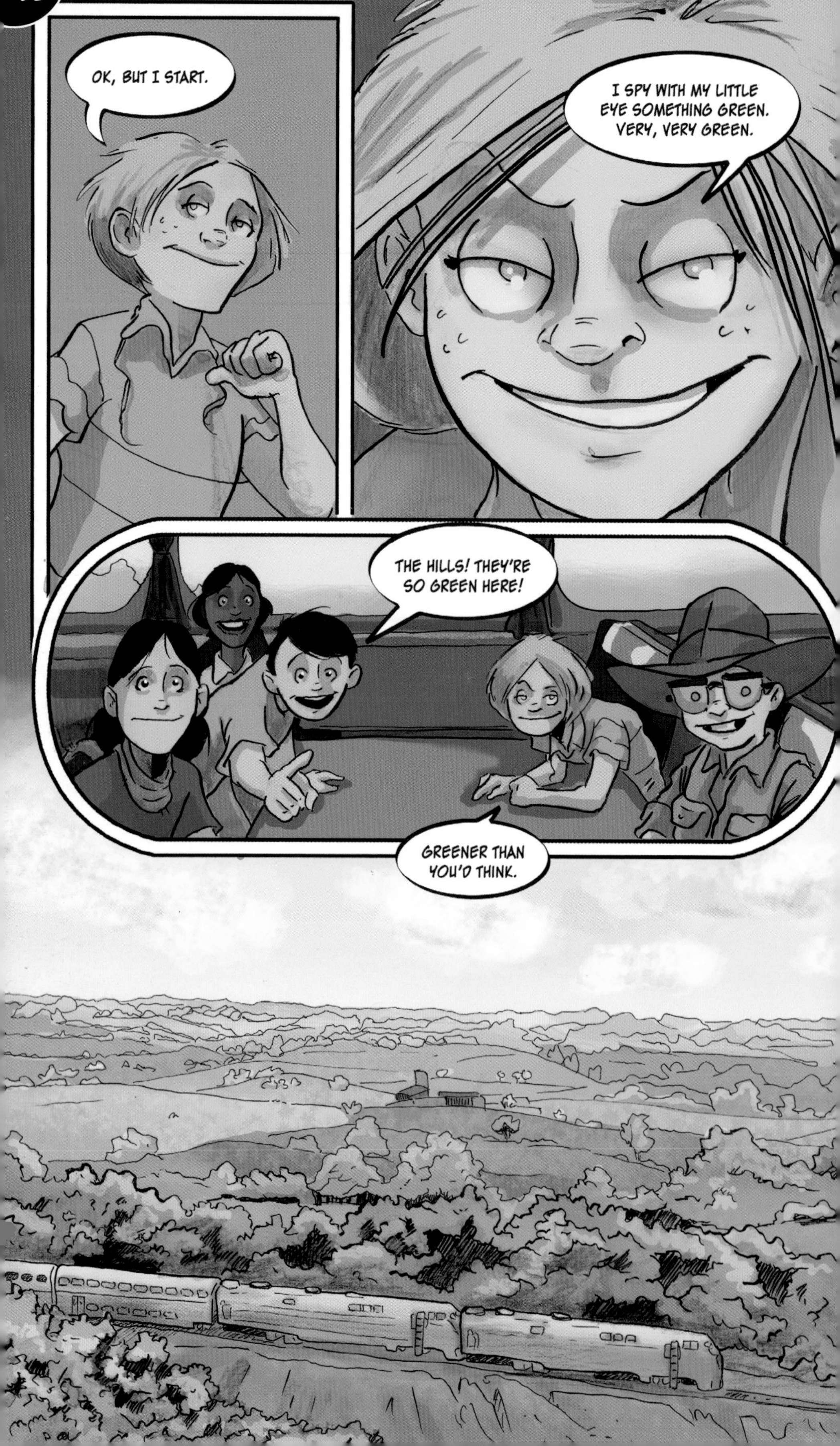
OK, BUT I START.
I SPY WITH MY LITTLE EYE SOMETHING GREEN. VERY, VERY GREEN.
THE HILLS! THEY'RE SO GREEN HERE!
GREENER THAN YOU'D THINK.

STUDENT HANDBOOK

Academy of
Planetary
Evolution

4

"Wallace's Line"

MONTAUK INDUSTRIES

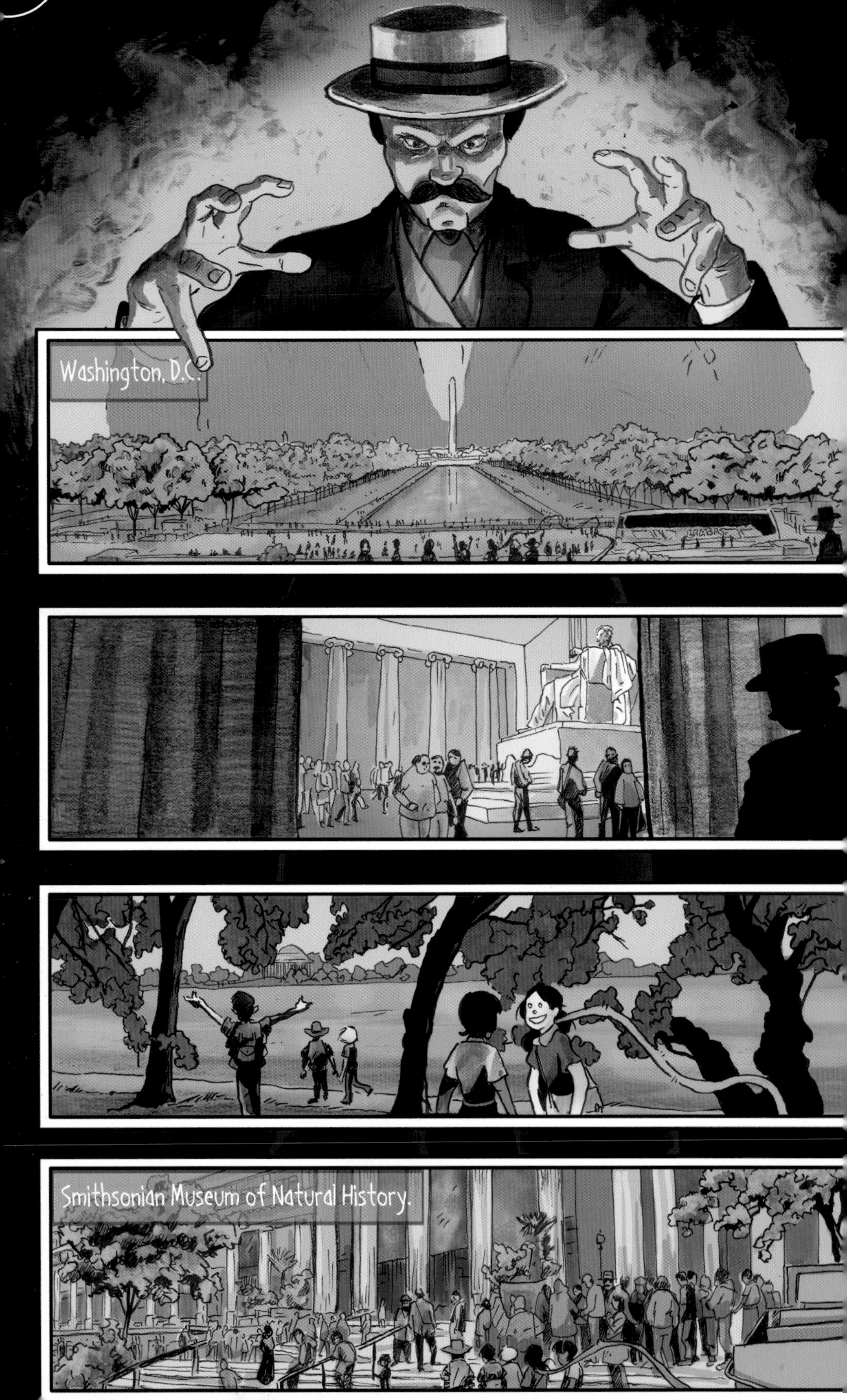
Washington, D.C.
Smithsonian Museum of Natural History.

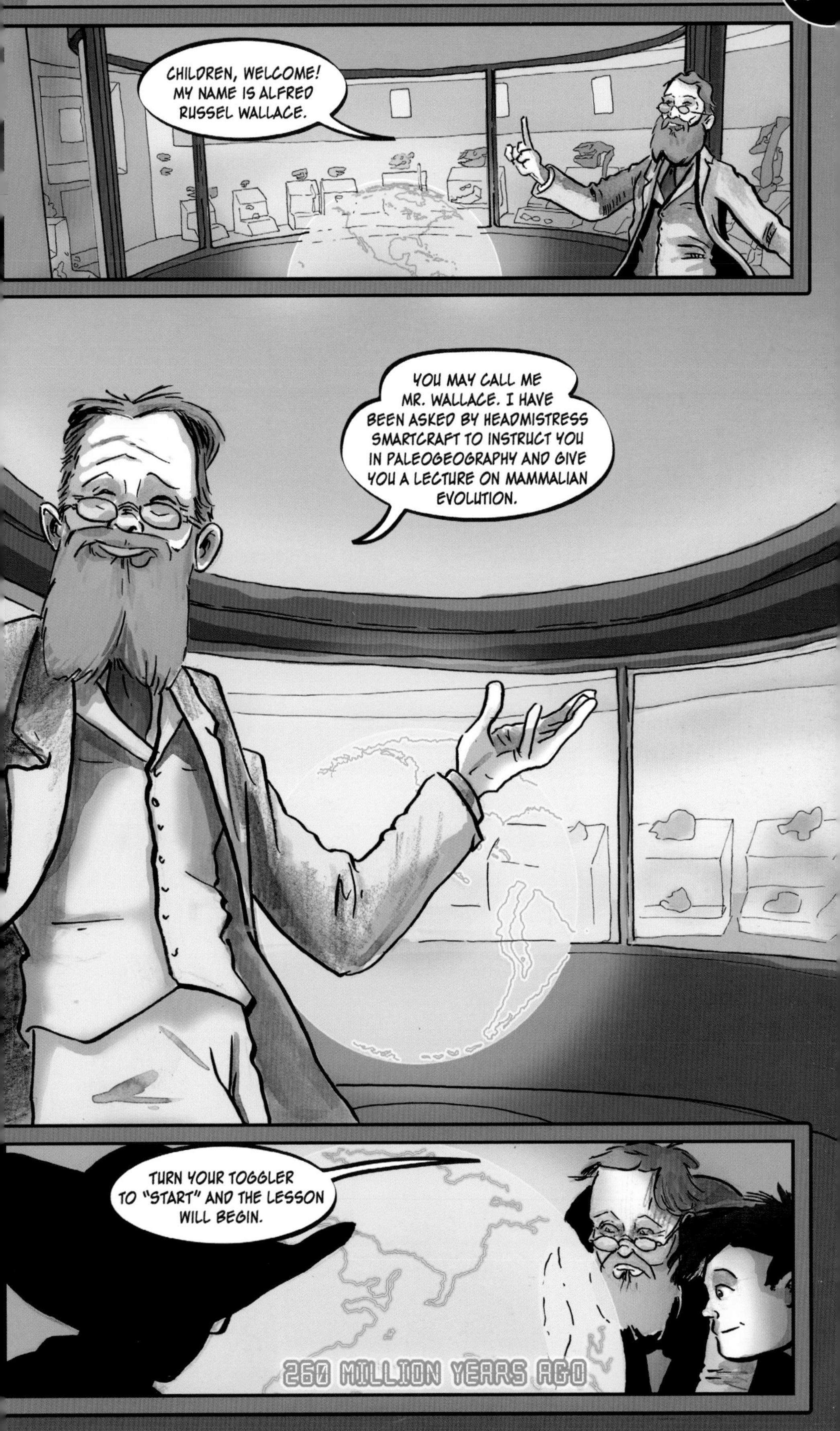
CHILDREN, WELCOME! MY NAME IS ALFRED RUSSEL WALLACE.
YOU MAY CALL ME MR. WALLACE. I HAVE BEEN ASKED BY HEADMISTRESS SMARTCRAFT TO INSTRUCT YOU IN PALEOGEOGRAPHY AND GIVE YOU A LECTURE ON MAMMALIAN EVOLUTION.
TURN YOUR TOGGLER TO "START" AND THE LESSON WILL BEGIN.
260 MILLION YEARS AGO

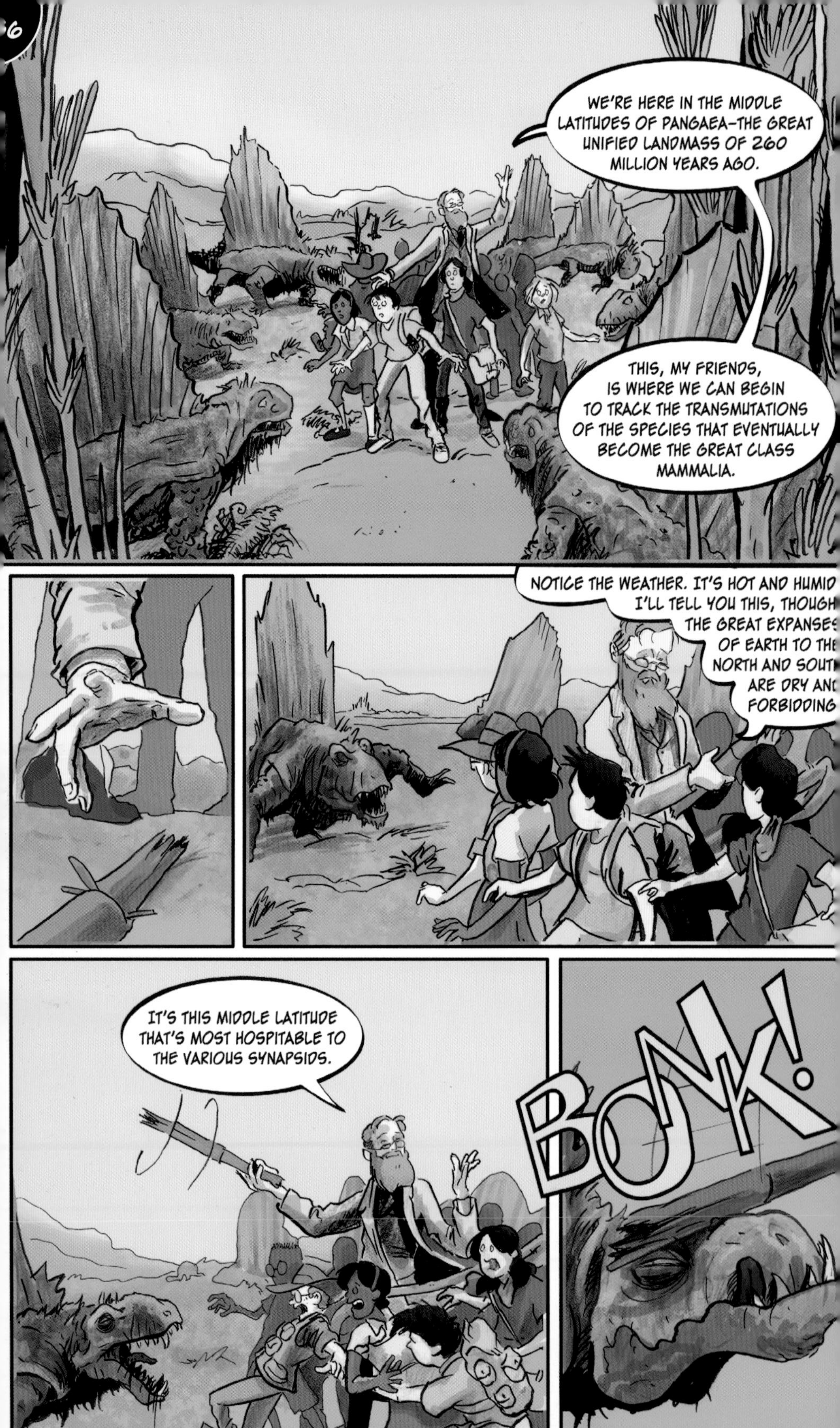
WE'RE HERE IN THE MIDDLE LATITUDES OF PANGAEA—THE GREAT UNIFIED LANDMASS OF 260 MILLION YEARS AGO.
THIS, MY FRIENDS, IS WHERE WE CAN BEGIN TO TRACK THE TRANSMUTATIONS OF THE SPECIES THAT EVENTUALLY BECOME THE GREAT CLASS MAMMALIA.
NOTICE THE WEATHER. IT'S HOT AND HUMID
I'LL TELL YOU THIS, THOUGH THE GREAT EXPANSES OF EARTH TO THE NORTH AND SOUTH ARE DRY AND FORBIDDING
IT'S THIS MIDDLE LATITUDE THAT'S MOST HOSPITABLE TO THE VARIOUS SYNAPSIDS.
BONK!

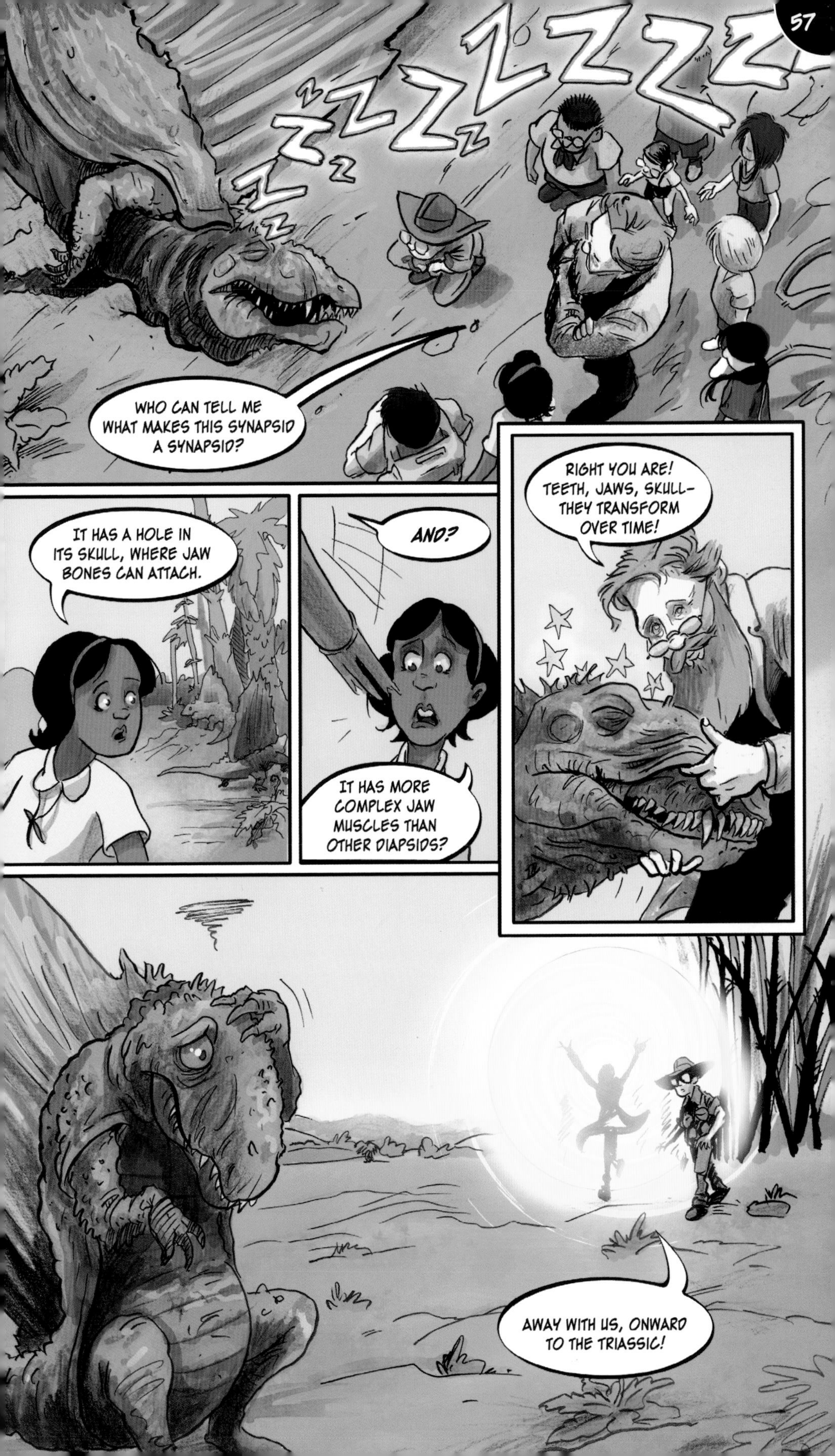
ZZZZZZZZZZZZZZ
WHO CAN TELL ME WHAT MAKES THIS SYNAPSID A SYNAPSID?
IT HAS A HOLE IN ITS SKULL, WHERE JAW BONES CAN ATTACH.
AND?
IT HAS MORE COMPLEX JAW MUSCLES THAN OTHER DIAPSIDS?
RIGHT YOU ARE! TEETH, JAWS, SKULL- THEY TRANSFORM OVER TIME!
AWAY WITH US, ONWARD TO THE TRIASSIC!

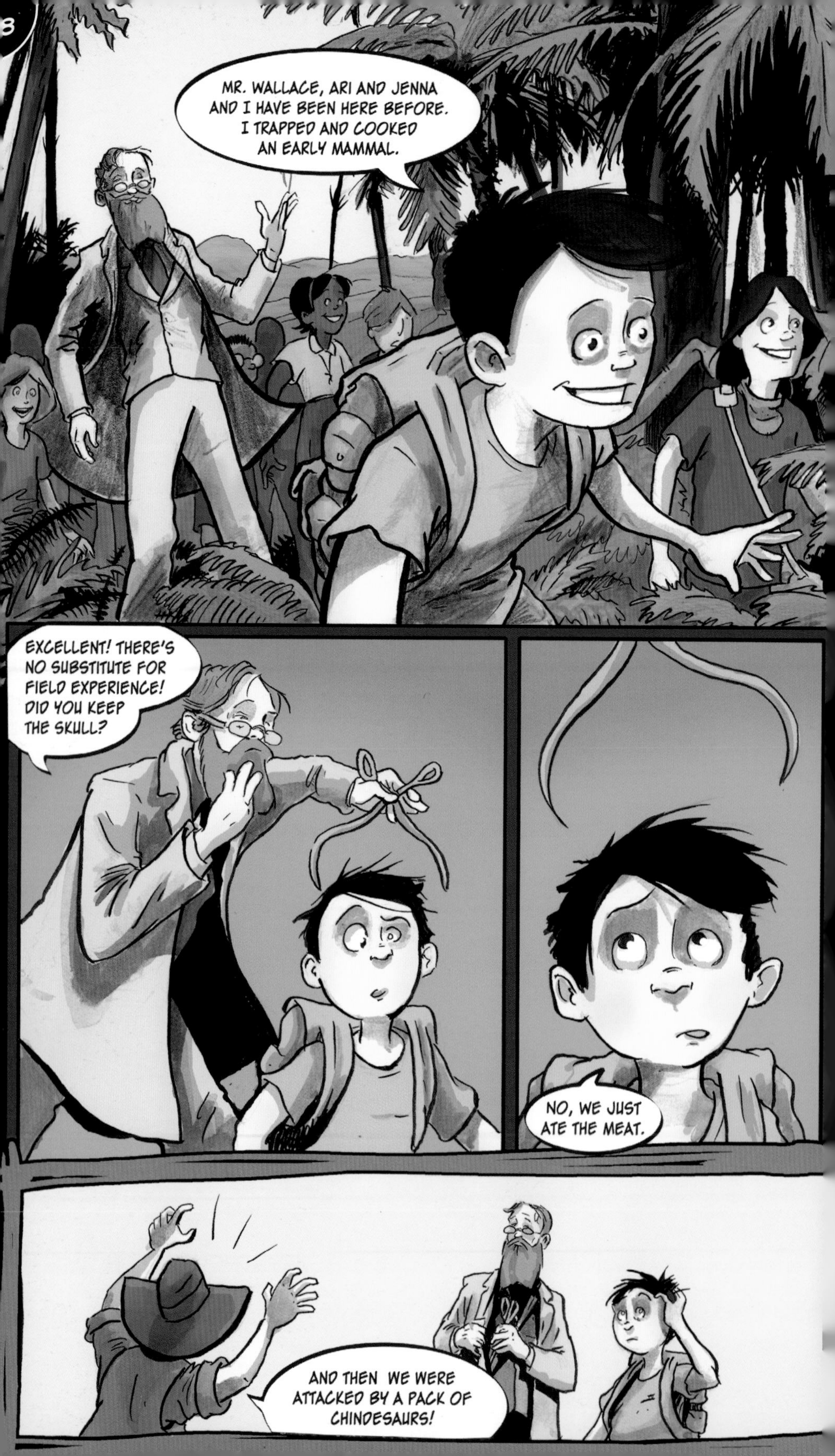
MR. WALLACE, ARI AND JENNA AND I HAVE BEEN HERE BEFORE. I TRAPPED AND COOKED AN EARLY MAMMAL.
EXCELLENT! THERE'S NO SUBSTITUTE FOR FIELD EXPERIENCE! DID YOU KEEP THE SKULL?
NO, WE JUST ATE THE MEAT.
AND THEN WE WERE ATTACKED BY A PACK OF CHINDESAURS!

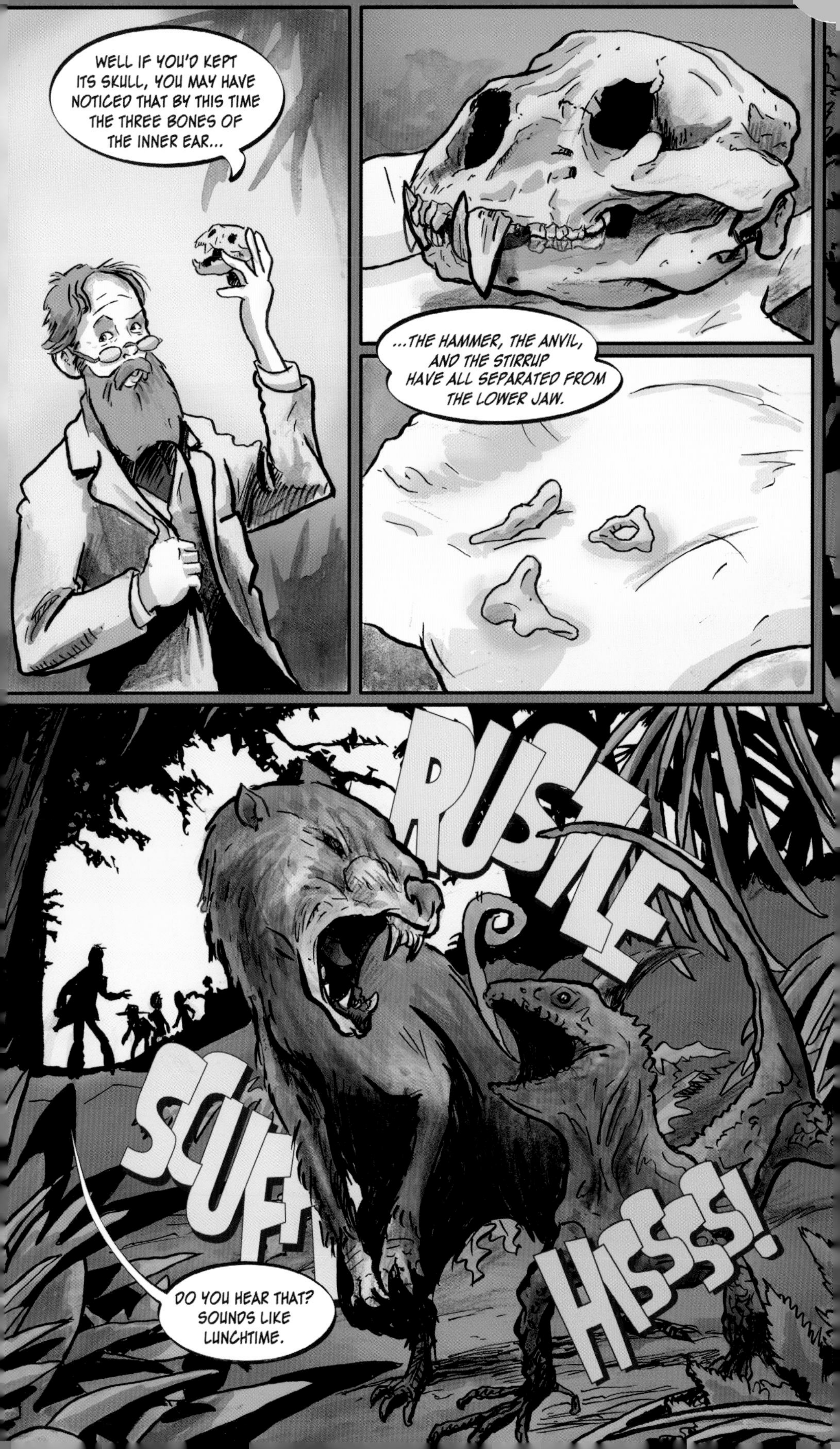
WELL IF YOU'D KEPT ITS SKULL, YOU MAY HAVE NOTICED THAT BY THIS TIME THE THREE BONES OF THE INNER EAR...
...THE HAMMER, THE ANVIL, AND THE STIRRUP HAVE ALL SEPARATED FROM THE LOWER JAW.
RUSTLE
SCUFF
HISSS!
DO YOU HEAR THAT? SOUNDS LIKE LUNCHTIME.

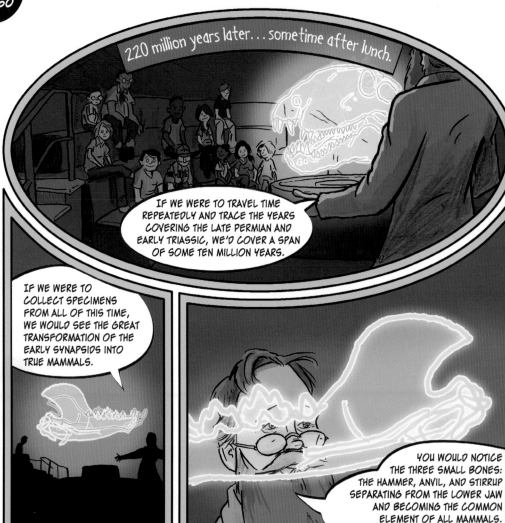

220 million years later... sometime after lunch.

IF WE WERE TO TRAVEL TIME REPEATEDLY AND TRACE THE YEARS COVERING THE LATE PERMIAN AND EARLY TRIASSIC, WE'D COVER A SPAN OF SOME TEN MILLION YEARS.

IF WE WERE TO COLLECT SPECIMENS FROM ALL OF THIS TIME, WE WOULD SEE THE GREAT TRANSFORMATION OF THE EARLY SYNAPSIDS INTO TRUE MAMMALS.

YOU WOULD NOTICE THE THREE SMALL BONES: THE HAMMER, ANVIL, AND STIRRUP SEPARATING FROM THE LOWER JAW AND BECOMING THE COMMON ELEMENT OF ALL MAMMALS.

THE EAR?

THAT IS CORRECT! THE INNER EAR TO BE PRECISE!

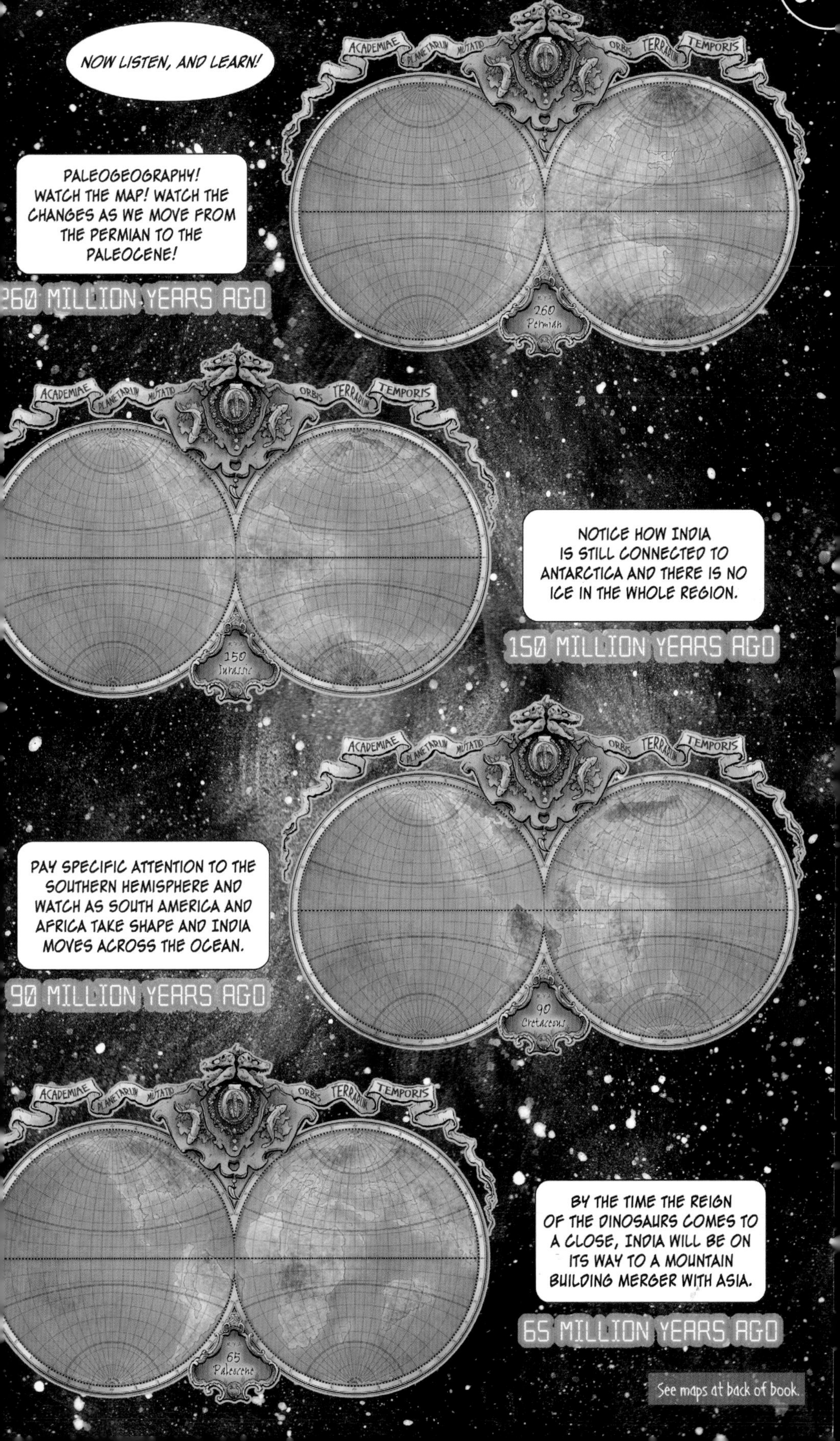
NOW LISTEN, AND LEARN!
ACADEMIAE PLANETARUM MUTATIO ORBIS TERRARUM TEMPORIS
PALEOGEOGRAPHY! WATCH THE MAP! WATCH THE CHANGES AS WE MOVE FROM THE PERMIAN TO THE PALEOCENE!
260 MILLION YEARS AGO
260 Permian
ACADEMIAE PLANETARUM MUTATIO ORBIS TERRARUM TEMPORIS
NOTICE HOW INDIA IS STILL CONNECTED TO ANTARCTICA AND THERE IS NO ICE IN THE WHOLE REGION.
150 Jurassic
150 MILLION YEARS AGO
ACADEMIAE PLANETARUM MUTATIO ORBIS TERRARUM TEMPORIS
PAY SPECIFIC ATTENTION TO THE SOUTHERN HEMISPHERE AND WATCH AS SOUTH AMERICA AND AFRICA TAKE SHAPE AND INDIA MOVES ACROSS THE OCEAN.
90 MILLION YEARS AGO
90 Cretaceous
ACADEMIAE PLANETARUM MUTATIO ORBIS TERRARUM TEMPORIS
BY THE TIME THE REIGN OF THE DINOSAURS COMES TO A CLOSE, INDIA WILL BE ON ITS WAY TO A MOUNTAIN BUILDING MERGER WITH ASIA.
65 MILLION YEARS AGO
65 Paleocene
See maps at back of book.

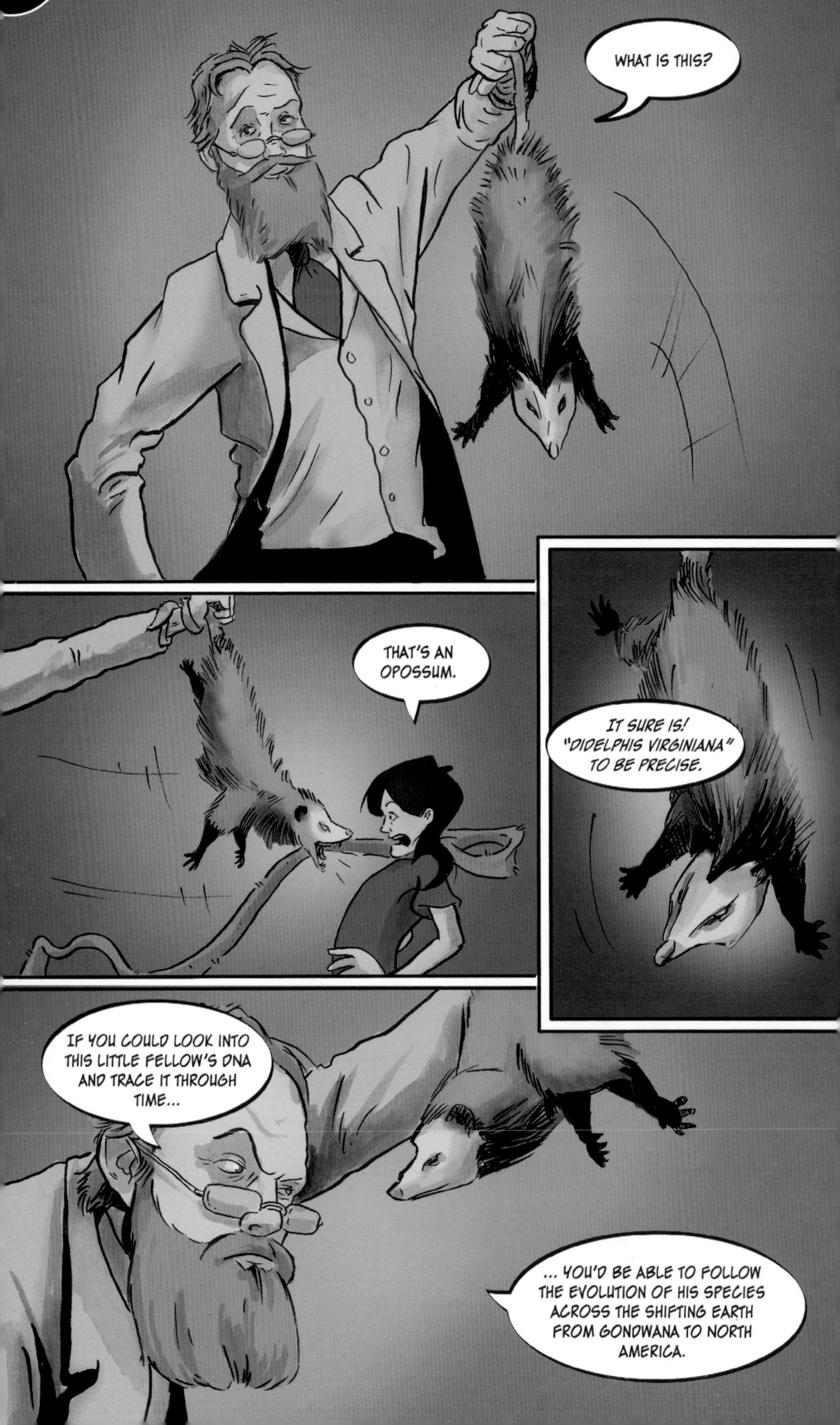
WHAT IS THIS?
THAT'S AN OPOSSUM.
IT SURE IS! "DIDELPHIS VIRGINIANA" TO BE PRECISE.
IF YOU COULD LOOK INTO THIS LITTLE FELLOW'S DNA AND TRACE IT THROUGH TIME...
... YOU'D BE ABLE TO FOLLOW THE EVOLUTION OF HIS SPECIES ACROSS THE SHIFTING EARTH FROM GONDWANA TO NORTH AMERICA.

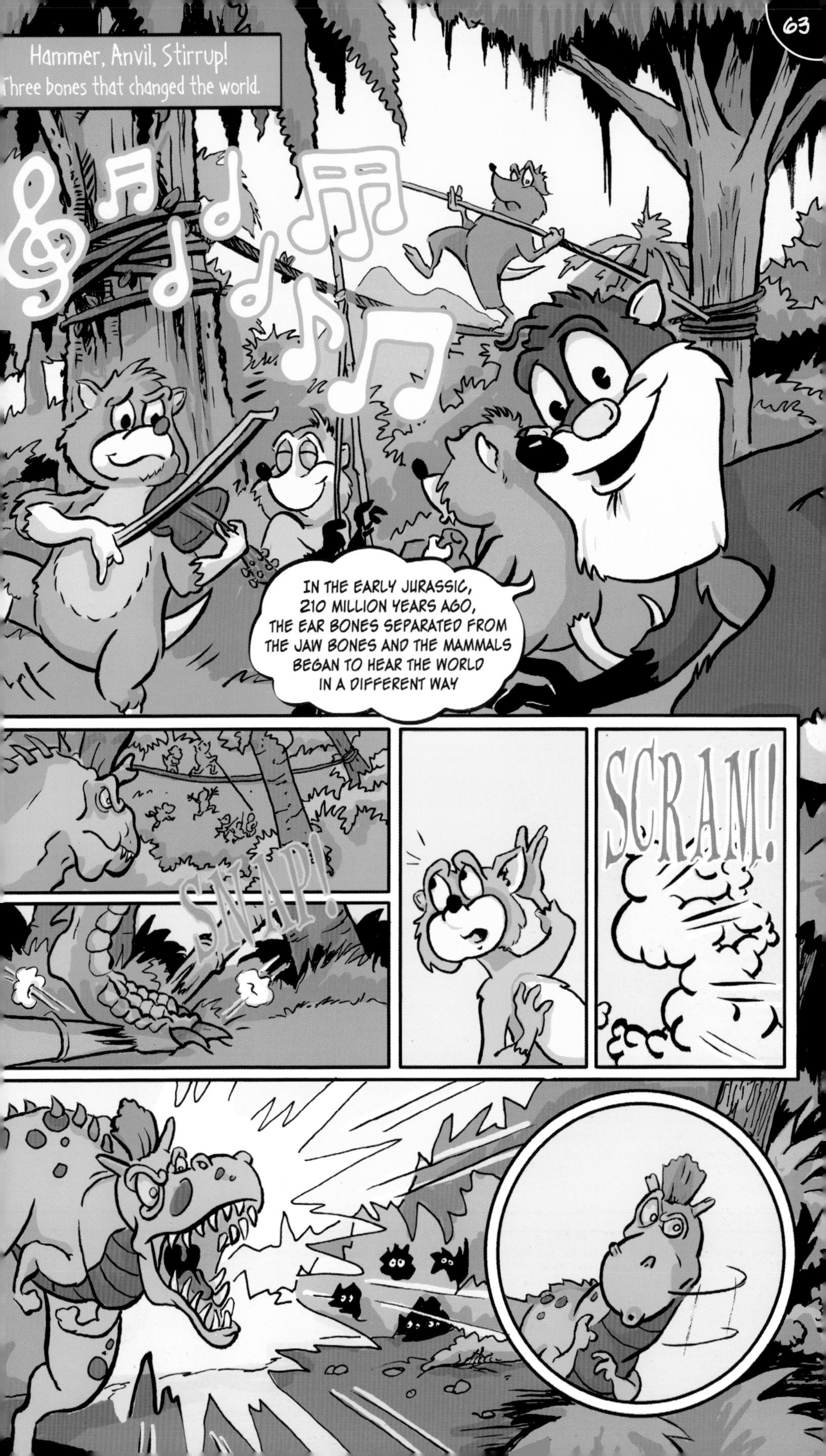
Hammer, Anvil, Stirrup!
Three bones that changed the world.
IN THE EARLY JURASSIC, 210 MILLION YEARS AGO, THE EAR BONES SEPARATED FROM THE JAW BONES AND THE MAMMALS BEGAN TO HEAR THE WORLD IN A DIFFERENT WAY
SNAP!
SCRAM!

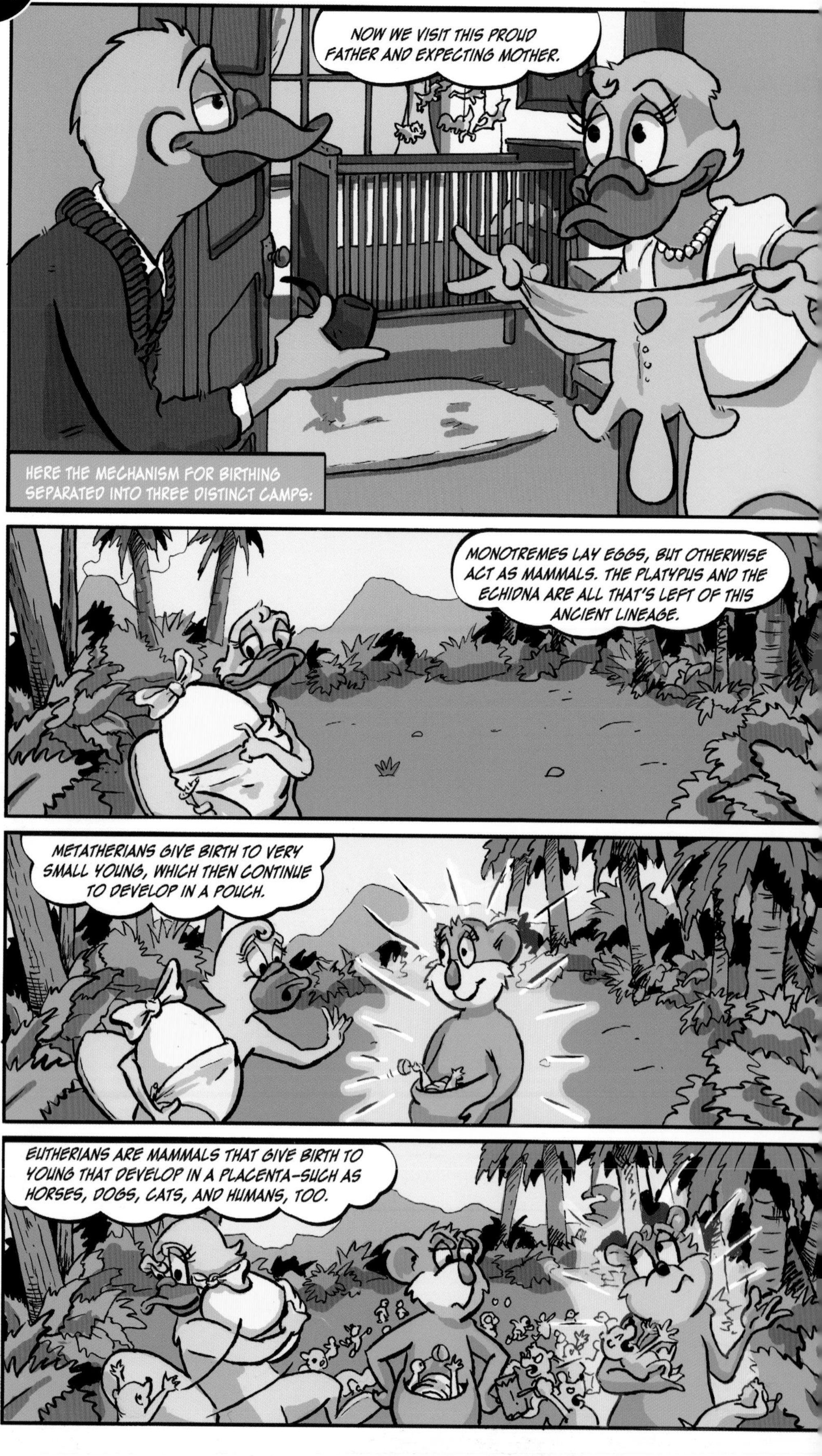
NOW WE VISIT THIS PROUD FATHER AND EXPECTING MOTHER.
HERE THE MECHANISM FOR BIRTHING SEPARATED INTO THREE DISTINCT CAMPS:
MONOTREMES LAY EGGS, BUT OTHERWISE ACT AS MAMMALS. THE PLATYPUS AND THE ECHIDNA ARE ALL THAT'S LEFT OF THIS ANCIENT LINEAGE.
METATHERIANS GIVE BIRTH TO VERY SMALL YOUNG, WHICH THEN CONTINUE TO DEVELOP IN A POUCH.
EUTHERIANS ARE MAMMALS THAT GIVE BIRTH TO YOUNG THAT DEVELOP IN A PLACENTA–SUCH AS HORSES, DOGS, CATS, AND HUMANS, TOO.

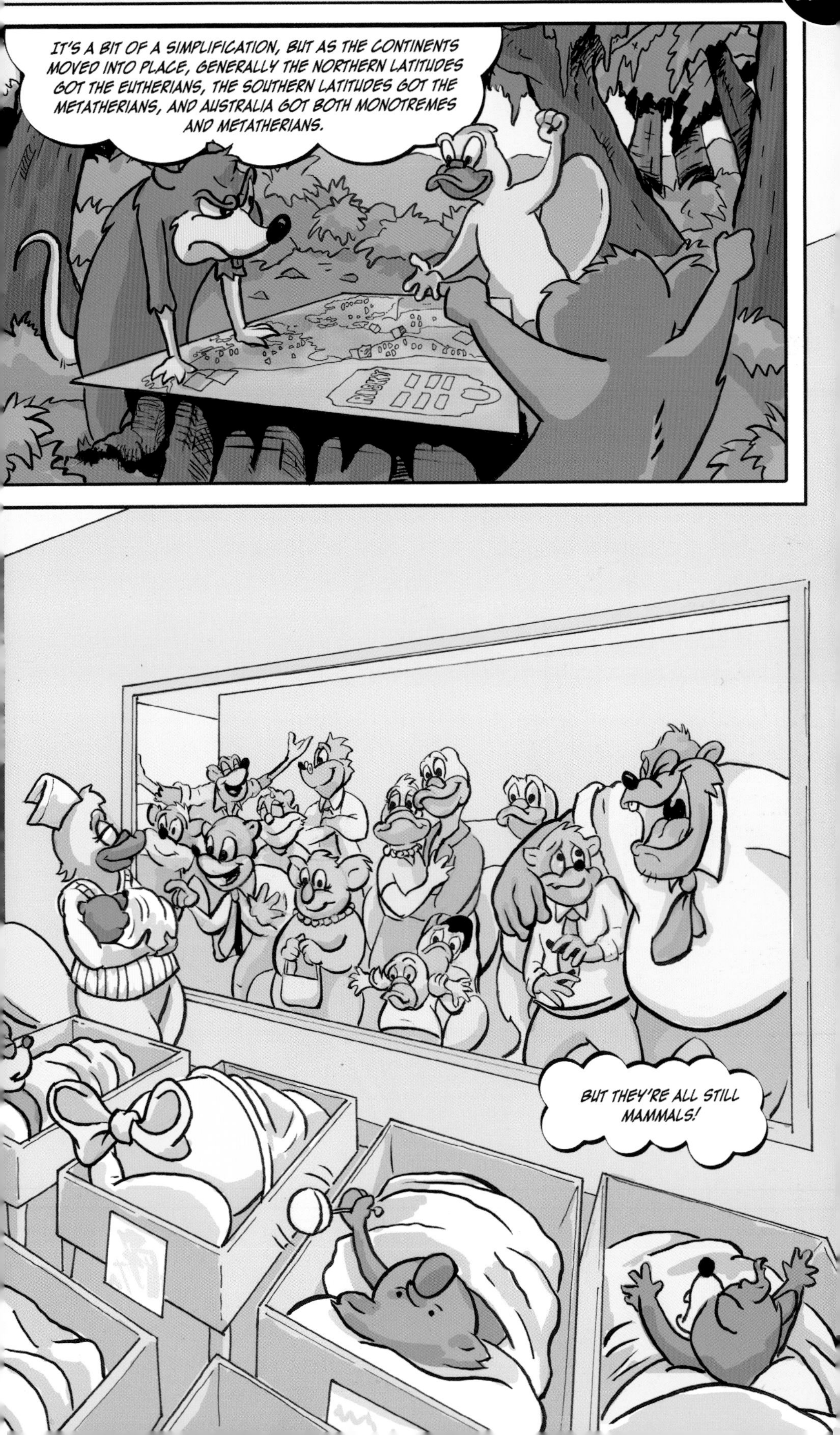
IT'S A BIT OF A SIMPLIFICATION, BUT AS THE CONTINENTS MOVED INTO PLACE, GENERALLY THE NORTHERN LATITUDES GOT THE EUTHERIANS, THE SOUTHERN LATITUDES GOT THE METATHERIANS, AND AUSTRALIA GOT BOTH MONOTREMES AND METATHERIANS.
BUT THEY'RE ALL STILL MAMMALS!

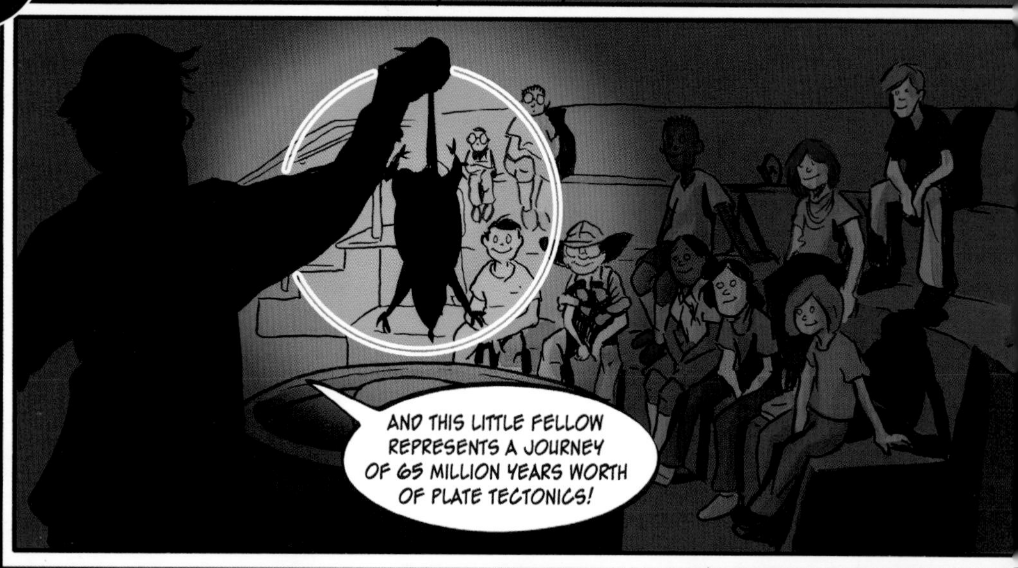
AND THIS LITTLE FELLOW REPRESENTS A JOURNEY OF 65 MILLION YEARS WORTH OF PLATE TECTONICS!

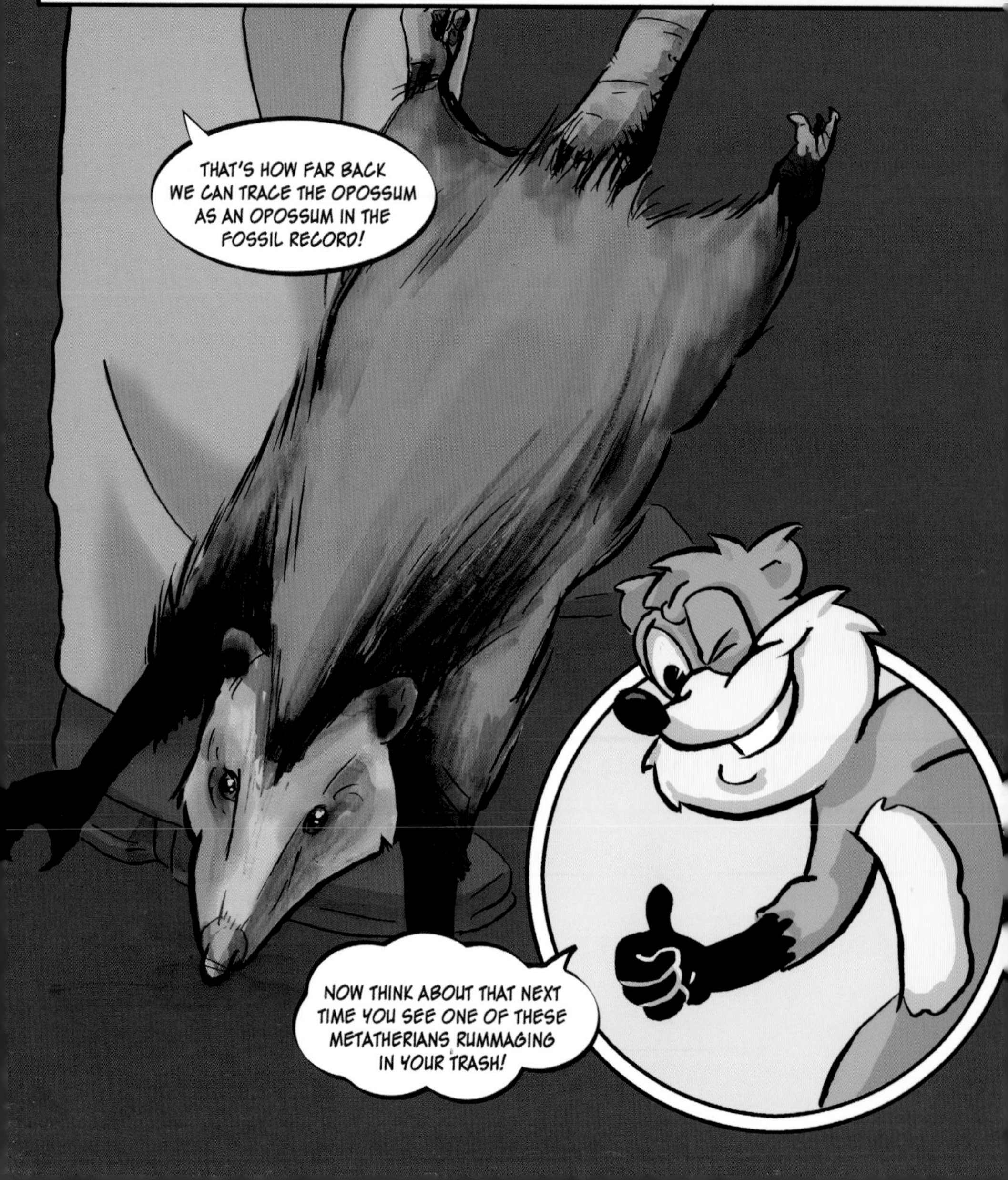
THAT'S HOW FAR BACK WE CAN TRACE THE OPOSSUM AS AN OPOSSUM IN THE FOSSIL RECORD!
NOW THINK ABOUT THAT NEXT TIME YOU SEE ONE OF THESE METATHERIANS RUMMAGING IN YOUR TRASH!

STUDENT HANDBOOK

Academy of Planetary Evolution

5

"REDI or Not"

5

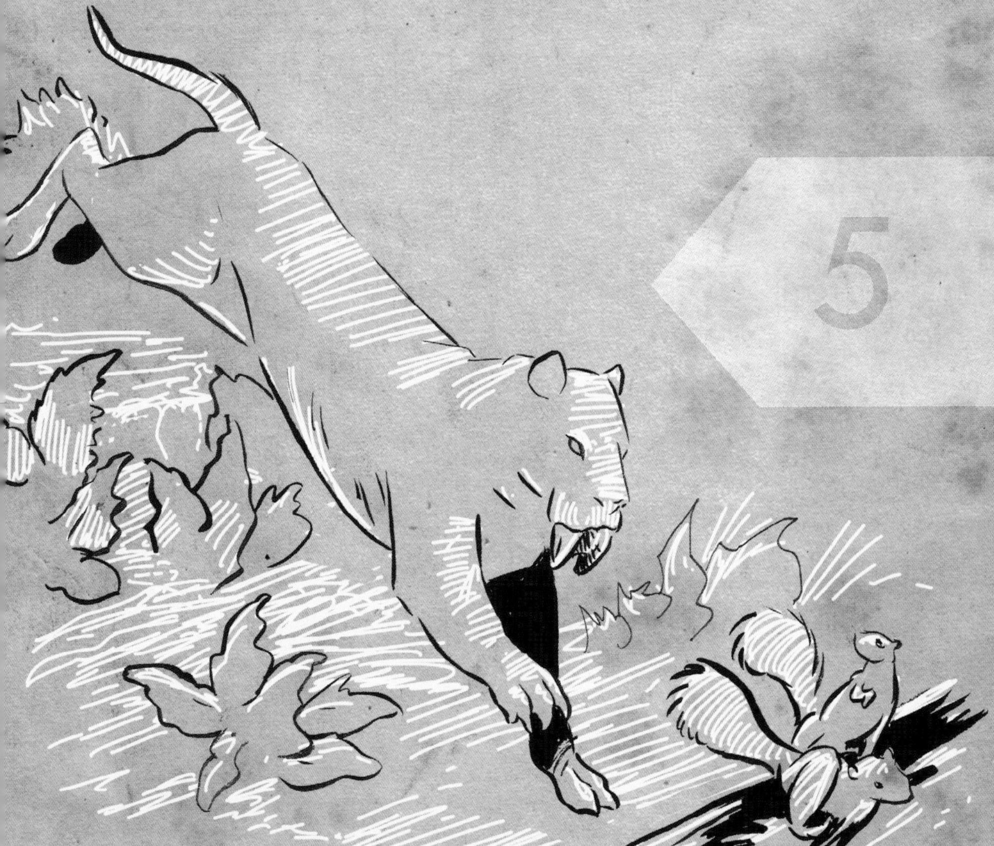

MONTAUK INDUSTRIES

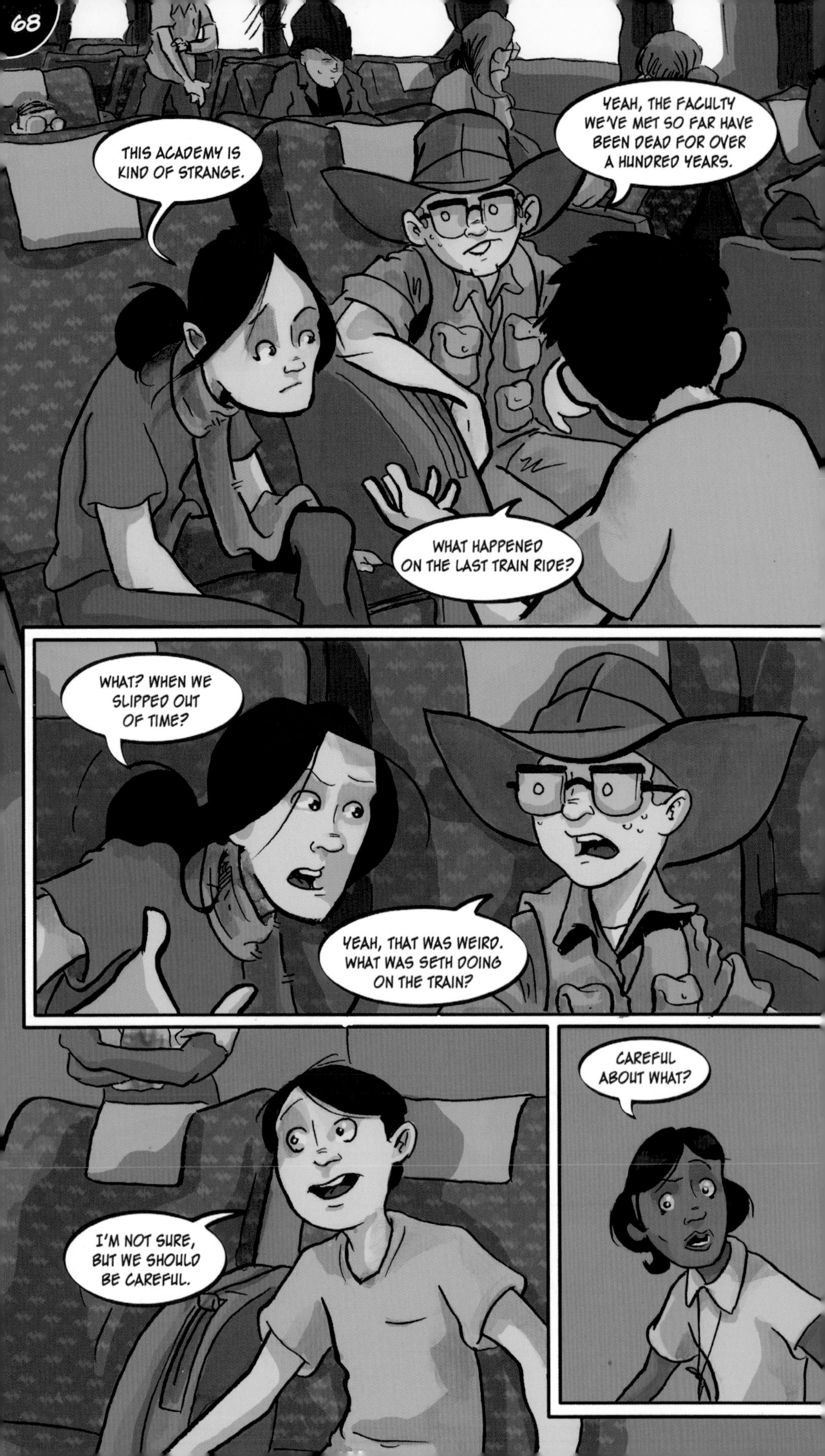
THIS ACADEMY IS KIND OF STRANGE.
YEAH, THE FACULTY WE'VE MET SO FAR HAVE BEEN DEAD FOR OVER A HUNDRED YEARS.
WHAT HAPPENED ON THE LAST TRAIN RIDE?
WHAT? WHEN WE SLIPPED OUT OF TIME?
YEAH, THAT WAS WEIRD. WHAT WAS SETH DOING ON THE TRAIN?
I'M NOT SURE, BUT WE SHOULD BE CAREFUL.
CAREFUL ABOUT WHAT?

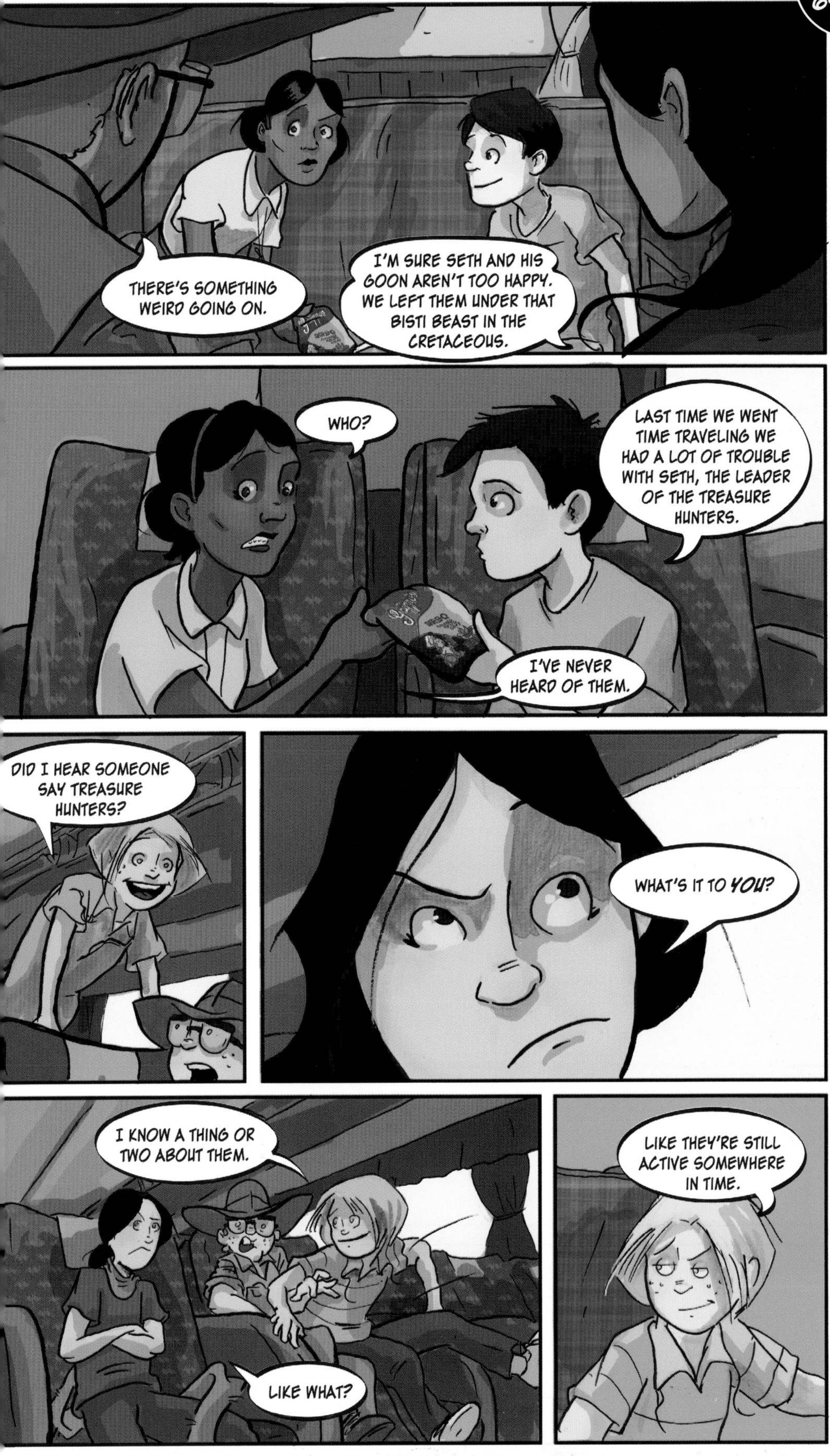
THERE'S SOMETHING WEIRD GOING ON.
I'M SURE SETH AND HIS GOON AREN'T TOO HAPPY. WE LEFT THEM UNDER THAT BISTI BEAST IN THE CRETACEOUS.
WHO?
LAST TIME WE WENT TIME TRAVELING WE HAD A LOT OF TROUBLE WITH SETH, THE LEADER OF THE TREASURE HUNTERS.
I'VE NEVER HEARD OF THEM.
DID I HEAR SOMEONE SAY TREASURE HUNTERS?
WHAT'S IT TO YOU?
I KNOW A THING OR TWO ABOUT THEM.
LIKE WHAT?
LIKE THEY'RE STILL ACTIVE SOMEWHERE IN TIME.

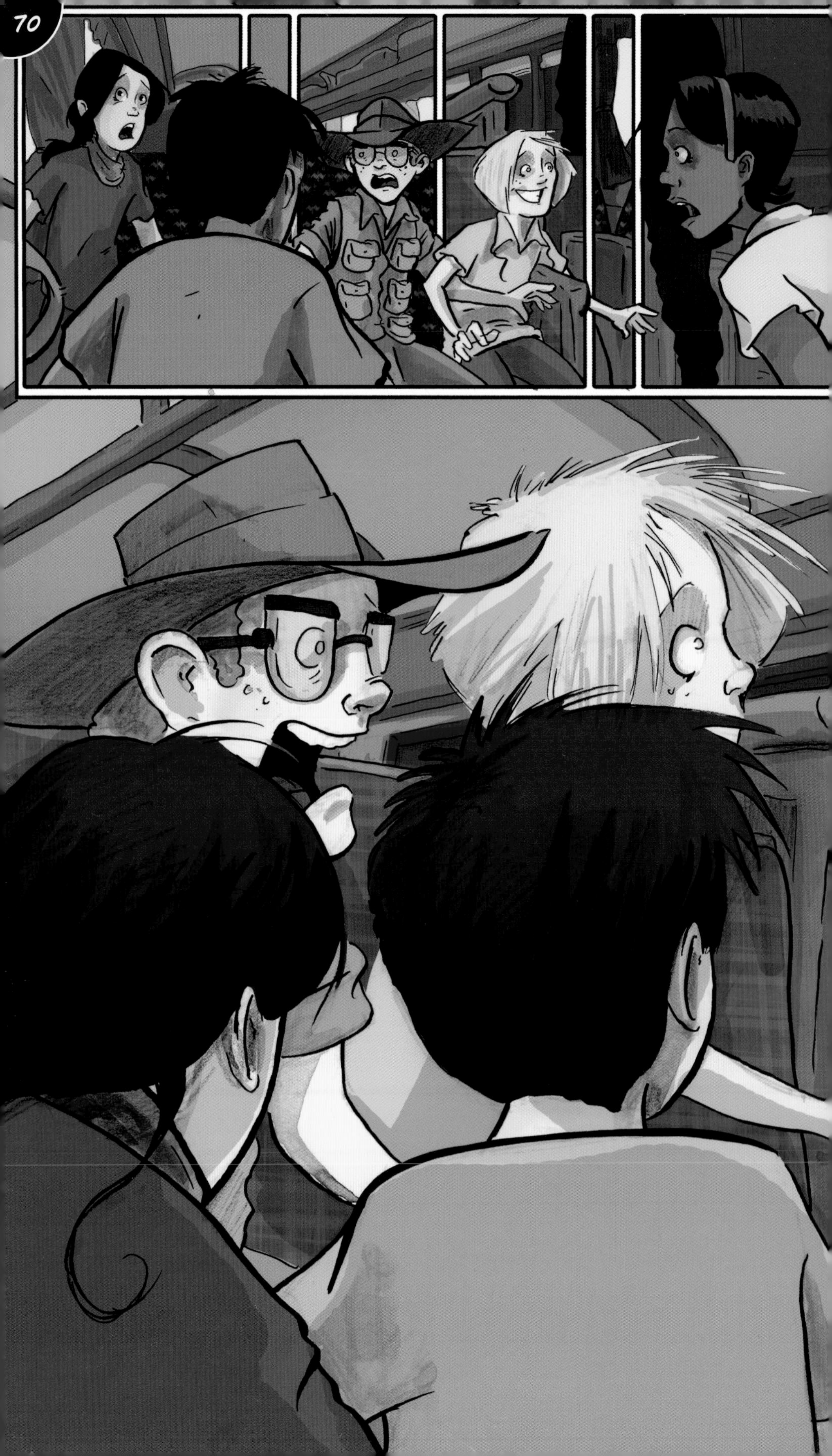

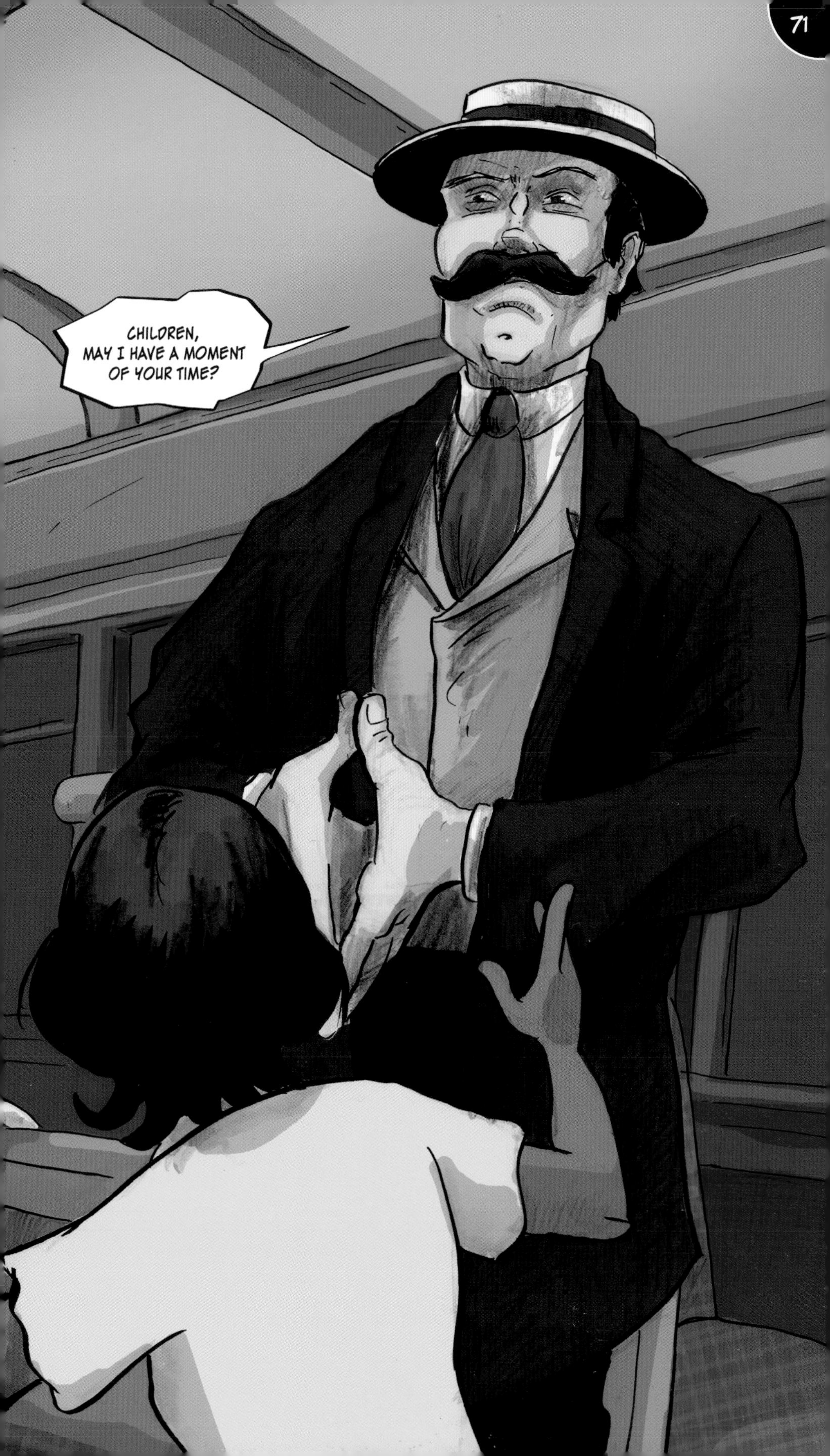
CHILDREN, MAY I HAVE A MOMENT OF YOUR TIME?

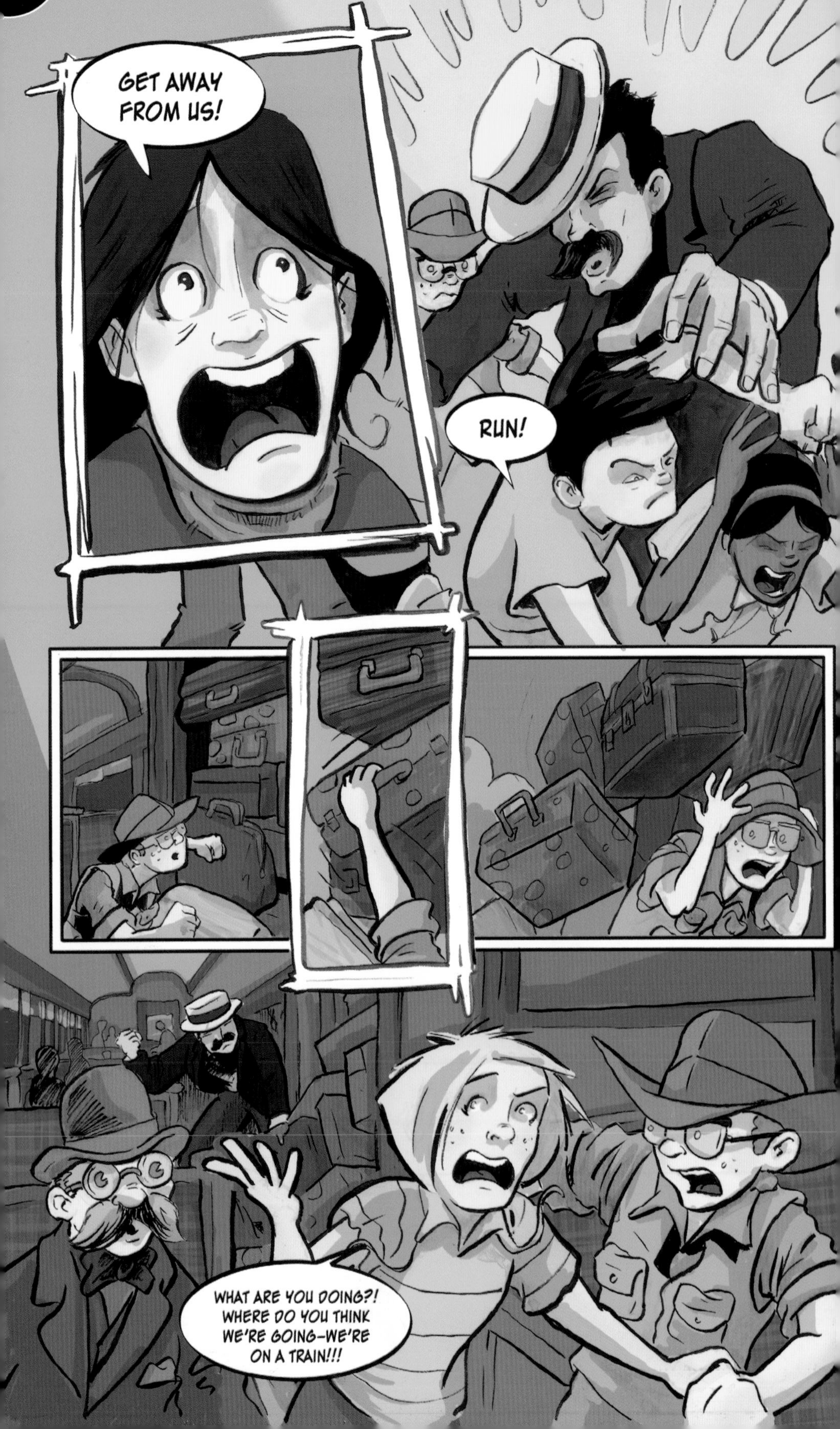
GET AWAY FROM US!
RUN!
WHAT ARE YOU DOING?! WHERE DO YOU THINK WE'RE GOING—WE'RE ON A TRAIN!!!

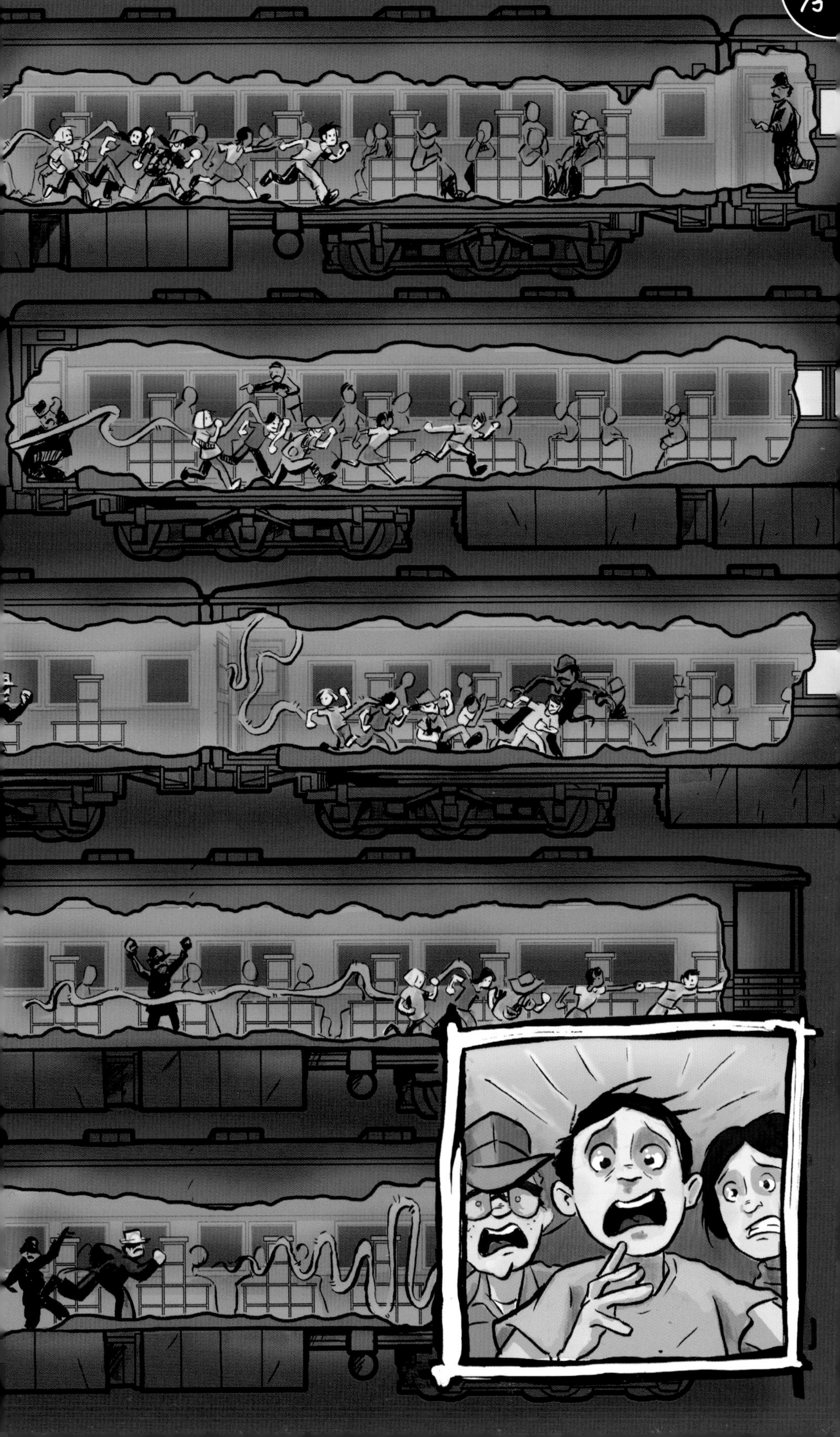

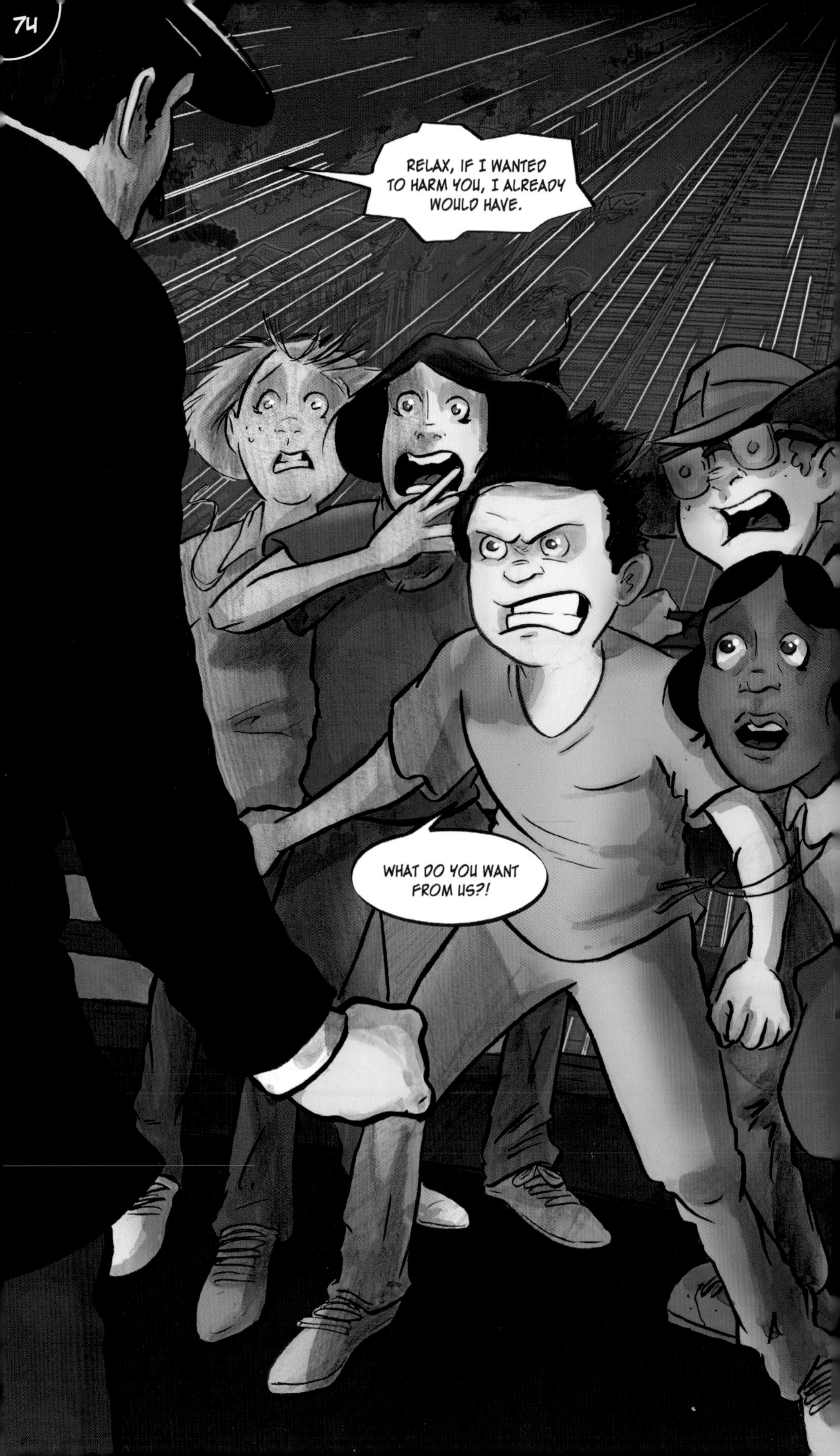
RELAX, IF I WANTED TO HARM YOU, I ALREADY WOULD HAVE.
WHAT DO YOU WANT FROM US?!

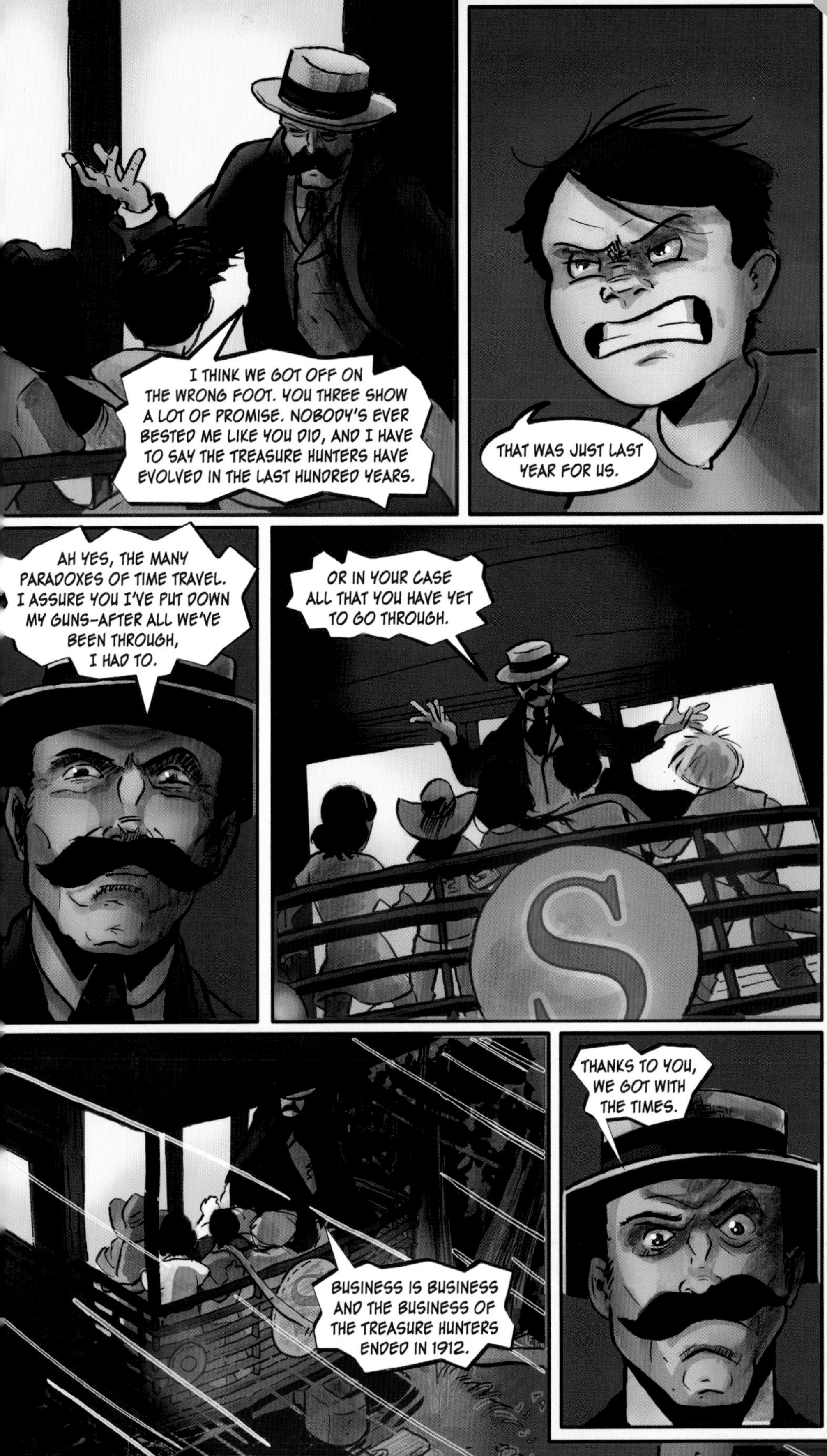

I THINK WE GOT OFF ON THE WRONG FOOT. YOU THREE SHOW A LOT OF PROMISE. NOBODY'S EVER BESTED ME LIKE YOU DID, AND I HAVE TO SAY THE TREASURE HUNTERS HAVE EVOLVED IN THE LAST HUNDRED YEARS.
THAT WAS JUST LAST YEAR FOR US.
AH YES, THE MANY PARADOXES OF TIME TRAVEL. I ASSURE YOU I'VE PUT DOWN MY GUNS–AFTER ALL WE'VE BEEN THROUGH, I HAD TO.
OR IN YOUR CASE ALL THAT YOU HAVE YET TO GO THROUGH.
BUSINESS IS BUSINESS AND THE BUSINESS OF THE TREASURE HUNTERS ENDED IN 1912.
THANKS TO YOU, WE GOT WITH THE TIMES.

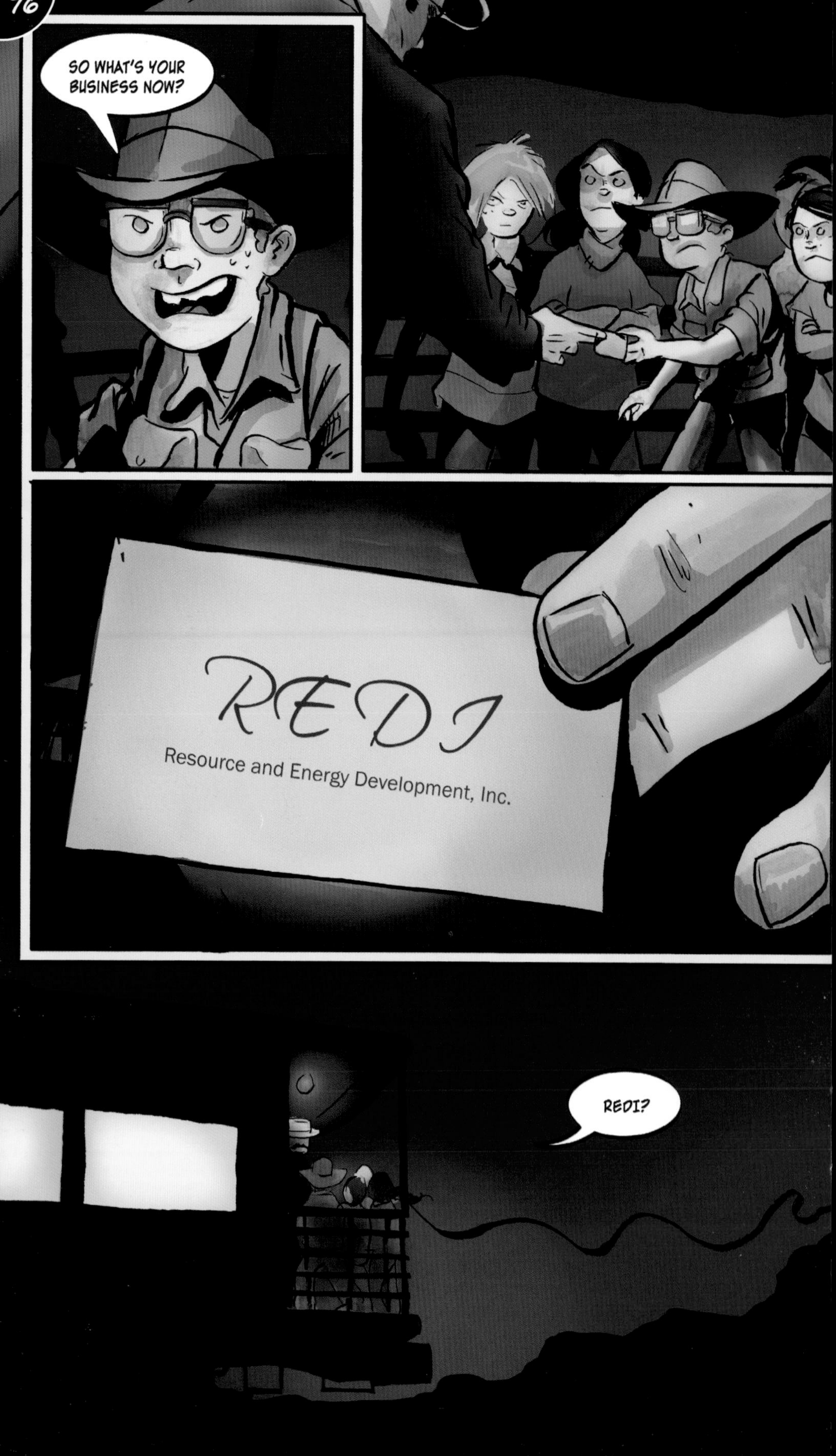
SO WHAT'S YOUR BUSINESS NOW?
REDI
Resource and Energy Development, Inc.
REDI?

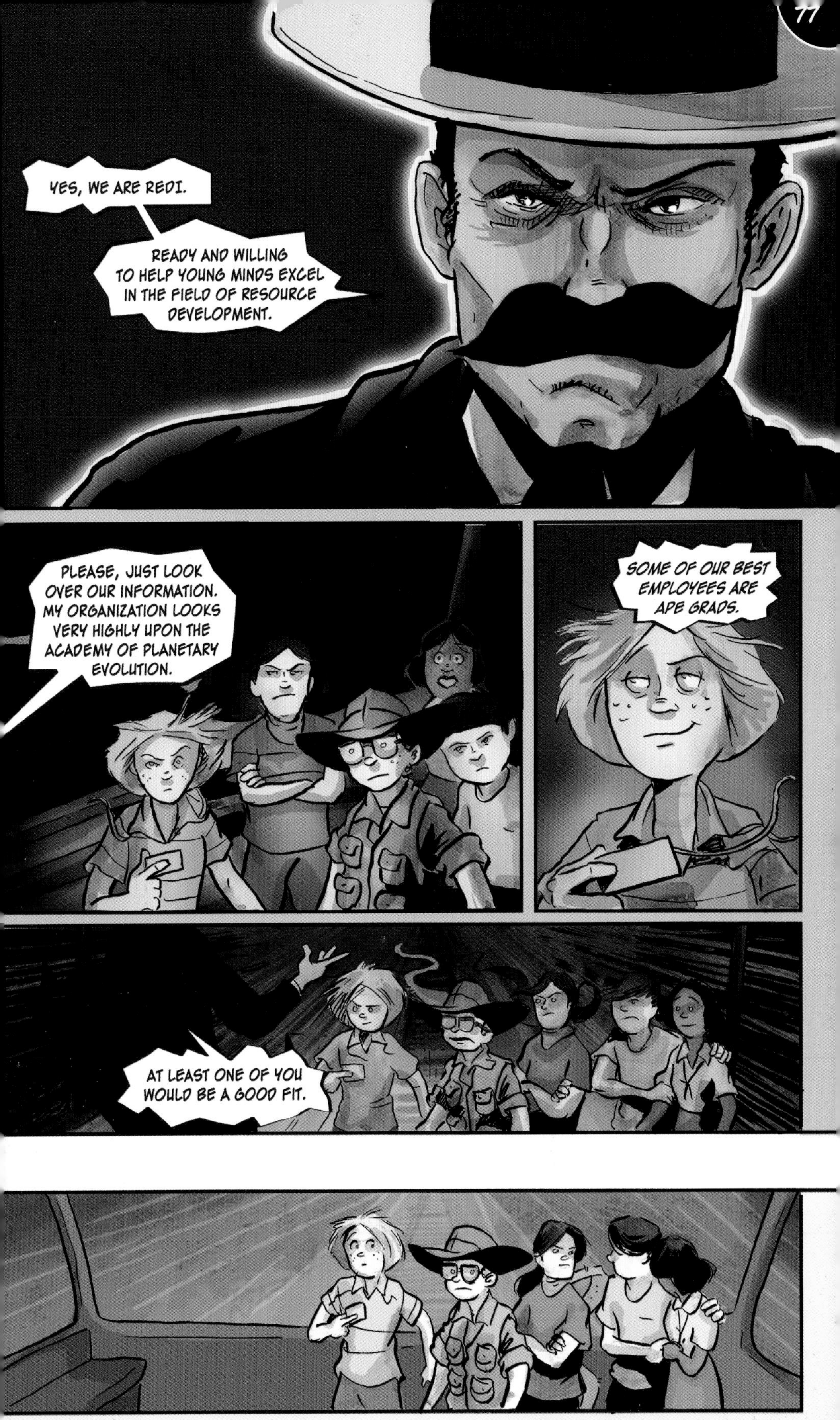
YES, WE ARE REDI.
READY AND WILLING TO HELP YOUNG MINDS EXCEL IN THE FIELD OF RESOURCE DEVELOPMENT.
PLEASE, JUST LOOK OVER OUR INFORMATION. MY ORGANIZATION LOOKS VERY HIGHLY UPON THE ACADEMY OF PLANETARY EVOLUTION.
SOME OF OUR BEST EMPLOYEES ARE APE GRADS.
AT LEAST ONE OF YOU WOULD BE A GOOD FIT.

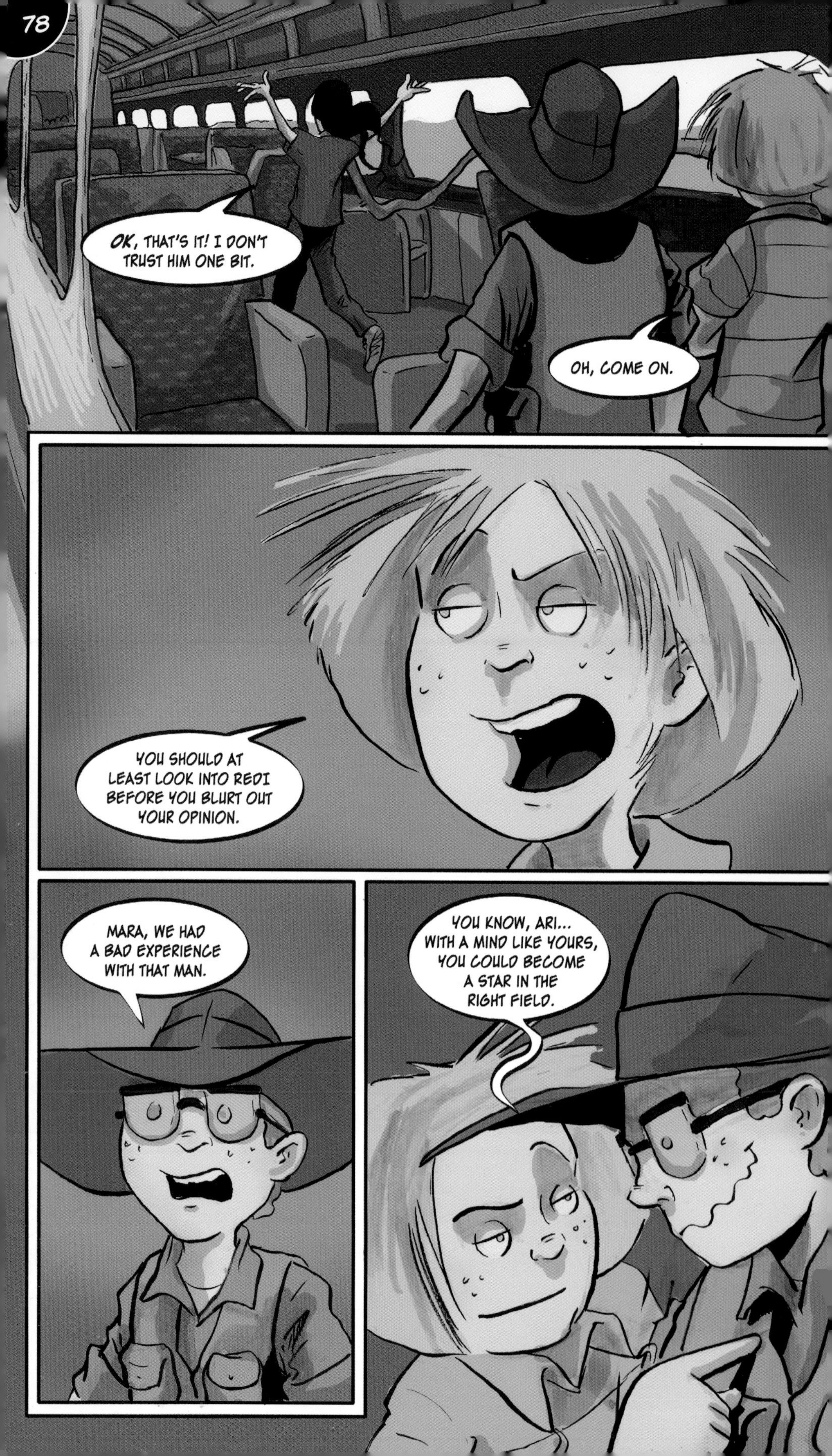
OK, THAT'S IT! I DON'T TRUST HIM ONE BIT.
OH, COME ON.
YOU SHOULD AT LEAST LOOK INTO REDI BEFORE YOU BLURT OUT YOUR OPINION.
MARA, WE HAD A BAD EXPERIENCE WITH THAT MAN.
YOU KNOW, ARI... WITH A MIND LIKE YOURS, YOU COULD BECOME A STAR IN THE RIGHT FIELD.

STUDENT HANDBOOK

Academy of
Planetary
Evolution

6

"The Philadelphia Project"

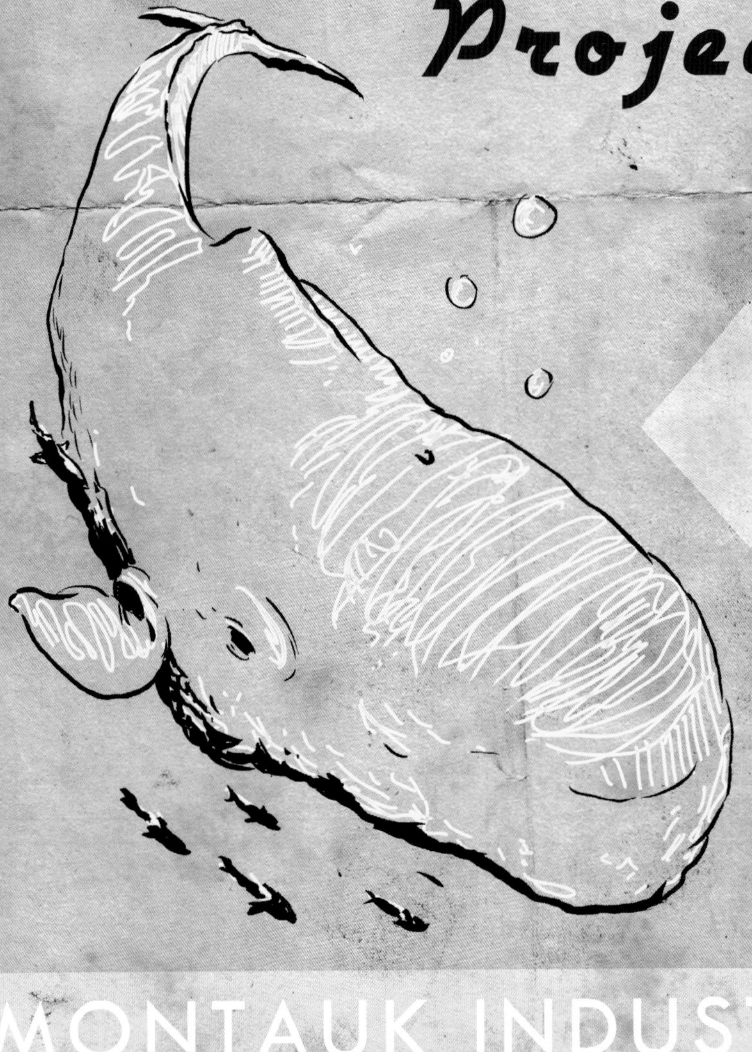

6

MONTAUK INDUSTRIES

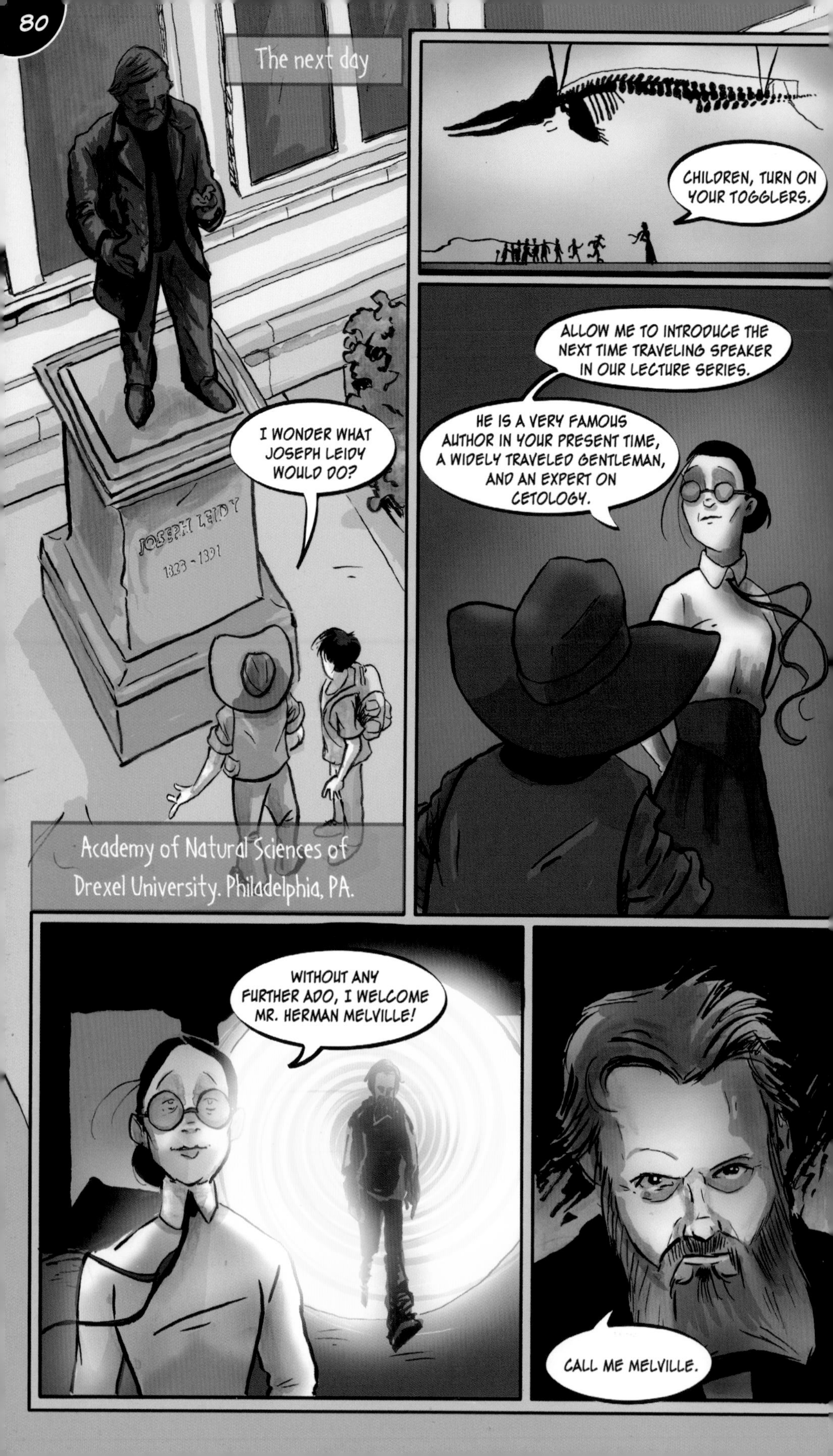
The next day
I WONDER WHAT JOSEPH LEIDY WOULD DO?
JOSEPH LEIDY
1823 - 1891
Academy of Natural Sciences of Drexel University. Philadelphia, PA.
CHILDREN, TURN ON YOUR TOGGLERS.
ALLOW ME TO INTRODUCE THE NEXT TIME TRAVELING SPEAKER IN OUR LECTURE SERIES.
HE IS A VERY FAMOUS AUTHOR IN YOUR PRESENT TIME, A WIDELY TRAVELED GENTLEMAN, AND AN EXPERT ON CETOLOGY.
WITHOUT ANY FURTHER ADO, I WELCOME MR. HERMAN MELVILLE!
CALL ME MELVILLE.

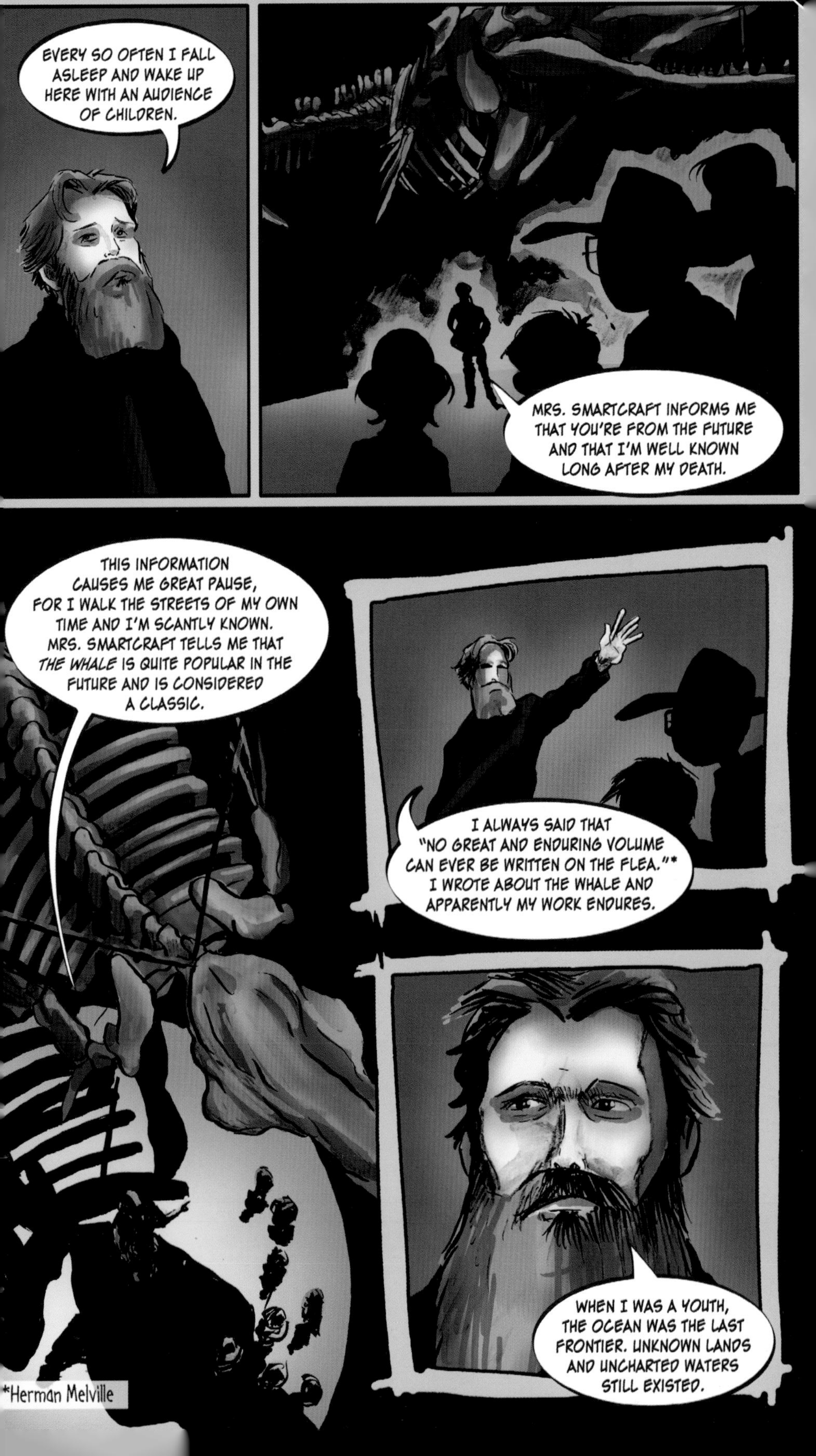
EVERY SO OFTEN I FALL ASLEEP AND WAKE UP HERE WITH AN AUDIENCE OF CHILDREN.
MRS. SMARTCRAFT INFORMS ME THAT YOU'RE FROM THE FUTURE AND THAT I'M WELL KNOWN LONG AFTER MY DEATH.
THIS INFORMATION CAUSES ME GREAT PAUSE, FOR I WALK THE STREETS OF MY OWN TIME AND I'M SCANTLY KNOWN. MRS. SMARTCRAFT TELLS ME THAT *THE WHALE* IS QUITE POPULAR IN THE FUTURE AND IS CONSIDERED A CLASSIC.
I ALWAYS SAID THAT "NO GREAT AND ENDURING VOLUME CAN EVER BE WRITTEN ON THE FLEA."* I WROTE ABOUT THE WHALE AND APPARENTLY MY WORK ENDURES.
WHEN I WAS A YOUTH, THE OCEAN WAS THE LAST FRONTIER. UNKNOWN LANDS AND UNCHARTED WATERS STILL EXISTED.
*Herman Melville

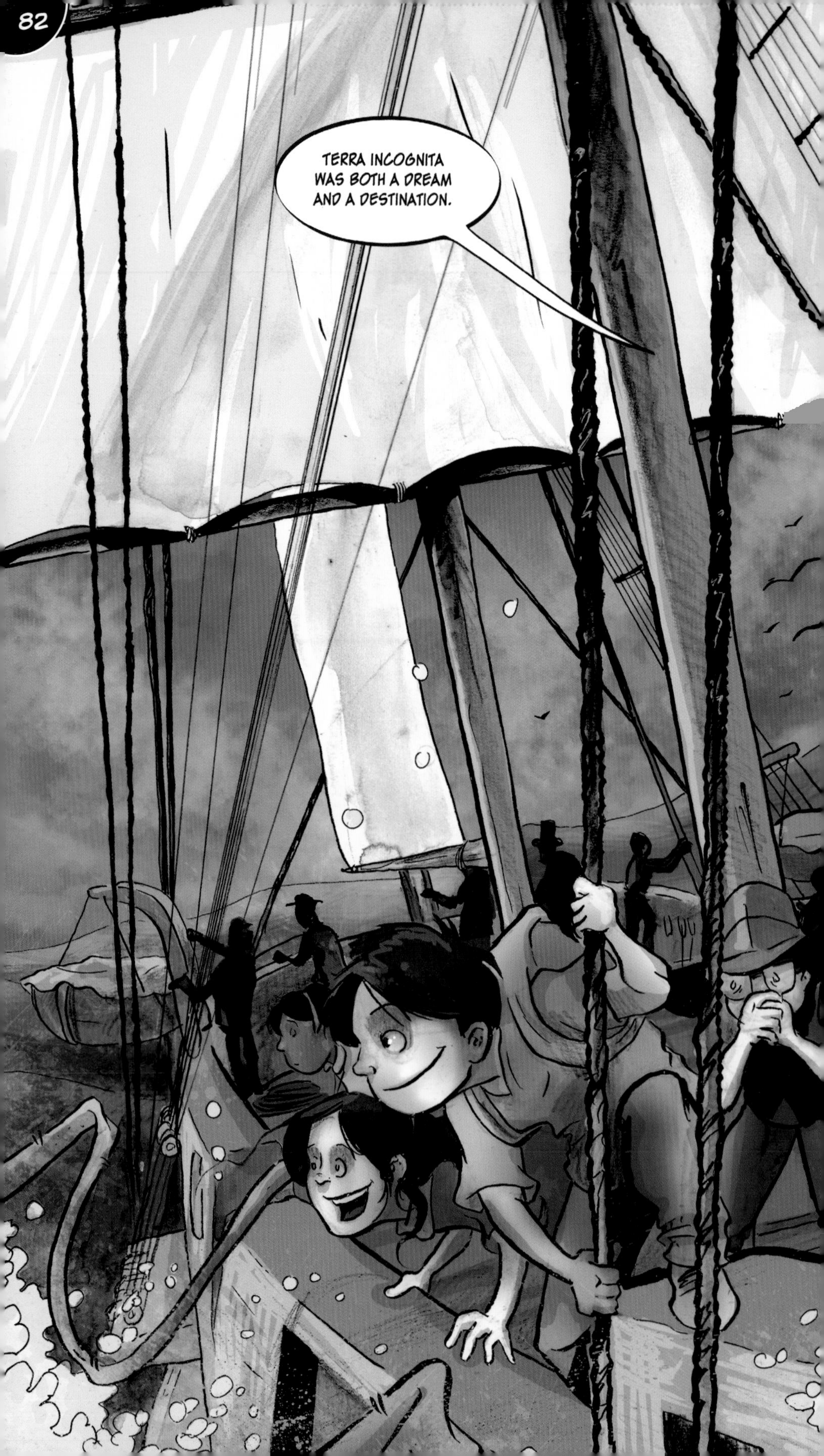
TERRA INCOGNITA
WAS BOTH A DREAM
AND A DESTINATION.

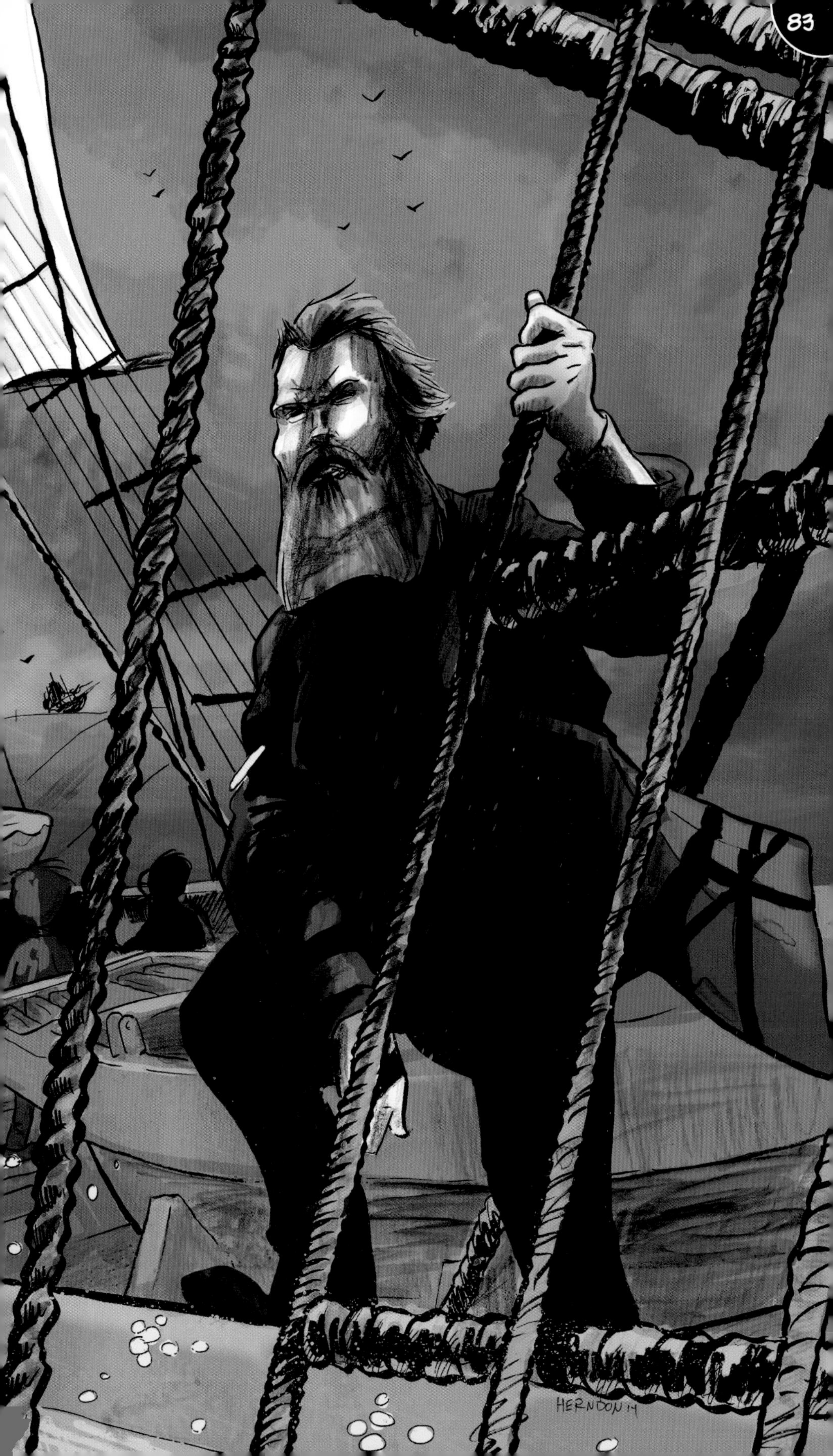
HERNDON 14

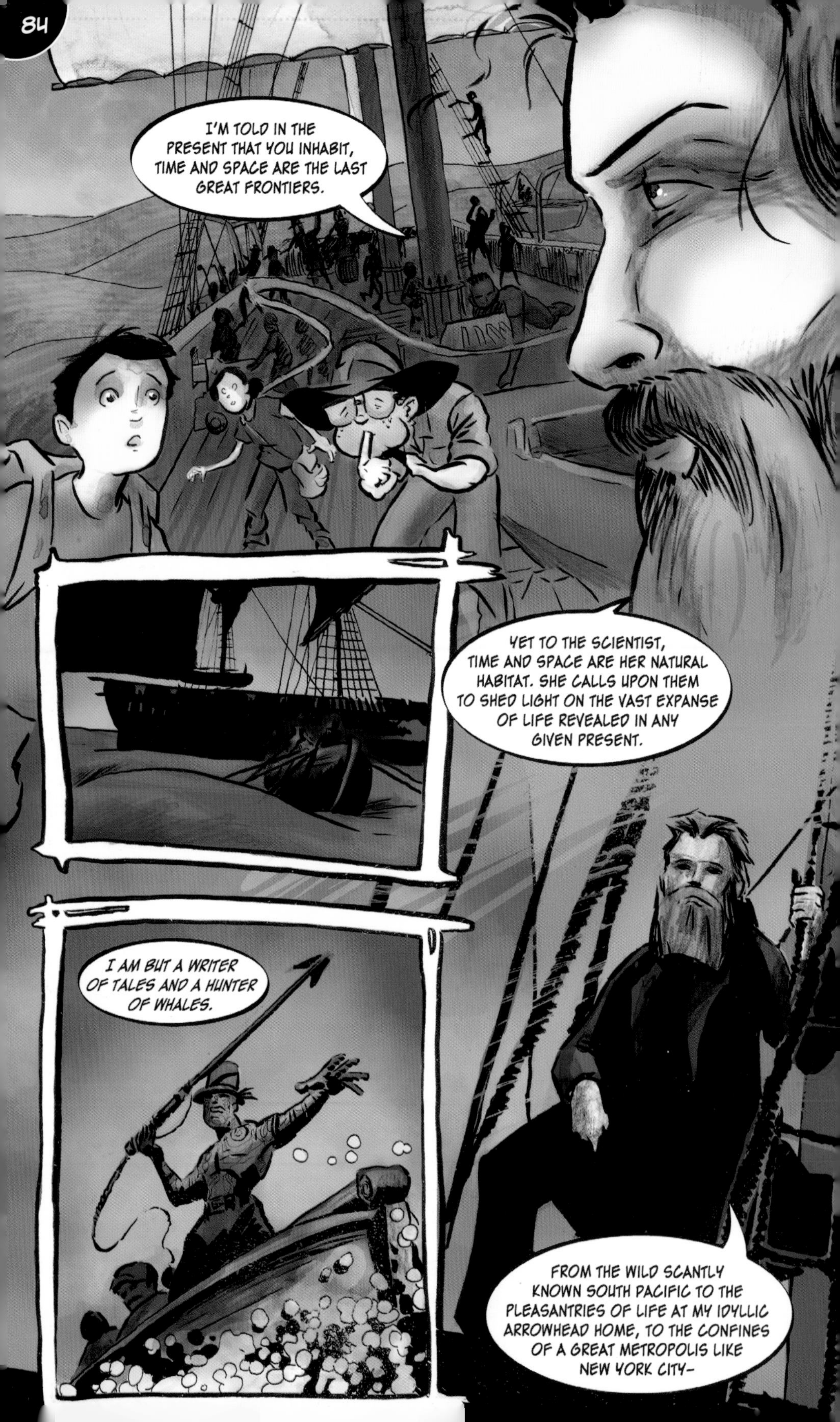
I'M TOLD IN THE PRESENT THAT YOU INHABIT, TIME AND SPACE ARE THE LAST GREAT FRONTIERS.
YET TO THE SCIENTIST, TIME AND SPACE ARE HER NATURAL HABITAT. SHE CALLS UPON THEM TO SHED LIGHT ON THE VAST EXPANSE OF LIFE REVEALED IN ANY GIVEN PRESENT.
I AM BUT A WRITER OF TALES AND A HUNTER OF WHALES.
FROM THE WILD SCANTLY KNOWN SOUTH PACIFIC TO THE PLEASANTRIES OF LIFE AT MY IDYLLIC ARROWHEAD HOME, TO THE CONFINES OF A GREAT METROPOLIS LIKE NEW YORK CITY–

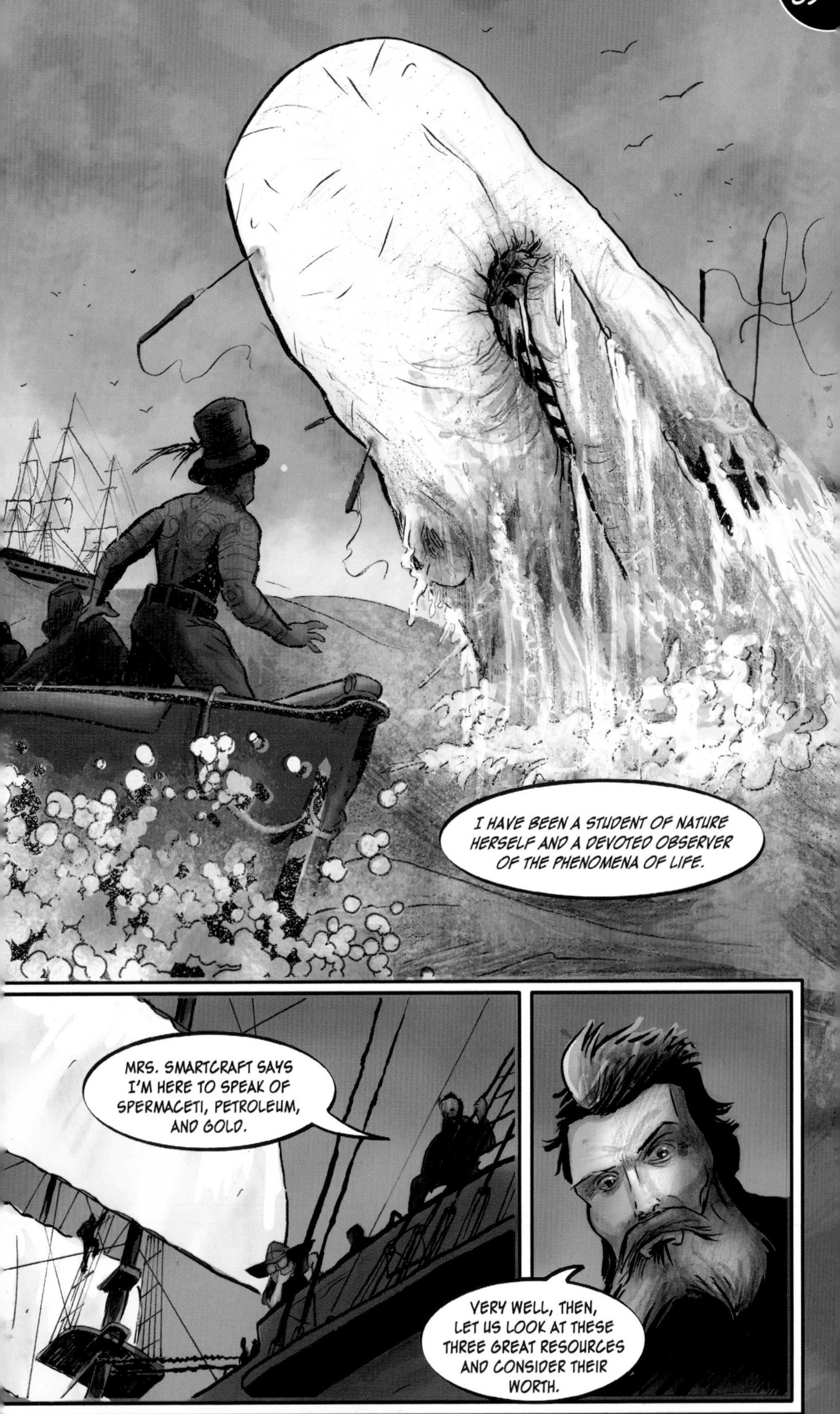
I HAVE BEEN A STUDENT OF NATURE HERSELF AND A DEVOTED OBSERVER OF THE PHENOMENA OF LIFE.
MRS. SMARTCRAFT SAYS I'M HERE TO SPEAK OF SPERMACETI, PETROLEUM, AND GOLD.
VERY WELL, THEN, LET US LOOK AT THESE THREE GREAT RESOURCES AND CONSIDER THEIR WORTH.

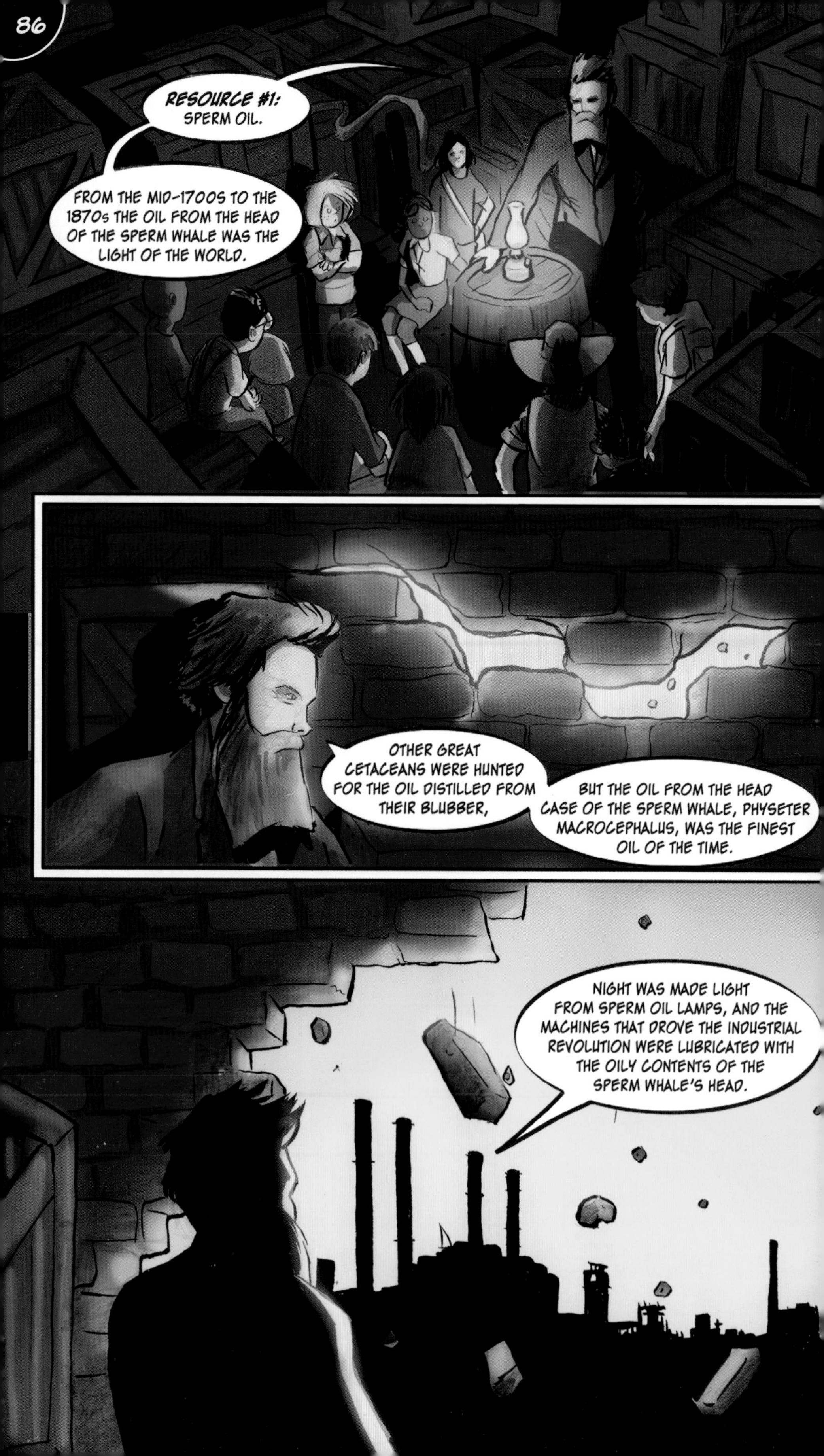
RESOURCE #1: SPERM OIL.
FROM THE MID-1700s TO THE 1870s THE OIL FROM THE HEAD OF THE SPERM WHALE WAS THE LIGHT OF THE WORLD.
OTHER GREAT CETACEANS WERE HUNTED FOR THE OIL DISTILLED FROM THEIR BLUBBER,
BUT THE OIL FROM THE HEAD CASE OF THE SPERM WHALE, PHYSETER MACROCEPHALUS, WAS THE FINEST OIL OF THE TIME.
NIGHT WAS MADE LIGHT FROM SPERM OIL LAMPS, AND THE MACHINES THAT DROVE THE INDUSTRIAL REVOLUTION WERE LUBRICATED WITH THE OILY CONTENTS OF THE SPERM WHALE'S HEAD.

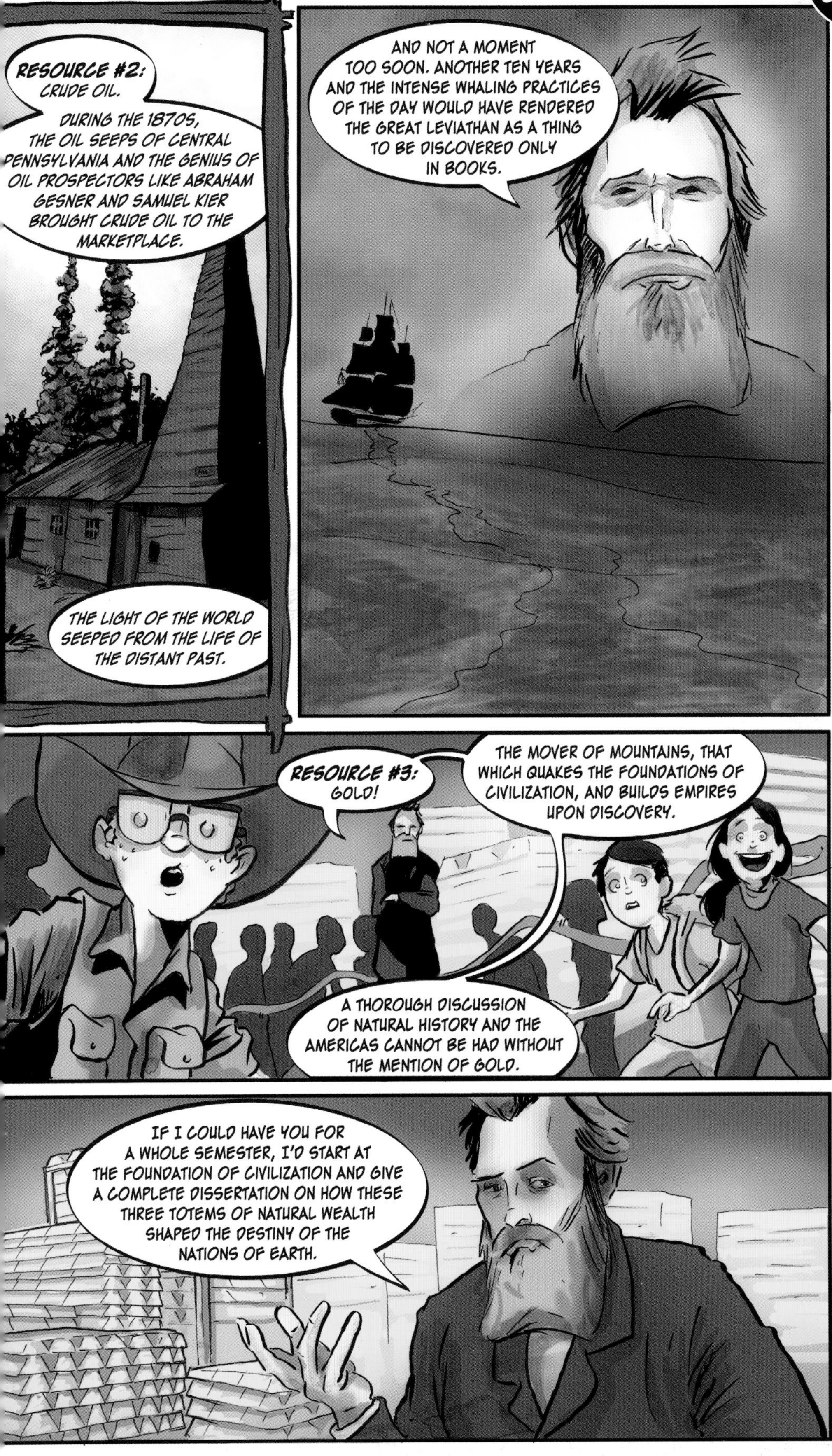
RESOURCE #2: CRUDE OIL.
DURING THE 1870S, THE OIL SEEPS OF CENTRAL PENNSYLVANIA AND THE GENIUS OF OIL PROSPECTORS LIKE ABRAHAM GESNER AND SAMUEL KIER BROUGHT CRUDE OIL TO THE MARKETPLACE.
THE LIGHT OF THE WORLD SEEPED FROM THE LIFE OF THE DISTANT PAST.
AND NOT A MOMENT TOO SOON. ANOTHER TEN YEARS AND THE INTENSE WHALING PRACTICES OF THE DAY WOULD HAVE RENDERED THE GREAT LEVIATHAN AS A THING TO BE DISCOVERED ONLY IN BOOKS.
RESOURCE #3: GOLD!
THE MOVER OF MOUNTAINS, THAT WHICH QUAKES THE FOUNDATIONS OF CIVILIZATION, AND BUILDS EMPIRES UPON DISCOVERY.
A THOROUGH DISCUSSION OF NATURAL HISTORY AND THE AMERICAS CANNOT BE HAD WITHOUT THE MENTION OF GOLD.
IF I COULD HAVE YOU FOR A WHOLE SEMESTER, I'D START AT THE FOUNDATION OF CIVILIZATION AND GIVE A COMPLETE DISSERTATION ON HOW THESE THREE TOTEMS OF NATURAL WEALTH SHAPED THE DESTINY OF THE NATIONS OF EARTH.

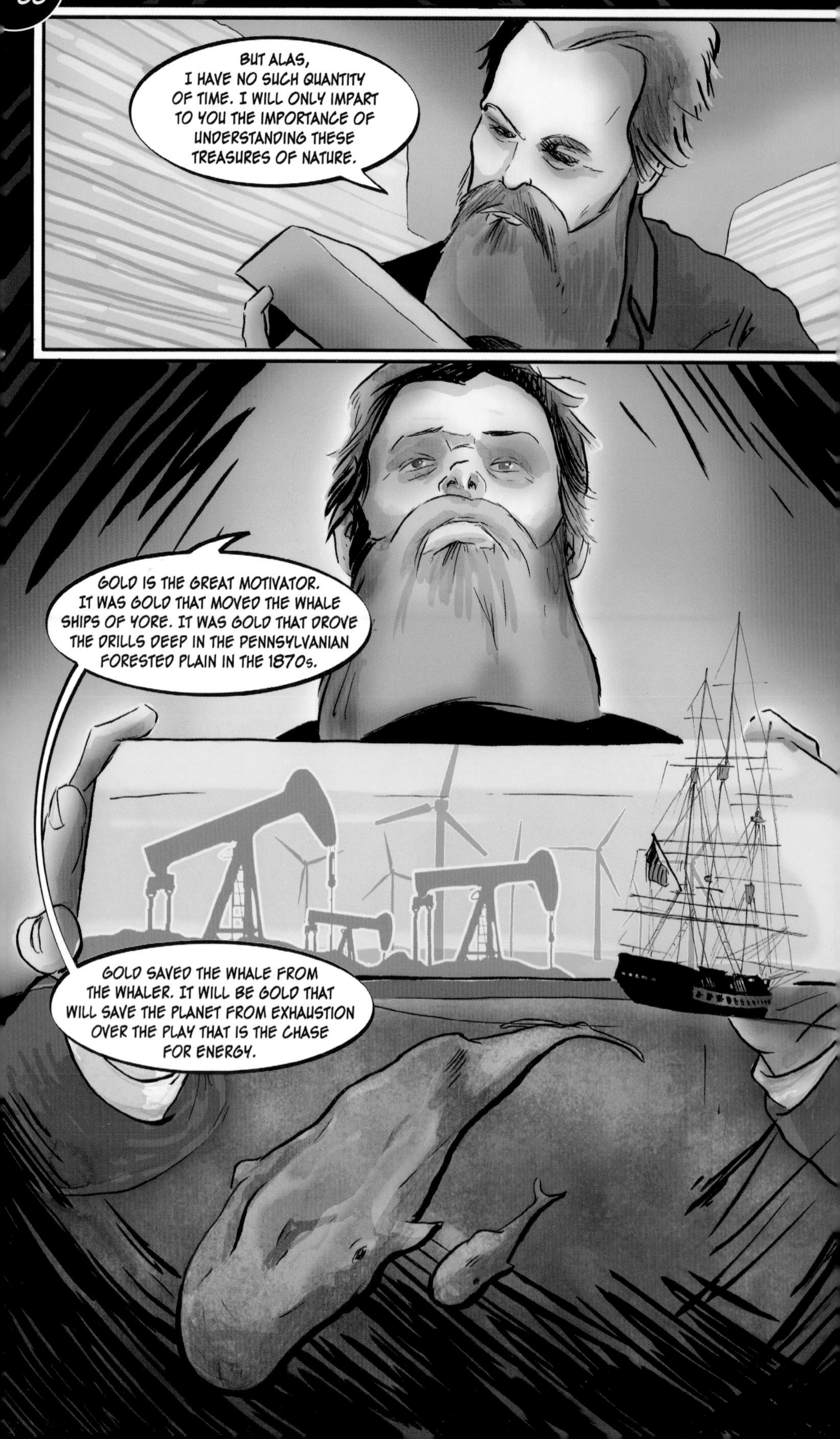
BUT ALAS, I HAVE NO SUCH QUANTITY OF TIME. I WILL ONLY IMPART TO YOU THE IMPORTANCE OF UNDERSTANDING THESE TREASURES OF NATURE.
GOLD IS THE GREAT MOTIVATOR. IT WAS GOLD THAT MOVED THE WHALE SHIPS OF YORE. IT WAS GOLD THAT DROVE THE DRILLS DEEP IN THE PENNSYLVANIAN FORESTED PLAIN IN THE 1870s.
GOLD SAVED THE WHALE FROM THE WHALER. IT WILL BE GOLD THAT WILL SAVE THE PLANET FROM EXHAUSTION OVER THE PLAY THAT IS THE CHASE FOR ENERGY.

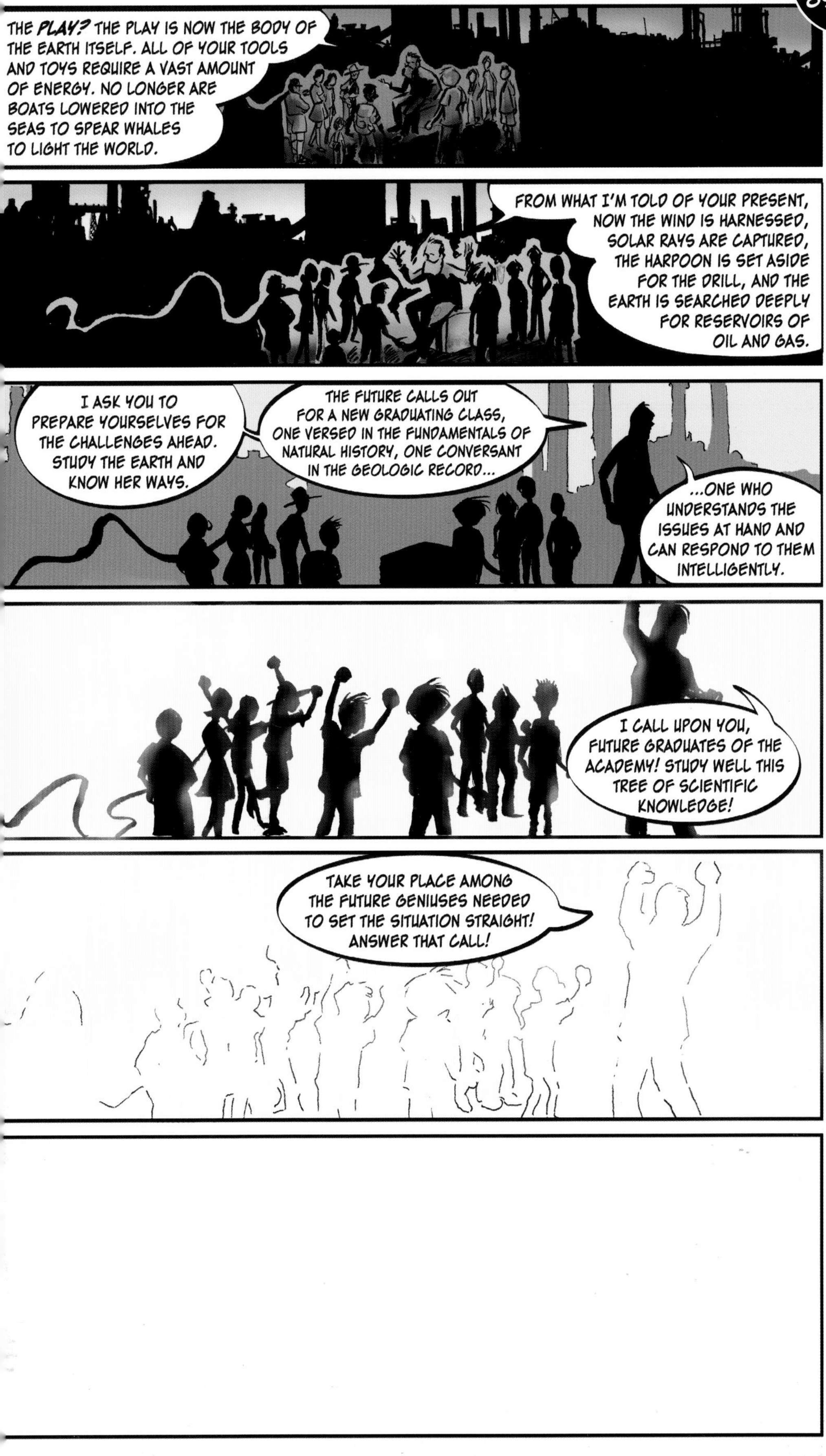
THE PLAY? THE PLAY IS NOW THE BODY OF THE EARTH ITSELF. ALL OF YOUR TOOLS AND TOYS REQUIRE A VAST AMOUNT OF ENERGY. NO LONGER ARE BOATS LOWERED INTO THE SEAS TO SPEAR WHALES TO LIGHT THE WORLD.
FROM WHAT I'M TOLD OF YOUR PRESENT, NOW THE WIND IS HARNESSED, SOLAR RAYS ARE CAPTURED, THE HARPOON IS SET ASIDE FOR THE DRILL, AND THE EARTH IS SEARCHED DEEPLY FOR RESERVOIRS OF OIL AND GAS.
I ASK YOU TO PREPARE YOURSELVES FOR THE CHALLENGES AHEAD. STUDY THE EARTH AND KNOW HER WAYS.
THE FUTURE CALLS OUT FOR A NEW GRADUATING CLASS, ONE VERSED IN THE FUNDAMENTALS OF NATURAL HISTORY, ONE CONVERSANT IN THE GEOLOGIC RECORD...
...ONE WHO UNDERSTANDS THE ISSUES AT HAND AND CAN RESPOND TO THEM INTELLIGENTLY.
I CALL UPON YOU, FUTURE GRADUATES OF THE ACADEMY! STUDY WELL THIS TREE OF SCIENTIFIC KNOWLEDGE!
TAKE YOUR PLACE AMONG THE FUTURE GENIUSES NEEDED TO SET THE SITUATION STRAIGHT! ANSWER THAT CALL!

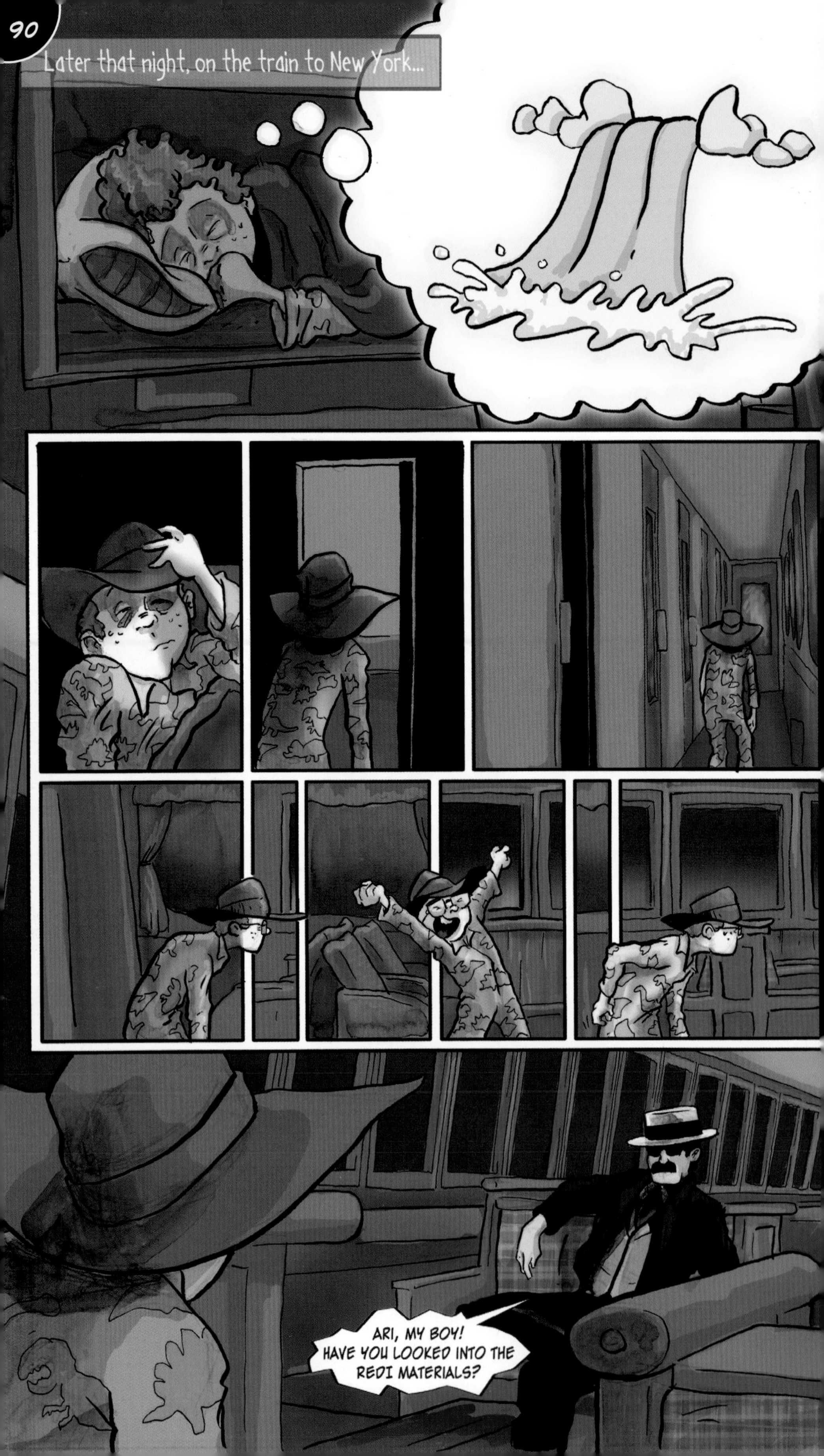
Later that night, on the train to New York...
ARI, MY BOY! HAVE YOU LOOKED INTO THE REDI MATERIALS?

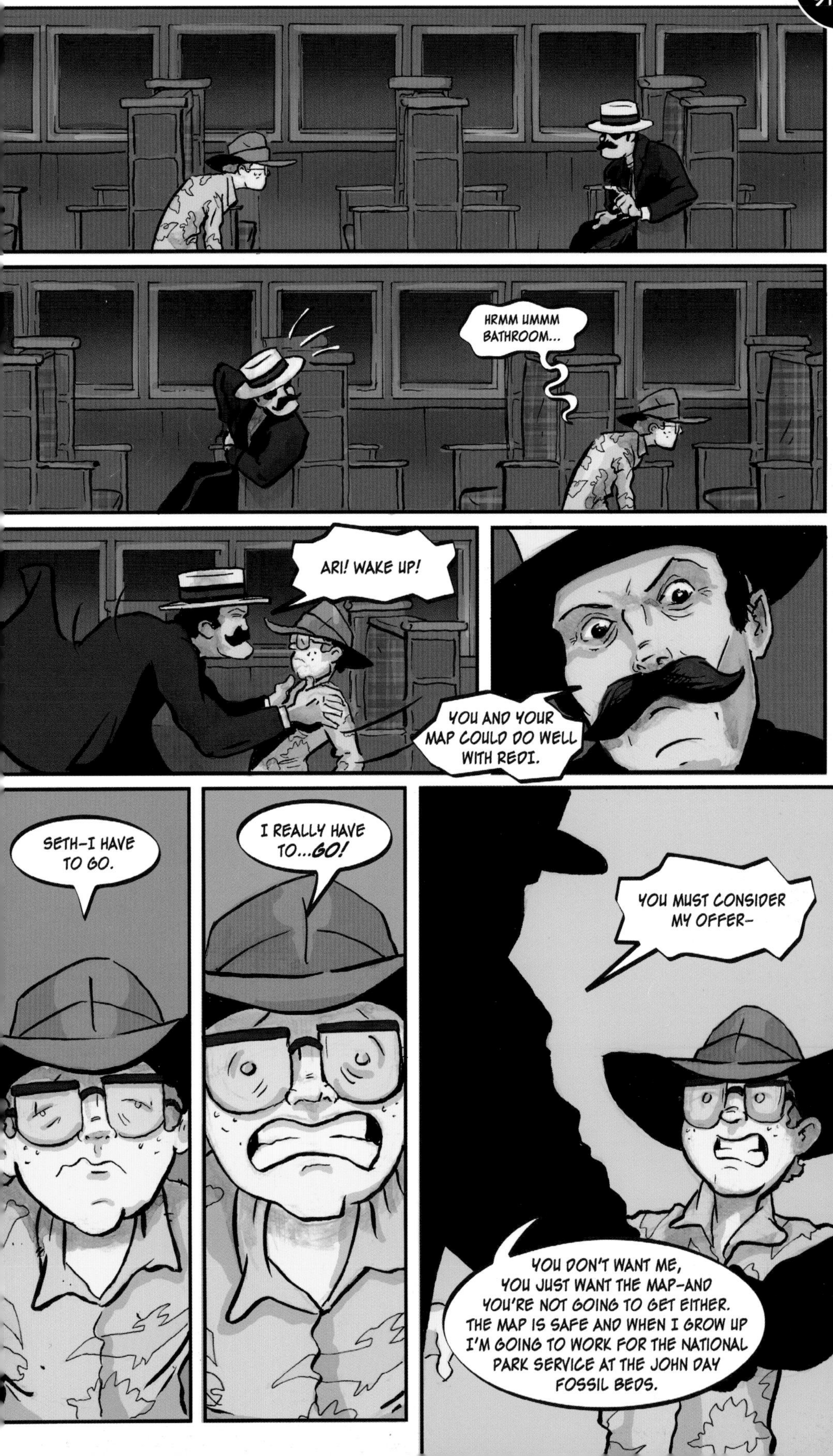
HRMM UMMM BATHROOM...
ARI! WAKE UP!
YOU AND YOUR MAP COULD DO WELL WITH REDI.
SETH–I HAVE TO GO.
I REALLY HAVE TO...GO!
YOU MUST CONSIDER MY OFFER–
YOU DON'T WANT ME, YOU JUST WANT THE MAP–AND YOU'RE NOT GOING TO GET EITHER. THE MAP IS SAFE AND WHEN I GROW UP I'M GOING TO WORK FOR THE NATIONAL PARK SERVICE AT THE JOHN DAY FOSSIL BEDS.

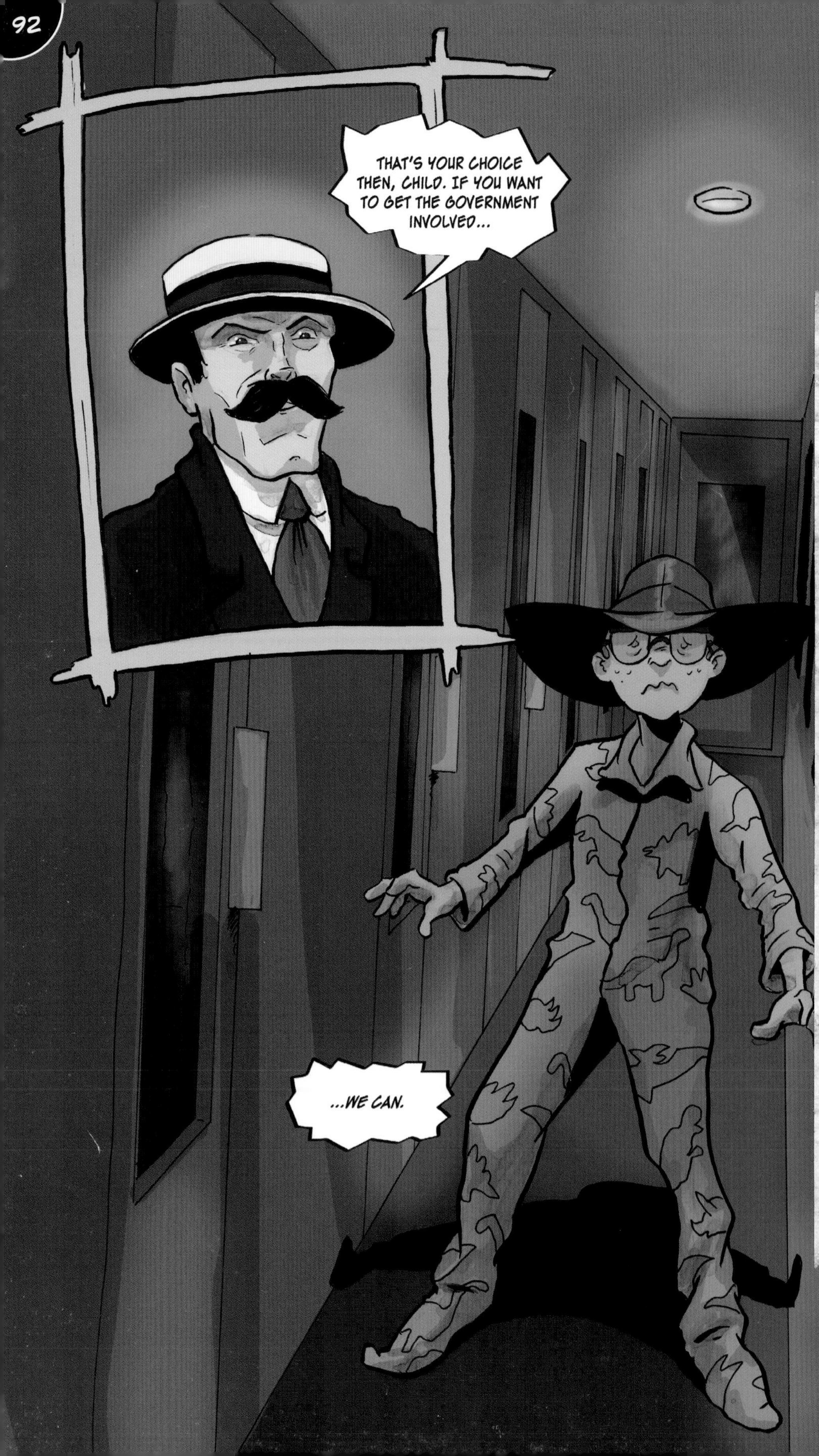
THAT'S YOUR CHOICE THEN, CHILD. IF YOU WANT TO GET THE GOVERNMENT INVOLVED...
...WE CAN.

STUDENT HANDBOOK

Academy of Planetary Evolution

7

"Cats and Dogs"

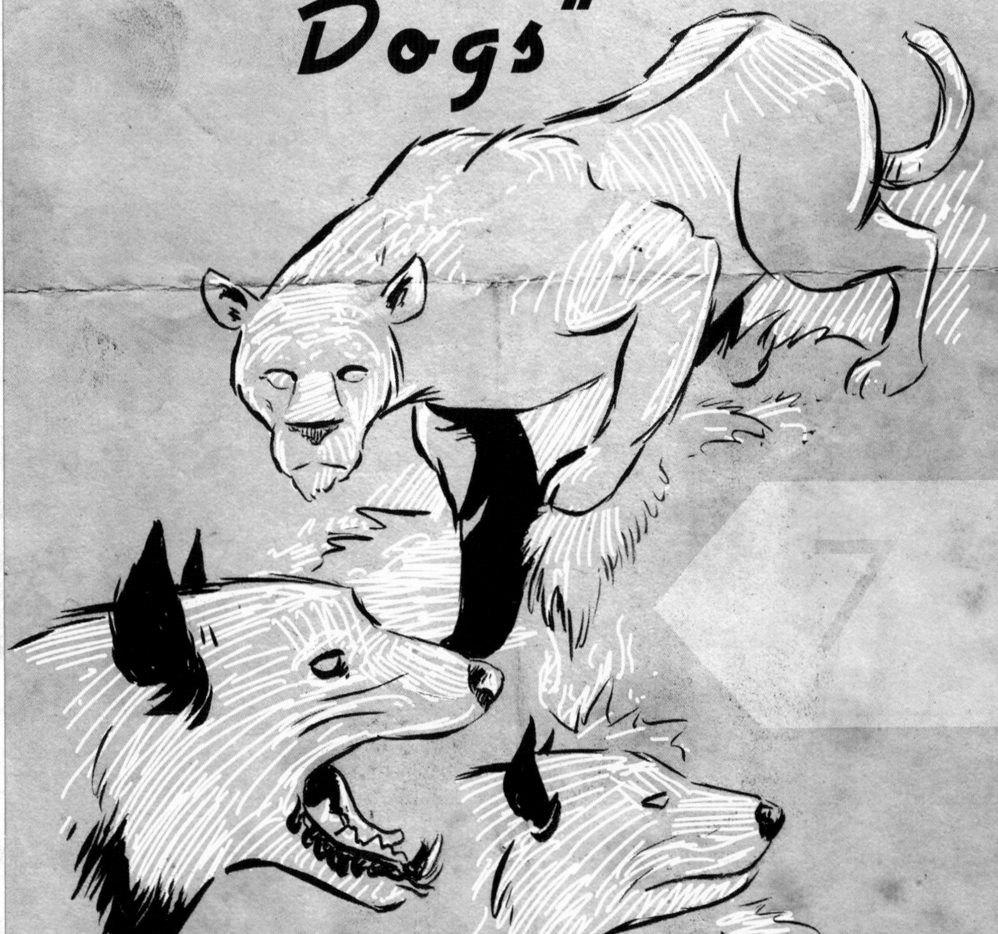

MONTAUK INDUSTRIES

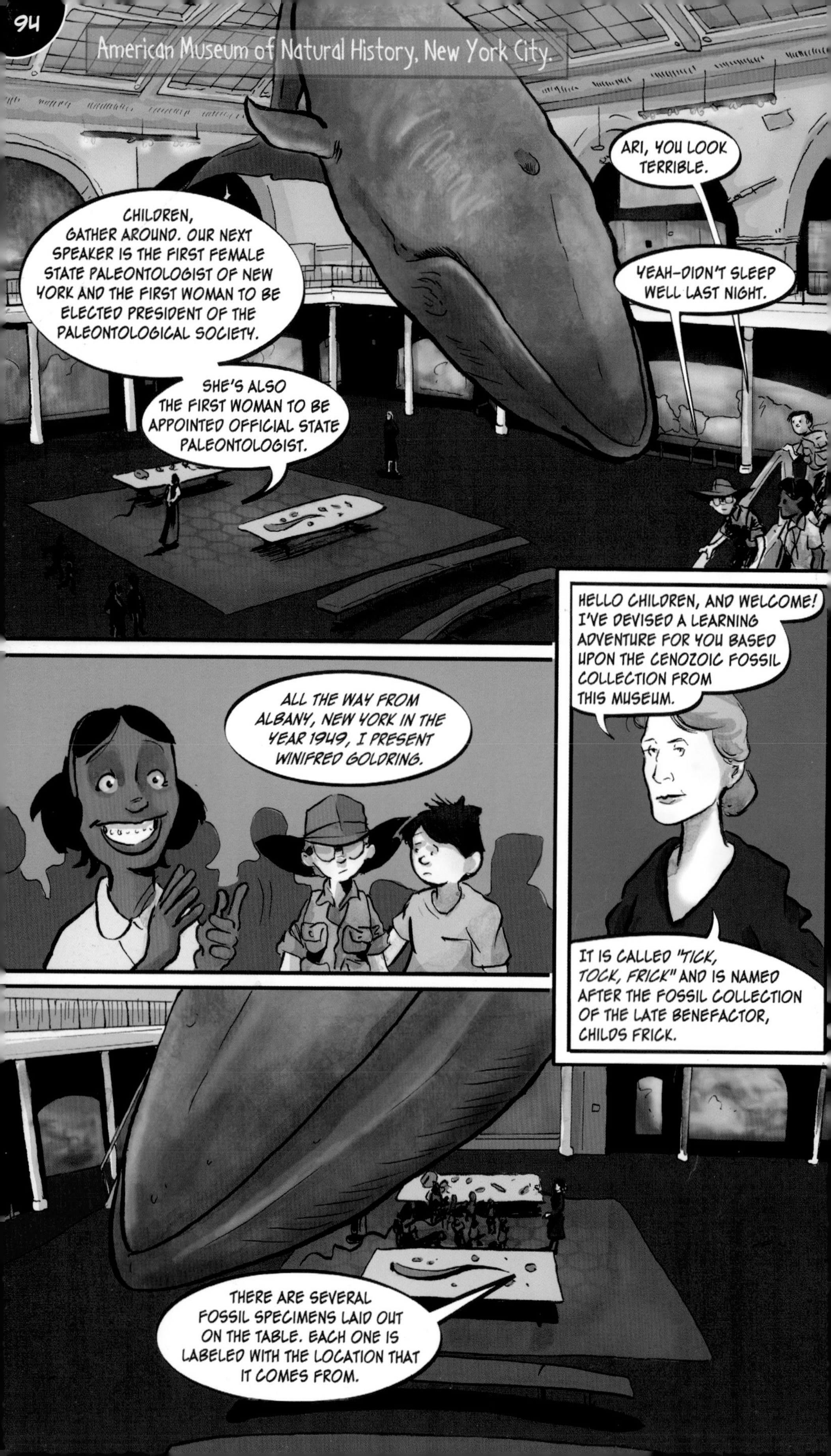
American Museum of Natural History, New York City.
CHILDREN, GATHER AROUND. OUR NEXT SPEAKER IS THE FIRST FEMALE STATE PALEONTOLOGIST OF NEW YORK AND THE FIRST WOMAN TO BE ELECTED PRESIDENT OF THE PALEONTOLOGICAL SOCIETY.
SHE'S ALSO THE FIRST WOMAN TO BE APPOINTED OFFICIAL STATE PALEONTOLOGIST.
ARI, YOU LOOK TERRIBLE.
YEAH—DIDN'T SLEEP WELL LAST NIGHT.
ALL THE WAY FROM ALBANY, NEW YORK IN THE YEAR 1949, I PRESENT WINIFRED GOLDRING.
HELLO CHILDREN, AND WELCOME! I'VE DEVISED A LEARNING ADVENTURE FOR YOU BASED UPON THE CENOZOIC FOSSIL COLLECTION FROM THIS MUSEUM.
IT IS CALLED "TICK, TOCK, FRICK" AND IS NAMED AFTER THE FOSSIL COLLECTION OF THE LATE BENEFACTOR, CHILDS FRICK.
THERE ARE SEVERAL FOSSIL SPECIMENS LAID OUT ON THE TABLE. EACH ONE IS LABELED WITH THE LOCATION THAT IT COMES FROM.

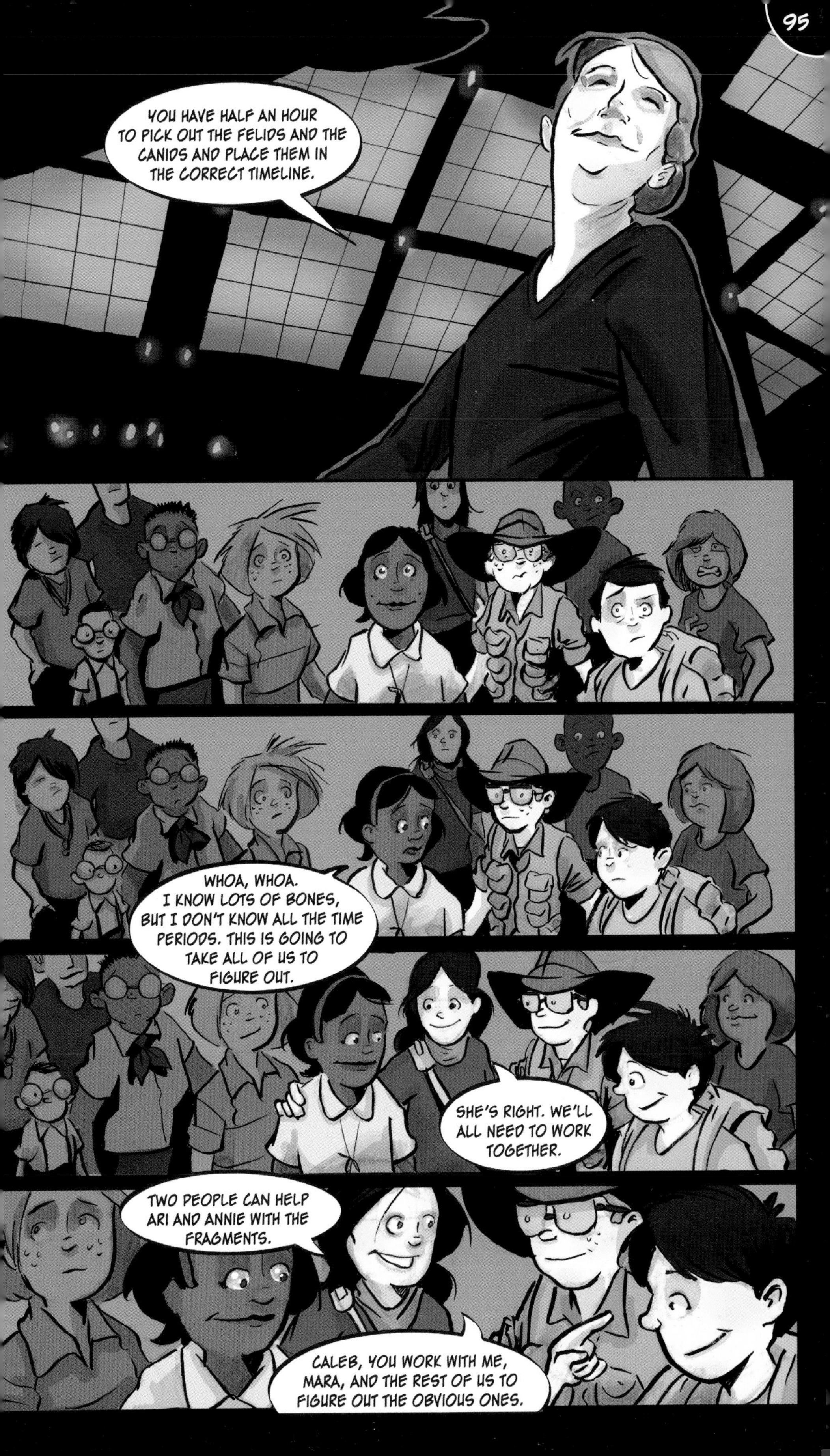
YOU HAVE HALF AN HOUR TO PICK OUT THE FELIDS AND THE CANIDS AND PLACE THEM IN THE CORRECT TIMELINE.
WHOA, WHOA. I KNOW LOTS OF BONES, BUT I DON'T KNOW ALL THE TIME PERIODS. THIS IS GOING TO TAKE ALL OF US TO FIGURE OUT.
SHE'S RIGHT. WE'LL ALL NEED TO WORK TOGETHER.
TWO PEOPLE CAN HELP ARI AND ANNIE WITH THE FRAGMENTS.
CALEB, YOU WORK WITH ME, MARA, AND THE REST OF US TO FIGURE OUT THE OBVIOUS ONES.

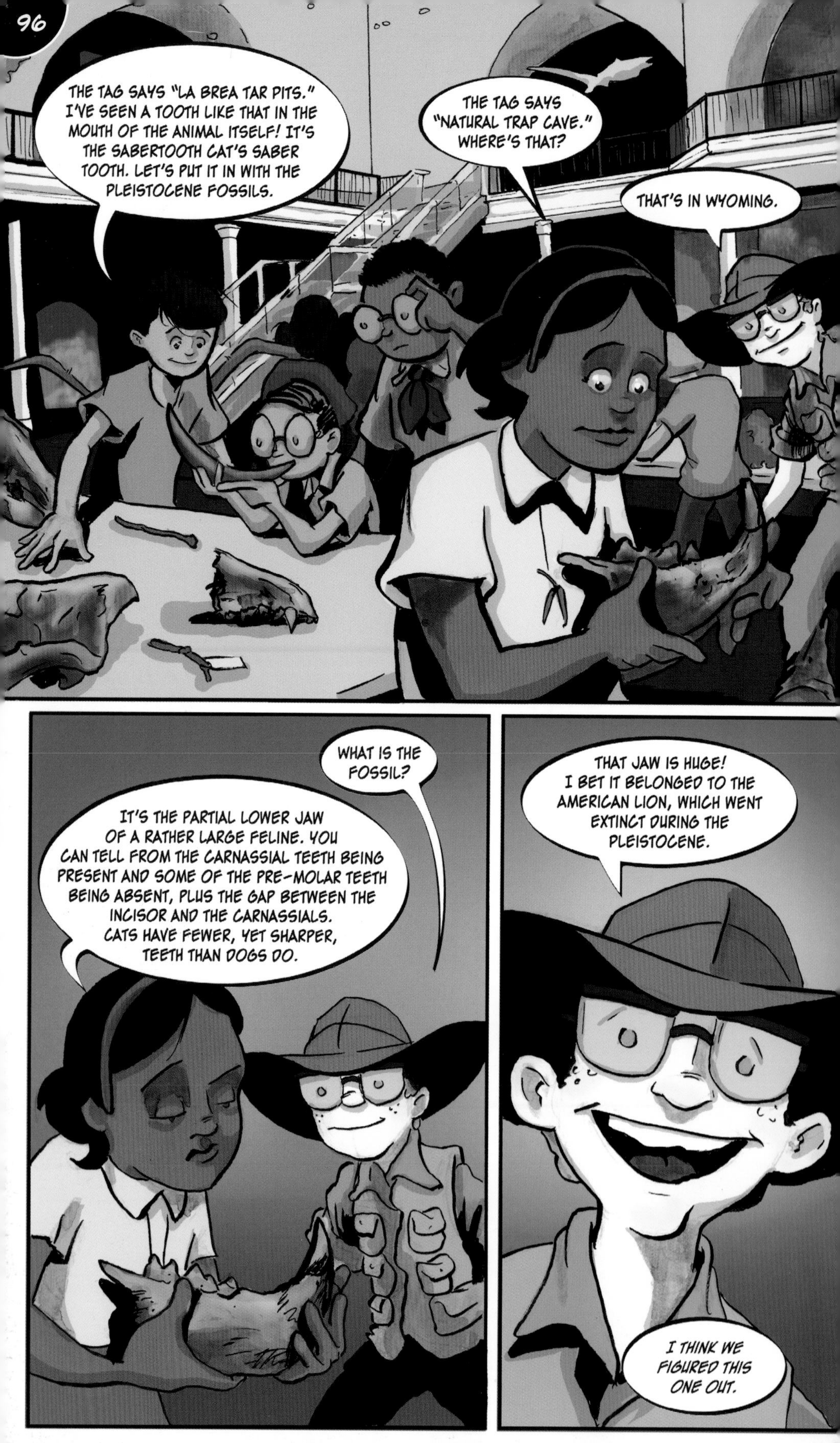
THE TAG SAYS "LA BREA TAR PITS." I'VE SEEN A TOOTH LIKE THAT IN THE MOUTH OF THE ANIMAL ITSELF! IT'S THE SABERTOOTH CAT'S SABER TOOTH. LET'S PUT IT IN WITH THE PLEISTOCENE FOSSILS.
THE TAG SAYS "NATURAL TRAP CAVE." WHERE'S THAT?
THAT'S IN WYOMING.
WHAT IS THE FOSSIL?
IT'S THE PARTIAL LOWER JAW OF A RATHER LARGE FELINE. YOU CAN TELL FROM THE CARNASSIAL TEETH BEING PRESENT AND SOME OF THE PRE-MOLAR TEETH BEING ABSENT, PLUS THE GAP BETWEEN THE INCISOR AND THE CARNASSIALS. CATS HAVE FEWER, YET SHARPER, TEETH THAN DOGS DO.
THAT JAW IS HUGE! I BET IT BELONGED TO THE AMERICAN LION, WHICH WENT EXTINCT DURING THE PLEISTOCENE.
I THINK WE FIGURED THIS ONE OUT.

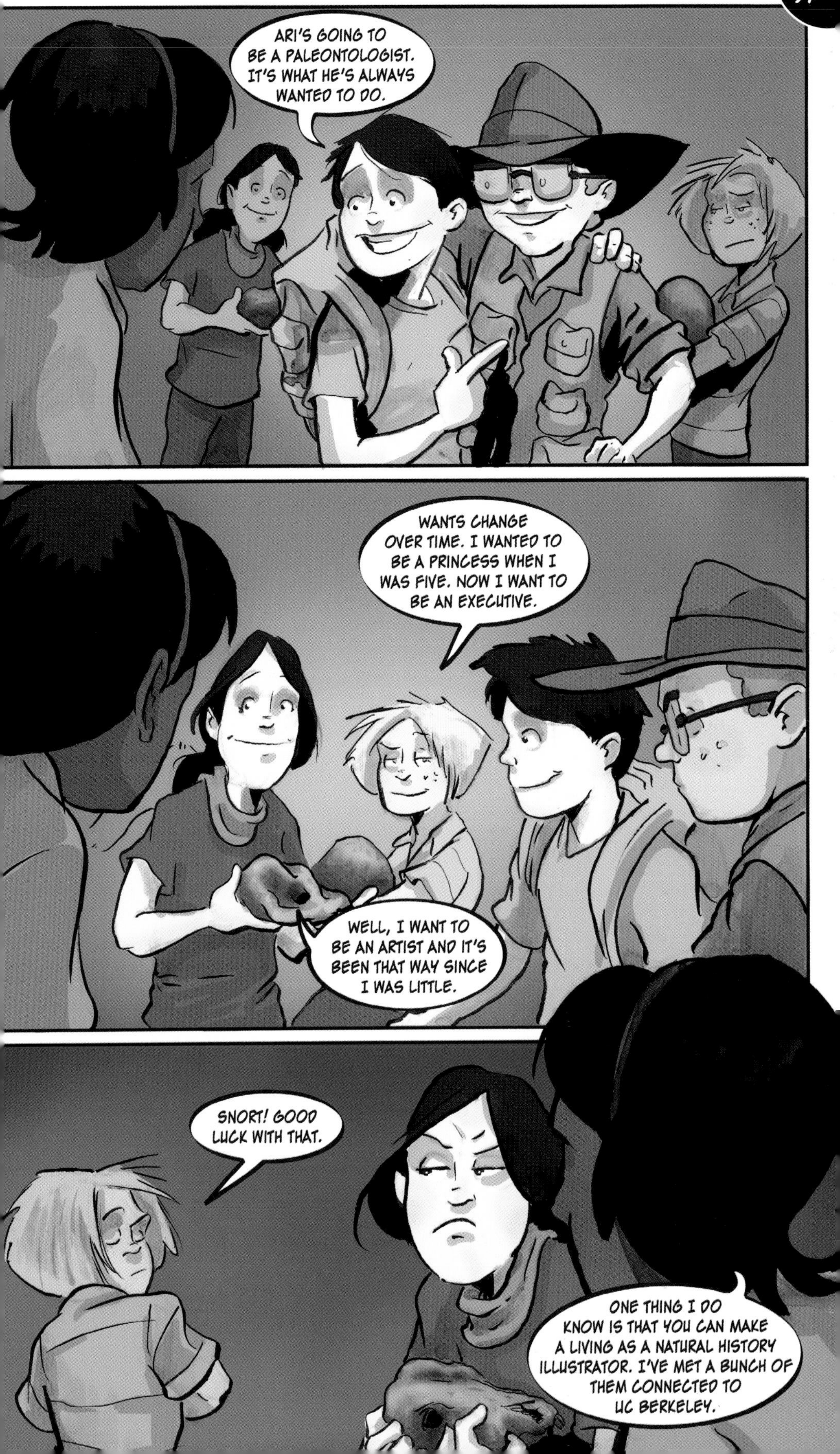
ARI'S GOING TO BE A PALEONTOLOGIST. IT'S WHAT HE'S ALWAYS WANTED TO DO.
WANTS CHANGE OVER TIME. I WANTED TO BE A PRINCESS WHEN I WAS FIVE. NOW I WANT TO BE AN EXECUTIVE.
WELL, I WANT TO BE AN ARTIST AND IT'S BEEN THAT WAY SINCE I WAS LITTLE.
SNORT! GOOD LUCK WITH THAT.
ONE THING I DO KNOW IS THAT YOU CAN MAKE A LIVING AS A NATURAL HISTORY ILLUSTRATOR. I'VE MET A BUNCH OF THEM CONNECTED TO UC BERKELEY.

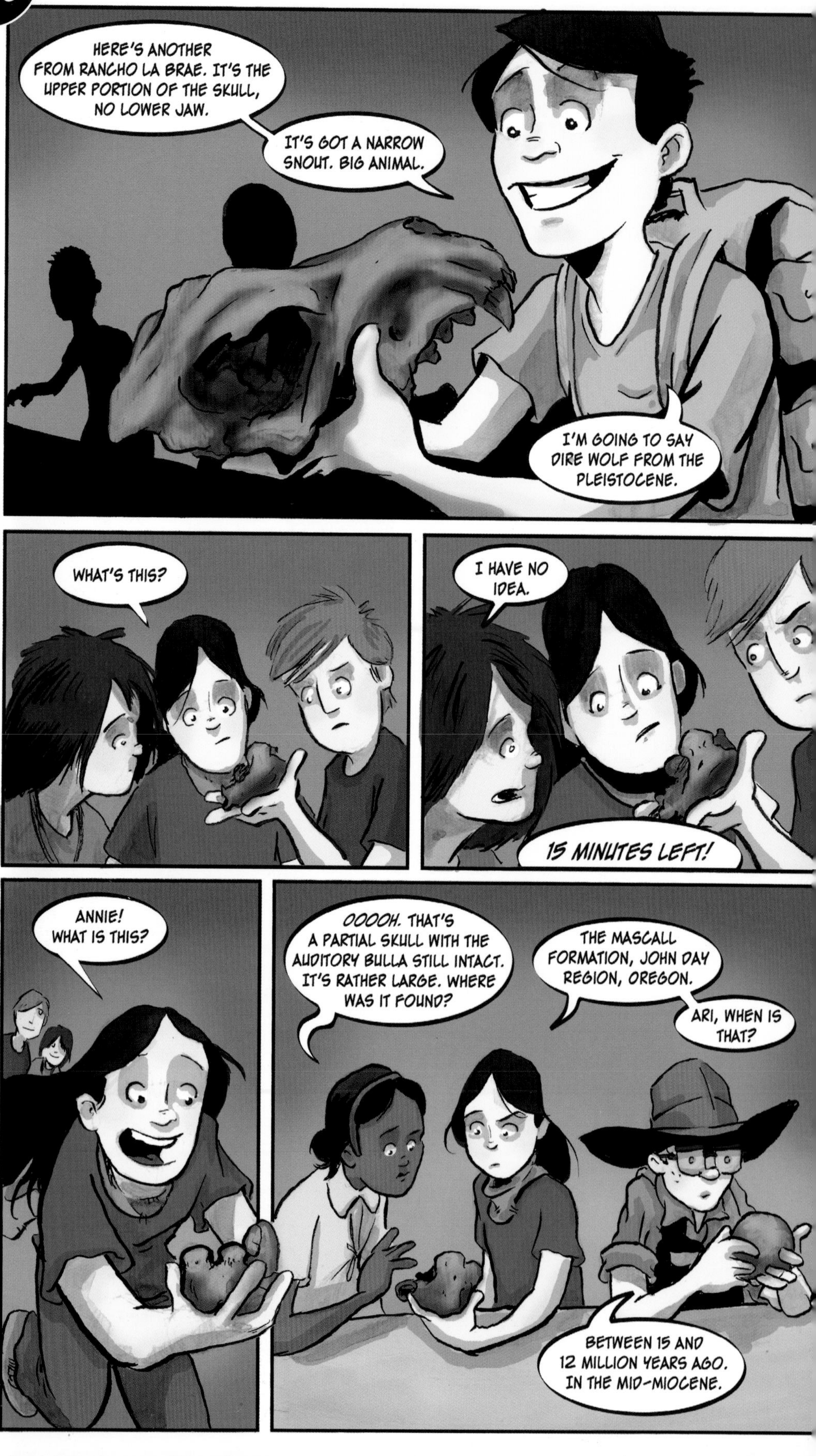
HERE'S ANOTHER FROM RANCHO LA BRAE. IT'S THE UPPER PORTION OF THE SKULL, NO LOWER JAW.
IT'S GOT A NARROW SNOUT. BIG ANIMAL.
I'M GOING TO SAY DIRE WOLF FROM THE PLEISTOCENE.
WHAT'S THIS?
I HAVE NO IDEA.
15 MINUTES LEFT!
ANNIE! WHAT IS THIS?
OOOOH. THAT'S A PARTIAL SKULL WITH THE AUDITORY BULLA STILL INTACT. IT'S RATHER LARGE. WHERE WAS IT FOUND?
THE MASCALL FORMATION, JOHN DAY REGION, OREGON.
ARI, WHEN IS THAT?
BETWEEN 15 AND 12 MILLION YEARS AGO. IN THE MID-MIOCENE.

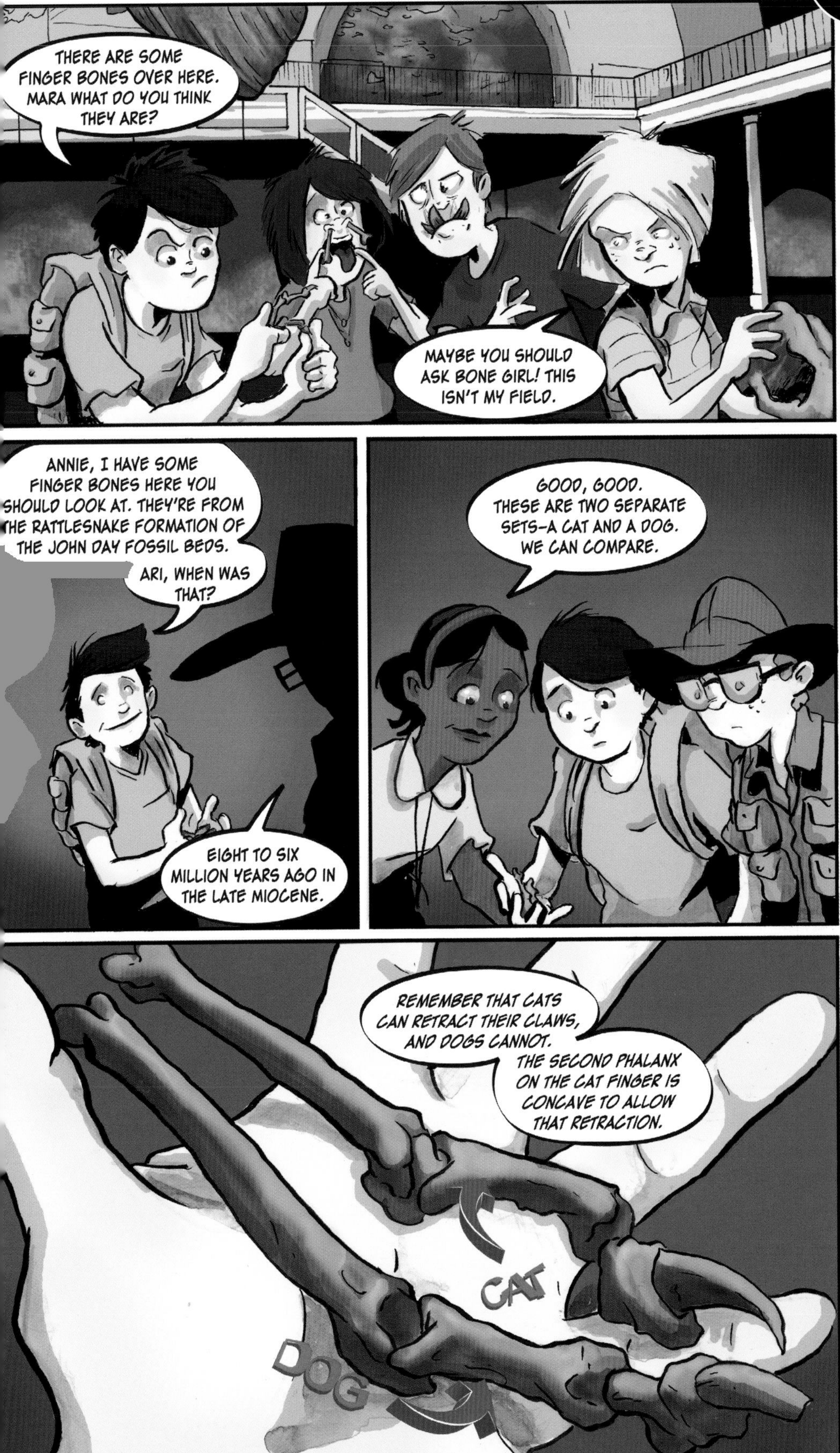
THERE ARE SOME FINGER BONES OVER HERE. MARA WHAT DO YOU THINK THEY ARE?
MAYBE YOU SHOULD ASK BONE GIRL! THIS ISN'T MY FIELD.
ANNIE, I HAVE SOME FINGER BONES HERE YOU SHOULD LOOK AT. THEY'RE FROM THE RATTLESNAKE FORMATION OF THE JOHN DAY FOSSIL BEDS.
ARI, WHEN WAS THAT?
EIGHT TO SIX MILLION YEARS AGO IN THE LATE MIOCENE.
GOOD, GOOD. THESE ARE TWO SEPARATE SETS—A CAT AND A DOG. WE CAN COMPARE.
REMEMBER THAT CATS CAN RETRACT THEIR CLAWS, AND DOGS CANNOT.
THE SECOND PHALANX ON THE CAT FINGER IS CONCAVE TO ALLOW THAT RETRACTION.
CAT
DOG

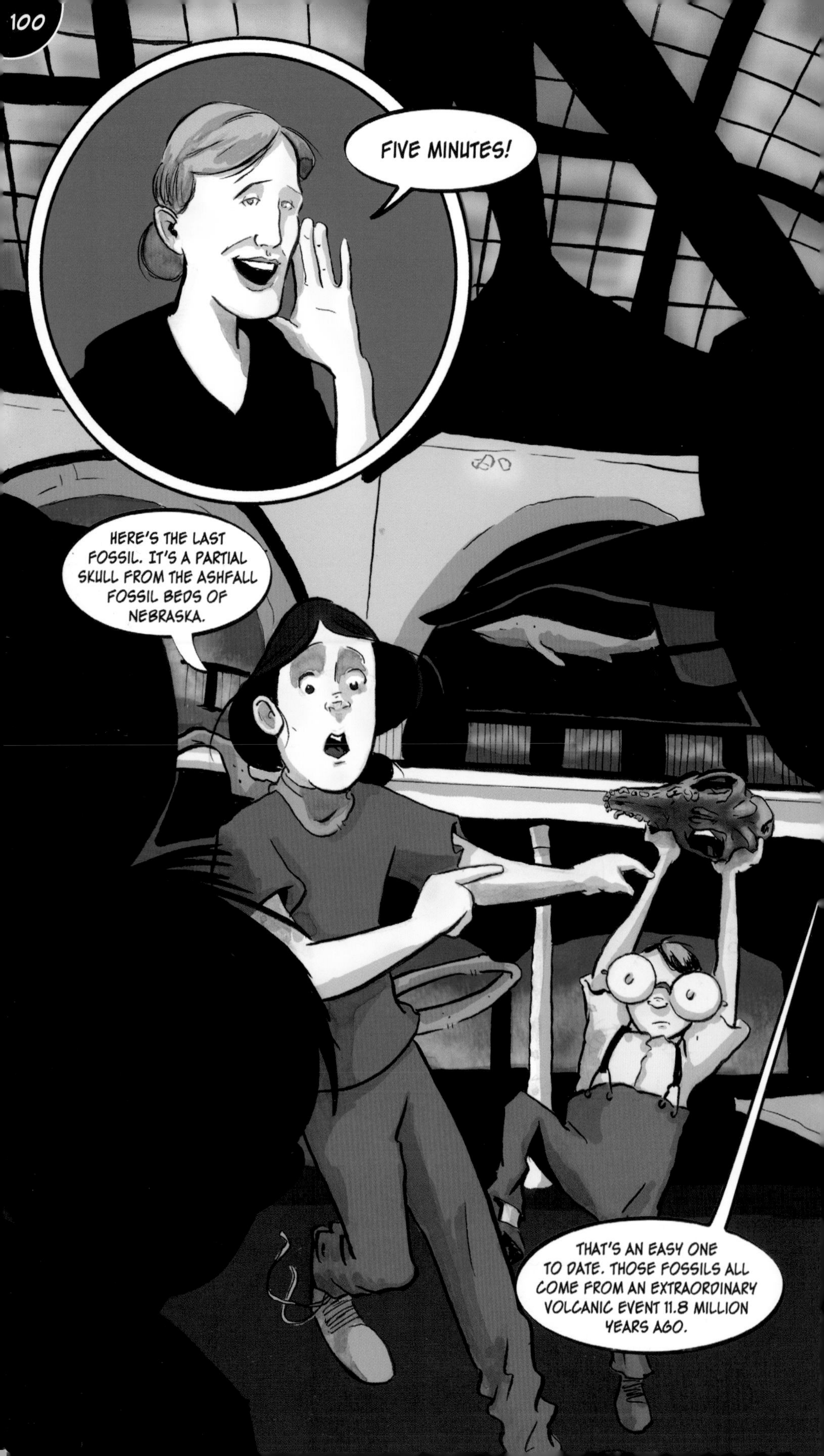
FIVE MINUTES!
HERE'S THE LAST FOSSIL. IT'S A PARTIAL SKULL FROM THE ASHFALL FOSSIL BEDS OF NEBRASKA.
THAT'S AN EASY ONE TO DATE. THOSE FOSSILS ALL COME FROM AN EXTRAORDINARY VOLCANIC EVENT 11.8 MILLION YEARS AGO.

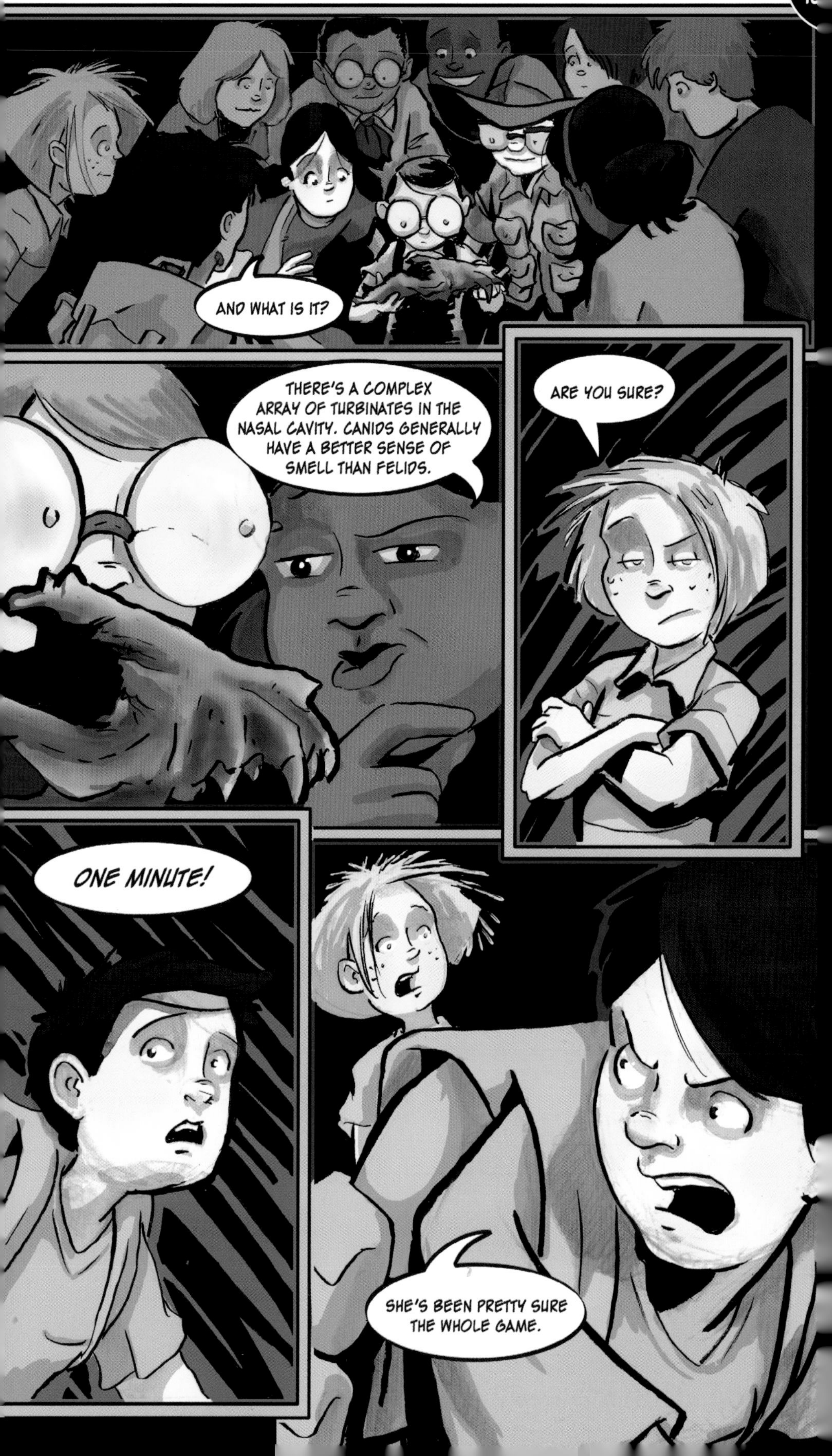
AND WHAT IS IT?
THERE'S A COMPLEX ARRAY OF TURBINATES IN THE NASAL CAVITY. CANIDS GENERALLY HAVE A BETTER SENSE OF SMELL THAN FELIDS.
ARE YOU SURE?
ONE MINUTE!
SHE'S BEEN PRETTY SURE THE WHOLE GAME.

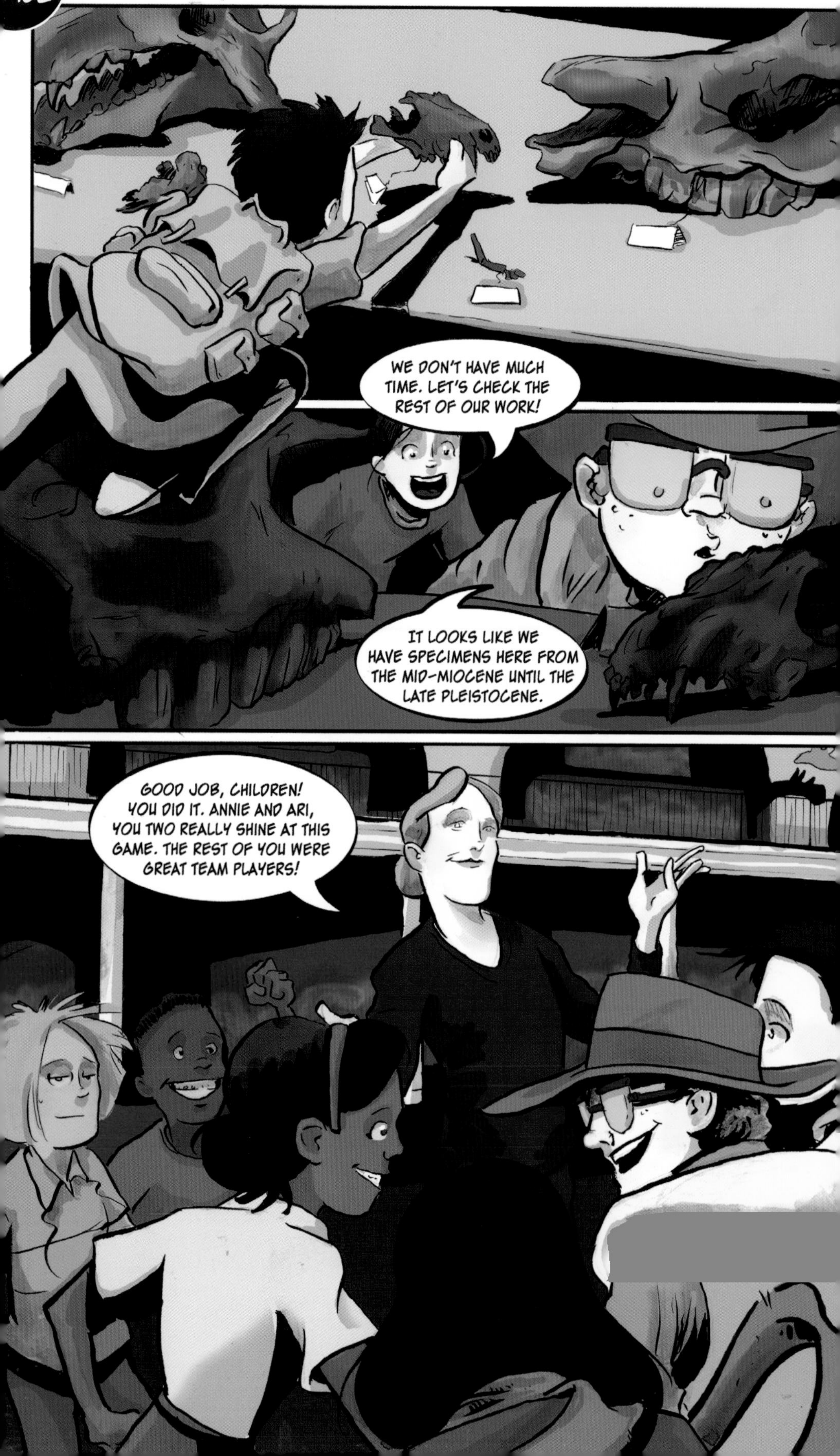
WE DON'T HAVE MUCH TIME. LET'S CHECK THE REST OF OUR WORK!
IT LOOKS LIKE WE HAVE SPECIMENS HERE FROM THE MID-MIOCENE UNTIL THE LATE PLEISTOCENE.
GOOD JOB, CHILDREN! YOU DID IT. ANNIE AND ARI, YOU TWO REALLY SHINE AT THIS GAME. THE REST OF YOU WERE GREAT TEAM PLAYERS!

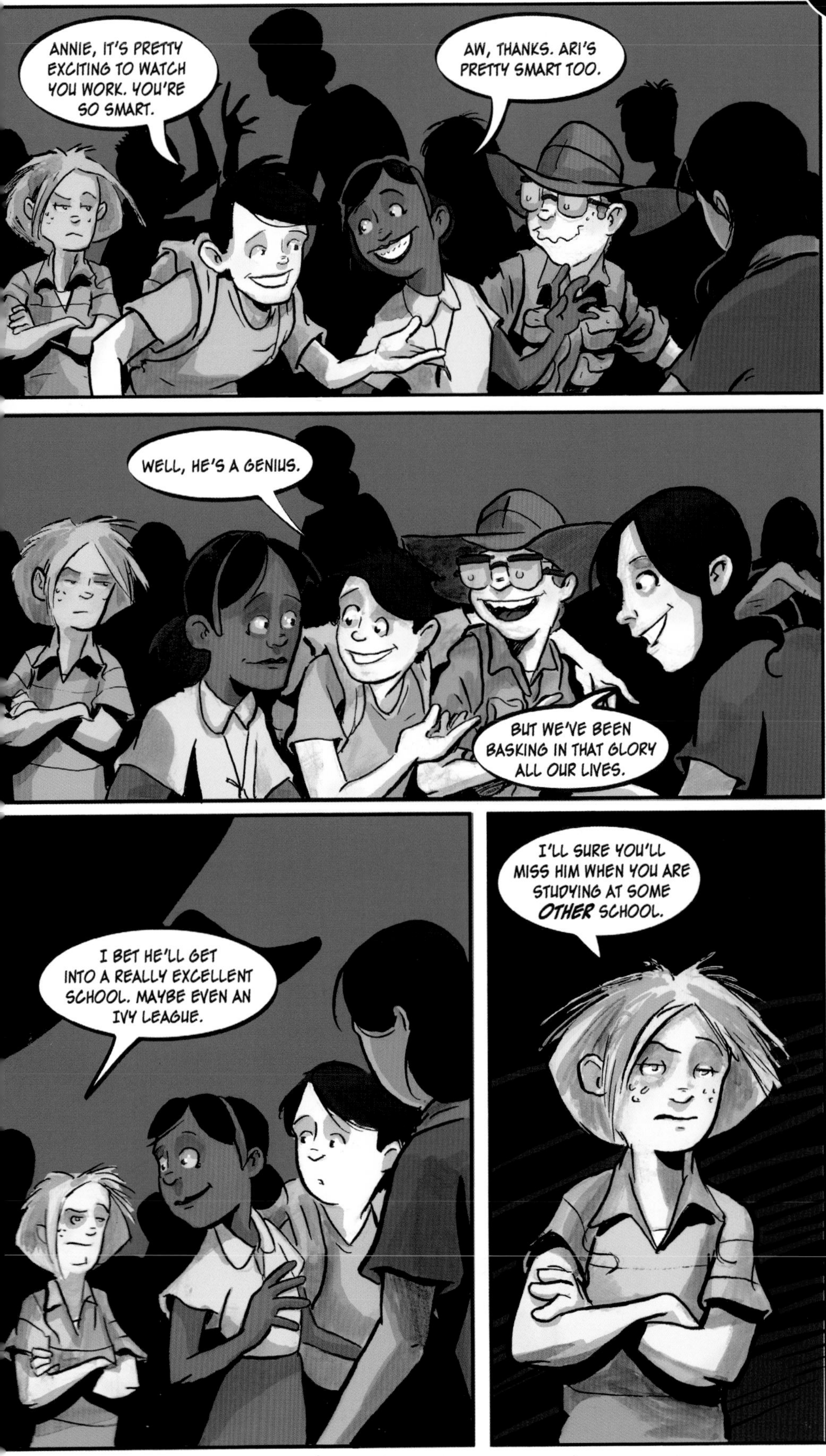
ANNIE, IT'S PRETTY EXCITING TO WATCH YOU WORK. YOU'RE SO SMART.
AW, THANKS. ARI'S PRETTY SMART TOO.
WELL, HE'S A GENIUS.
BUT WE'VE BEEN BASKING IN THAT GLORY ALL OUR LIVES.
I BET HE'LL GET INTO A REALLY EXCELLENT SCHOOL. MAYBE EVEN AN IVY LEAGUE.
I'LL SURE YOU'LL MISS HIM WHEN YOU ARE STUDYING AT SOME *OTHER* SCHOOL.

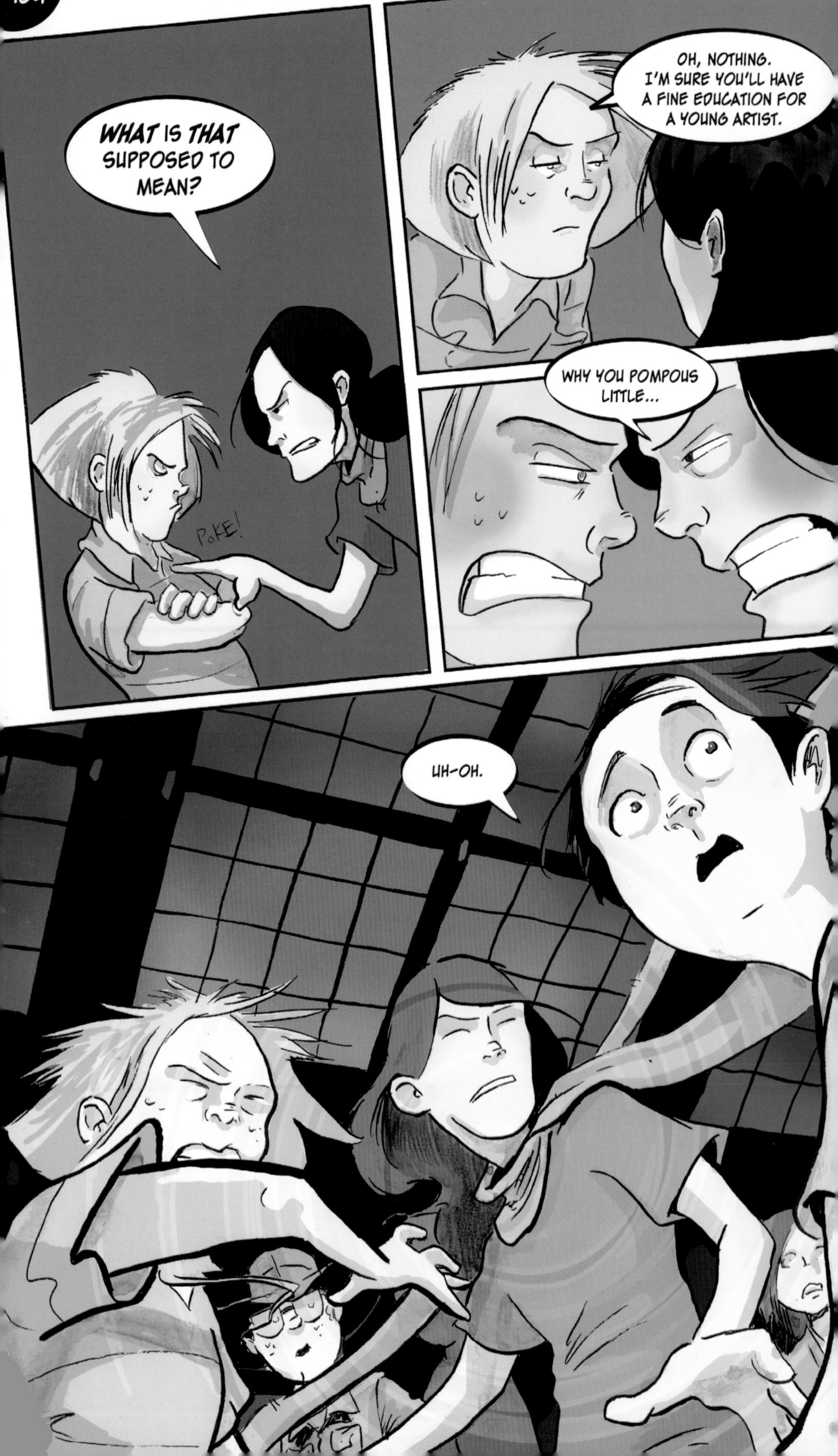
WHAT IS THAT SUPPOSED TO MEAN?
POKE!
OH, NOTHING. I'M SURE YOU'LL HAVE A FINE EDUCATION FOR A YOUNG ARTIST.
WHY YOU POMPOUS LITTLE...
UH-OH.

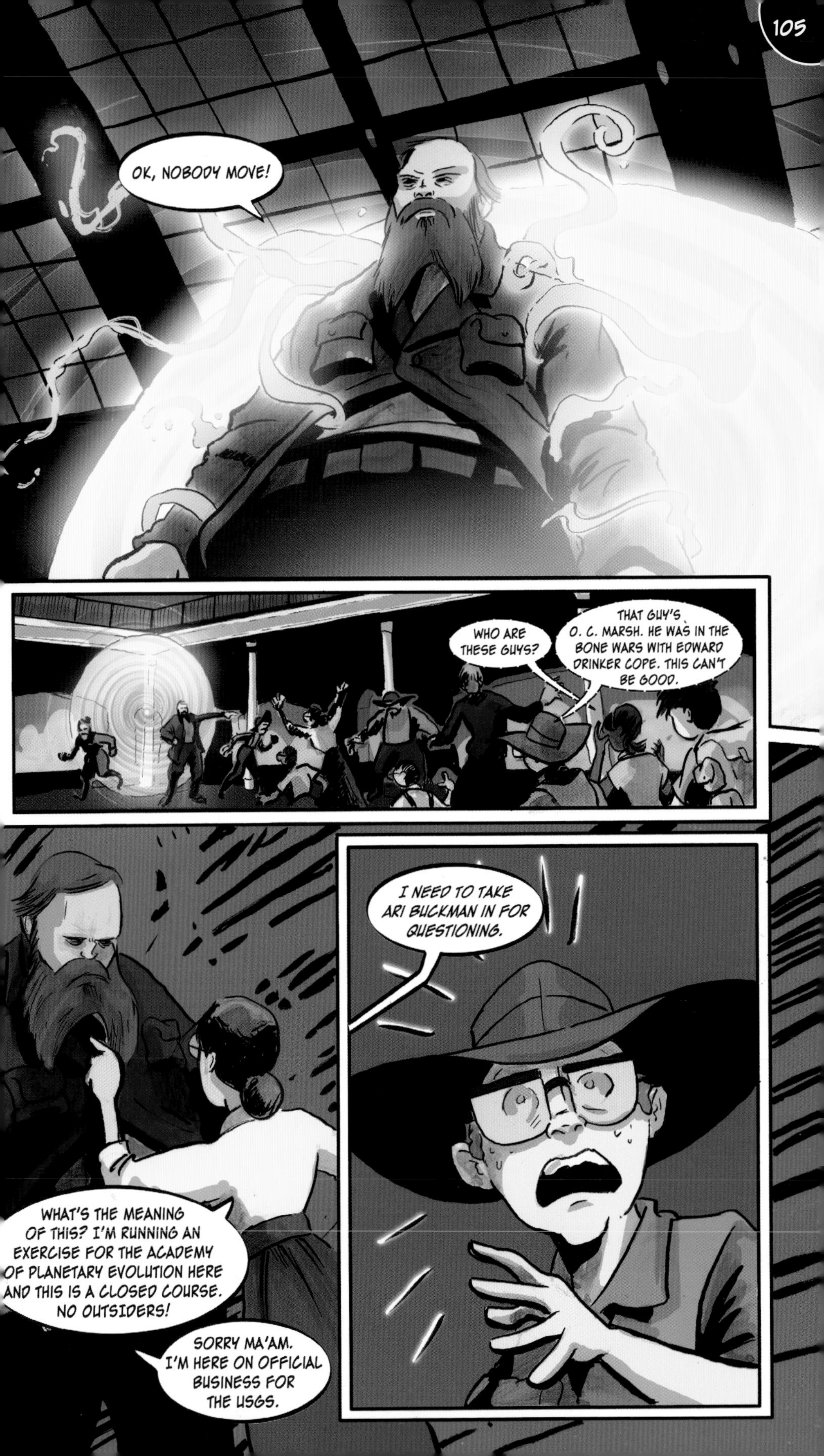
OK, NOBODY MOVE!
WHO ARE THESE GUYS?
THAT GUY'S O. C. MARSH. HE WAS IN THE BONE WARS WITH EDWARD DRINKER COPE. THIS CAN'T BE GOOD.
WHAT'S THE MEANING OF THIS? I'M RUNNING AN EXERCISE FOR THE ACADEMY OF PLANETARY EVOLUTION HERE AND THIS IS A CLOSED COURSE. NO OUTSIDERS!
SORRY MA'AM. I'M HERE ON OFFICIAL BUSINESS FOR THE USGS.
I NEED TO TAKE ARI BUCKMAN IN FOR QUESTIONING.

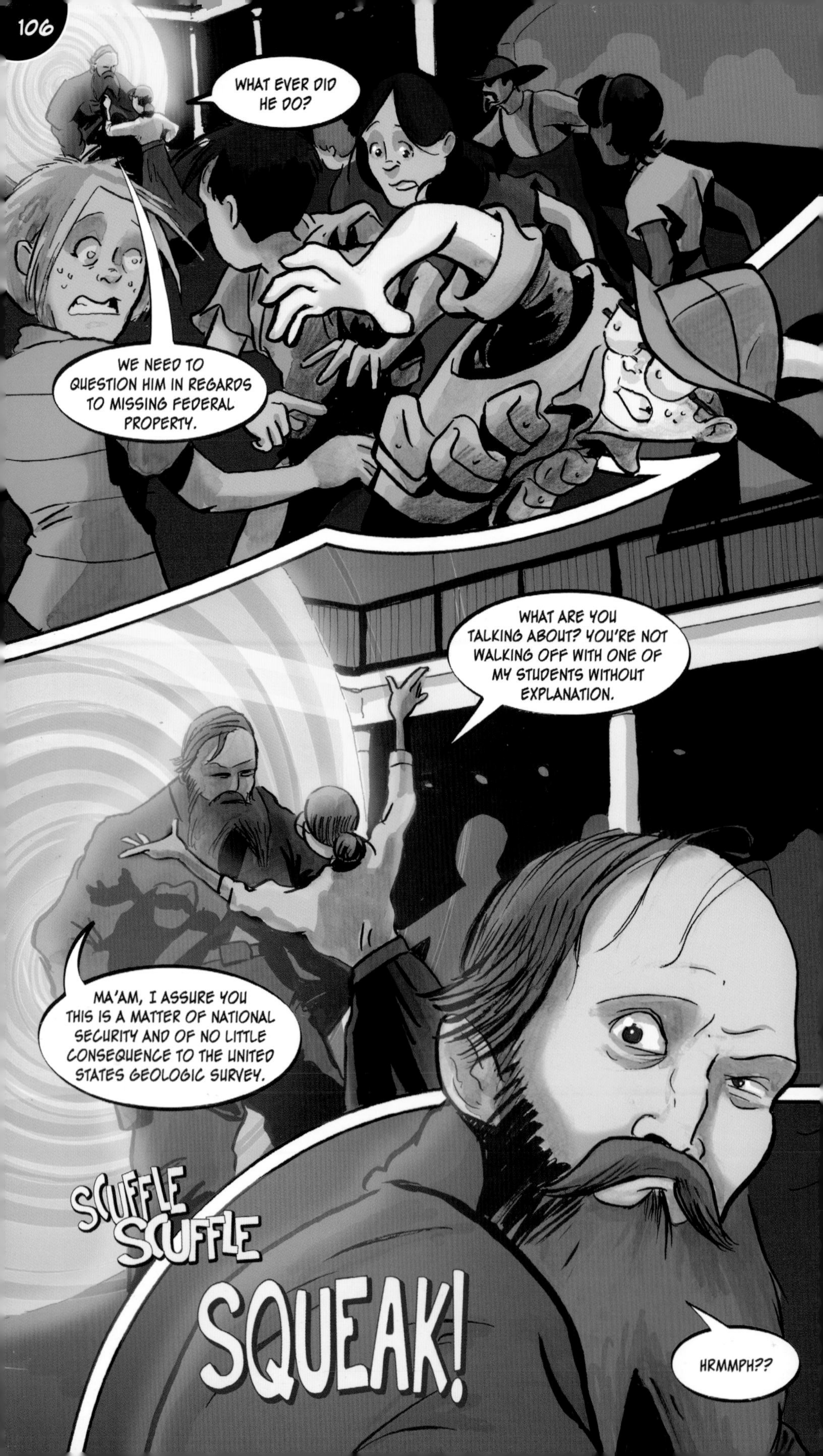
WHAT EVER DID HE DO?
WE NEED TO QUESTION HIM IN REGARDS TO MISSING FEDERAL PROPERTY.
WHAT ARE YOU TALKING ABOUT? YOU'RE NOT WALKING OFF WITH ONE OF MY STUDENTS WITHOUT EXPLANATION.
MA'AM, I ASSURE YOU THIS IS A MATTER OF NATIONAL SECURITY AND OF NO LITTLE CONSEQUENCE TO THE UNITED STATES GEOLOGIC SURVEY.
SCUFFLE SCUFFLE
SQUEAK!
HRMMPH??

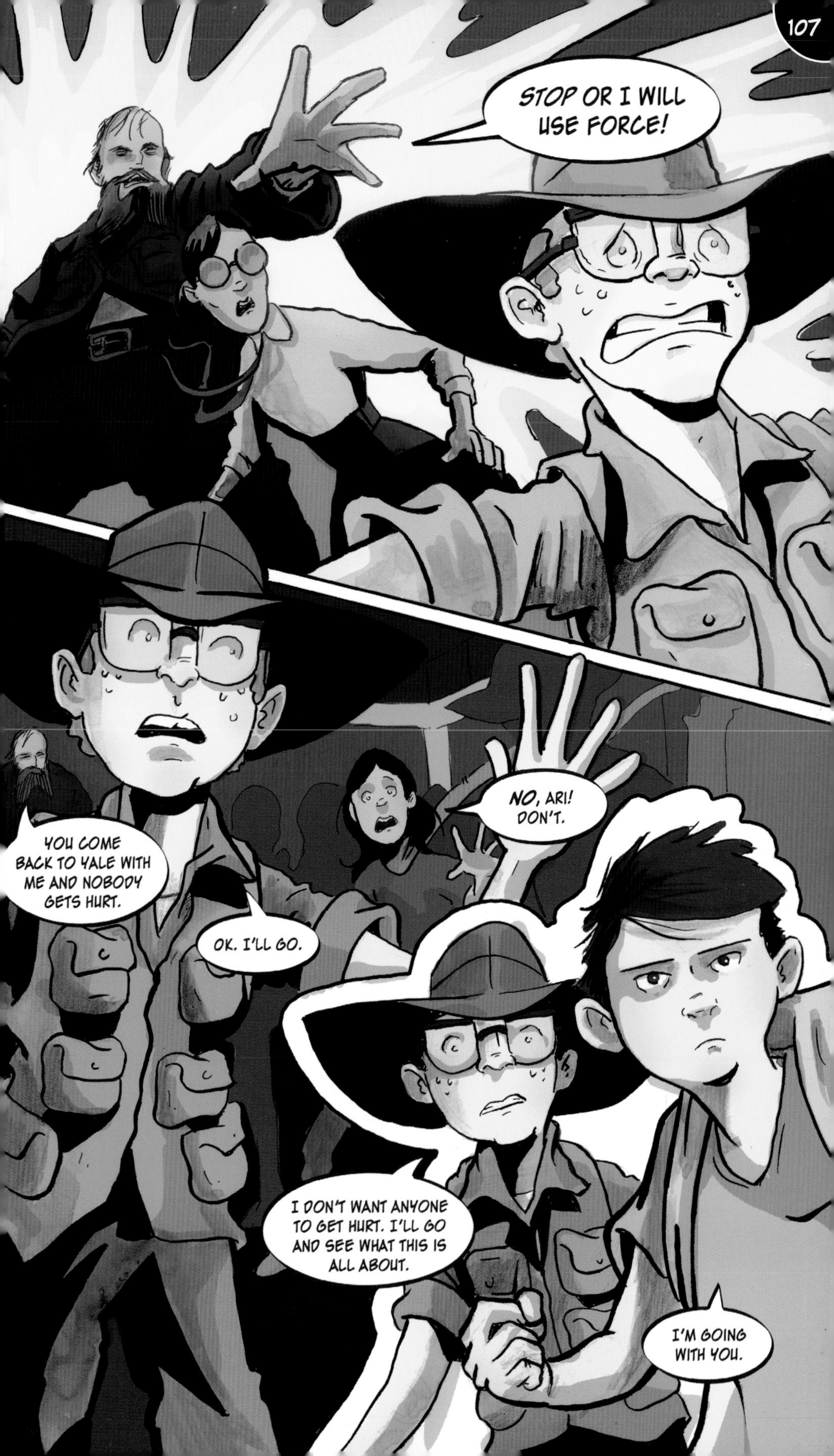
STOP OR I WILL USE FORCE!
YOU COME BACK TO YALE WITH ME AND NOBODY GETS HURT.
NO, ARI! DON'T.
OK. I'LL GO.
I DON'T WANT ANYONE TO GET HURT. I'LL GO AND SEE WHAT THIS IS ALL ABOUT.
I'M GOING WITH YOU.

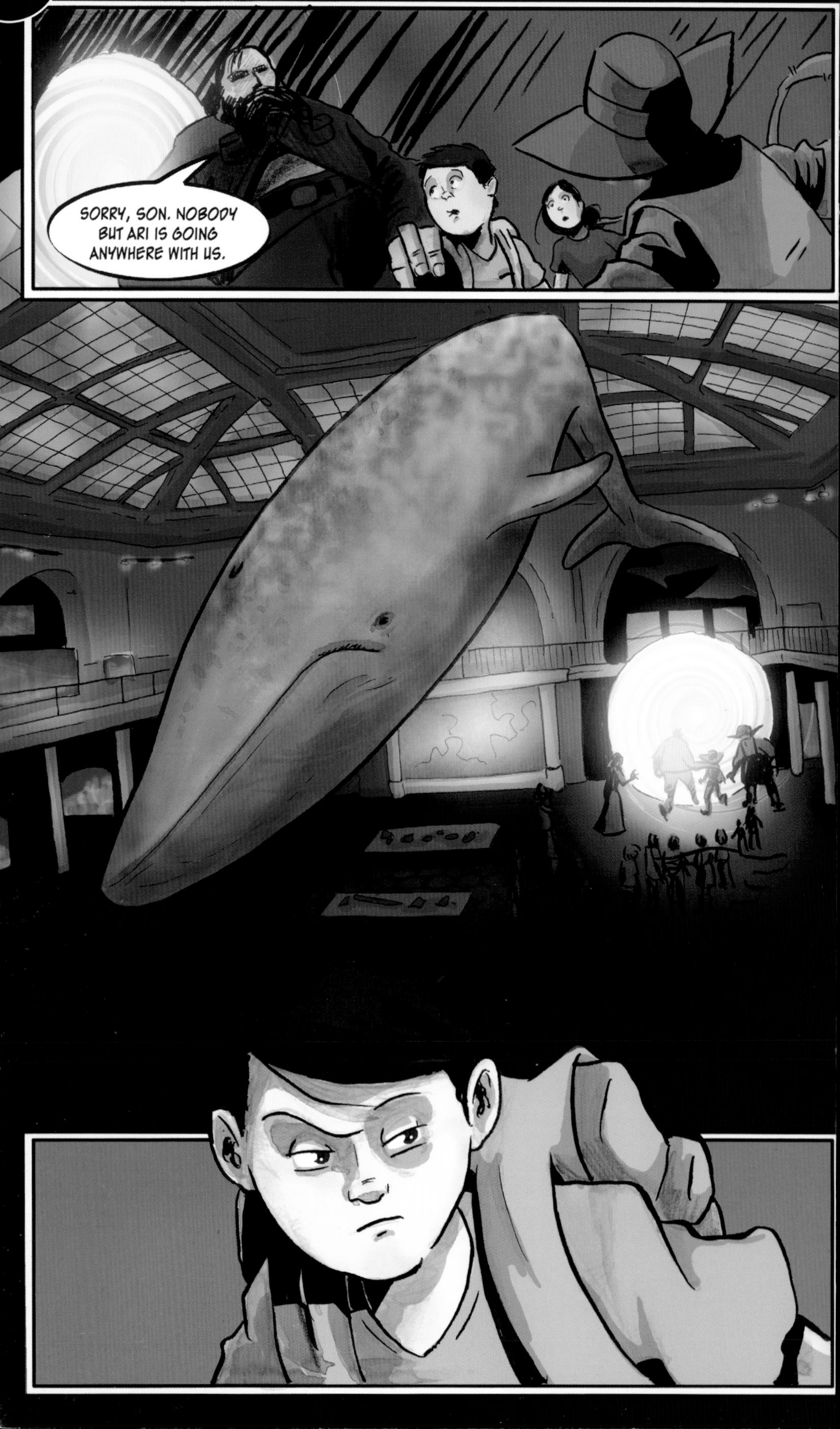
SORRY, SON. NOBODY BUT ARI IS GOING ANYWHERE WITH US.

STUDENT HANDBOOK

Academy of
Planetary
Evolution

8

"Switching Tracks"

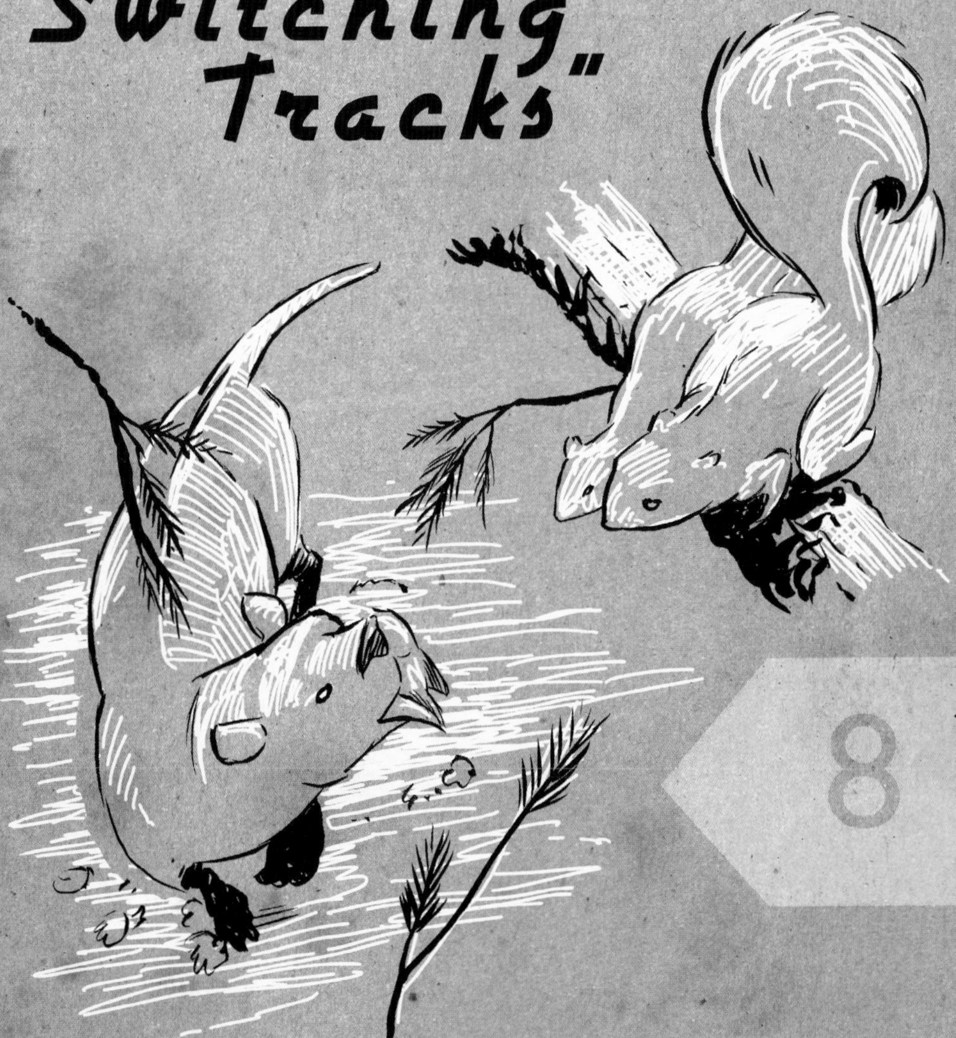
8

MONTAUK INDUSTRIES

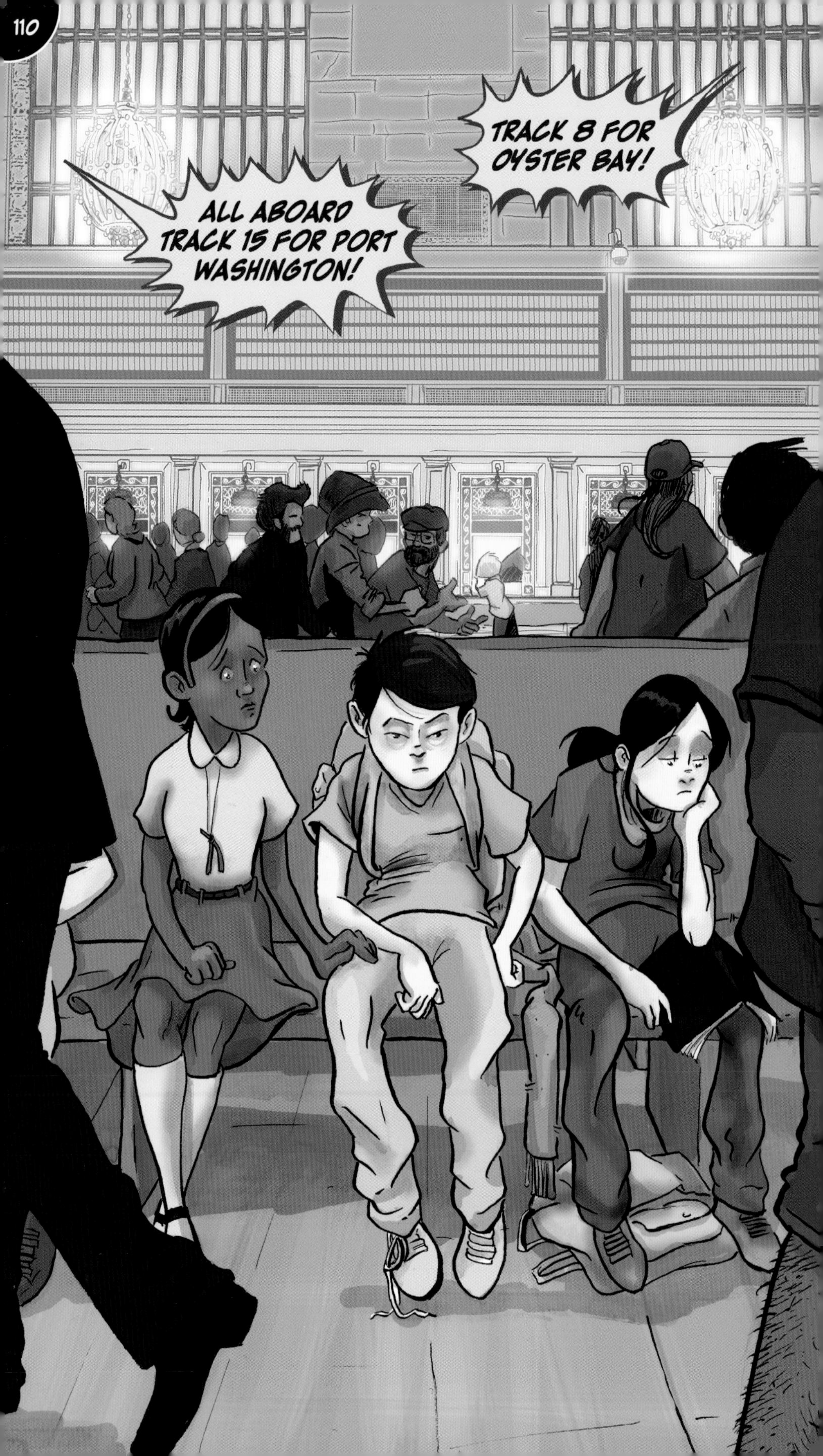
ALL ABOARD TRACK 15 FOR PORT WASHINGTON!
TRACK 8 FOR OYSTER BAY!

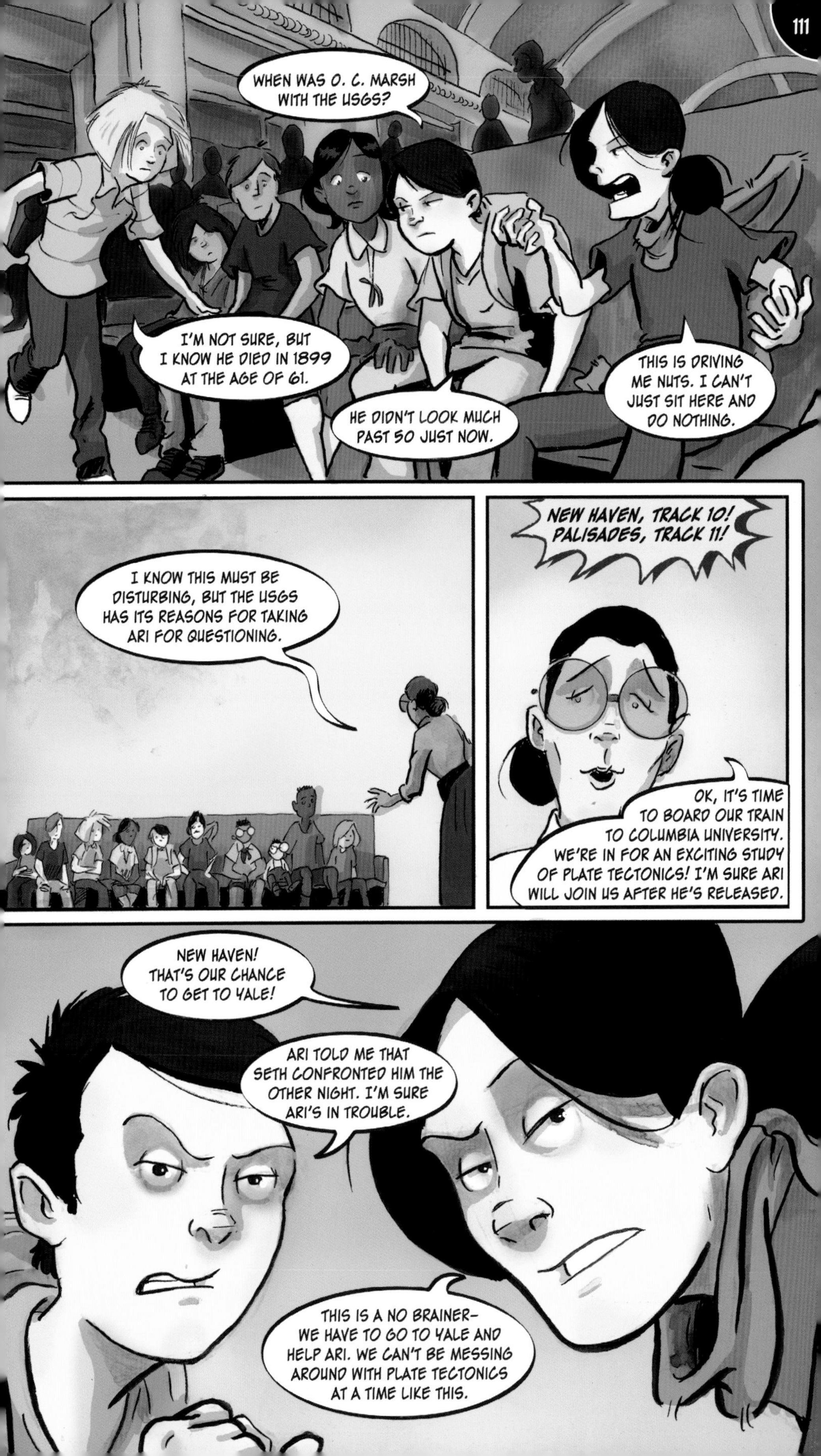
WHEN WAS O. C. MARSH WITH THE USGS?
I'M NOT SURE, BUT I KNOW HE DIED IN 1899 AT THE AGE OF 61.
HE DIDN'T LOOK MUCH PAST 50 JUST NOW.
THIS IS DRIVING ME NUTS. I CAN'T JUST SIT HERE AND DO NOTHING.
I KNOW THIS MUST BE DISTURBING, BUT THE USGS HAS ITS REASONS FOR TAKING ARI FOR QUESTIONING.
NEW HAVEN, TRACK 10! PALISADES, TRACK 11!
OK, IT'S TIME TO BOARD OUR TRAIN TO COLUMBIA UNIVERSITY. WE'RE IN FOR AN EXCITING STUDY OF PLATE TECTONICS! I'M SURE ARI WILL JOIN US AFTER HE'S RELEASED.
NEW HAVEN! THAT'S OUR CHANCE TO GET TO YALE!
ARI TOLD ME THAT SETH CONFRONTED HIM THE OTHER NIGHT. I'M SURE ARI'S IN TROUBLE.
THIS IS A NO BRAINER– WE HAVE TO GO TO YALE AND HELP ARI. WE CAN'T BE MESSING AROUND WITH PLATE TECTONICS AT A TIME LIKE THIS.

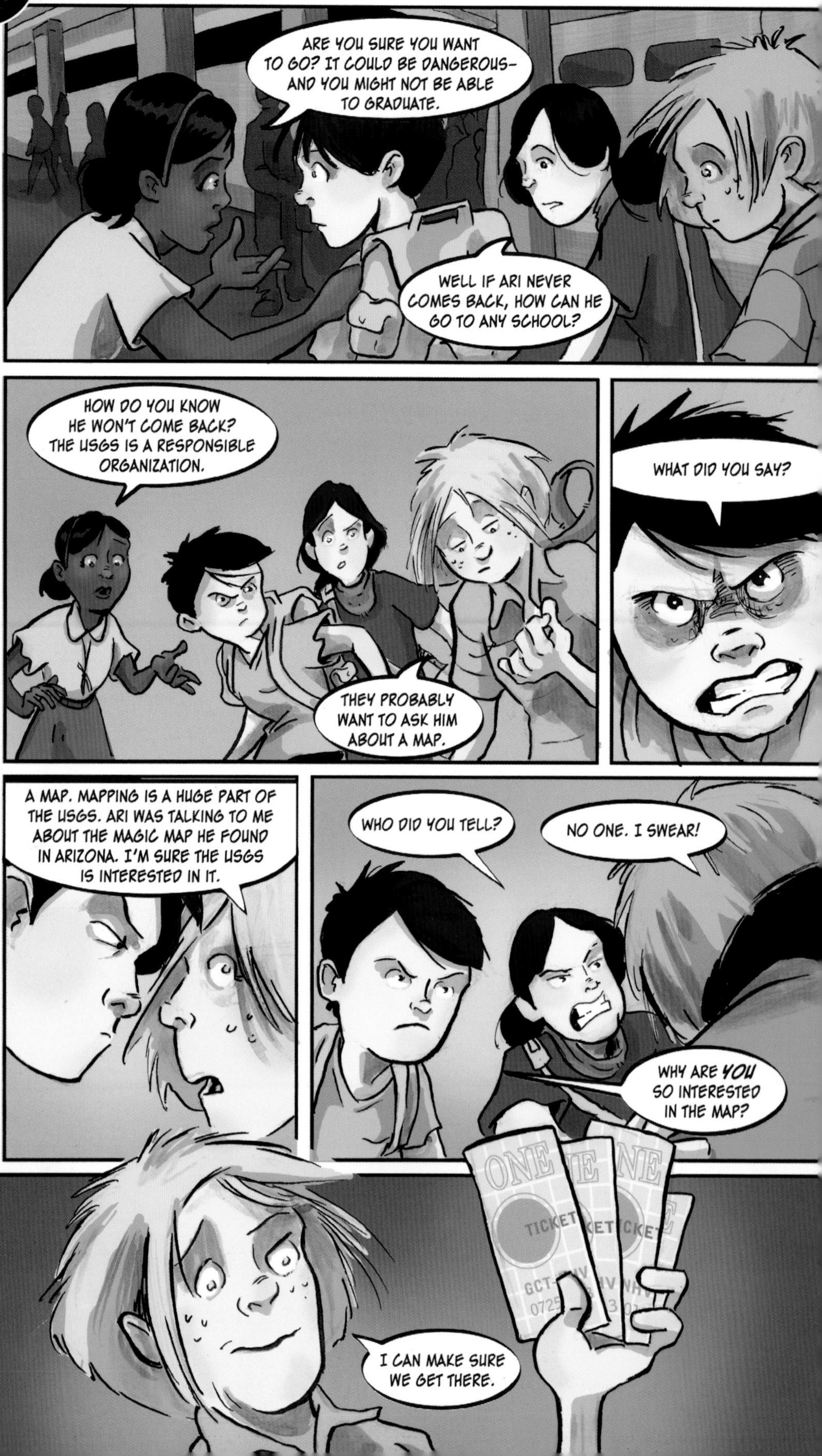
ARE YOU SURE YOU WANT TO GO? IT COULD BE DANGEROUS-AND YOU MIGHT NOT BE ABLE TO GRADUATE.
WELL IF ARI NEVER COMES BACK, HOW CAN HE GO TO ANY SCHOOL?
HOW DO YOU KNOW HE WON'T COME BACK? THE USGS IS A RESPONSIBLE ORGANIZATION.
THEY PROBABLY WANT TO ASK HIM ABOUT A MAP.
WHAT DID YOU SAY?
A MAP. MAPPING IS A HUGE PART OF THE USGS. ARI WAS TALKING TO ME ABOUT THE MAGIC MAP HE FOUND IN ARIZONA. I'M SURE THE USGS IS INTERESTED IN IT.
WHO DID YOU TELL?
NO ONE. I SWEAR!
WHY ARE *YOU* SO INTERESTED IN THE MAP?
ONE
TICKET
I CAN MAKE SURE WE GET THERE.

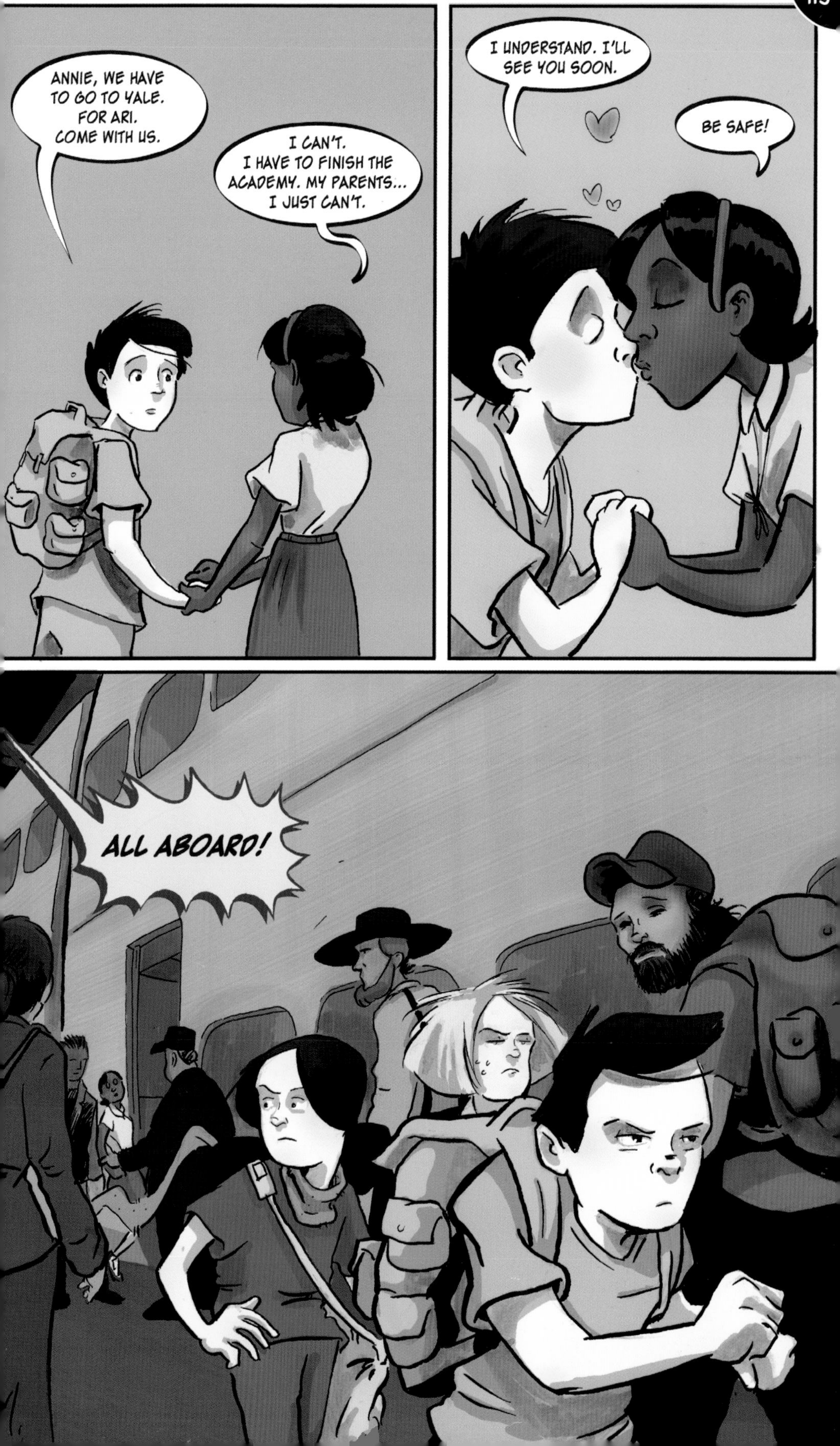
ANNIE, WE HAVE TO GO TO YALE. FOR ARI. COME WITH US.
I CAN'T. I HAVE TO FINISH THE ACADEMY. MY PARENTS... I JUST CAN'T.
I UNDERSTAND. I'LL SEE YOU SOON.
BE SAFE!
ALL ABOARD!

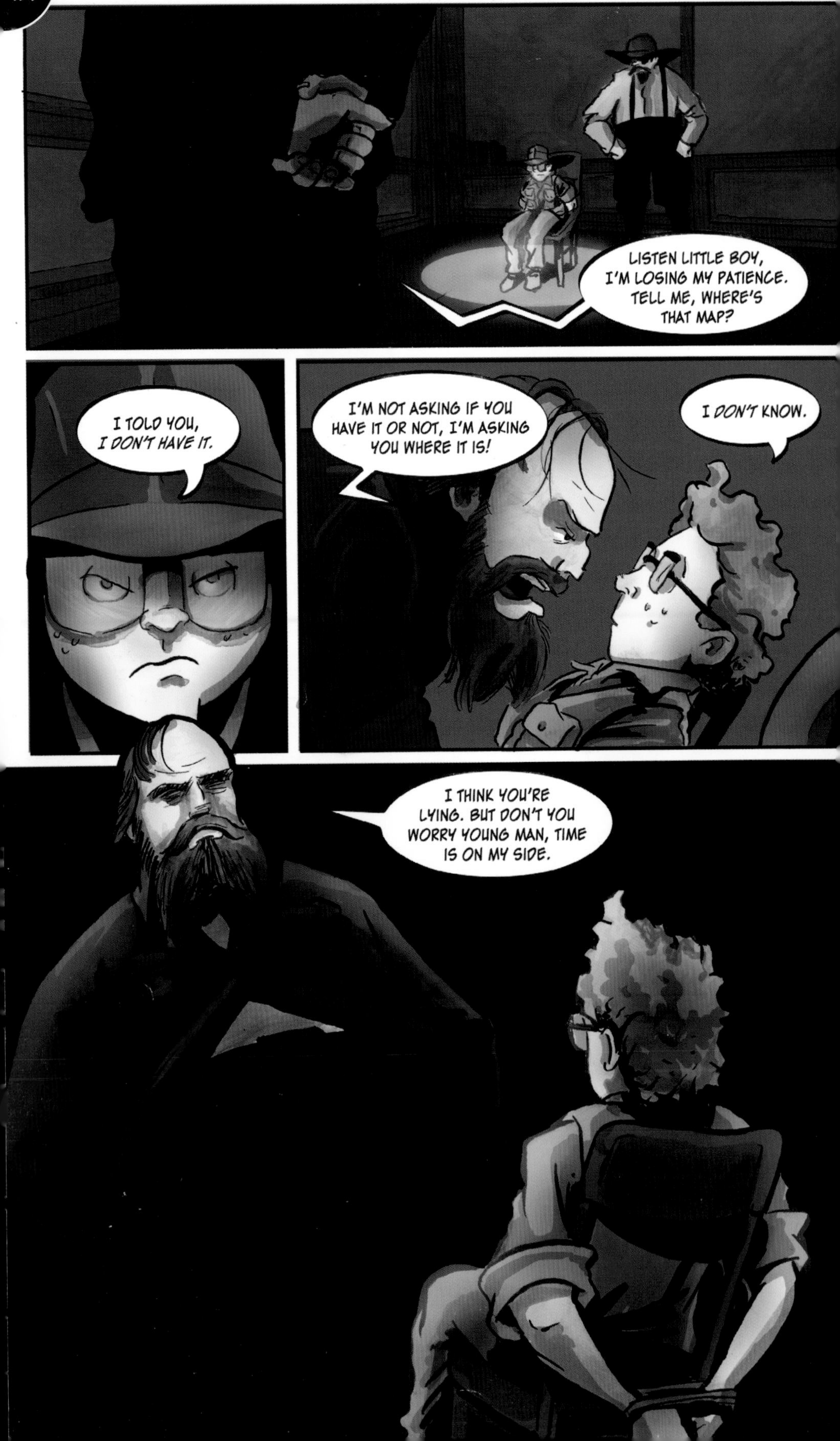
LISTEN LITTLE BOY, I'M LOSING MY PATIENCE. TELL ME, WHERE'S THAT MAP?
I TOLD YOU, I DON'T HAVE IT.
I'M NOT ASKING IF YOU HAVE IT OR NOT, I'M ASKING YOU WHERE IT IS!
I DON'T KNOW.
I THINK YOU'RE LYING. BUT DON'T YOU WORRY YOUNG MAN, TIME IS ON MY SIDE.

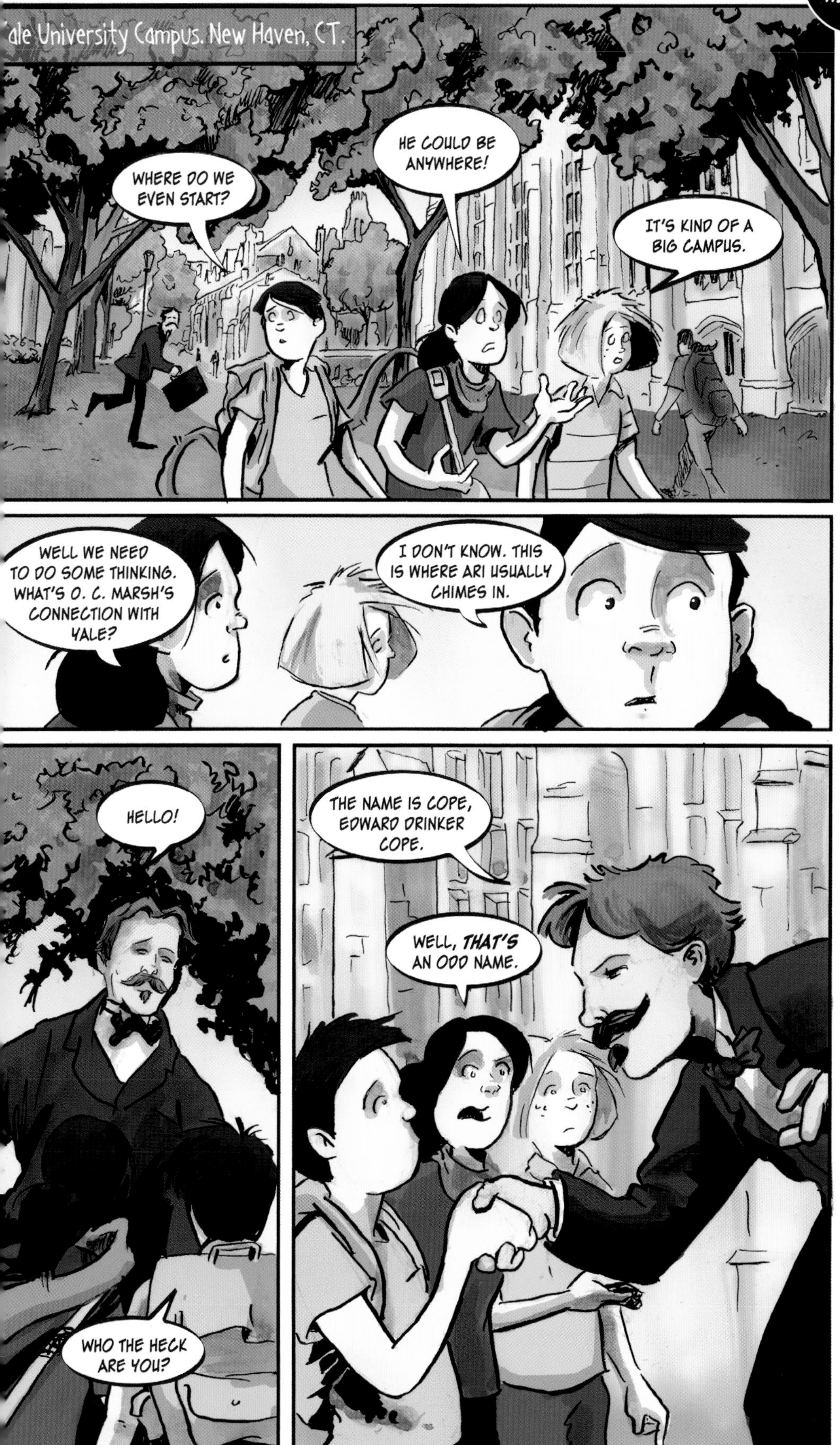
ale University Campus. New Haven, CT.
WHERE DO WE EVEN START?
HE COULD BE ANYWHERE!
IT'S KIND OF A BIG CAMPUS.
WELL WE NEED TO DO SOME THINKING. WHAT'S O. C. MARSH'S CONNECTION WITH YALE?
I DON'T KNOW. THIS IS WHERE ARI USUALLY CHIMES IN.
HELLO!
WHO THE HECK ARE YOU?
THE NAME IS COPE, EDWARD DRINKER COPE.
WELL, *THAT'S* AN ODD NAME.

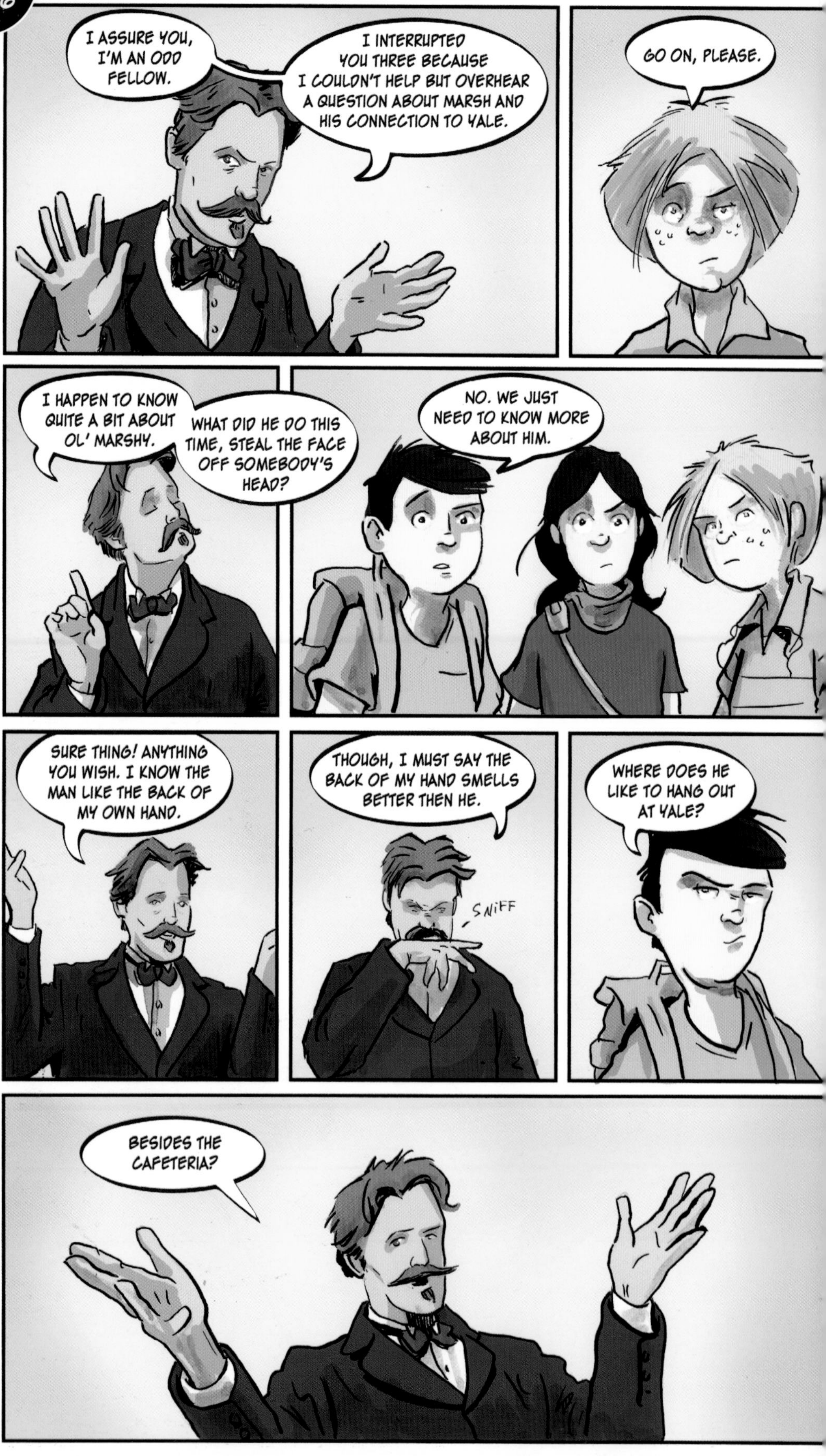
I ASSURE YOU, I'M AN ODD FELLOW.
I INTERRUPTED YOU THREE BECAUSE I COULDN'T HELP BUT OVERHEAR A QUESTION ABOUT MARSH AND HIS CONNECTION TO YALE.
GO ON, PLEASE.
I HAPPEN TO KNOW QUITE A BIT ABOUT OL' MARSHY.
WHAT DID HE DO THIS TIME, STEAL THE FACE OFF SOMEBODY'S HEAD?
NO. WE JUST NEED TO KNOW MORE ABOUT HIM.
SURE THING! ANYTHING YOU WISH. I KNOW THE MAN LIKE THE BACK OF MY OWN HAND.
THOUGH, I MUST SAY THE BACK OF MY HAND SMELLS BETTER THEN HE.
SNIFF
WHERE DOES HE LIKE TO HANG OUT AT YALE?
BESIDES THE CAFETERIA?

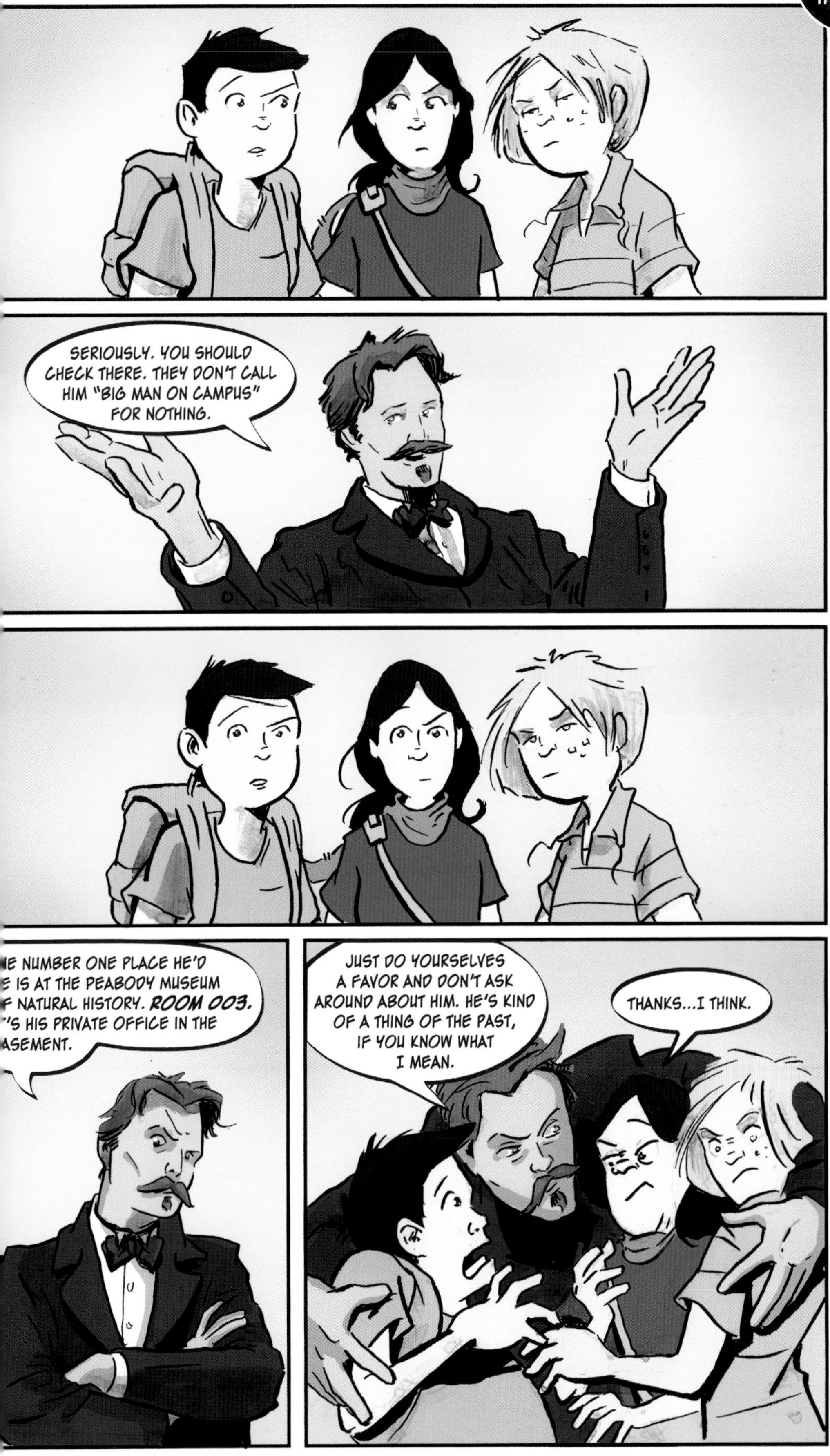
SERIOUSLY. YOU SHOULD CHECK THERE. THEY DON'T CALL HIM "BIG MAN ON CAMPUS" FOR NOTHING.
E NUMBER ONE PLACE HE'D E IS AT THE PEABODY MUSEUM F NATURAL HISTORY. ROOM 003. 'S HIS PRIVATE OFFICE IN THE ASEMENT.
JUST DO YOURSELVES A FAVOR AND DON'T ASK AROUND ABOUT HIM. HE'S KIND OF A THING OF THE PAST, IF YOU KNOW WHAT I MEAN.
THANKS...I THINK.

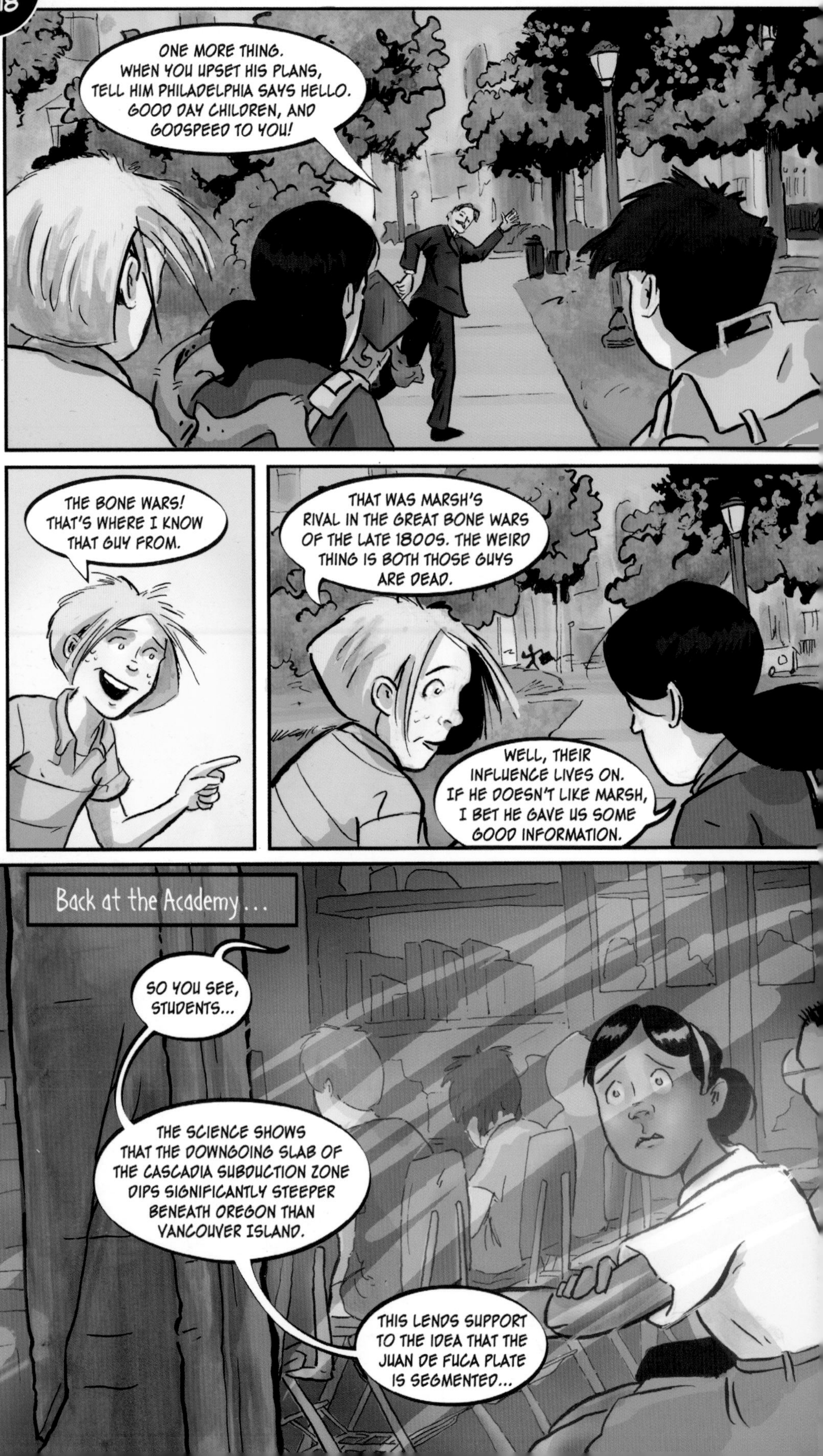
ONE MORE THING. WHEN YOU UPSET HIS PLANS, TELL HIM PHILADELPHIA SAYS HELLO. GOOD DAY CHILDREN, AND GODSPEED TO YOU!
THE BONE WARS! THAT'S WHERE I KNOW THAT GUY FROM.
THAT WAS MARSH'S RIVAL IN THE GREAT BONE WARS OF THE LATE 1800S. THE WEIRD THING IS BOTH THOSE GUYS ARE DEAD.
WELL, THEIR INFLUENCE LIVES ON. IF HE DOESN'T LIKE MARSH, I BET HE GAVE US SOME GOOD INFORMATION.
Back at the Academy . . .
SO YOU SEE, STUDENTS...
THE SCIENCE SHOWS THAT THE DOWNGOING SLAB OF THE CASCADIA SUBDUCTION ZONE DIPS SIGNIFICANTLY STEEPER BENEATH OREGON THAN VANCOUVER ISLAND.
THIS LENDS SUPPORT TO THE IDEA THAT THE JUAN DE FUCA PLATE IS SEGMENTED...

STUDENT HANDBOOK

Academy of
Planetary
Evolution

9

"Campus Rumpus"

MONTAUK INDUSTRIES

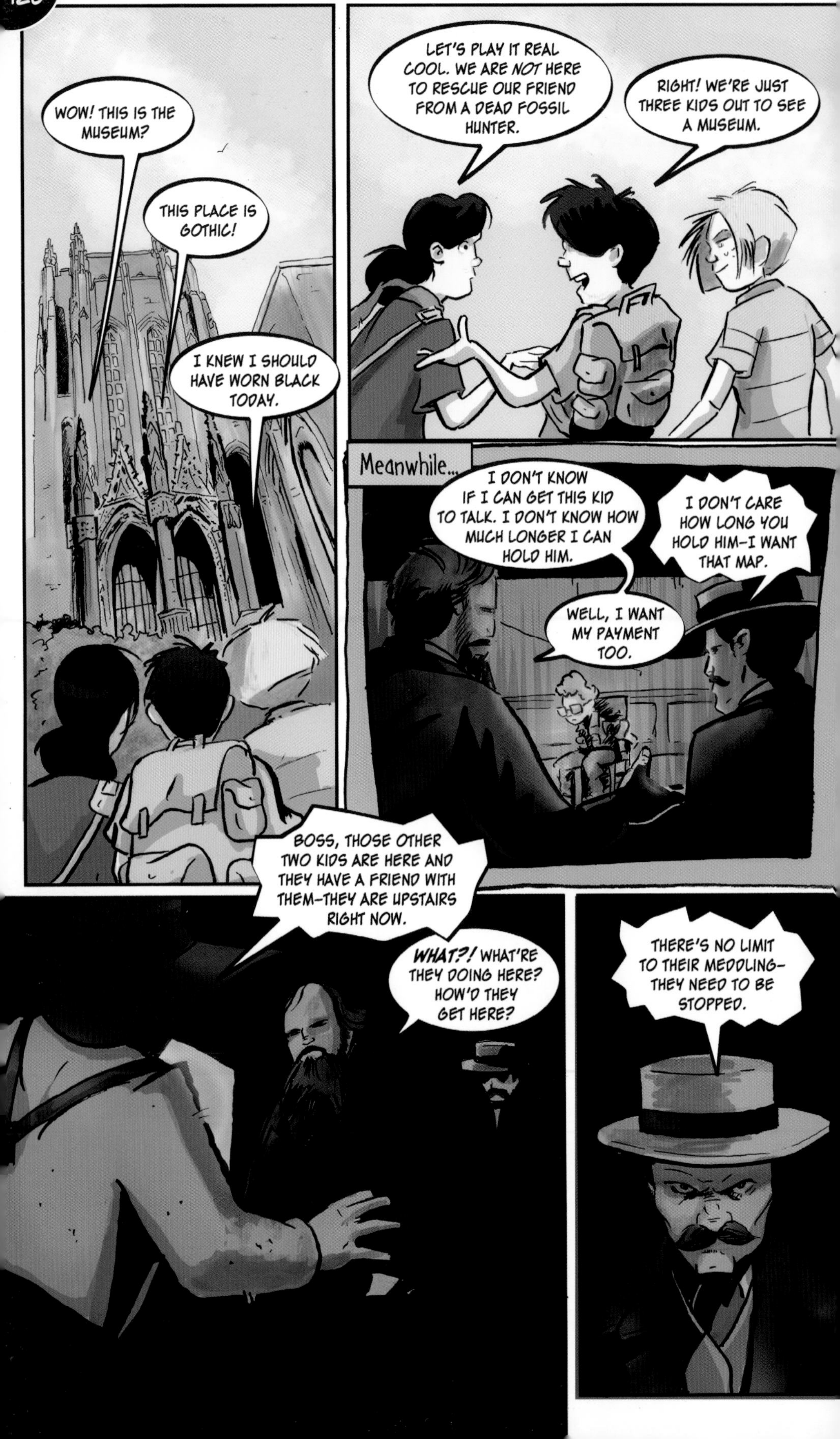
WOW! THIS IS THE MUSEUM?
THIS PLACE IS GOTHIC!
I KNEW I SHOULD HAVE WORN BLACK TODAY.
LET'S PLAY IT REAL COOL. WE ARE NOT HERE TO RESCUE OUR FRIEND FROM A DEAD FOSSIL HUNTER.
RIGHT! WE'RE JUST THREE KIDS OUT TO SEE A MUSEUM.
Meanwhile...
I DON'T KNOW IF I CAN GET THIS KID TO TALK. I DON'T KNOW HOW MUCH LONGER I CAN HOLD HIM.
I DON'T CARE HOW LONG YOU HOLD HIM—I WANT THAT MAP.
WELL, I WANT MY PAYMENT TOO.
BOSS, THOSE OTHER TWO KIDS ARE HERE AND THEY HAVE A FRIEND WITH THEM—THEY ARE UPSTAIRS RIGHT NOW.
WHAT?! WHAT'RE THEY DOING HERE? HOW'D THEY GET HERE?
THERE'S NO LIMIT TO THEIR MEDDLING—THEY NEED TO BE STOPPED.

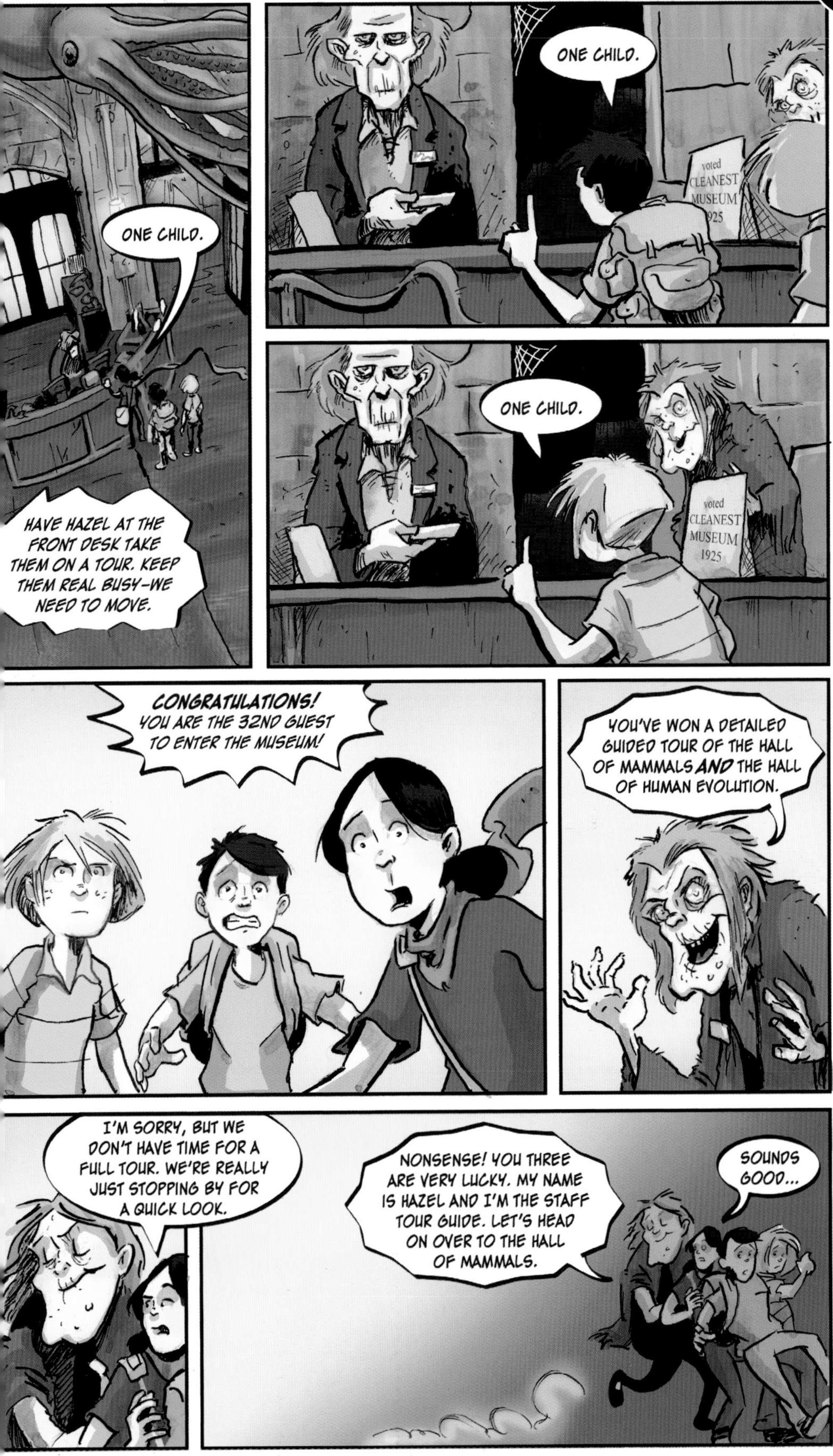
ONE CHILD.
HAVE HAZEL AT THE FRONT DESK TAKE THEM ON A TOUR. KEEP THEM REAL BUSY—WE NEED TO MOVE.
ONE CHILD.
voted CLEANEST MUSEUM 1925
ONE CHILD.
voted CLEANEST MUSEUM 1925
CONGRATULATIONS! YOU ARE THE 32ND GUEST TO ENTER THE MUSEUM!
YOU'VE WON A DETAILED GUIDED TOUR OF THE HALL OF MAMMALS AND THE HALL OF HUMAN EVOLUTION.
I'M SORRY, BUT WE DON'T HAVE TIME FOR A FULL TOUR. WE'RE REALLY JUST STOPPING BY FOR A QUICK LOOK.
NONSENSE! YOU THREE ARE VERY LUCKY. MY NAME IS HAZEL AND I'M THE STAFF TOUR GUIDE. LET'S HEAD ON OVER TO THE HALL OF MAMMALS.
SOUNDS GOOD...

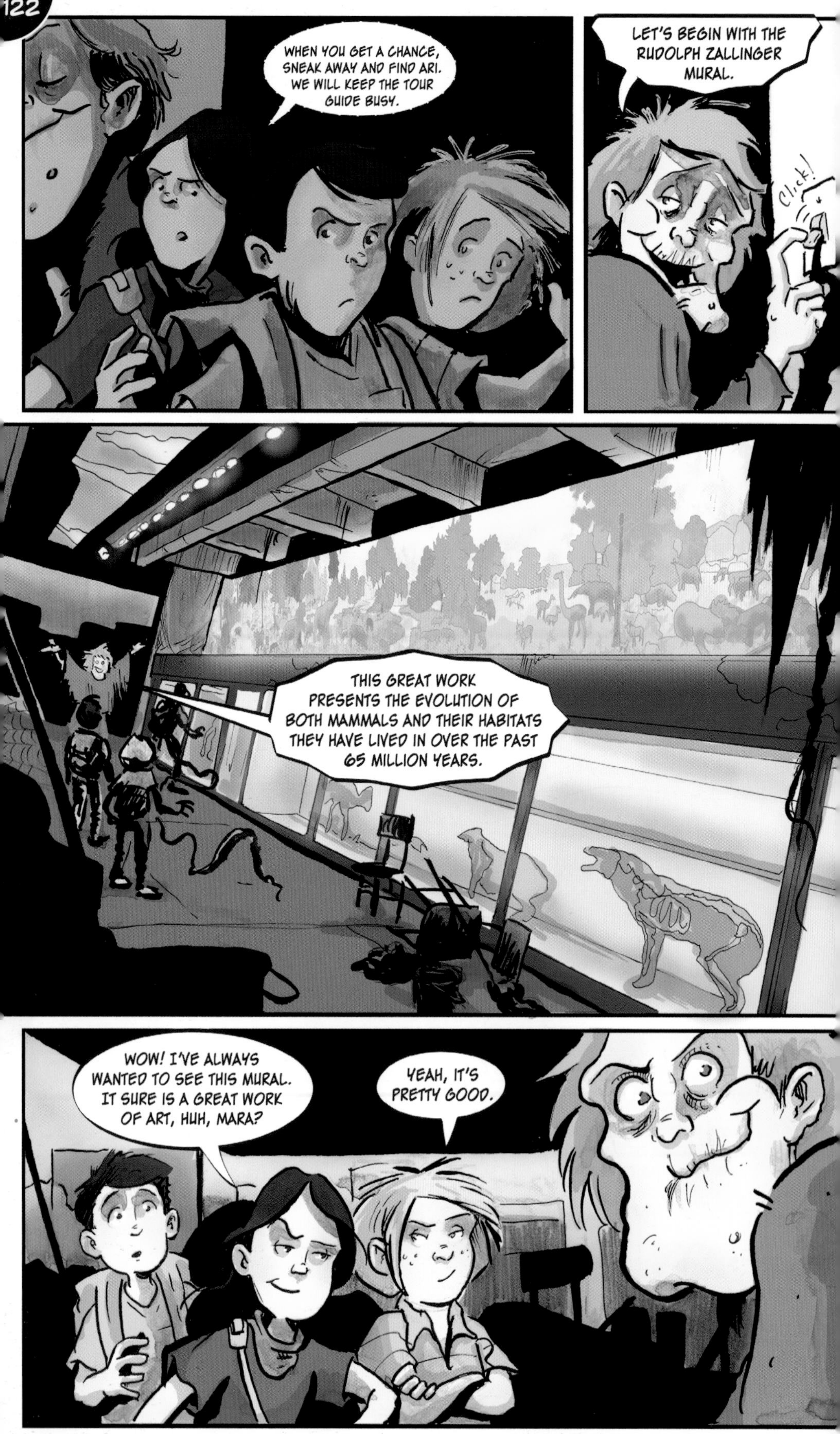
WHEN YOU GET A CHANCE, SNEAK AWAY AND FIND ARI. WE WILL KEEP THE TOUR GUIDE BUSY.
LET'S BEGIN WITH THE RUDOLPH ZALLINGER MURAL.
Click!
THIS GREAT WORK PRESENTS THE EVOLUTION OF BOTH MAMMALS AND THEIR HABITATS THEY HAVE LIVED IN OVER THE PAST 65 MILLION YEARS.
WOW! I'VE ALWAYS WANTED TO SEE THIS MURAL. IT SURE IS A GREAT WORK OF ART, HUH, MARA?
YEAH, IT'S PRETTY GOOD.

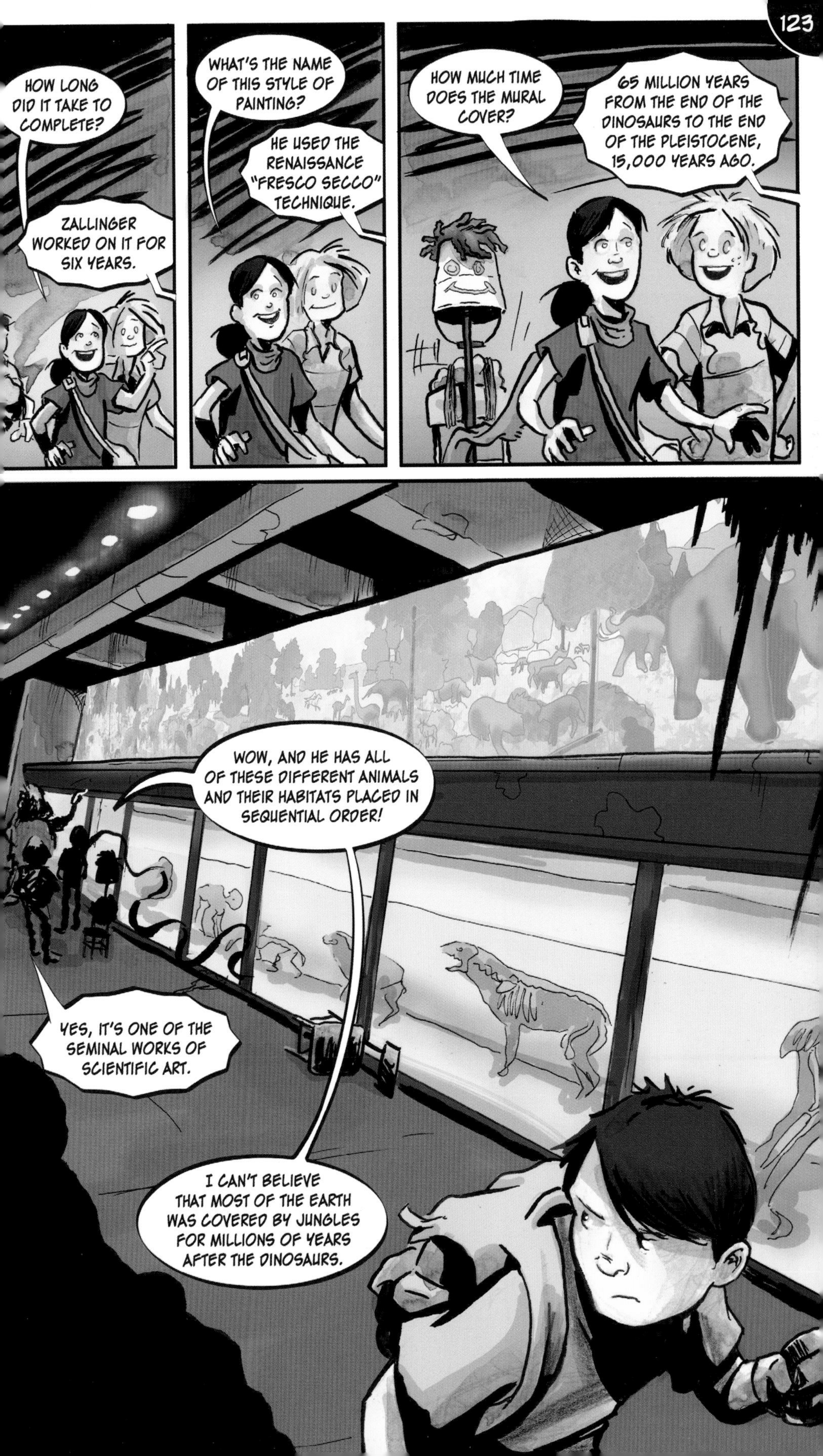
HOW LONG DID IT TAKE TO COMPLETE?
ZALLINGER WORKED ON IT FOR SIX YEARS.
WHAT'S THE NAME OF THIS STYLE OF PAINTING?
HE USED THE RENAISSANCE "FRESCO SECCO" TECHNIQUE.
HOW MUCH TIME DOES THE MURAL COVER?
65 MILLION YEARS FROM THE END OF THE DINOSAURS TO THE END OF THE PLEISTOCENE, 15,000 YEARS AGO.
WOW, AND HE HAS ALL OF THESE DIFFERENT ANIMALS AND THEIR HABITATS PLACED IN SEQUENTIAL ORDER!
YES, IT'S ONE OF THE SEMINAL WORKS OF SCIENTIFIC ART.
I CAN'T BELIEVE THAT MOST OF THE EARTH WAS COVERED BY JUNGLES FOR MILLIONS OF YEARS AFTER THE DINOSAURS.

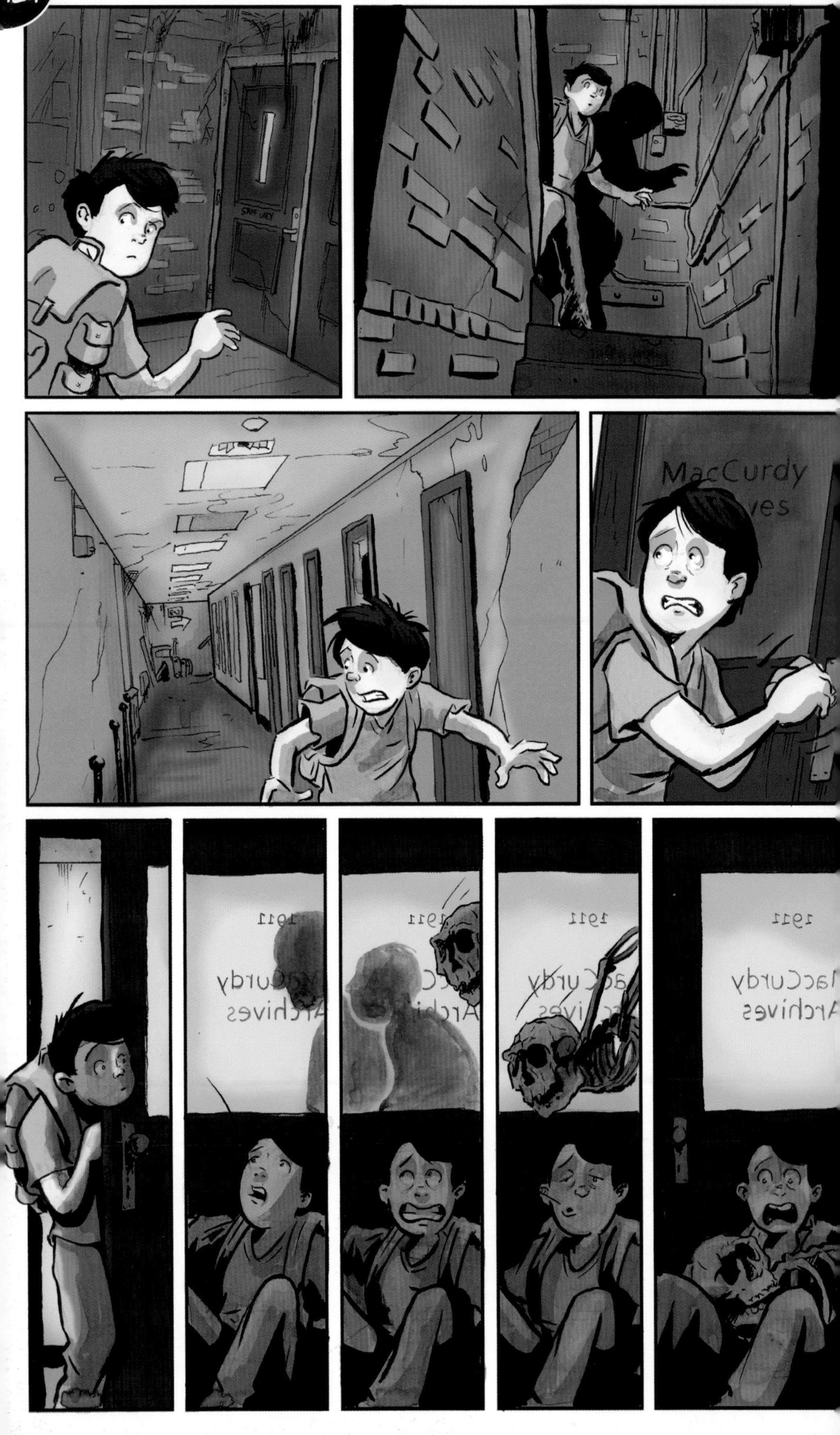
MacCurdy
ves

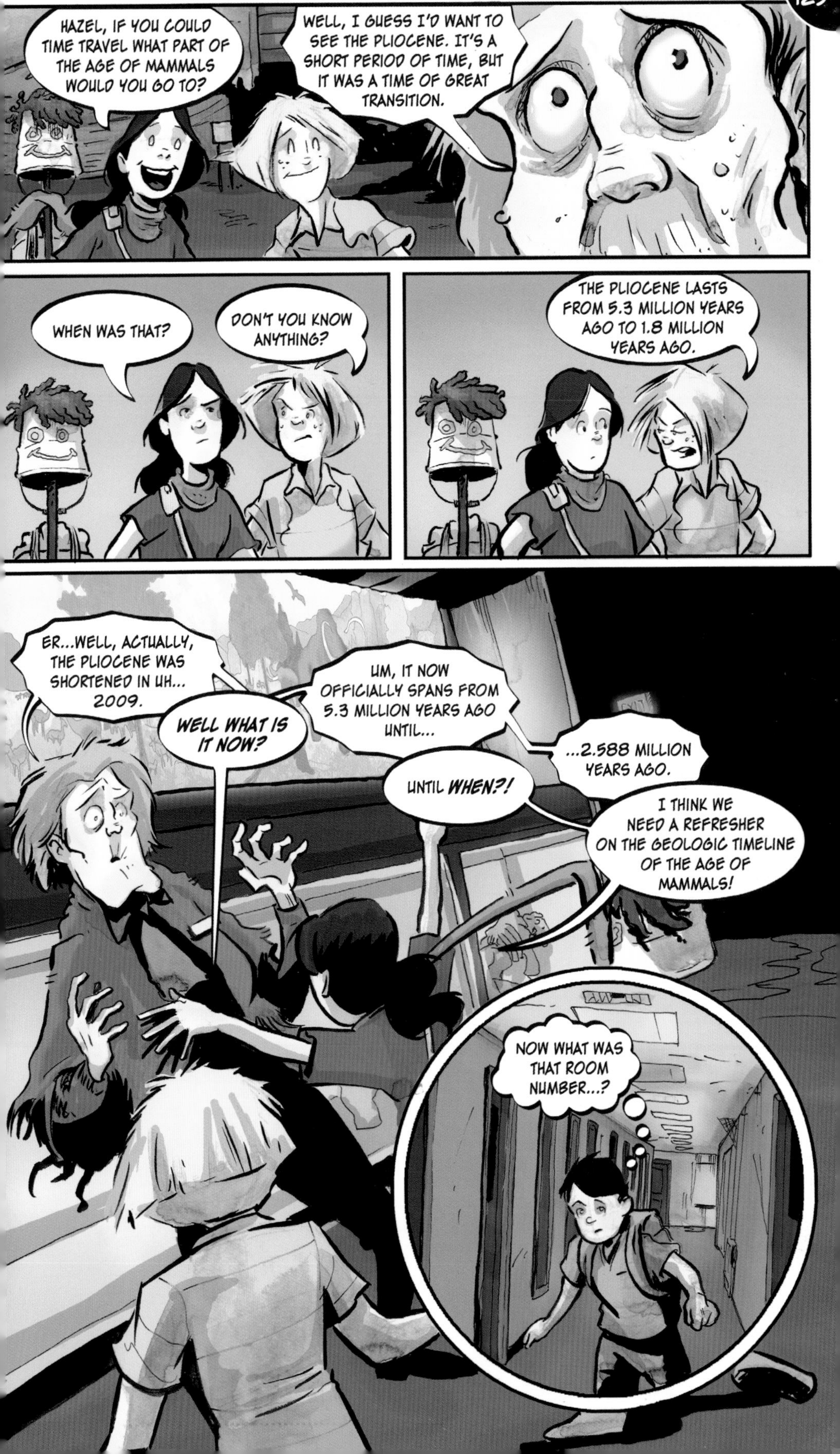
HAZEL, IF YOU COULD TIME TRAVEL WHAT PART OF THE AGE OF MAMMALS WOULD YOU GO TO?
WELL, I GUESS I'D WANT TO SEE THE PLIOCENE. IT'S A SHORT PERIOD OF TIME, BUT IT WAS A TIME OF GREAT TRANSITION.
WHEN WAS THAT?
DON'T YOU KNOW ANYTHING?
THE PLIOCENE LASTS FROM 5.3 MILLION YEARS AGO TO 1.8 MILLION YEARS AGO.
ER...WELL, ACTUALLY, THE PLIOCENE WAS SHORTENED IN UH... 2009.
WELL WHAT IS IT NOW?
UM, IT NOW OFFICIALLY SPANS FROM 5.3 MILLION YEARS AGO UNTIL...
UNTIL WHEN?!
...2.588 MILLION YEARS AGO.
I THINK WE NEED A REFRESHER ON THE GEOLOGIC TIMELINE OF THE AGE OF MAMMALS!
NOW WHAT WAS THAT ROOM NUMBER...?

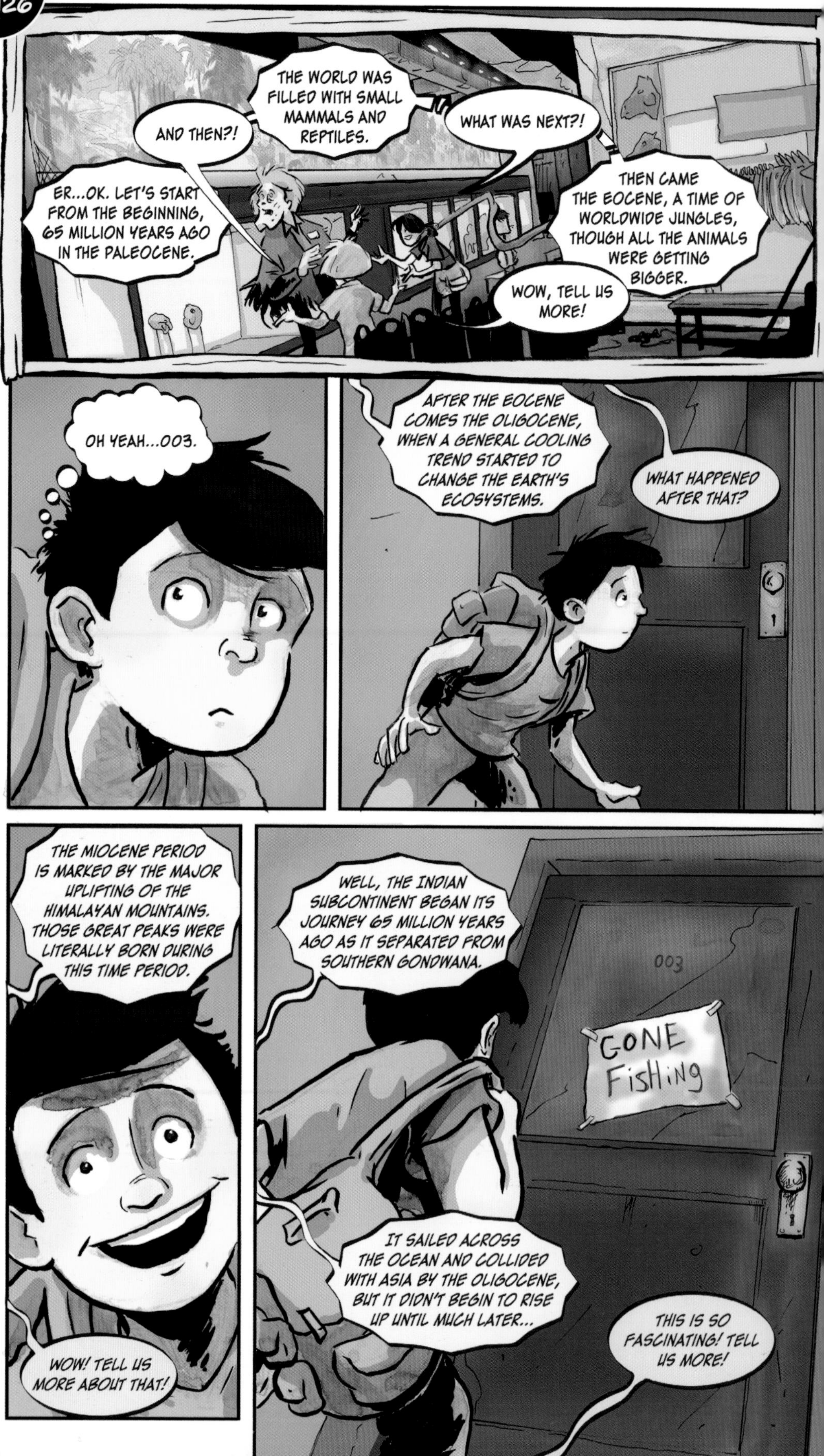
ER...OK. LET'S START FROM THE BEGINNING, 65 MILLION YEARS AGO IN THE PALEOCENE.
AND THEN?!
THE WORLD WAS FILLED WITH SMALL MAMMALS AND REPTILES.
WHAT WAS NEXT?!
THEN CAME THE EOCENE, A TIME OF WORLDWIDE JUNGLES, THOUGH ALL THE ANIMALS WERE GETTING BIGGER.
WOW, TELL US MORE!
OH YEAH...003.
AFTER THE EOCENE COMES THE OLIGOCENE, WHEN A GENERAL COOLING TREND STARTED TO CHANGE THE EARTH'S ECOSYSTEMS.
WHAT HAPPENED AFTER THAT?
THE MIOCENE PERIOD IS MARKED BY THE MAJOR UPLIFTING OF THE HIMALAYAN MOUNTAINS. THOSE GREAT PEAKS WERE LITERALLY BORN DURING THIS TIME PERIOD.
WOW! TELL US MORE ABOUT THAT!
WELL, THE INDIAN SUBCONTINENT BEGAN ITS JOURNEY 65 MILLION YEARS AGO AS IT SEPARATED FROM SOUTHERN GONDWANA.
003
GONE FISHING
IT SAILED ACROSS THE OCEAN AND COLLIDED WITH ASIA BY THE OLIGOCENE, BUT IT DIDN'T BEGIN TO RISE UP UNTIL MUCH LATER...
THIS IS SO FASCINATING! TELL US MORE!

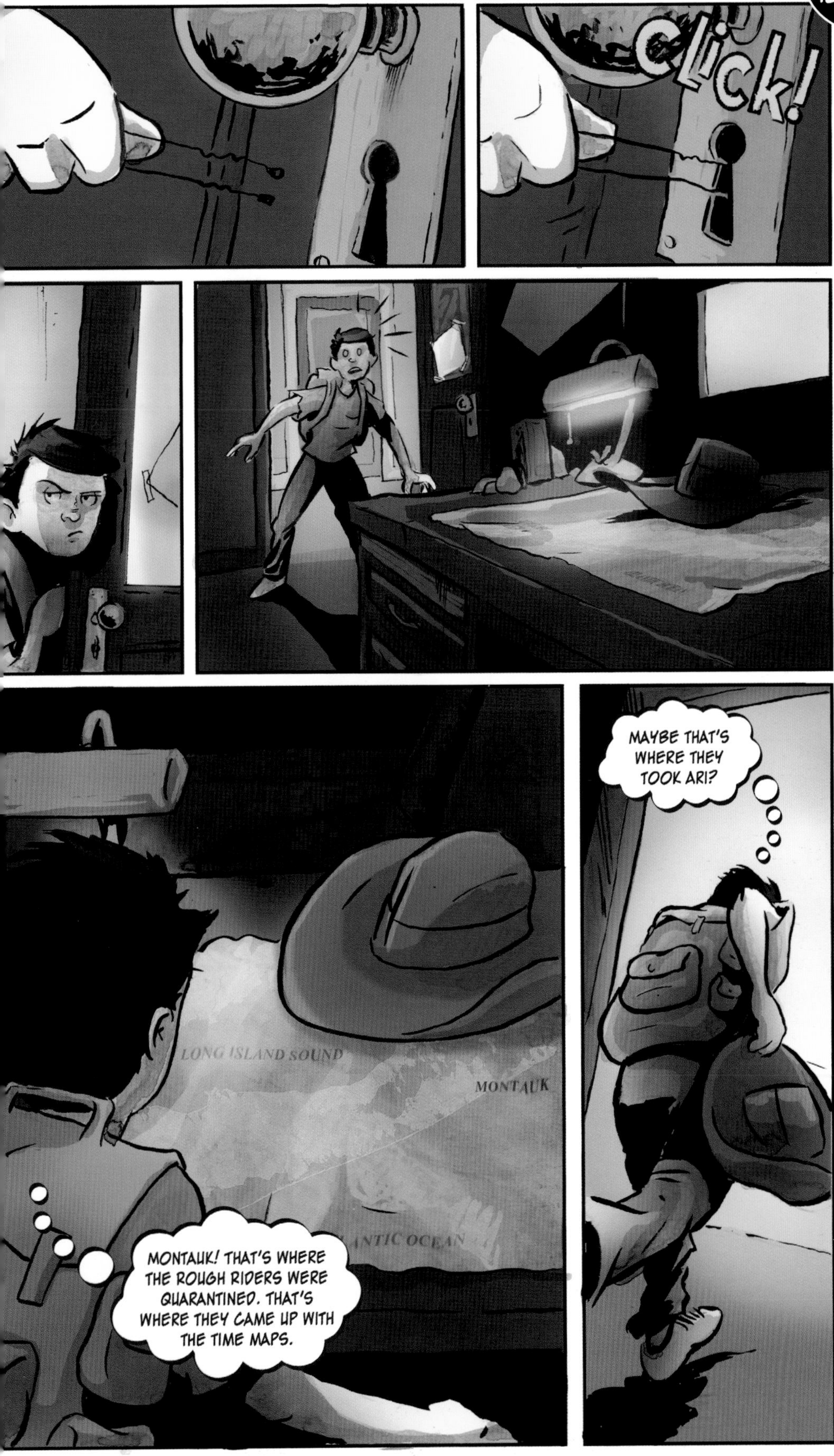
CLICK!
LONG ISLAND SOUND
MONTAUK
MONTAUK! THAT'S WHERE THE ROUGH RIDERS WERE QUARANTINED. THAT'S WHERE THEY CAME UP WITH THE TIME MAPS.
MAYBE THAT'S WHERE THEY TOOK ARI?

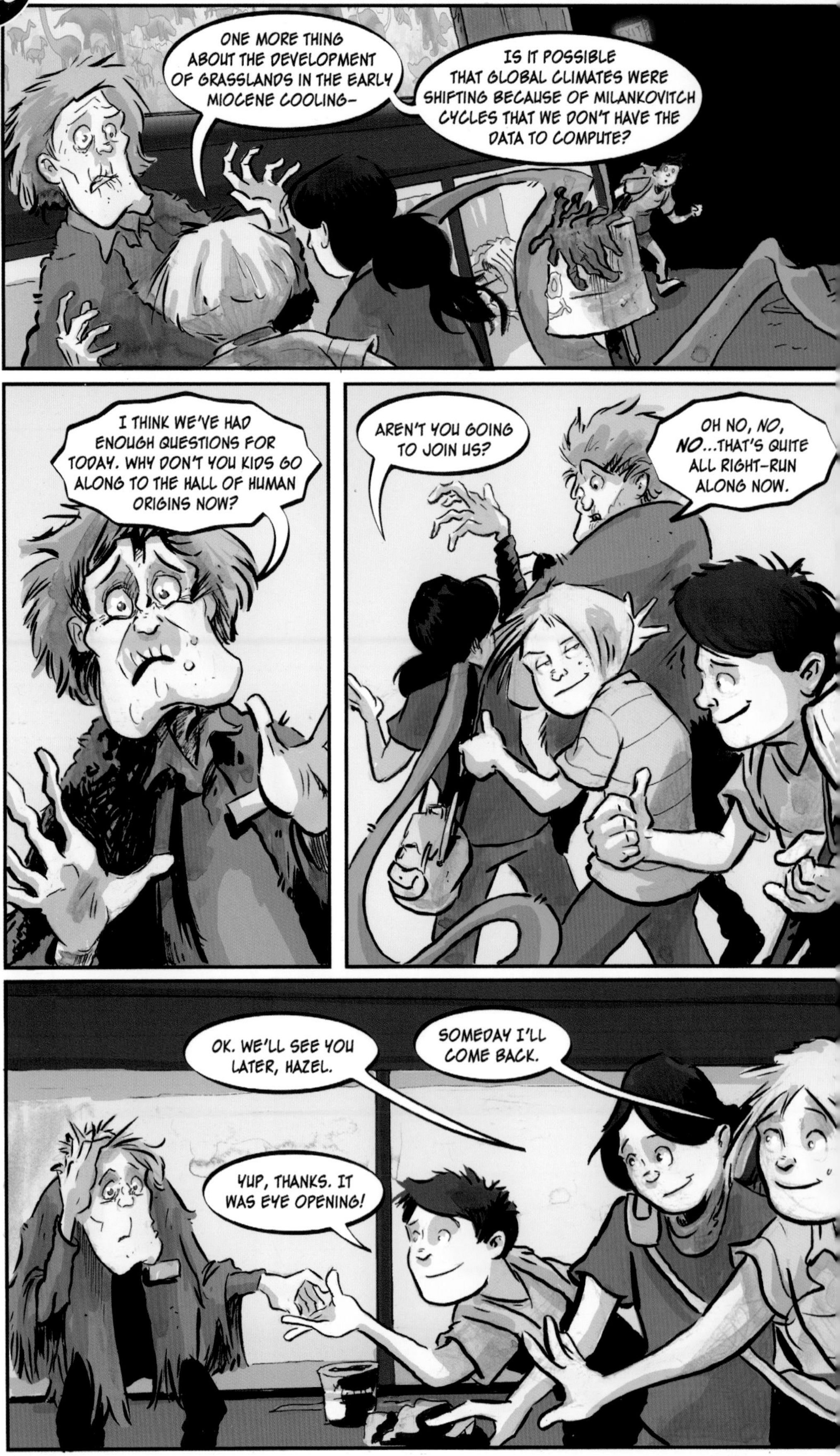
ONE MORE THING ABOUT THE DEVELOPMENT OF GRASSLANDS IN THE EARLY MIOCENE COOLING–
IS IT POSSIBLE THAT GLOBAL CLIMATES WERE SHIFTING BECAUSE OF MILANKOVITCH CYCLES THAT WE DON'T HAVE THE DATA TO COMPUTE?
EXIT
I THINK WE'VE HAD ENOUGH QUESTIONS FOR TODAY. WHY DON'T YOU KIDS GO ALONG TO THE HALL OF HUMAN ORIGINS NOW?
AREN'T YOU GOING TO JOIN US?
OH NO, *NO*, ***NO***...THAT'S QUITE ALL RIGHT–RUN ALONG NOW.
OK. WE'LL SEE YOU LATER, HAZEL.
SOMEDAY I'LL COME BACK.
YUP, THANKS. IT WAS EYE OPENING!

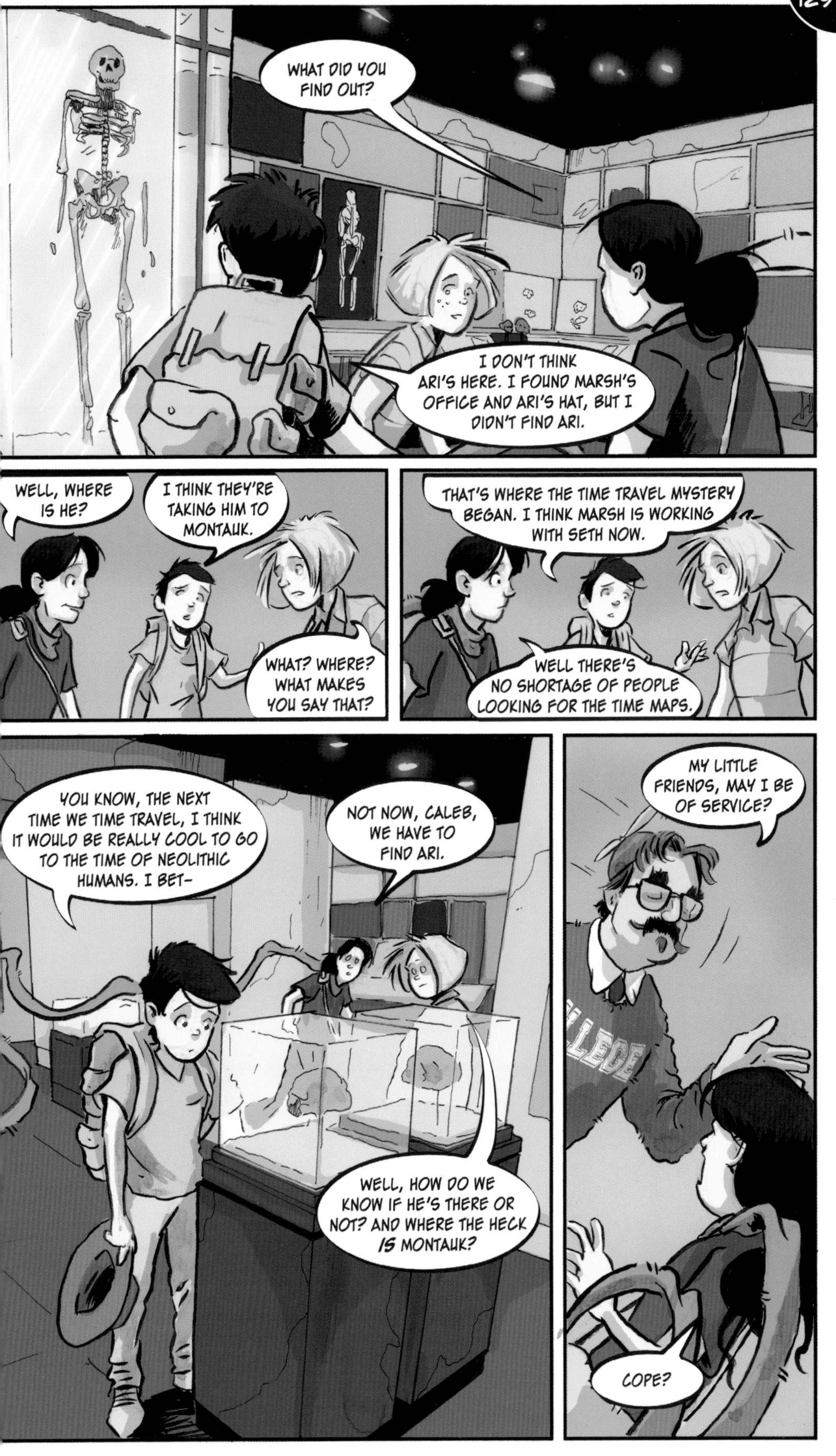
WHAT DID YOU FIND OUT?
I DON'T THINK ARI'S HERE. I FOUND MARSH'S OFFICE AND ARI'S HAT, BUT I DIDN'T FIND ARI.
WELL, WHERE IS HE?
I THINK THEY'RE TAKING HIM TO MONTAUK.
WHAT? WHERE? WHAT MAKES YOU SAY THAT?
THAT'S WHERE THE TIME TRAVEL MYSTERY BEGAN. I THINK MARSH IS WORKING WITH SETH NOW.
WELL THERE'S NO SHORTAGE OF PEOPLE LOOKING FOR THE TIME MAPS.
YOU KNOW, THE NEXT TIME WE TIME TRAVEL, I THINK IT WOULD BE REALLY COOL TO GO TO THE TIME OF NEOLITHIC HUMANS. I BET–
NOT NOW, CALEB, WE HAVE TO FIND ARI.
WELL, HOW DO WE KNOW IF HE'S THERE OR NOT? AND WHERE THE HECK *IS* MONTAUK?
MY LITTLE FRIENDS, MAY I BE OF SERVICE?
LLEGE
COPE?

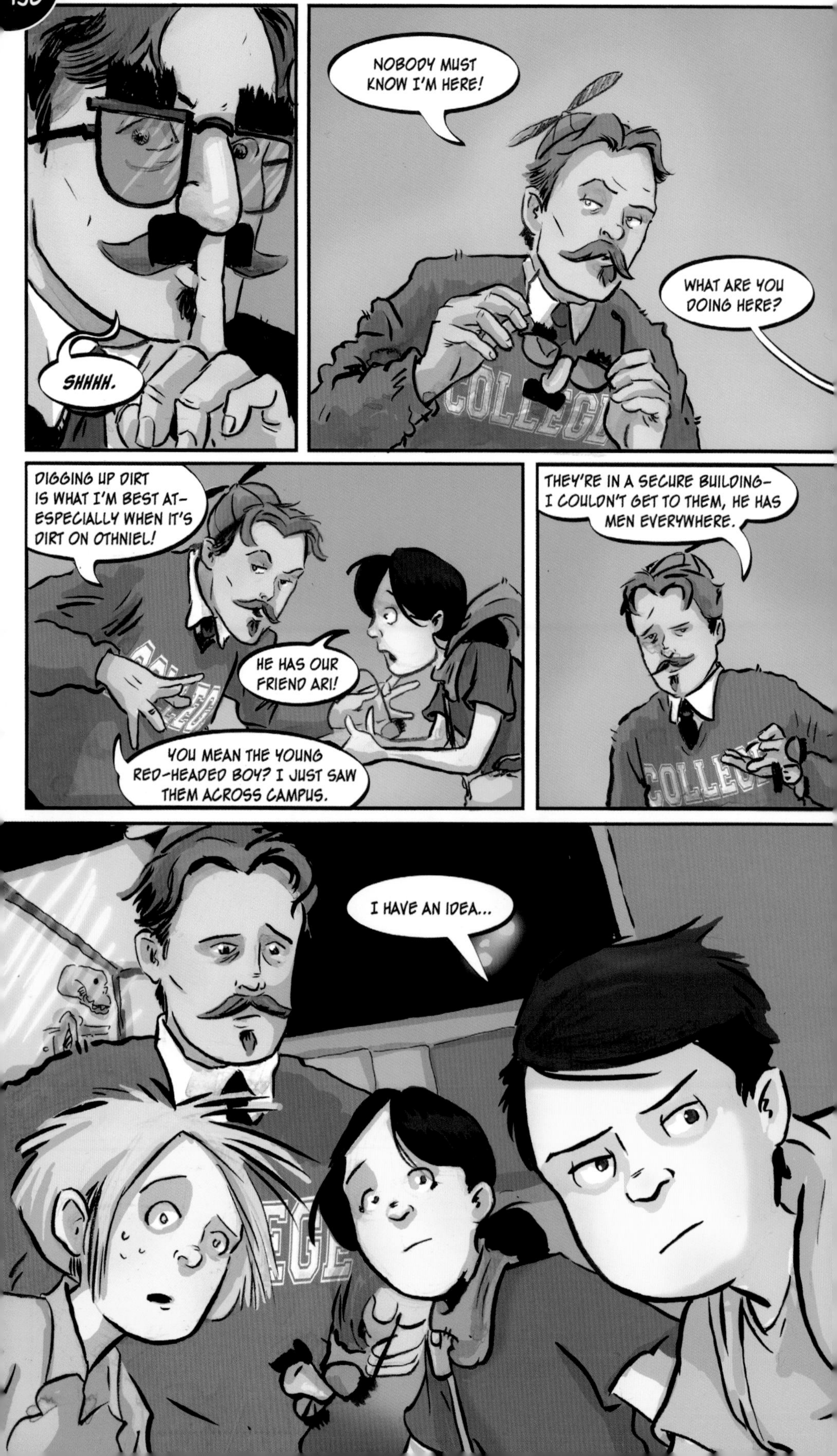
SHHHH.
NOBODY MUST KNOW I'M HERE!
WHAT ARE YOU DOING HERE?
COLLEGE
DIGGING UP DIRT IS WHAT I'M BEST AT- ESPECIALLY WHEN IT'S DIRT ON OTHNIEL!
HE HAS OUR FRIEND ARI!
YOU MEAN THE YOUNG RED-HEADED BOY? I JUST SAW THEM ACROSS CAMPUS.
THEY'RE IN A SECURE BUILDING- I COULDN'T GET TO THEM, HE HAS MEN EVERYWHERE.
I HAVE AN IDEA...

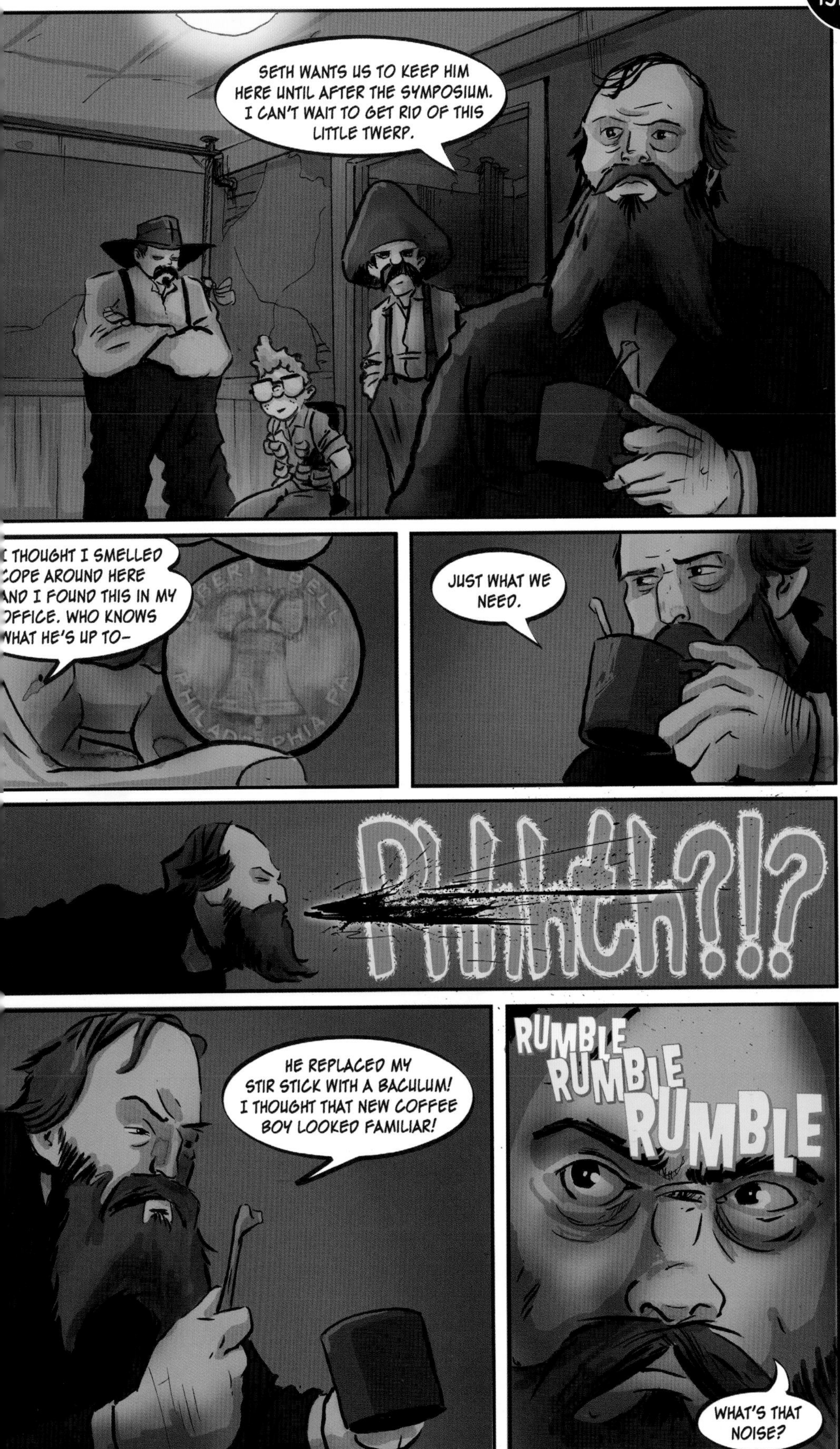
SETH WANTS US TO KEEP HIM HERE UNTIL AFTER THE SYMPOSIUM. I CAN'T WAIT TO GET RID OF THIS LITTLE TWERP.
I THOUGHT I SMELLED COPE AROUND HERE AND I FOUND THIS IN MY OFFICE. WHO KNOWS WHAT HE'S UP TO-
LIBERTY BELL
PHILADELPHIA PA
JUST WHAT WE NEED.
PHHHCH?!?
HE REPLACED MY STIR STICK WITH A BACULUM! I THOUGHT THAT NEW COFFEE BOY LOOKED FAMILIAR!
RUMBLE RUMBLE RUMBLE
WHAT'S THAT NOISE?

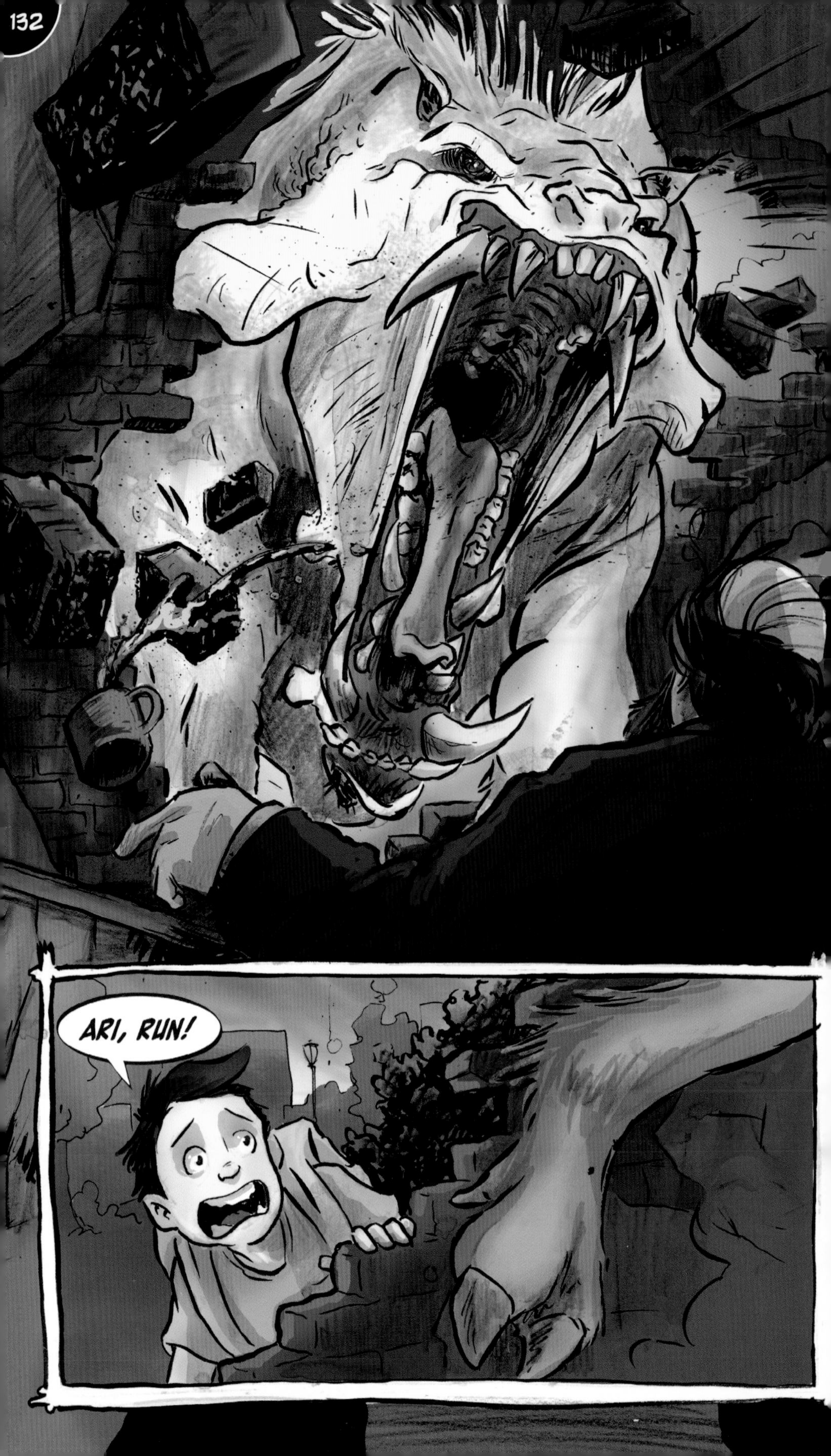
ARI, RUN!

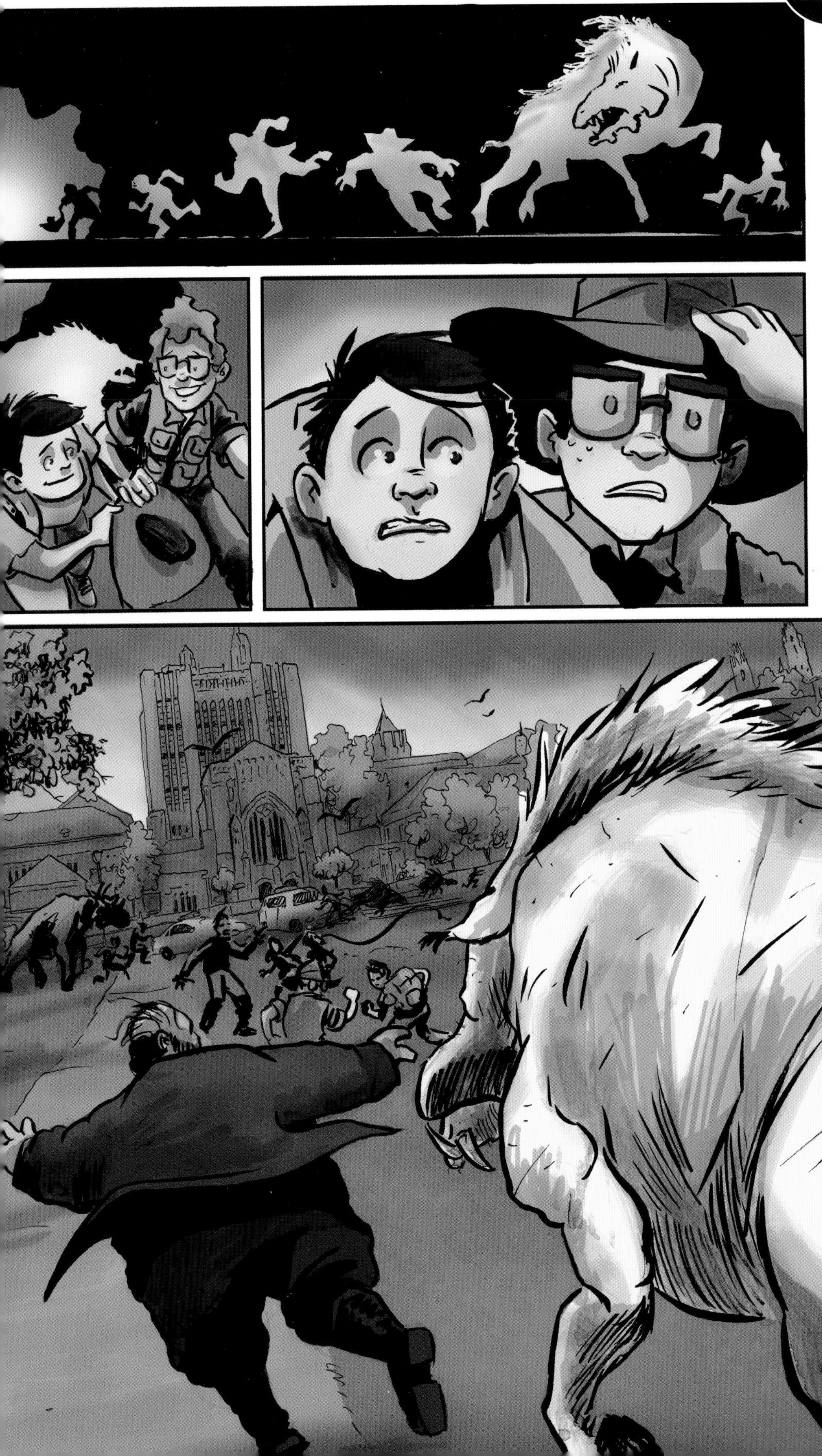

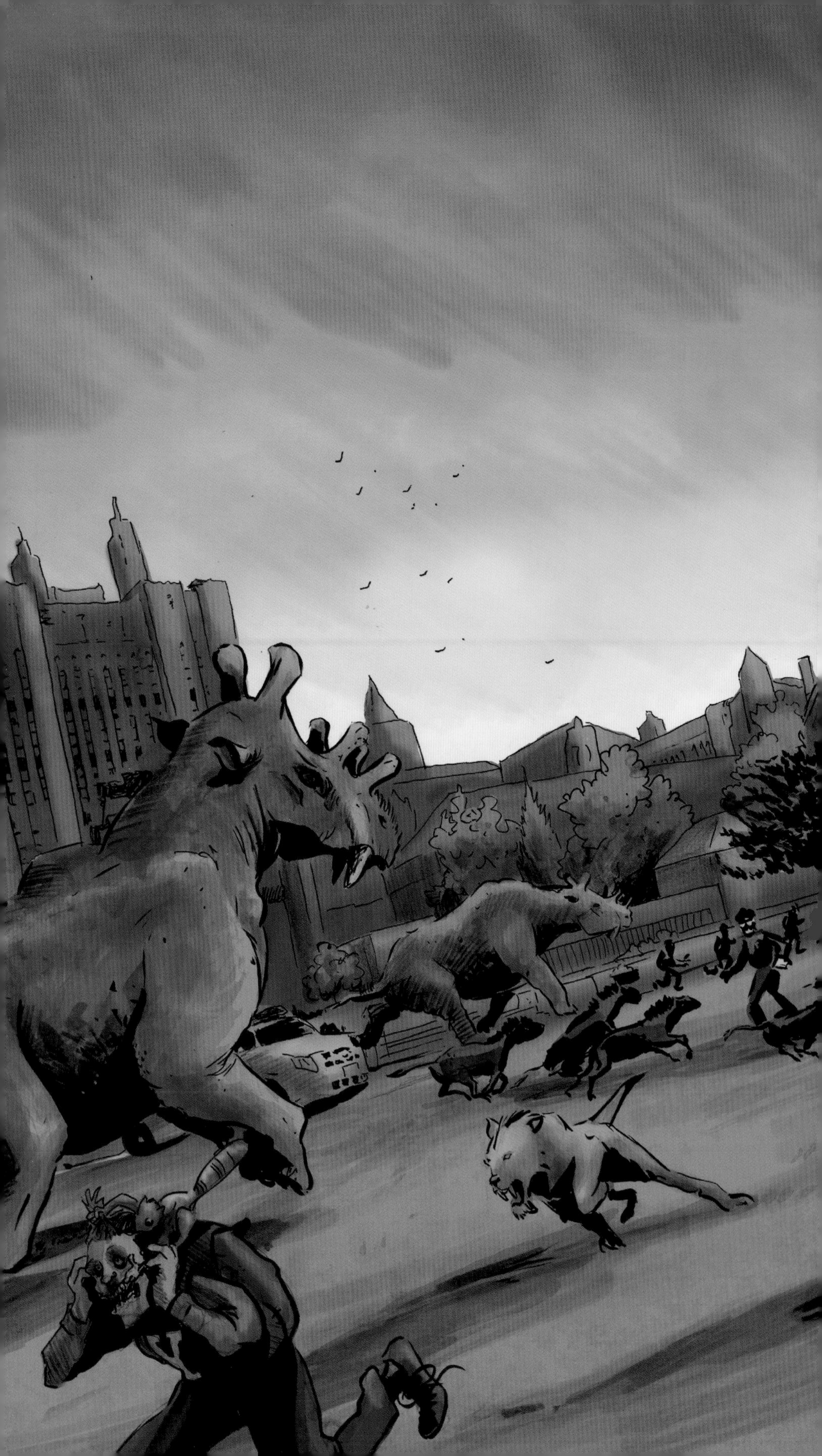

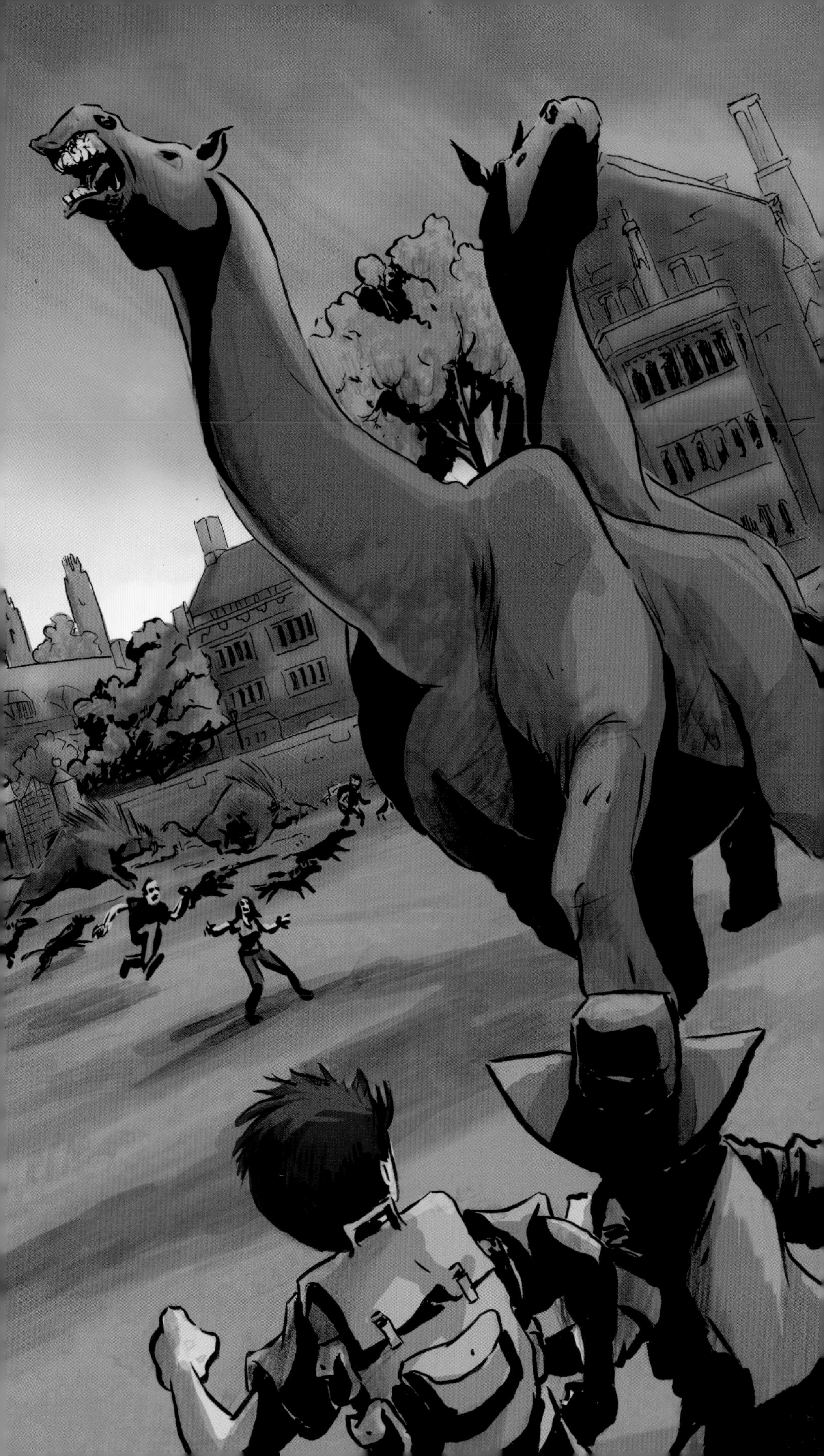

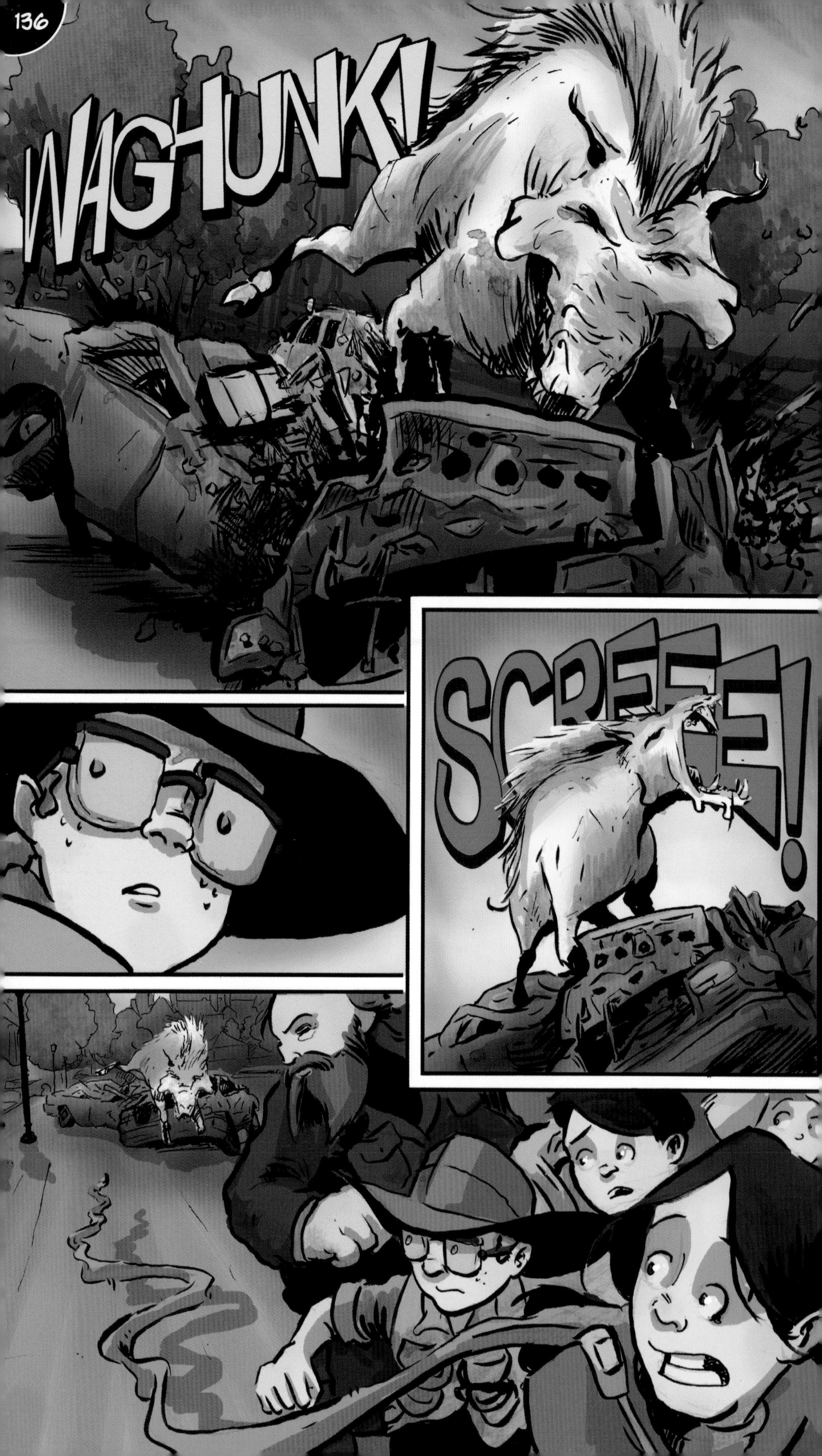
WAGHUNK!
SCREEE!

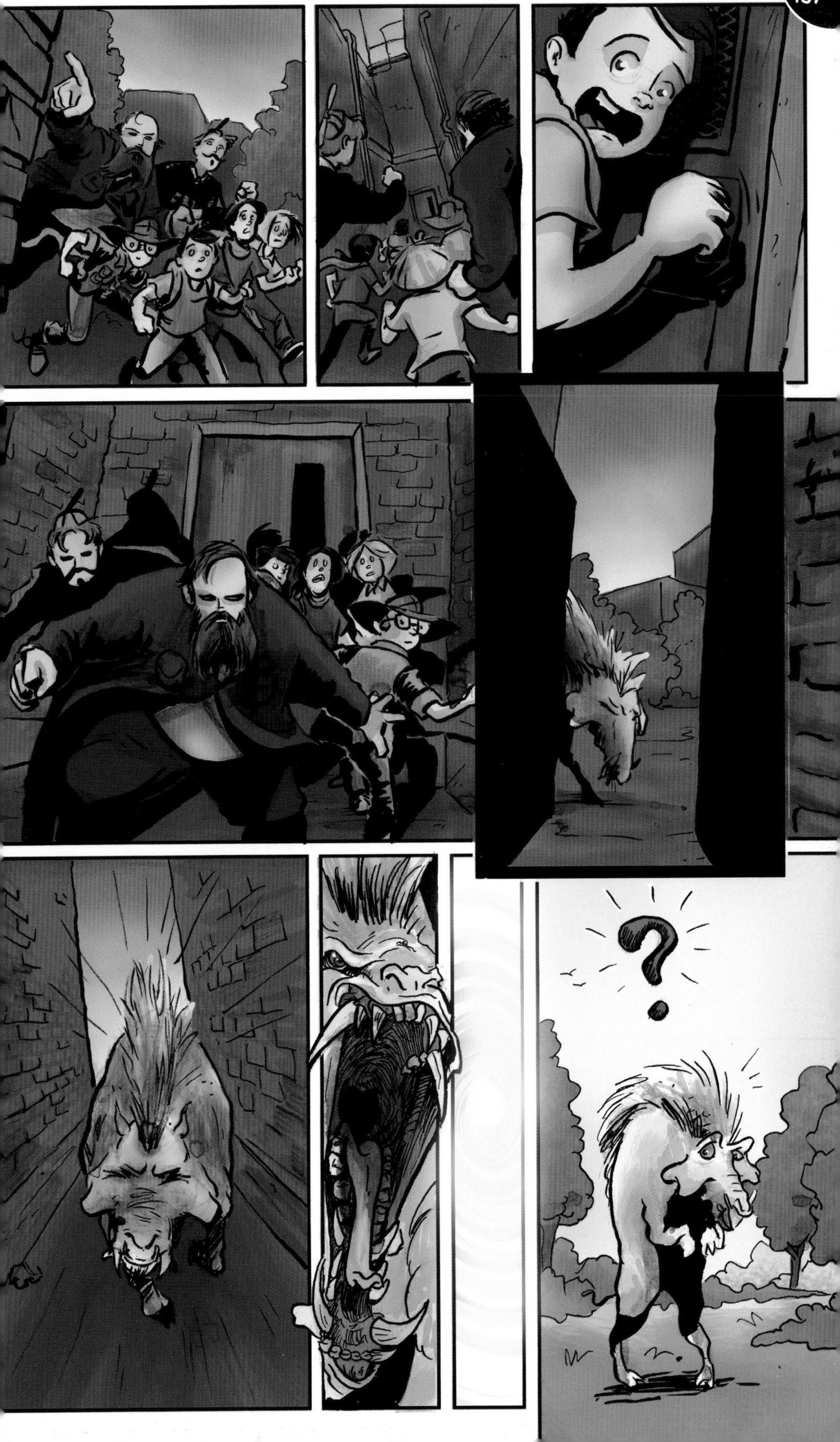

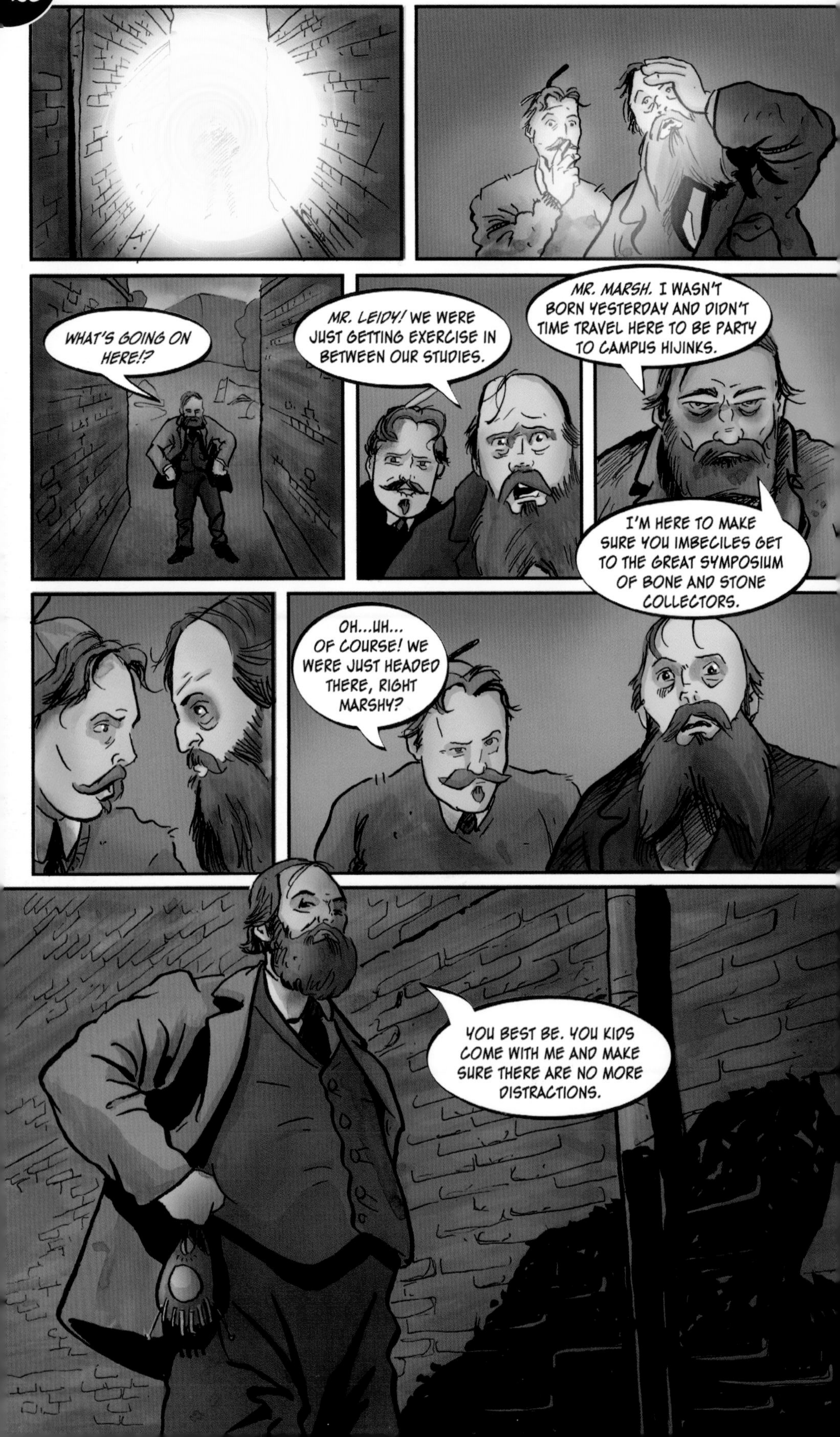
WHAT'S GOING ON HERE!?
MR. LEIDY! WE WERE JUST GETTING EXERCISE IN BETWEEN OUR STUDIES.
MR. MARSH. I WASN'T BORN YESTERDAY AND DIDN'T TIME TRAVEL HERE TO BE PARTY TO CAMPUS HIJINKS.
I'M HERE TO MAKE SURE YOU IMBECILES GET TO THE GREAT SYMPOSIUM OF BONE AND STONE COLLECTORS.
OH...UH... OF COURSE! WE WERE JUST HEADED THERE, RIGHT MARSHY?
YOU BEST BE. YOU KIDS COME WITH ME AND MAKE SURE THERE ARE NO MORE DISTRACTIONS.

STUDENT HANDBOOK

Academy of
Planetary
Evolution

10

"Great Symposium"

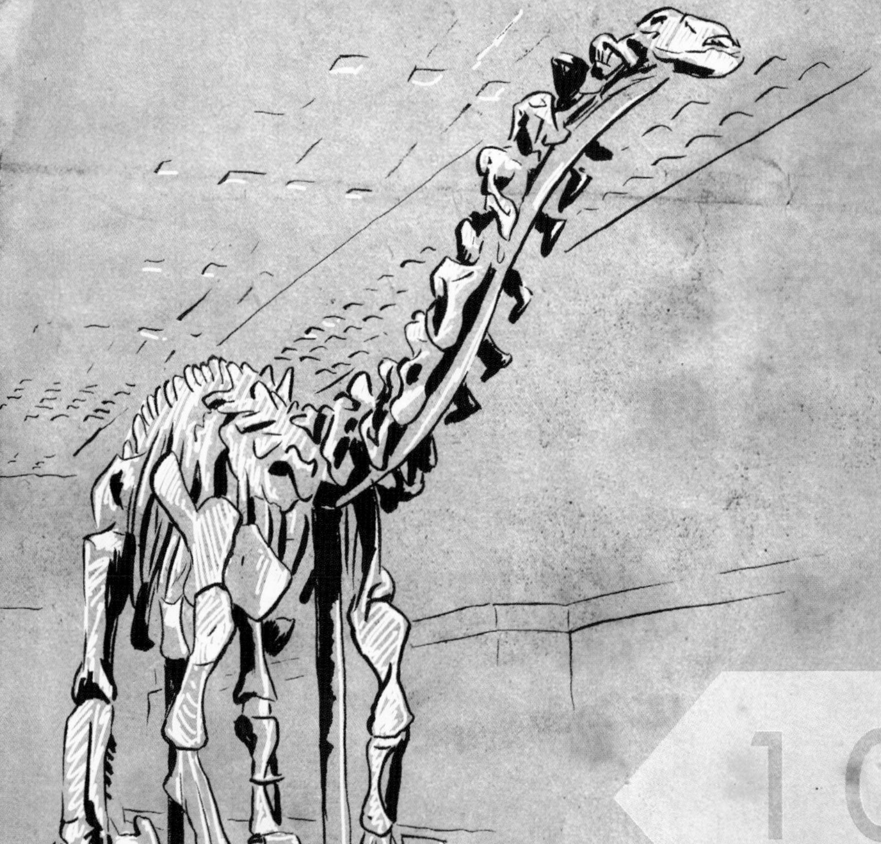

10

MONTAUK INDUSTRIES

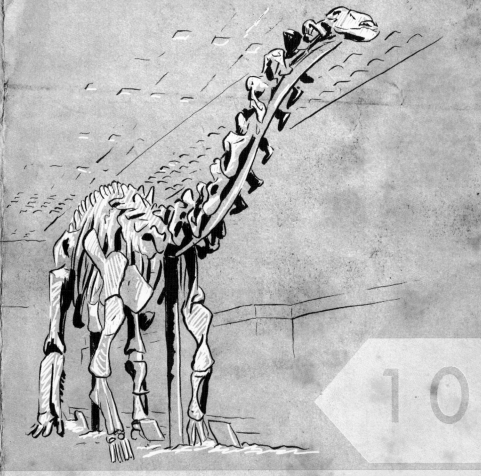

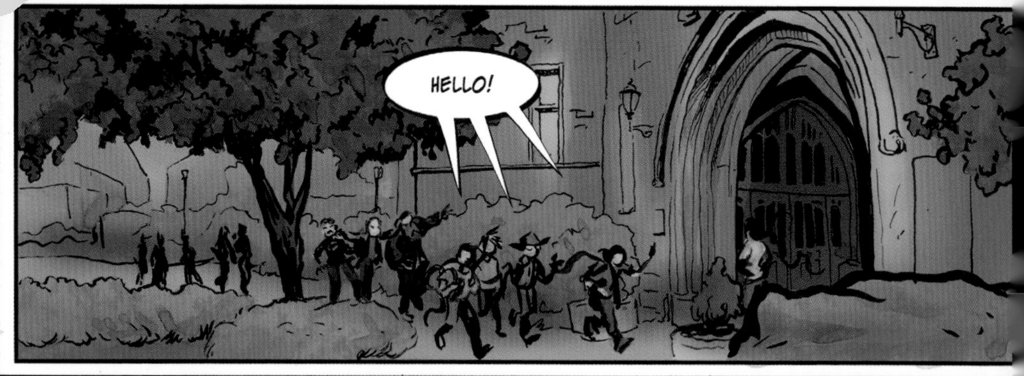
HELLO!

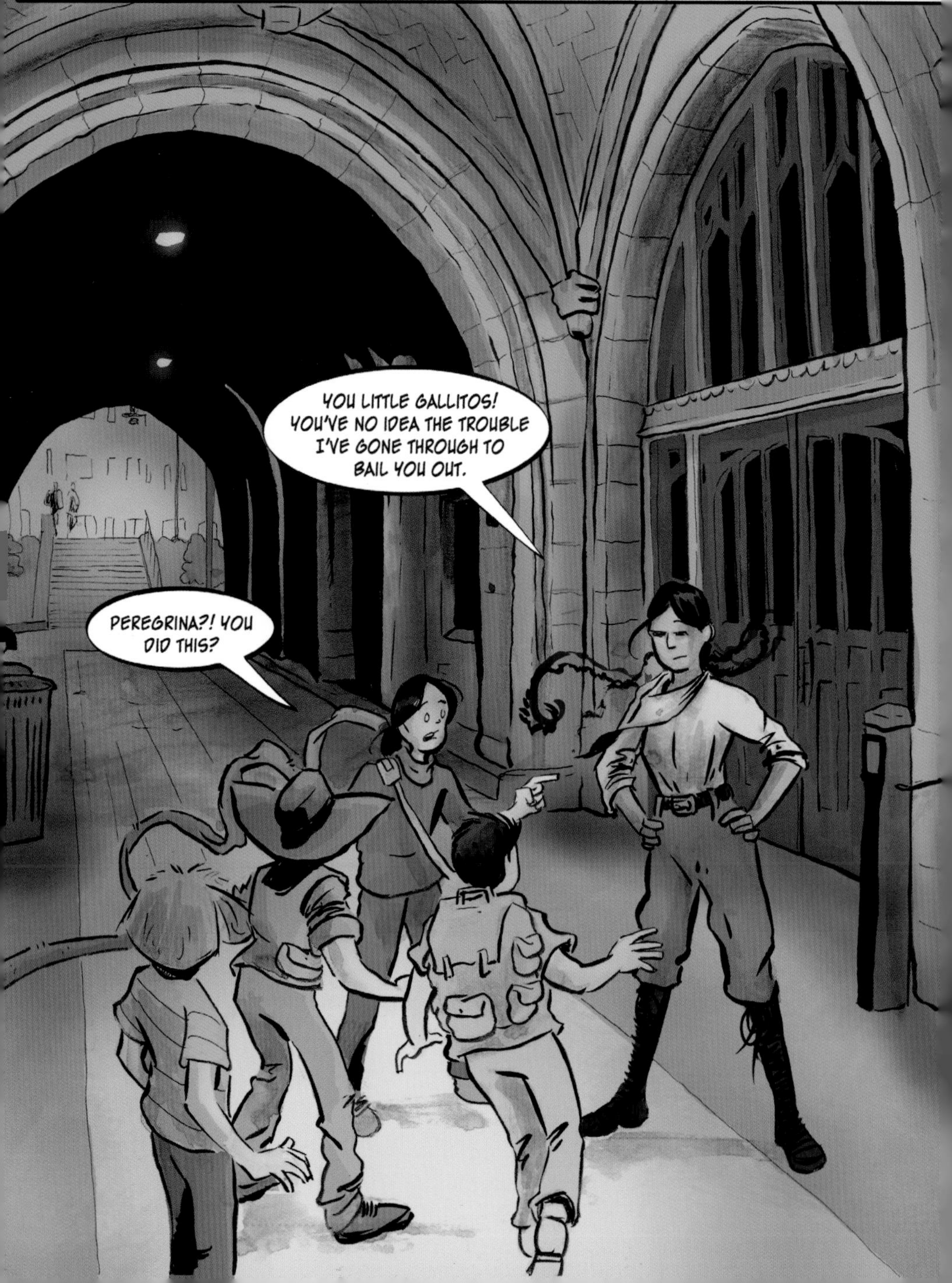
YOU LITTLE GALLITOS! YOU'VE NO IDEA THE TROUBLE I'VE GONE THROUGH TO BAIL YOU OUT.
PEREGRINA?! YOU DID THIS?

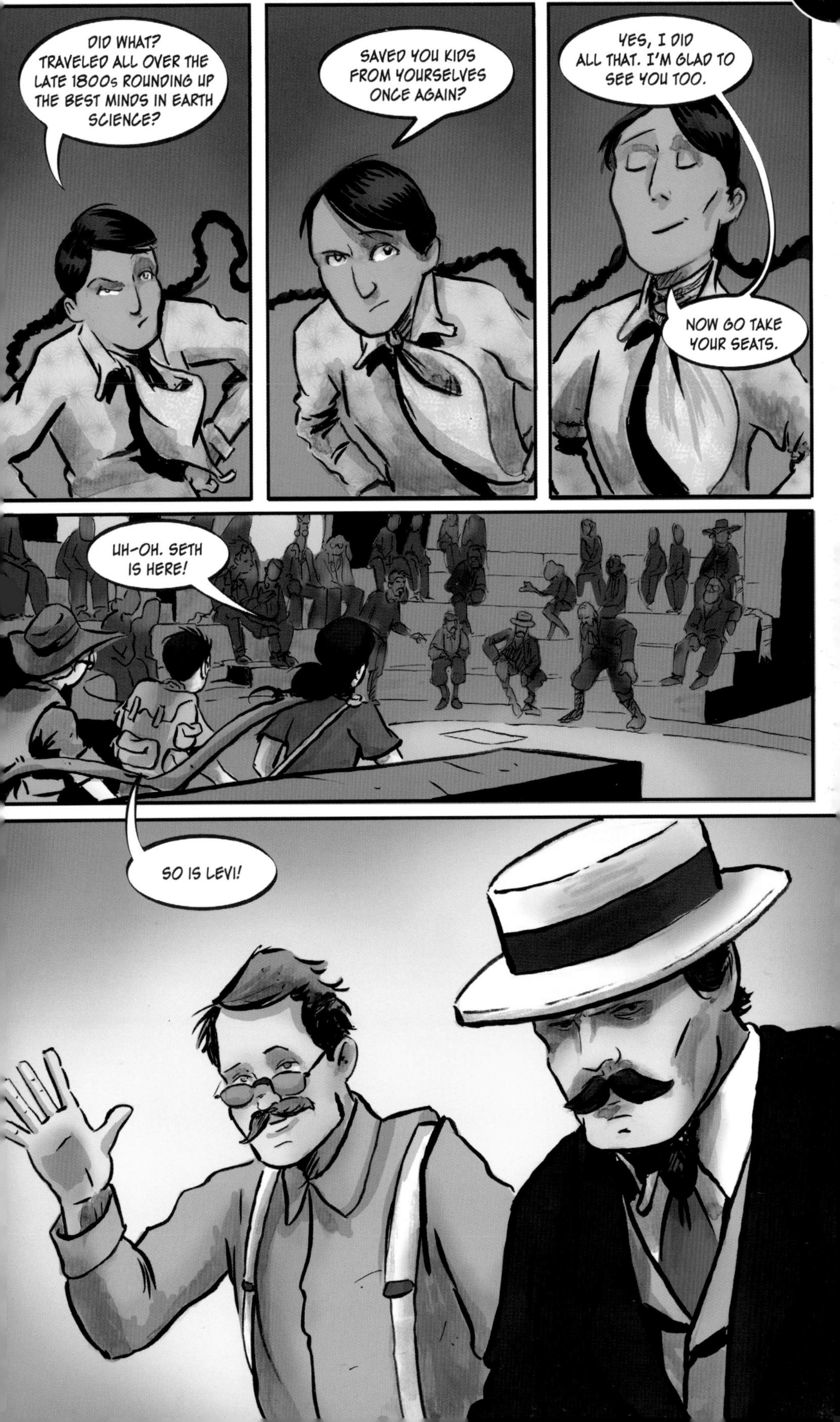
DID WHAT? TRAVELED ALL OVER THE LATE 1800s ROUNDING UP THE BEST MINDS IN EARTH SCIENCE?
SAVED YOU KIDS FROM YOURSELVES ONCE AGAIN?
YES, I DID ALL THAT. I'M GLAD TO SEE YOU TOO.
NOW GO TAKE YOUR SEATS.
UH-OH. SETH IS HERE!
SO IS LEVI!

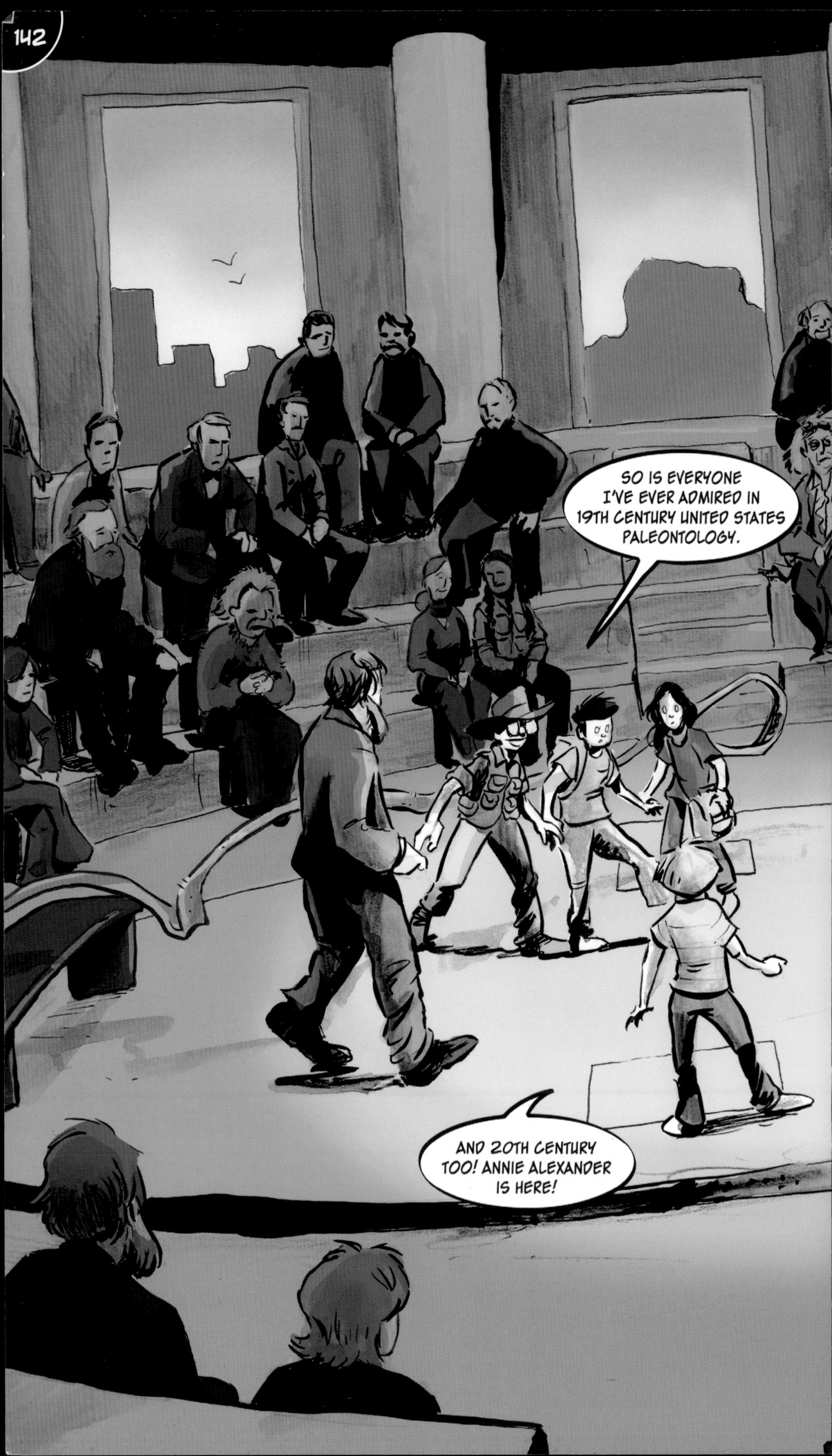
SO IS EVERYONE I'VE EVER ADMIRED IN 19TH CENTURY UNITED STATES PALEONTOLOGY.
AND 20TH CENTURY TOO! ANNIE ALEXANDER IS HERE!

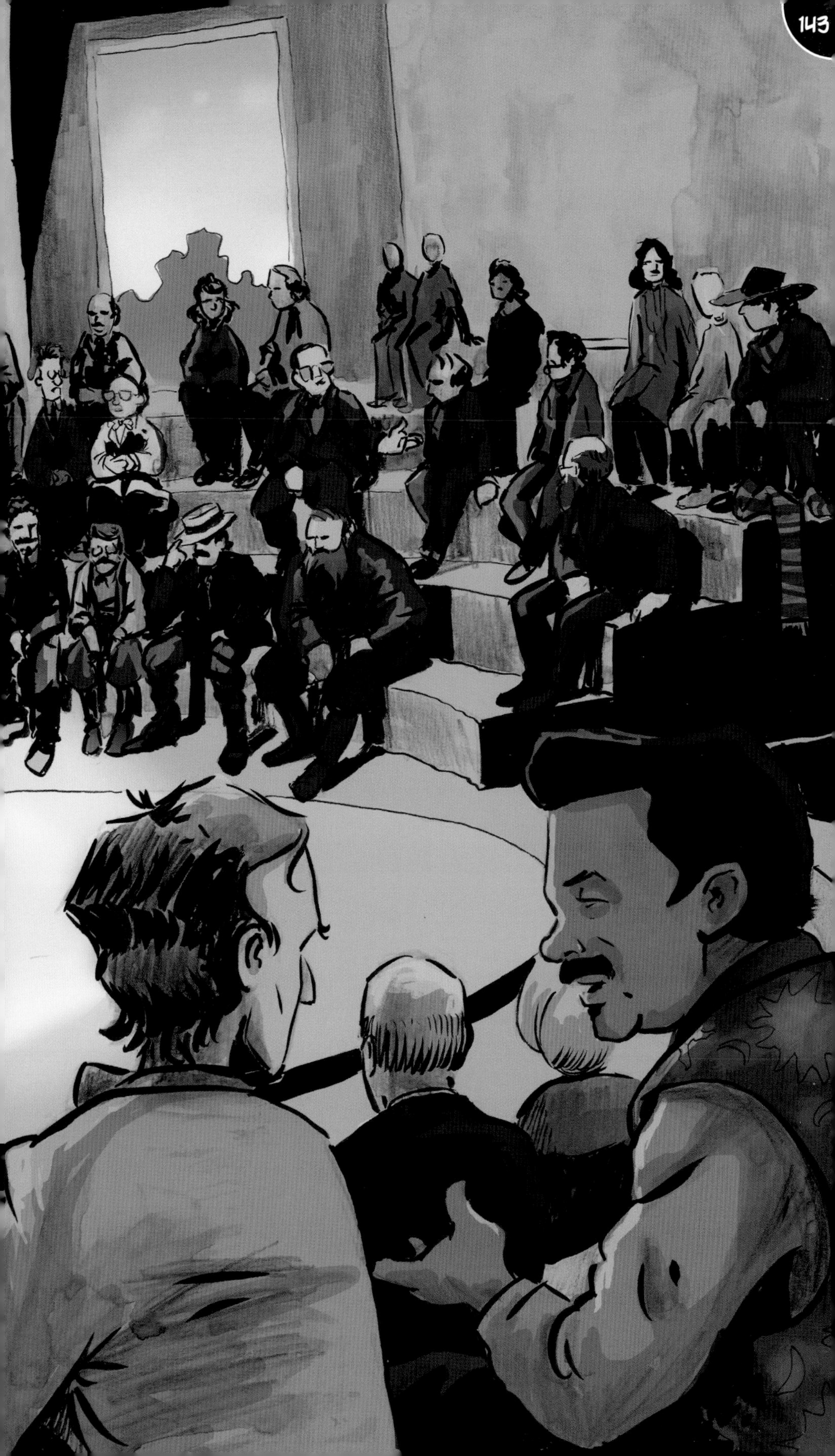

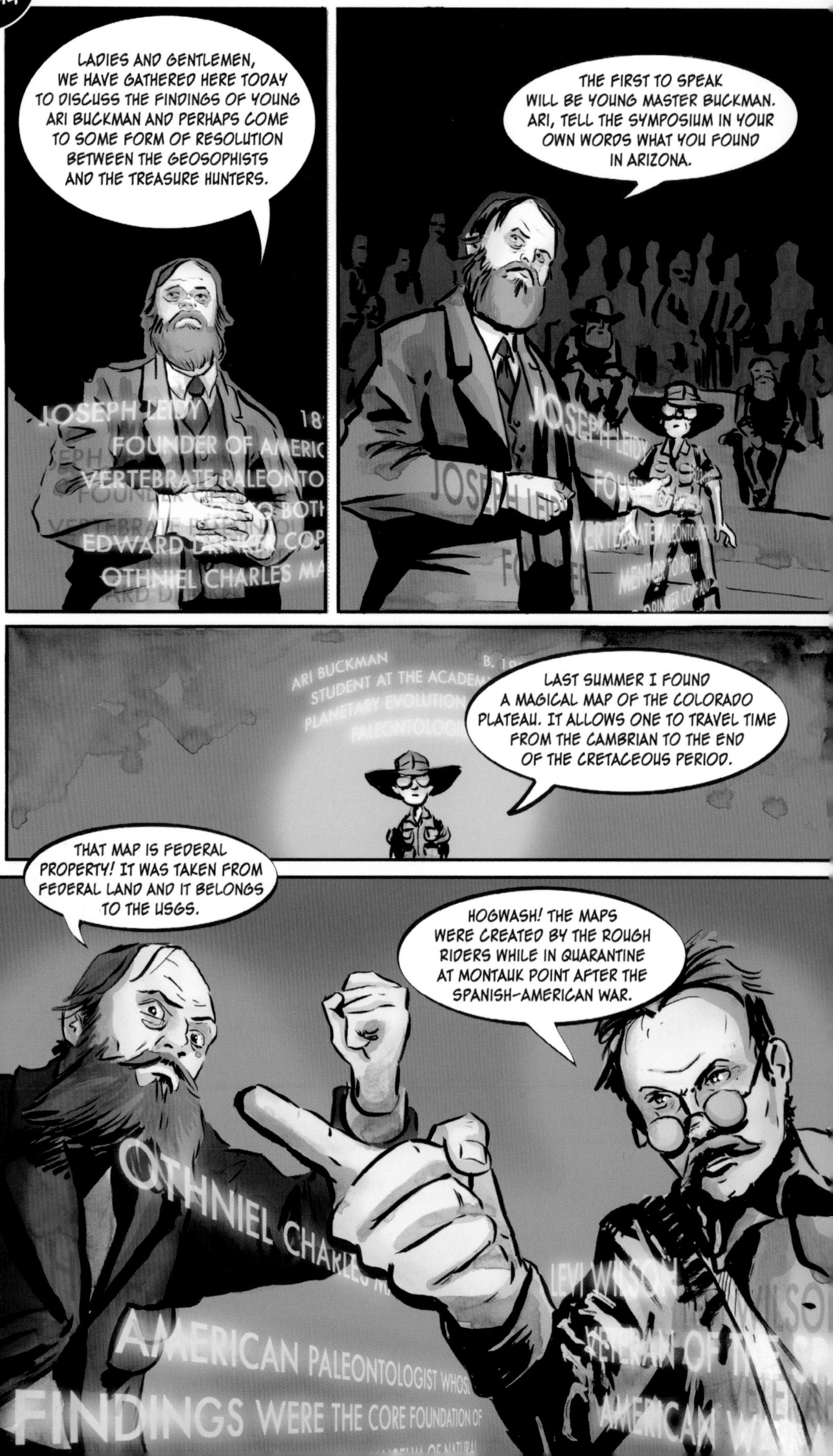
LADIES AND GENTLEMEN, WE HAVE GATHERED HERE TODAY TO DISCUSS THE FINDINGS OF YOUNG ARI BUCKMAN AND PERHAPS COME TO SOME FORM OF RESOLUTION BETWEEN THE GEOSOPHISTS AND THE TREASURE HUNTERS.
THE FIRST TO SPEAK WILL BE YOUNG MASTER BUCKMAN. ARI, TELL THE SYMPOSIUM IN YOUR OWN WORDS WHAT YOU FOUND IN ARIZONA.
LAST SUMMER I FOUND A MAGICAL MAP OF THE COLORADO PLATEAU. IT ALLOWS ONE TO TRAVEL TIME FROM THE CAMBRIAN TO THE END OF THE CRETACEOUS PERIOD.
THAT MAP IS FEDERAL PROPERTY! IT WAS TAKEN FROM FEDERAL LAND AND IT BELONGS TO THE USGS.
HOGWASH! THE MAPS WERE CREATED BY THE ROUGH RIDERS WHILE IN QUARANTINE AT MONTAUK POINT AFTER THE SPANISH-AMERICAN WAR.

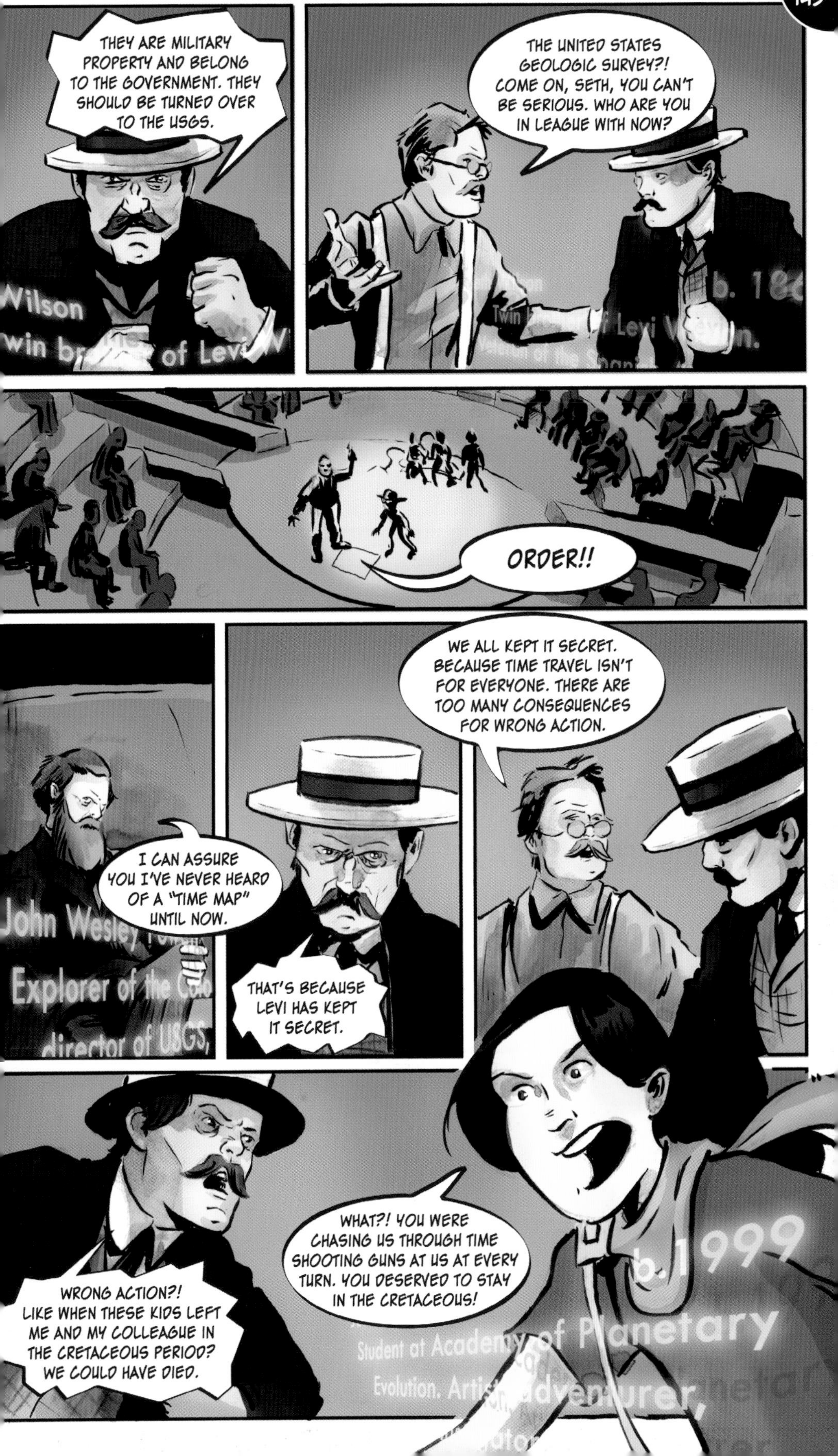
THEY ARE MILITARY PROPERTY AND BELONG TO THE GOVERNMENT. THEY SHOULD BE TURNED OVER TO THE USGS.
Wilson
THE UNITED STATES GEOLOGIC SURVEY?! COME ON, SETH, YOU CAN'T BE SERIOUS. WHO ARE YOU IN LEAGUE WITH NOW?
ORDER!!
I CAN ASSURE YOU I'VE NEVER HEARD OF A "TIME MAP" UNTIL NOW.
THAT'S BECAUSE LEVI HAS KEPT IT SECRET.
WE ALL KEPT IT SECRET. BECAUSE TIME TRAVEL ISN'T FOR EVERYONE. THERE ARE TOO MANY CONSEQUENCES FOR WRONG ACTION.
WRONG ACTION?! LIKE WHEN THESE KIDS LEFT ME AND MY COLLEAGUE IN THE CRETACEOUS PERIOD? WE COULD HAVE DIED.
WHAT?! YOU WERE CHASING US THROUGH TIME SHOOTING GUNS AT US AT EVERY TURN. YOU DESERVED TO STAY IN THE CRETACEOUS!
b.1999
Student at Academy of Planetary

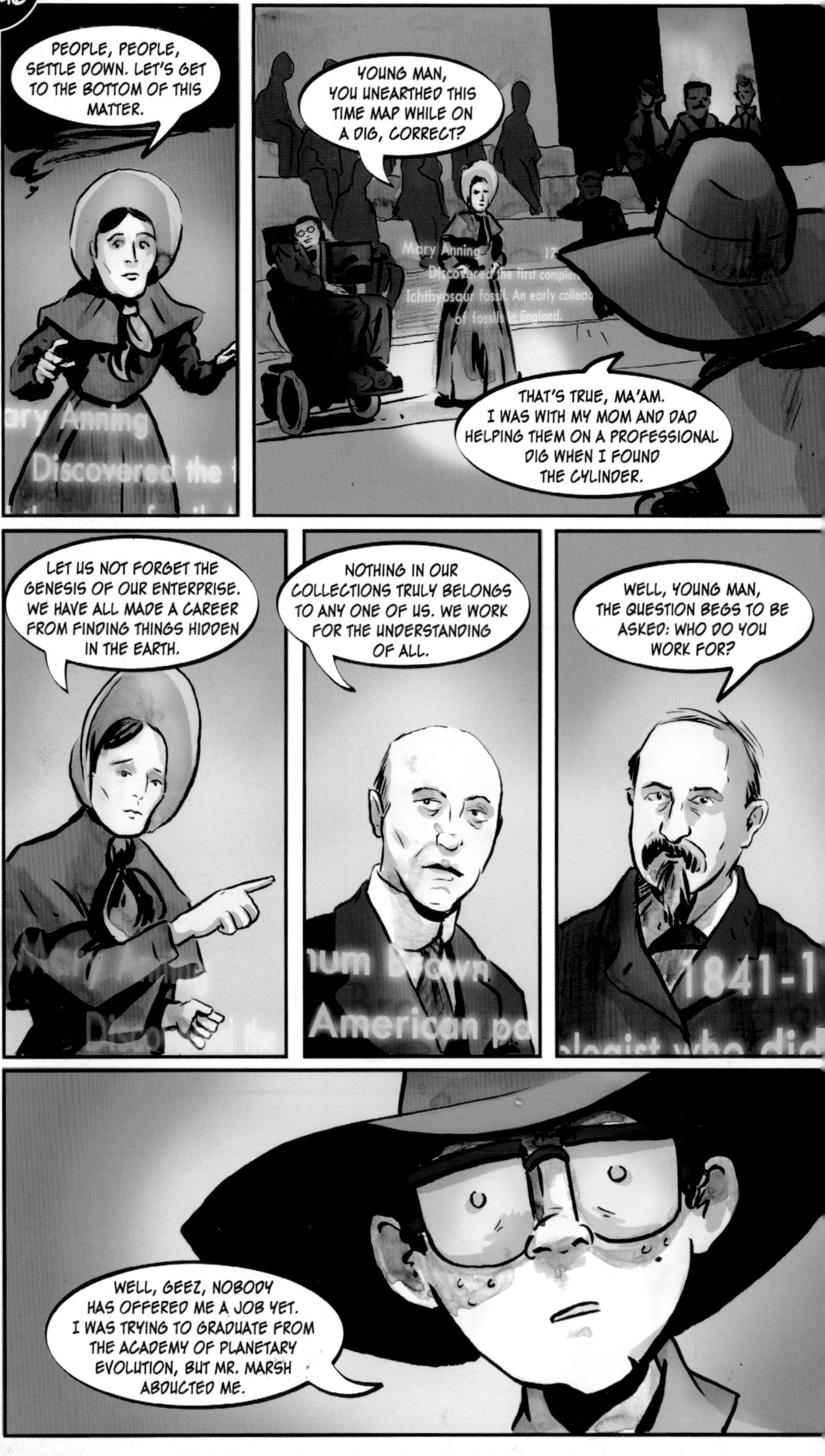
PEOPLE, PEOPLE, SETTLE DOWN. LET'S GET TO THE BOTTOM OF THIS MATTER.
YOUNG MAN, YOU UNEARTHED THIS TIME MAP WHILE ON A DIG, CORRECT?
Mary Anning
THAT'S TRUE, MA'AM. I WAS WITH MY MOM AND DAD HELPING THEM ON A PROFESSIONAL DIG WHEN I FOUND THE CYLINDER.
LET US NOT FORGET THE GENESIS OF OUR ENTERPRISE. WE HAVE ALL MADE A CAREER FROM FINDING THINGS HIDDEN IN THE EARTH.
NOTHING IN OUR COLLECTIONS TRULY BELONGS TO ANY ONE OF US. WE WORK FOR THE UNDERSTANDING OF ALL.
WELL, YOUNG MAN, THE QUESTION BEGS TO BE ASKED: WHO DO YOU WORK FOR?
WELL, GEEZ, NOBODY HAS OFFERED ME A JOB YET. I WAS TRYING TO GRADUATE FROM THE ACADEMY OF PLANETARY EVOLUTION, BUT MR. MARSH ABDUCTED ME.

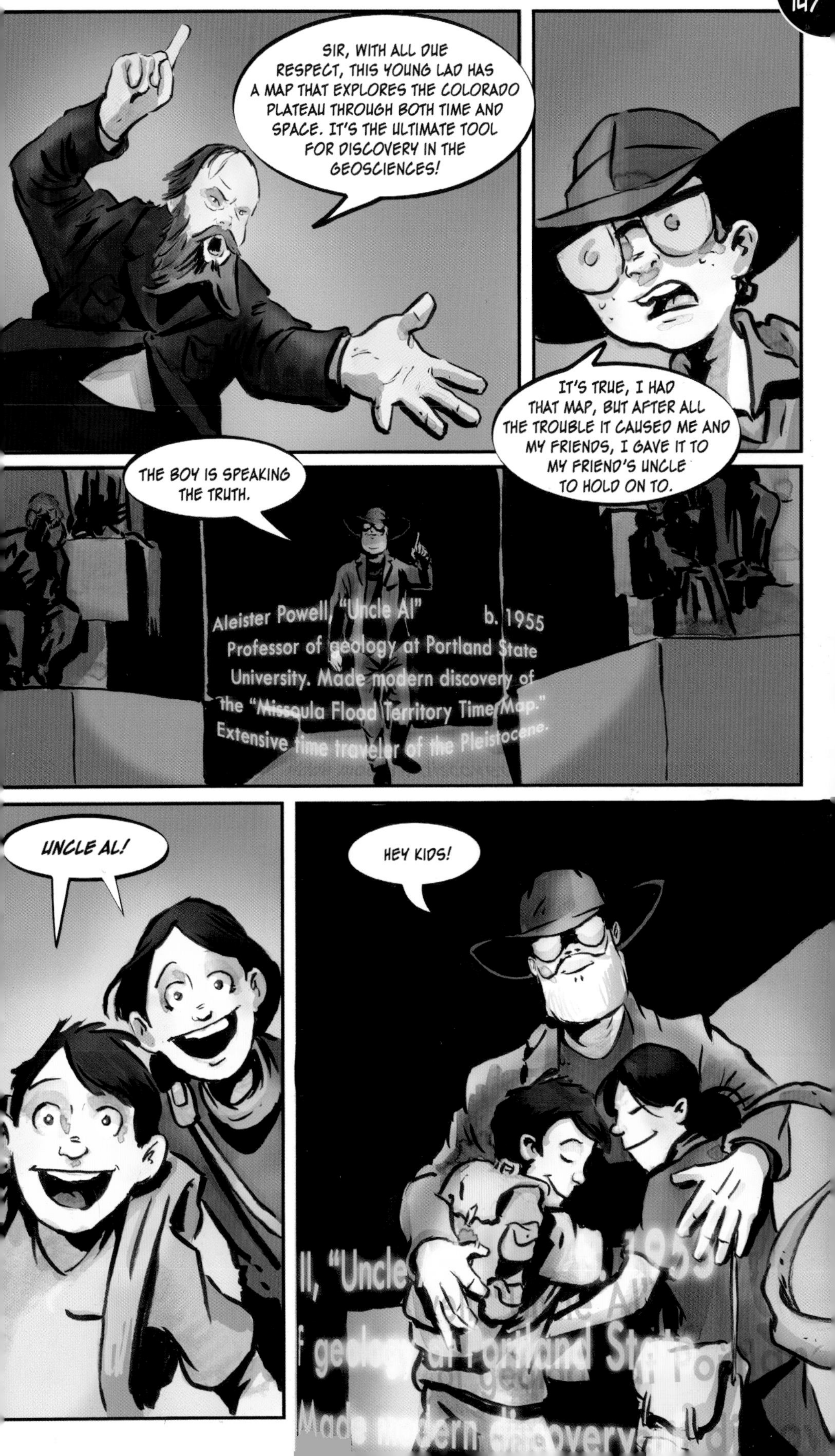
SIR, WITH ALL DUE RESPECT, THIS YOUNG LAD HAS A MAP THAT EXPLORES THE COLORADO PLATEAU THROUGH BOTH TIME AND SPACE. IT'S THE ULTIMATE TOOL FOR DISCOVERY IN THE GEOSCIENCES!
IT'S TRUE, I HAD THAT MAP, BUT AFTER ALL THE TROUBLE IT CAUSED ME AND MY FRIENDS, I GAVE IT TO MY FRIEND'S UNCLE TO HOLD ON TO.
THE BOY IS SPEAKING THE TRUTH.
Aleister Powell, “Uncle Al” b. 1955
Professor of geology at Portland State University. Made modern discovery of the “Missoula Flood Territory Time Map.” Extensive time traveler of the Pleistocene.
UNCLE AL!
HEY KIDS!

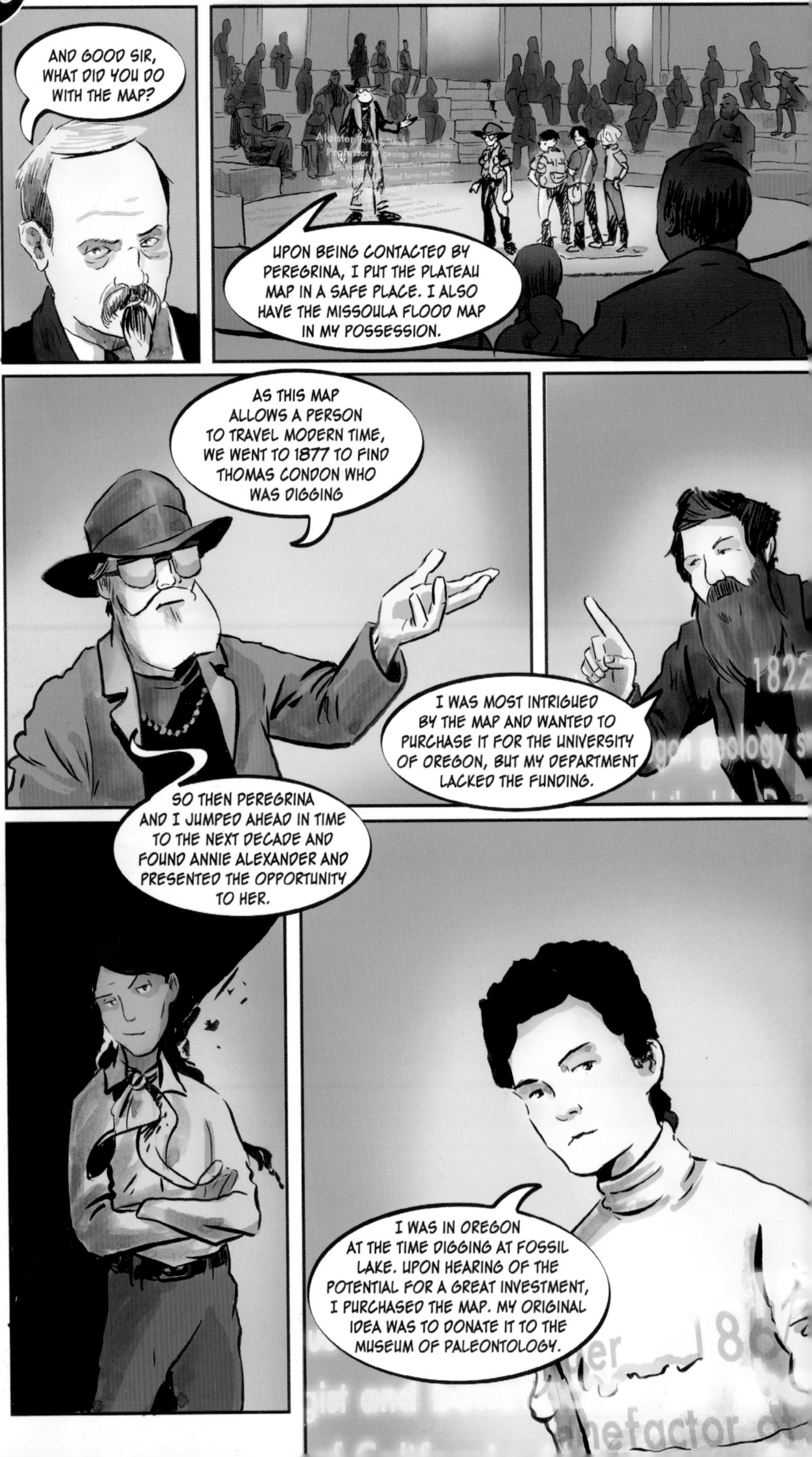
AND GOOD SIR, WHAT DID YOU DO WITH THE MAP?
UPON BEING CONTACTED BY PEREGRINA, I PUT THE PLATEAU MAP IN A SAFE PLACE. I ALSO HAVE THE MISSOULA FLOOD MAP IN MY POSSESSION.
AS THIS MAP ALLOWS A PERSON TO TRAVEL MODERN TIME, WE WENT TO 1877 TO FIND THOMAS CONDON WHO WAS DIGGING
I WAS MOST INTRIGUED BY THE MAP AND WANTED TO PURCHASE IT FOR THE UNIVERSITY OF OREGON, BUT MY DEPARTMENT LACKED THE FUNDING.
SO THEN PEREGRINA AND I JUMPED AHEAD IN TIME TO THE NEXT DECADE AND FOUND ANNIE ALEXANDER AND PRESENTED THE OPPORTUNITY TO HER.
I WAS IN OREGON AT THE TIME DIGGING AT FOSSIL LAKE. UPON HEARING OF THE POTENTIAL FOR A GREAT INVESTMENT, I PURCHASED THE MAP. MY ORIGINAL IDEA WAS TO DONATE IT TO THE MUSEUM OF PALEONTOLOGY.

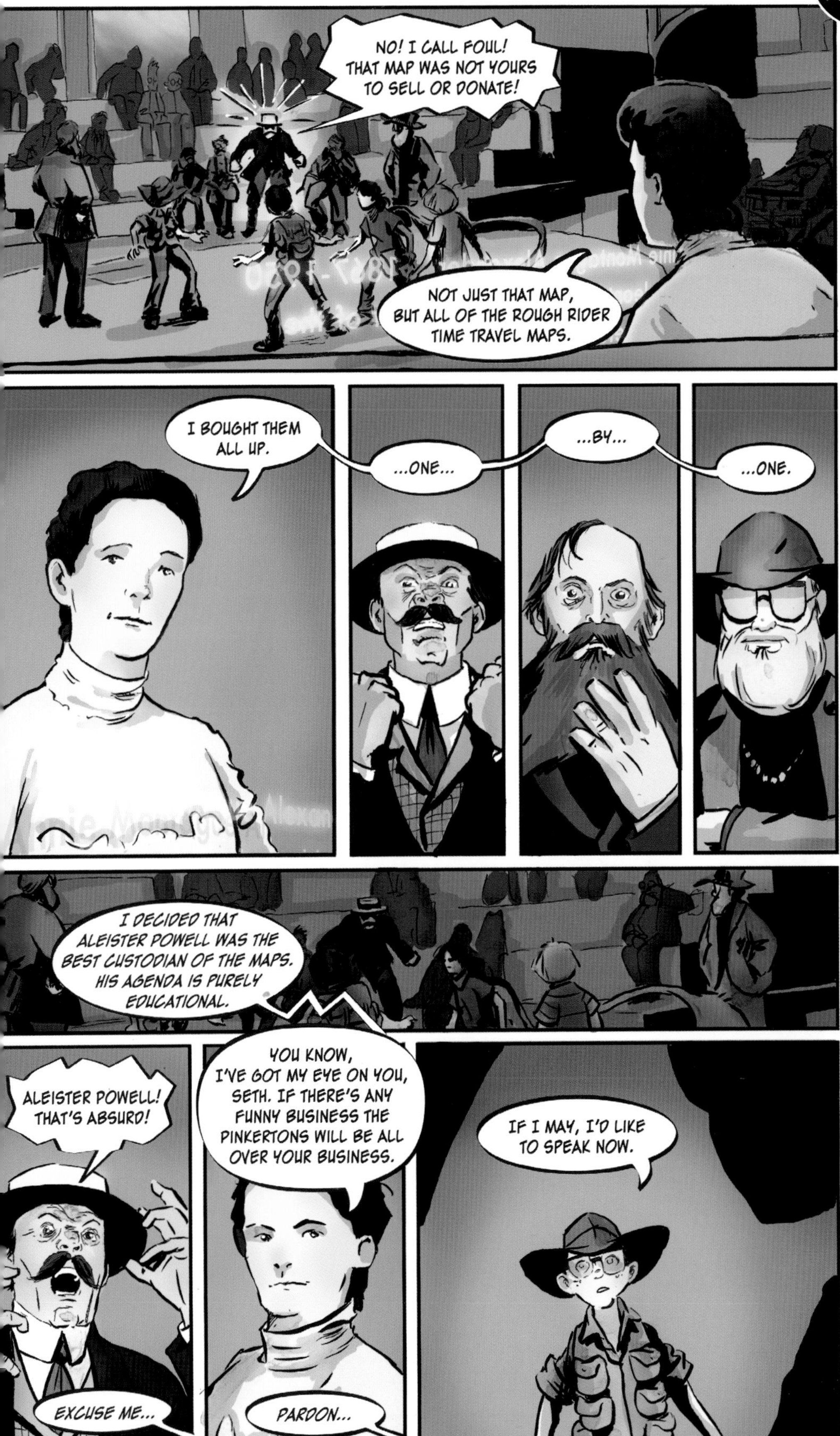
NO! I CALL FOUL! THAT MAP WAS NOT YOURS TO SELL OR DONATE!
NOT JUST THAT MAP, BUT ALL OF THE ROUGH RIDER TIME TRAVEL MAPS.
I BOUGHT THEM ALL UP.
...ONE...
...BY...
...ONE.
I DECIDED THAT ALEISTER POWELL WAS THE BEST CUSTODIAN OF THE MAPS. HIS AGENDA IS PURELY EDUCATIONAL.
ALEISTER POWELL! THAT'S ABSURD!
EXCUSE ME...
YOU KNOW, I'VE GOT MY EYE ON YOU, SETH. IF THERE'S ANY FUNNY BUSINESS THE PINKERTONS WILL BE ALL OVER YOUR BUSINESS.
PARDON...
IF I MAY, I'D LIKE TO SPEAK NOW.

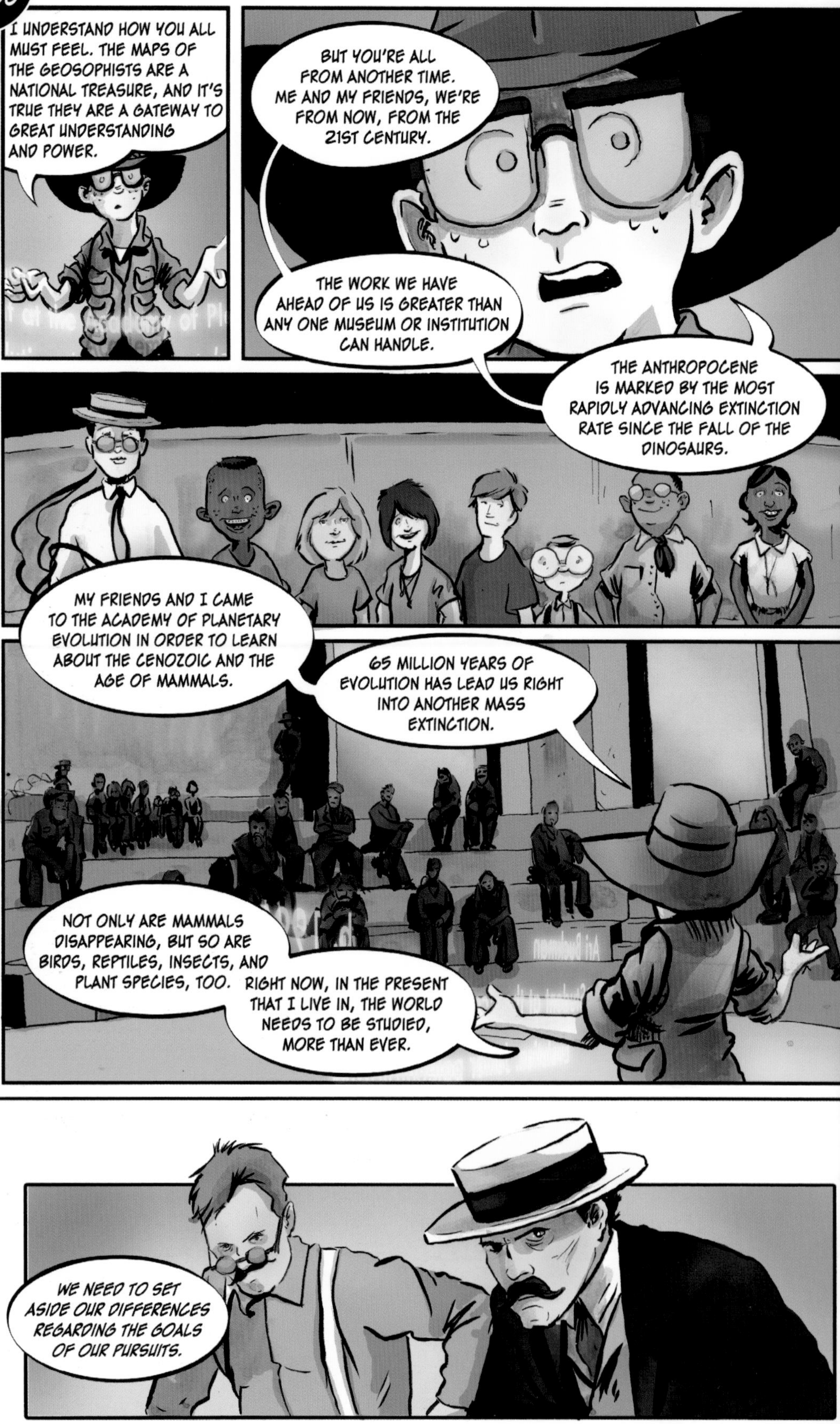
I UNDERSTAND HOW YOU ALL MUST FEEL. THE MAPS OF THE GEOSOPHISTS ARE A NATIONAL TREASURE, AND IT'S TRUE THEY ARE A GATEWAY TO GREAT UNDERSTANDING AND POWER.
BUT YOU'RE ALL FROM ANOTHER TIME. ME AND MY FRIENDS, WE'RE FROM NOW, FROM THE 21ST CENTURY.
THE WORK WE HAVE AHEAD OF US IS GREATER THAN ANY ONE MUSEUM OR INSTITUTION CAN HANDLE.
THE ANTHROPOCENE IS MARKED BY THE MOST RAPIDLY ADVANCING EXTINCTION RATE SINCE THE FALL OF THE DINOSAURS.
MY FRIENDS AND I CAME TO THE ACADEMY OF PLANETARY EVOLUTION IN ORDER TO LEARN ABOUT THE CENOZOIC AND THE AGE OF MAMMALS.
65 MILLION YEARS OF EVOLUTION HAS LEAD US RIGHT INTO ANOTHER MASS EXTINCTION.
NOT ONLY ARE MAMMALS DISAPPEARING, BUT SO ARE BIRDS, REPTILES, INSECTS, AND PLANT SPECIES, TOO.
RIGHT NOW, IN THE PRESENT THAT I LIVE IN, THE WORLD NEEDS TO BE STUDIED, MORE THAN EVER.
WE NEED TO SET ASIDE OUR DIFFERENCES REGARDING THE GOALS OF OUR PURSUITS.

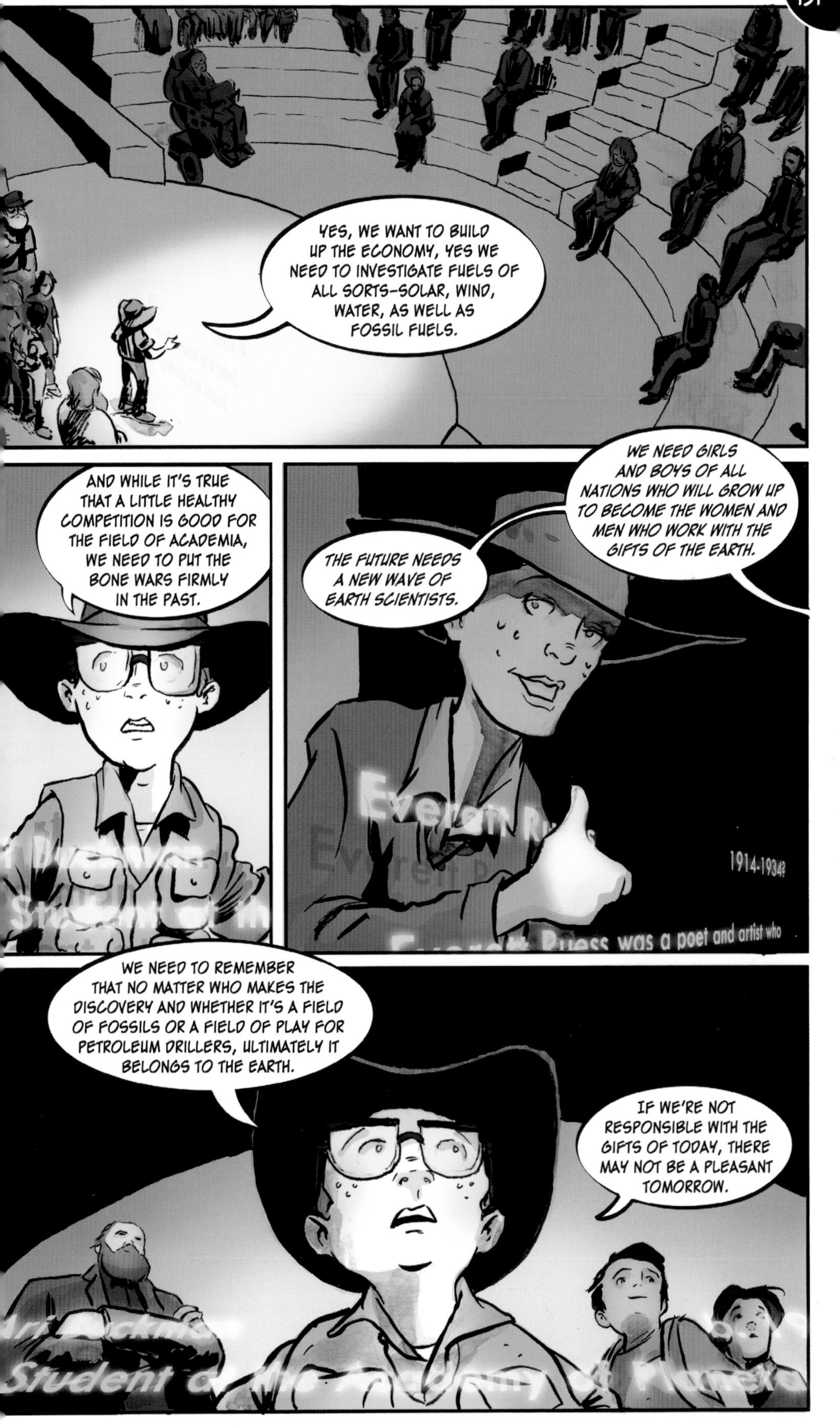
YES, WE WANT TO BUILD UP THE ECONOMY, YES WE NEED TO INVESTIGATE FUELS OF ALL SORTS–SOLAR, WIND, WATER, AS WELL AS FOSSIL FUELS.
AND WHILE IT'S TRUE THAT A LITTLE HEALTHY COMPETITION IS GOOD FOR THE FIELD OF ACADEMIA, WE NEED TO PUT THE BONE WARS FIRMLY IN THE PAST.
THE FUTURE NEEDS A NEW WAVE OF EARTH SCIENTISTS.
WE NEED GIRLS AND BOYS OF ALL NATIONS WHO WILL GROW UP TO BECOME THE WOMEN AND MEN WHO WORK WITH THE GIFTS OF THE EARTH.
1914-1934?
was a poet and artist who
WE NEED TO REMEMBER THAT NO MATTER WHO MAKES THE DISCOVERY AND WHETHER IT'S A FIELD OF FOSSILS OR A FIELD OF PLAY FOR PETROLEUM DRILLERS, ULTIMATELY IT BELONGS TO THE EARTH.
IF WE'RE NOT RESPONSIBLE WITH THE GIFTS OF TODAY, THERE MAY NOT BE A PLEASANT TOMORROW.

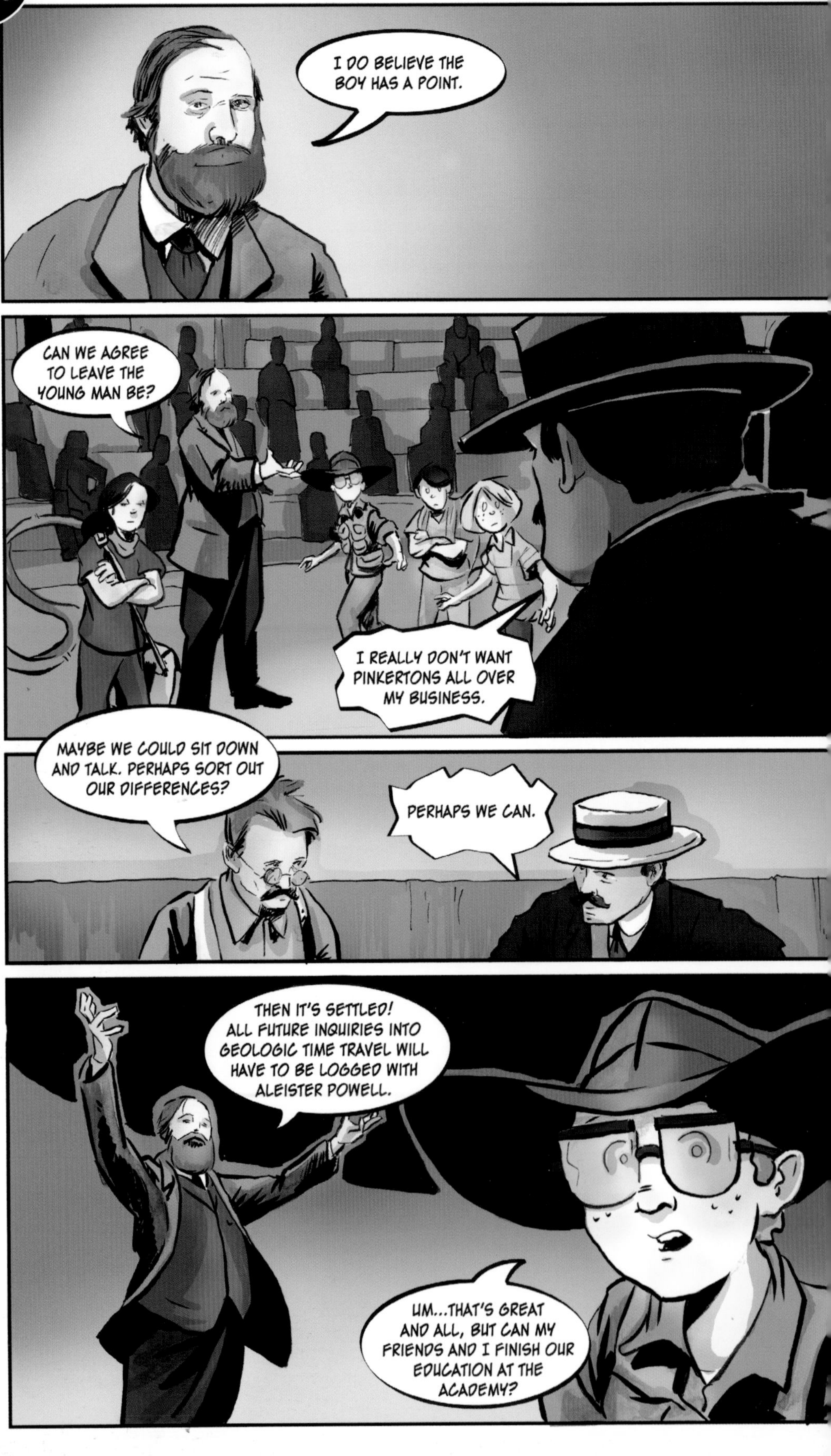
I DO BELIEVE THE BOY HAS A POINT.
CAN WE AGREE TO LEAVE THE YOUNG MAN BE?
I REALLY DON'T WANT PINKERTONS ALL OVER MY BUSINESS.
MAYBE WE COULD SIT DOWN AND TALK. PERHAPS SORT OUT OUR DIFFERENCES?
PERHAPS WE CAN.
THEN IT'S SETTLED! ALL FUTURE INQUIRIES INTO GEOLOGIC TIME TRAVEL WILL HAVE TO BE LOGGED WITH ALEISTER POWELL.
UM...THAT'S GREAT AND ALL, BUT CAN MY FRIENDS AND I FINISH OUR EDUCATION AT THE ACADEMY?

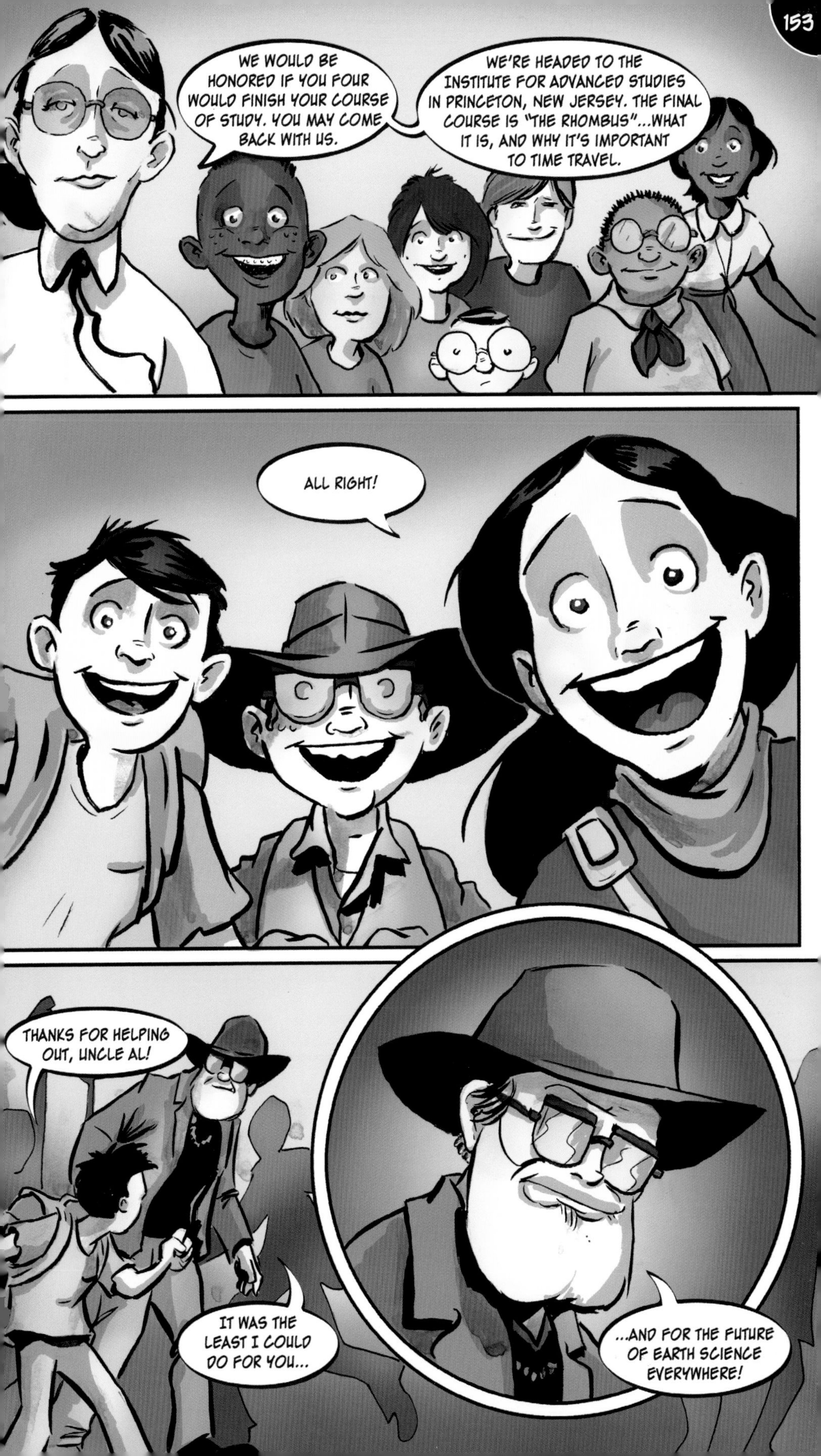
WE WOULD BE HONORED IF YOU FOUR WOULD FINISH YOUR COURSE OF STUDY. YOU MAY COME BACK WITH US.
WE'RE HEADED TO THE INSTITUTE FOR ADVANCED STUDIES IN PRINCETON, NEW JERSEY. THE FINAL COURSE IS "THE RHOMBUS"...WHAT IT IS, AND WHY IT'S IMPORTANT TO TIME TRAVEL.
ALL RIGHT!
THANKS FOR HELPING OUT, UNCLE AL!
IT WAS THE LEAST I COULD DO FOR YOU...
...AND FOR THE FUTURE OF EARTH SCIENCE EVERYWHERE!

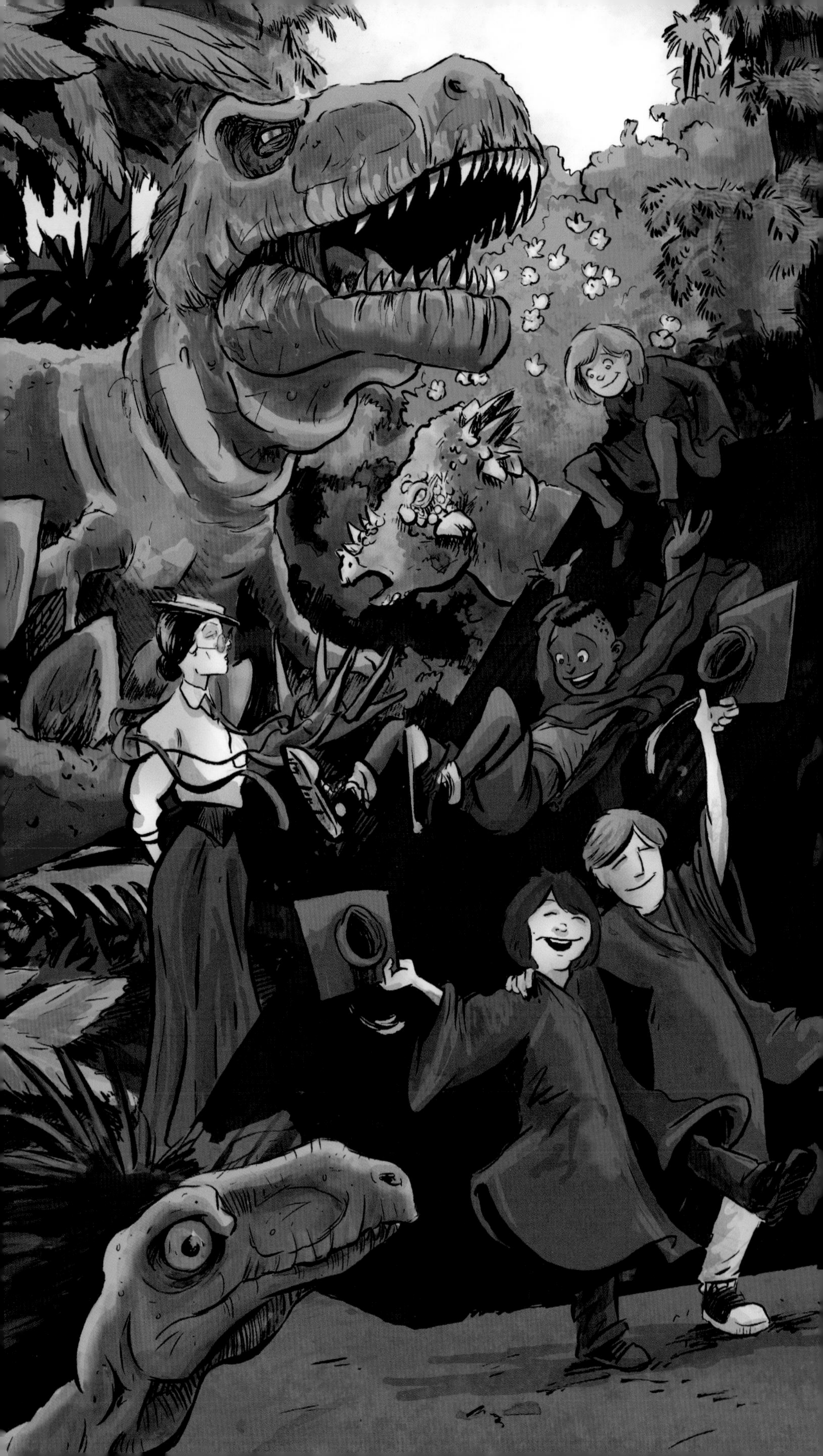

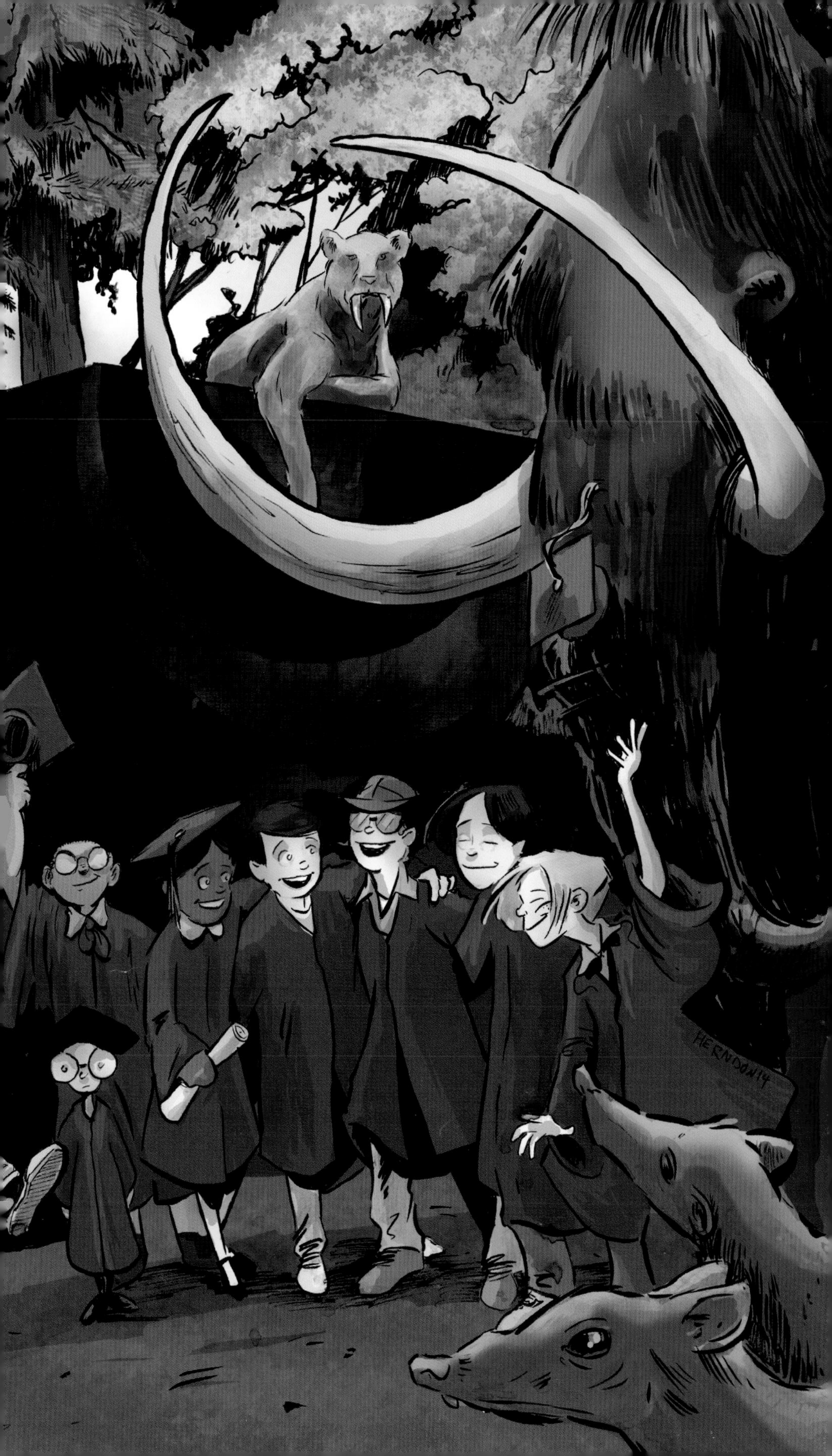
HERNDON'14

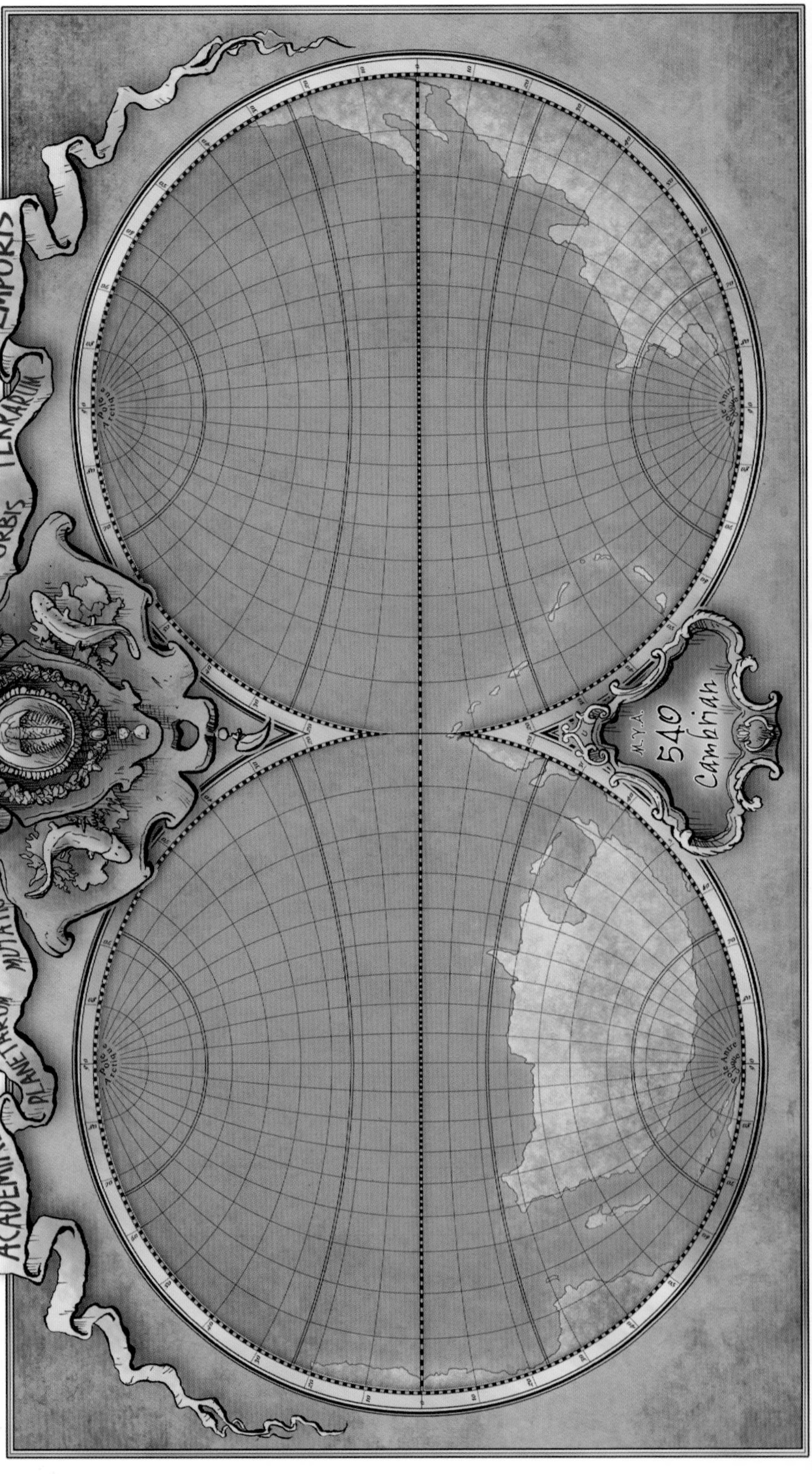
ACADEMIAE PLANETARUM MUTATIO ORBIS TERRARUM TEMPORIS
M.Y.A.
540
Cambrian

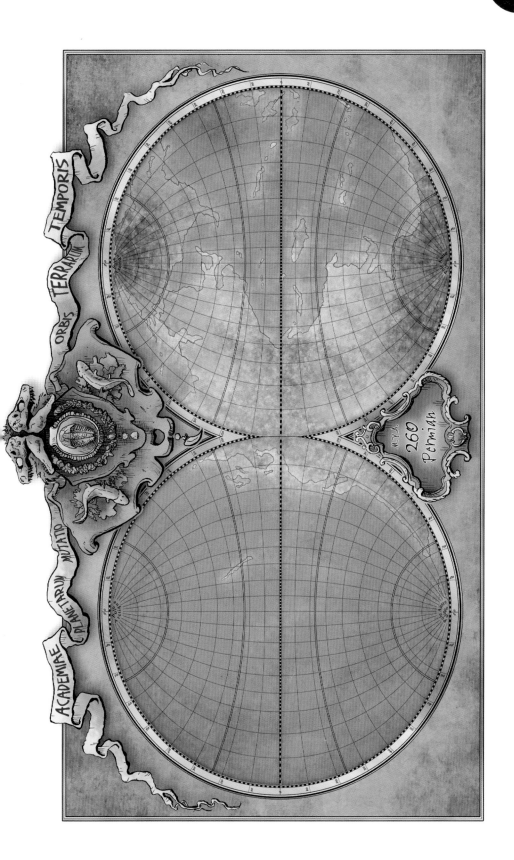

ORBIS TERRARUM TEMPORIS

ACADEMIAE PLANETARUM MUTATIO

M.Y.A.
260
Permian

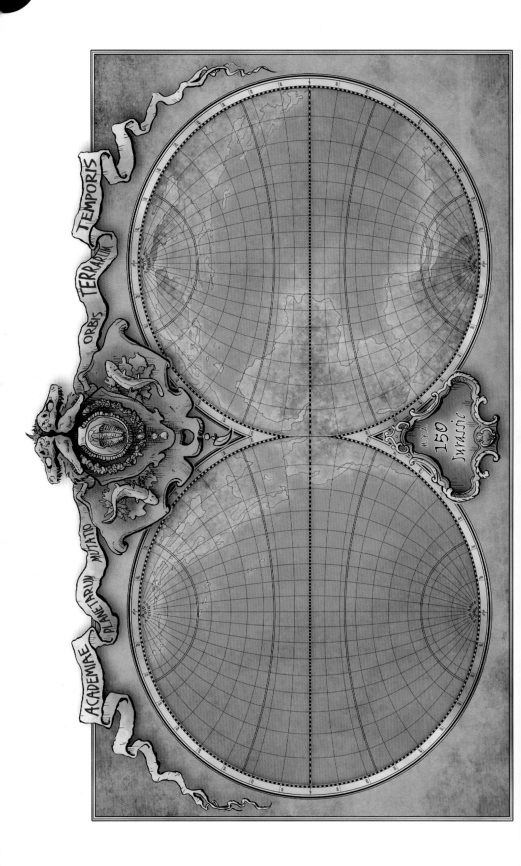

ORBIS TERRARUM TEMPORIS

ACADEMIAE PLANETARUM MUTATIO

MYA 150 Jurassic

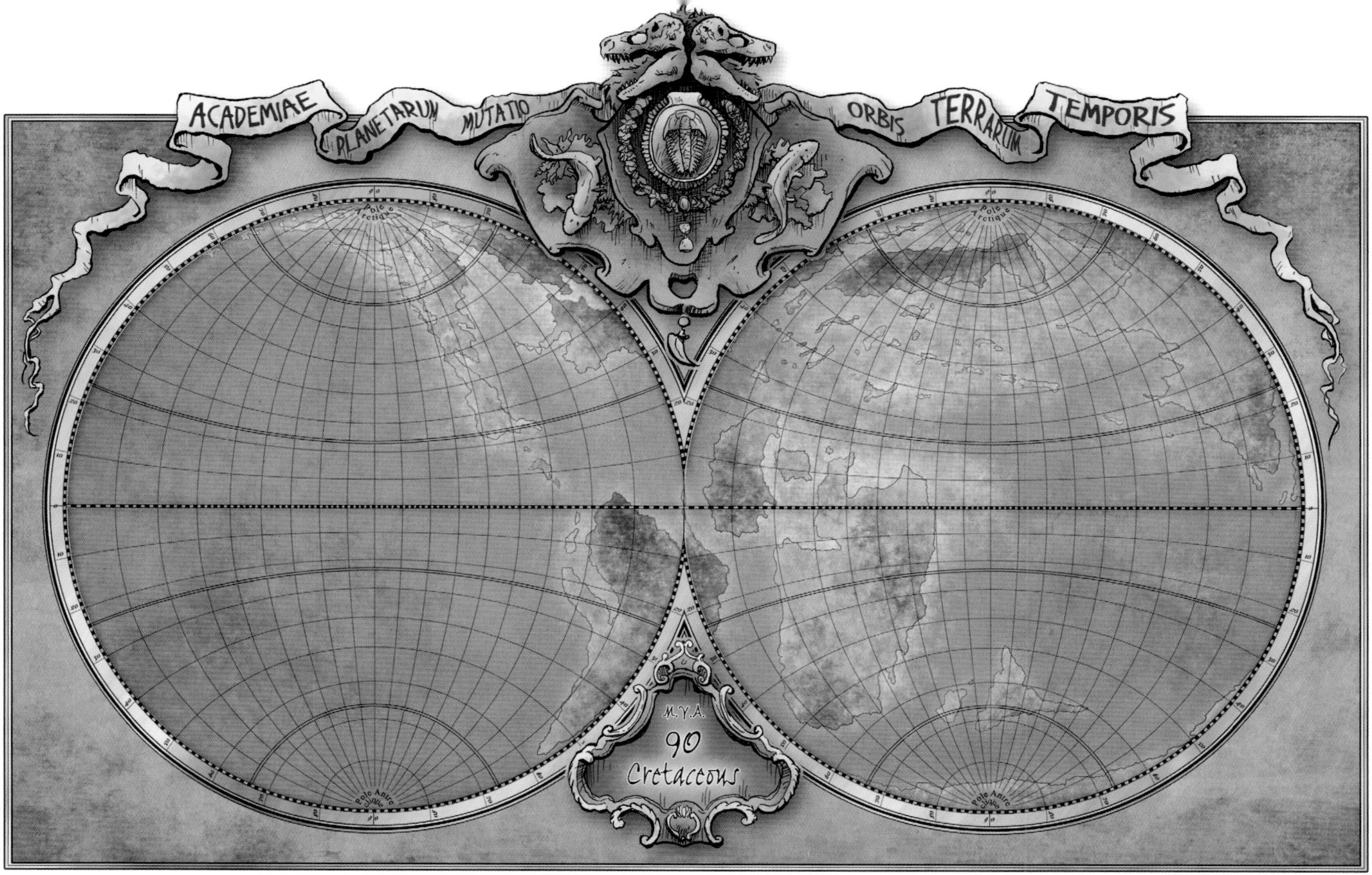
ACADEMIAE PLANETARUM MUTATIO ORBIS TERRARUM TEMPORIS
Pole Arctique
Pole Arctique
Pole Antarctique
Pole Antarctique
M.Y.A.
90
Cretaceous

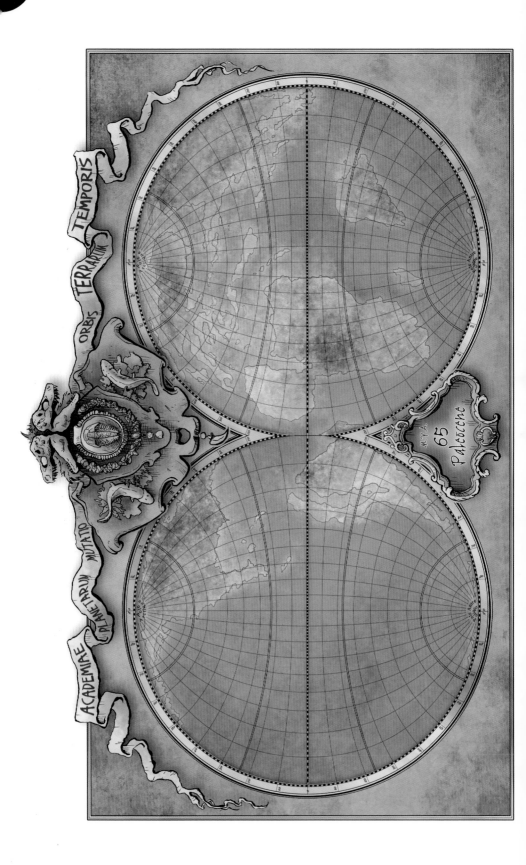

ORBIS TERRARUM TEMPORIS

ACADEMIAE PLANETARUM MUTATIO

65
Palæocene

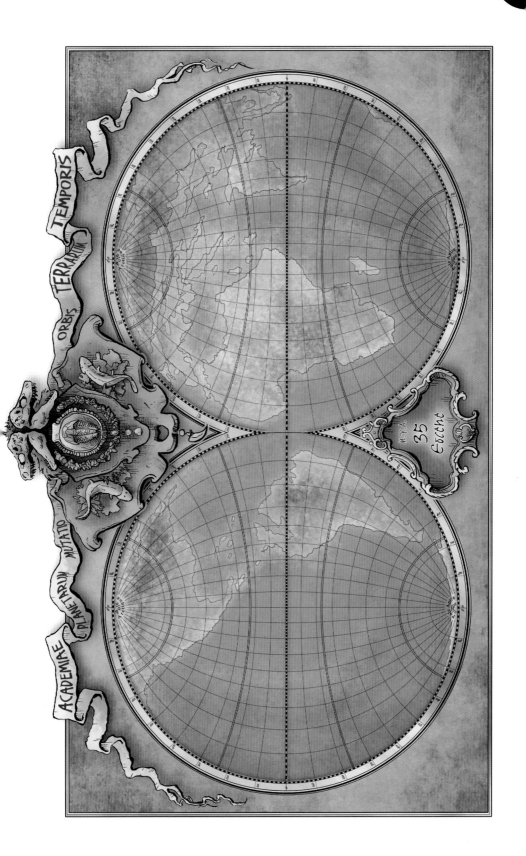

TEMPORIS

ORBIS TERRARUM

ACADEMIAE PLANETARUM MUTATIO

M.Y.A
35
Eocene

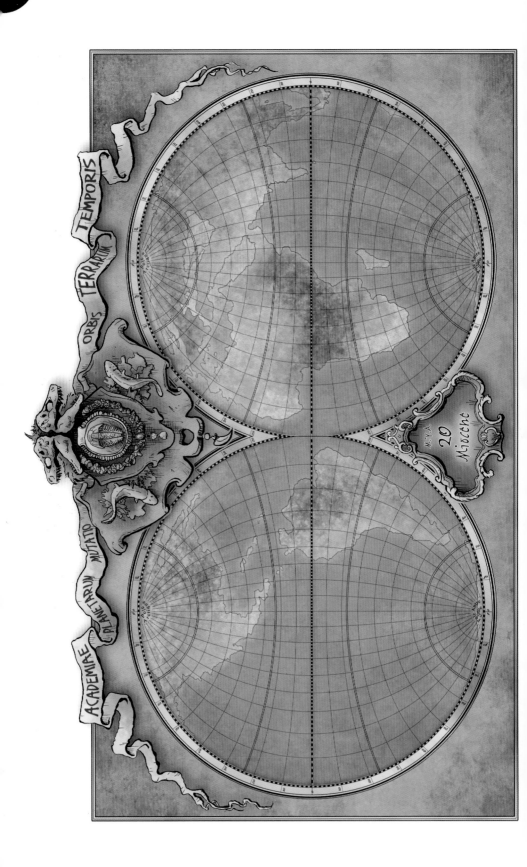

ORBIS TERRARUM TEMPORIS

ACADEMIAE PLANETARUM MUTATIO

M.Y.A.
20
Miocene

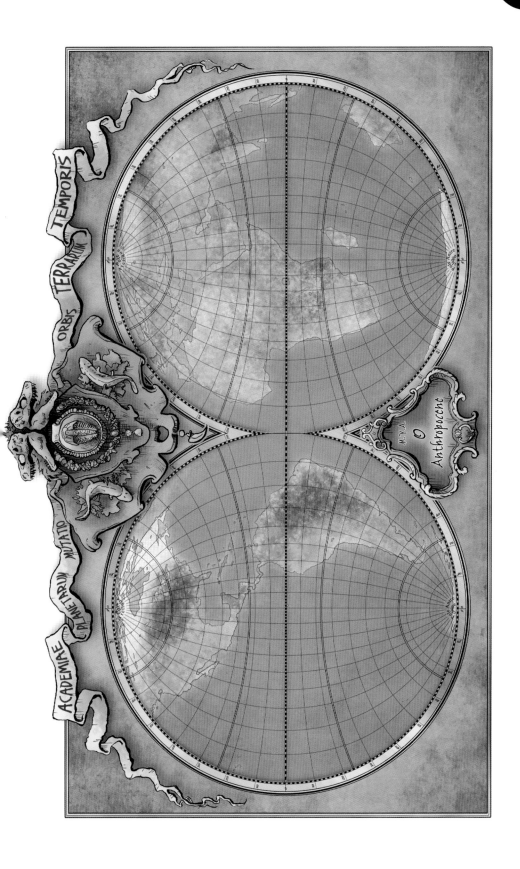

ORBIS TERRARUM TEMPORIS

ACADEMIAE PLANETARUM MUTATIO

M.Y.A. 0

Anthropocene

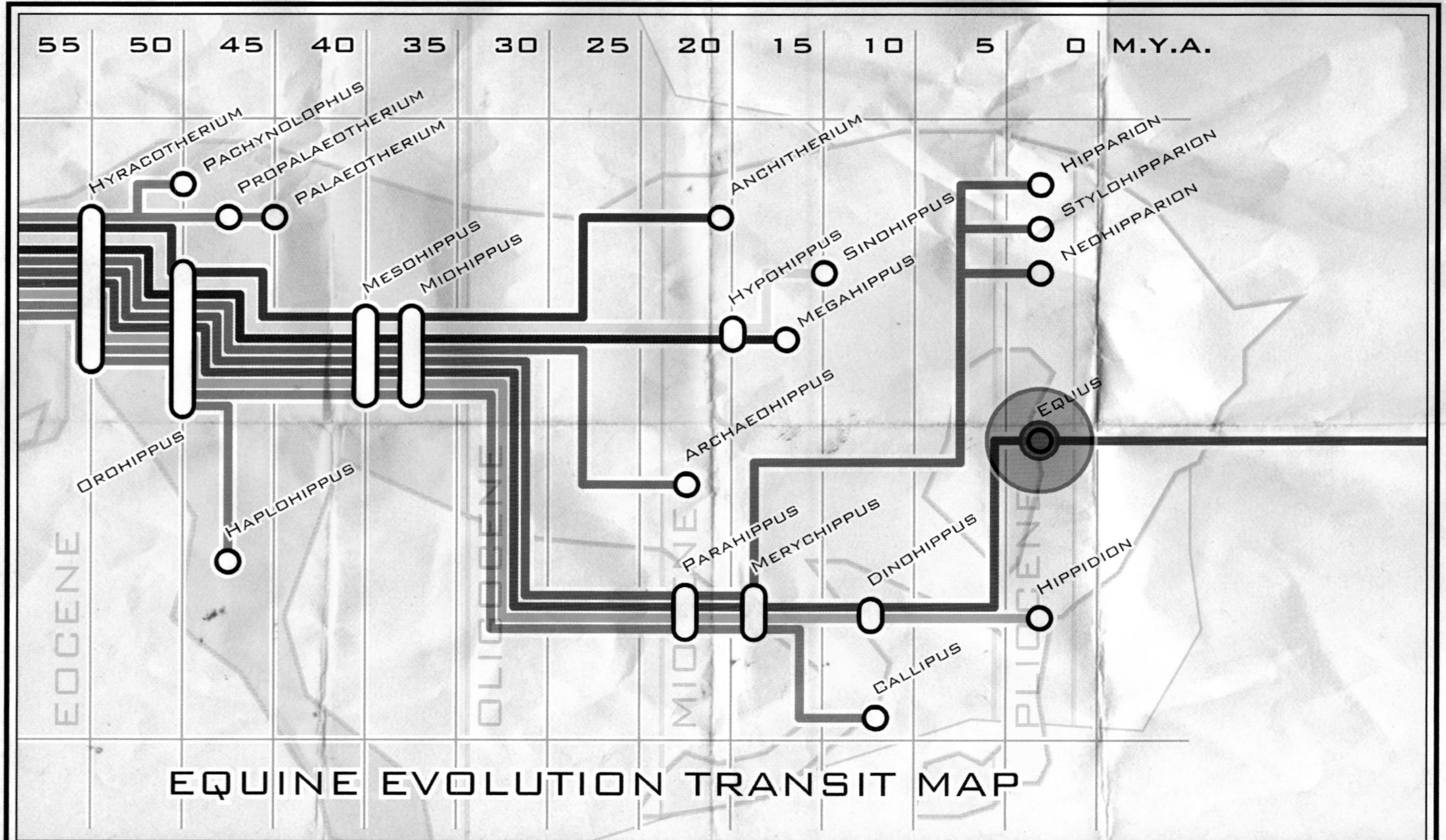
55
50
45
40
35
30
25
20
15
10
5
0
M.Y.A.
HYRACOTHERIUM
PACHYNOLOPHUS
PROPALAEOTHERIUM
PALAEOTHERIUM
MESOHIPPUS
MIOHIPPUS
ANCHITHERIUM
HYPOHIPPUS
SINOHIPPUS
MEGAHIPPUS
HIPPARION
STYLOHIPPARION
NEOHIPPARION
EQUUS
ARCHAEOHIPPUS
OROHIPPUS
HAPLOHIPPUS
PARAHIPPUS
MERYCHIPPUS
DINOHIPPUS
HIPPIDION
CALLIPUS
EOCENE
OLIGOCENE
MIOCENE
PLIOCENE
EQUINE EVOLUTION TRANSIT MAP

BIOS

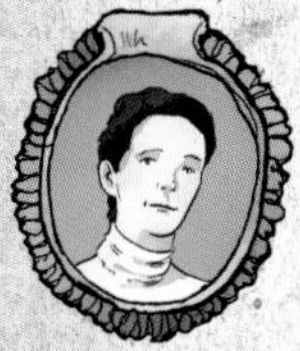

Annie Montague Alexander 1867-1950
Paleontologist and benefactor of the University of California Museum of Paleontology.

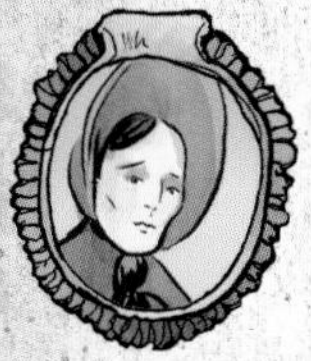

Mary Anning 1799-1847
Discovered the first complete Ichthyosaur fossil. An early collector of fossils in England.

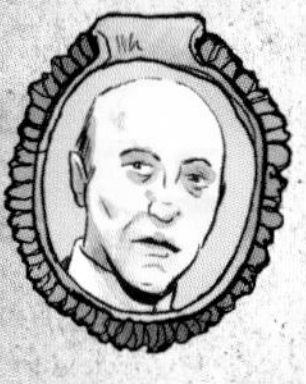

Barnum Brown 1873-1963
American paleontologist that discovered the first remains of a Tyrannosaurus rex.

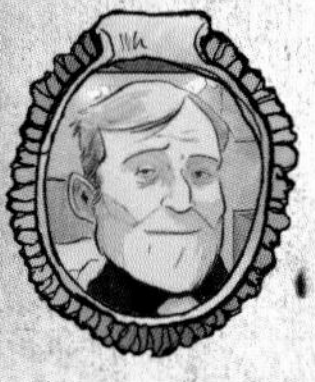

Andrew Carnegie 1835-1919
Scottish-American industrialist who was the richest man in the world before retiring and committing himself to philanthropy. Millions of people have benefited from his foresighted generosity.

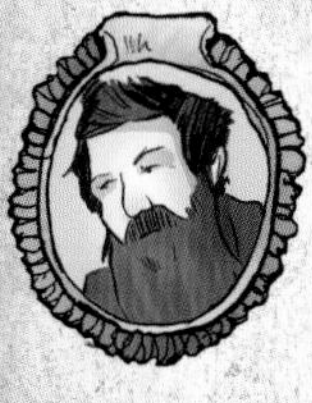

Thomas Condon 1822-1907
Grandfather of Oregon geology studies. First scientist to work the John Day Fossil Beds in Oregon, a major repository of Cenozoic fossils.

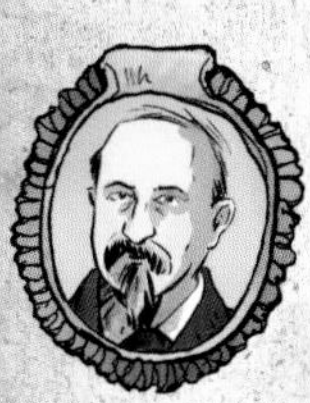

Clarence Dutton 1841-1912
American geologist who did extensive mapping of the Colorado Plateau.

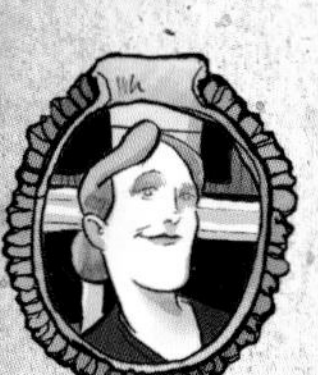

Winifred Goldring 1888-1971
Pioneering female paleontologist whose work on the Gilboa fossils of New York was very important for understanding Devonian Period flora and fauna. Through her work of creating museum exhibits for the New York State Museum, she helped expose many young minds to the wonders of the ancient past.

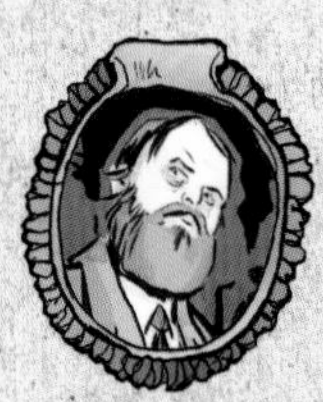

Joseph Leidy 1823-1891
Founder of American vertebrate paleontology. Mentor to both Edward Drinker Cope and Othniel Charles Marsh.

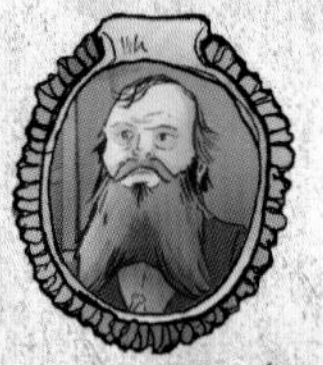

Othniel Charles Marsh 1831-1899
American paleontologist whose findings were the core foundation of the Yale Peabody Museum of Natural History. Infamous for his involvement in the "Bone Wars" against Edward Drinker Cope.

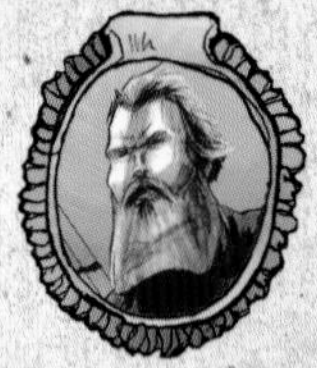

Herman Melville 1819-1891
American novelist, poet, and writer of short stories. Traveled extensively as a young man to the South Pacific where his studies of nature and the people of the region strongly influenced his writing career. Avid student of nature throughout his life.

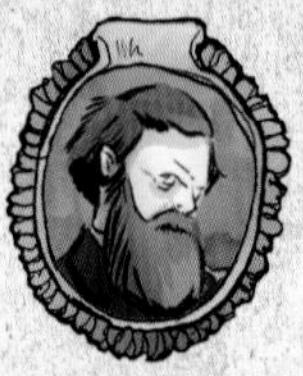

John Wesley Powell 1834-1902
Explorer of the Colorado River and director of United States Geological Survey from 1881-1894.

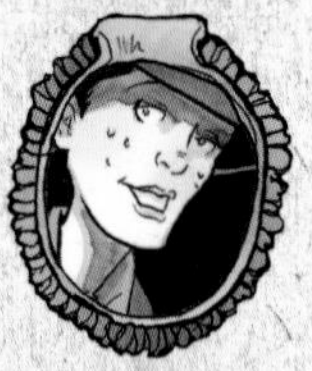

Everett Ruess 1914 – 1934?
A poet and artist who disappeared in the Utah Canyon Country in the 1930s.

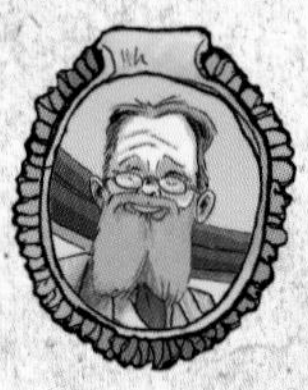

Alfred Russel Wallace 1823-1913
British naturalist and explorer who logged many years of field-work studying all aspects of nature in both South America and the Malay Archipelago. He was the 19th century's expert on the geographical distribution of animals and is considered the father of biogeography, the study of the geological distribution of plants and animals. He is the lesser-known co-founder of the theory of evolution through natural selection.

GLOSSARY

Anthropology: The scientific study of the origin, behavior, physical, cultural, and social development of humans.

Anthropocene: Earth's most recent geologic time period beginning approximately 8,000 years ago.

Auditory bulla: The hollow bony structure that encloses the inner ear in mammals.

Bacteria: Microscopic, single celled organisms.

Billion: 1,000,000,000, or one thousand million.

Cambrian explosion: The rapid diversification of multicellular life that occurred at the beginning of the Cambrian Period roughly 542 million years ago.

Canid: A mammal of the dog family.

Carnassial: The large, sharp molar and pre-molar tooth found in many carnivorous mammals used for shredding meat.

Complex life: Life forms that are multicellular.

Continents: The principle landmasses of Earth; usually regarded as including Africa, Antarctica, Asia, Australia, Europe, North America, and South America.

Felid: A mammal of the cat family.

Galaxy: A system of millions or billions of stars held together by gravity.

Gravity: The force that attracts a body toward any other physical body having mass.

Hemisphere: Half of the terrestrial globe divided into a northern and southern hemisphere along the equator but also eastern and western hemisphere along the Prime meridian.

Latitude: The angular distance north or south from the earth's equator, measured in degrees up to 90 degrees, as on a map or a globe.

Marcellus Formation: Unit of marine sedimentary rock rich in natural gas resources in the eastern United States.

Milankovitch cycles: The hypothesis that when parts of the cyclic variations (i.e. Earth's rotations varying over time) are combined and occur at the same time, they are responsible for major changes to the Earth's climate. See *Terra Tempo: Ice Age Cataclysm*.

Million: 1,000,000.

Paleogeography: A cross-disciplinary study that incorporates the fossil record and the study of geography across time to understand what the earth looked like millions of years ago.

Paleontological Society: An international non-profit organization founded in 1908 and dedicated exclusively to the advancement of the science of paleontology.

Pangaea: The hypothetical supercontinent that included all of the world's landmasses. Evidence points to its existing between 300 and 200 million years ago; purportedly Pangaea broke into two mega-continents named Gondwanaland and Laurasia.

Paradox: A seemingly contradictory statement that nonetheless may be true.

Petroleum: The liquid mixture that is present in certain rock strata that, once brought to the surface, can be refined into gasoline, kerosene, and diesel fuel.

Phalanx: The series of long bones in a finger or toe that make up the hands and feet of vertebrates.

Pinkertons: A private security and detective agency founded in 1850. At the height of its power, Pinkerton's National Detective Agency was the largest private law enforcement agency in the world.

Planet: A large round celestial body revolving in an orbit around a star.

Plate tectonics: The scientific theory that declares that the outer surface of the earth is divided into separate plates that rest upon the magma below. The grinding of these plates causes earthquakes.

Ring of Fire: An extensive zone of volcanic activity that circles the Pacific Ocean and nearby landmasses.

Solar System: A system of planets or celestial bodies orbiting a sun.

Spermaceti: A white, waxy substance obtained from the head of the sperm whale and used for making candles, oils, and much more.

Star: Any one of the objects in space that are made of burning gas.

Subduction zone: An area where one tectonic plate slides beneath another tectonic plate.

Terra incognita: Literally means "unknown land," but can mean anywhere that is unknown or uncharted.

Turbinate: Small, curved bone housed in the nasal cavity of mammals.

Universe: The totality of all objects and elements in space.

USGS: The United States Geological Survey; a scientific agency of the US government that studies the landscape, natural resources, and the natural hazards of the United States.

CREATORS

Writer **David R. Shapiro** is the founder of Craigmore Creations. He has worked as an animal tracker, interpretive guide, youth educator, and summer camp director. David is the author of the graphic novel series Terra Tempo; a web comic series, *Around the World with Haley Zoic*; several children's picture books; and an illustrated book of sonnets. He lives in Portland, Oregon, and travels often to be a part of the rest of the world.

Illustrator **Christopher Herndon** is an artist, monster maker, musician, and more. He is the creator of two comic book series and illustrator for numerous album covers, games, and magazines. Previous works include the children's book, *Tool. Time. Twist.*, the Terra Tempo graphic novel series, *Blunderbuss Wanderlust,* and *Living with Zombies.* Herndon currently lives in Portland, Oregon. Visit his website at www.christopherherndon.com.

Colorist **Erica Melville** has a MFA in visual art from Rutgers University and currently lives in Burlington, Vermont. Erica's experience as a painter and editor have helped her develop her ability to seamlessly integrate color to the Terra Tempo graphic novel series, bringing the illustrations and text to life. She has a wide skill set in art, design, and editing, with a love for nature and good stories. Erica is a painter of abstract art with exhibitions on both coasts. You can see her work at www.ericamelville.com.

AT THE ACADEMY, THE JOURNEY IS THE DESTINATION.

TERRA TEMPO

DON'T MISS THE ORIGINAL ACTION-PACKED ADVENTURES OF JENNA, CALEB, AND ARI!

CHECK OUT VOLUMES 1 AND 2 WITH BONUS MAPS. FULL COLOR!

SHAPIRO MELVILLE HERNDON
TERRA TEMPO

Terra Tempo: Ice Age Cataclysm
(Vol. 1 in the series)
ISBN 9780984442218

SHAPIRO HERNDON MELVILLE
TERRA TEMPO
THE FOUR CORNERS OF TIME

Terra Tempo: The Four Corners of Time
(Vol. 2 in the series)
ISBN 9780984442263

AVAILABLE AT YOUR LOCAL COMICS SHOP OR BOOKSTORE.

CREATIONS

www.craigmorecreations.com

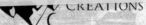

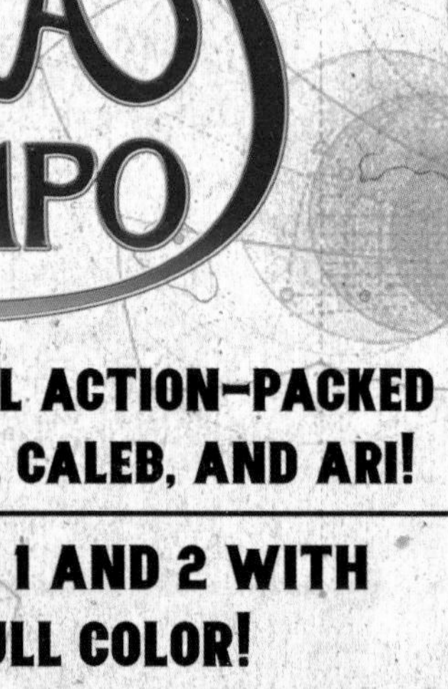